The City of London in Fantasy and Fiction

Tales of Magic, Murder and Macabre upon the Streets of England's Capital

British Library Cataloguing-in-Publication Data
A catalogue record for this book is available from
the British Library

Contents

THE BATTLE OF DORKING

G. T. *Chesney*

You ask me to tell you, my grandchildren, something about my own
share in the great events that happened fifty years ago. 'Tis sad work
turning back to that bitter page in our history, but you may perhaps
take profit in your new homes from the lesson it teaches. For us in
England it came too late. And yet we had plenty of warnings, if we
had only made use of them. The danger did not come on us unawares.
It burst on us suddenly, 'tis true; but its coming was foreshadowed
plainly enough to open our eyes, if we had not been wilfully blind.
We English have only ourselves to blame for the humiliation which
has been brought on the land. Venerable old age! Dishonourable old
age, I say, when it follows a manhood dishonoured as ours has been.
I declare, even now, though fifty years have passed, I can hardly
look a young man in the face when I think I am one of those in
whose youth happened this degradation of Old England—one of
those who betrayed the trust handed down to us unstained by our
forefathers.

What a proud and happy country was this fifty years ago! Free-
trade had been working for more than a quarter of a century, and
there seemed to be no end to the riches it was bringing us. London
was growing bigger and bigger; you could not build houses fast
enough for the rich people who wanted to live in them, the merchants
who made the money and came from all parts of the world to settle
there, and the lawyers and doctors and engineers and others, and
trades-people who got their share out of the profits. The streets
reached down to Croydon and Wimbledon, which my father could
remember quite country places; and people used to say that Kingston
and Reigate would soon be joined to London. We thought we could

1

go on building and multiplying for ever. 'Tis true that even then there was no lack of poverty; the people who had no money went on increasing as fast as the rich, and pauperism was already beginning to be a difficulty; but if the rates were high, there was plenty of money to pay them with; and as for what were called the middle classes, there really seemed no limit to their increase and prosperity. People in those days thought it quite a matter of course to bring a dozen of children into the world—or, as it used to be said, Providence sent them that number of babies; and if they couldn't always marry on all the daughters, they used to manage to provide for the sons, for there were new openings to be found in all the professions, or in the Government offices, which went on steadily getting larger. Besides, in those days young men could be sent out to India, or into the army or navy; and even then emigration was not uncommon, although not the regular custom it is now. Schoolmasters, like all other professional classes, drove a capital trade. They did not teach very much, to be sure, but new schools with their four or five hundred boys were springing up all over the country.

Fools that we were! We thought that all this wealth and prosperity were sent us by Providence, and could not stop coming. In our blindness we did not see that we were merely a big workshop, making up the things which came from all parts of the world; and that if other nations stopped sending us raw goods to work up, we could not produce them ourselves. True, we had in those days an advantage in our cheap coal and iron; and had we taken care not to waste the fuel, it might have lasted us longer. But even then there were signs that coal and iron would soon become cheaper in foreign parts; while as to food and other things, England was not better off than it is now. We were so rich simply because other nations from all parts of the world were in the habit of sending their goods to us to be sold or manufactured; and we thought that this would last for ever. And so, perhaps, it might have lasted, if we had only taken proper means to keep it; but, in our folly, we were too careless even to insure our prosperity, and after the course of trade was turned away it would not come back again.

And yet, if ever a nation had a plain warning, we had. If we were the greatest trading country, our neighbours were the leading military power in Europe. They were driving a good trade, too, for this was before their foolish communism (about which you will hear when you are older) had ruined the rich without benefiting the poor, and they were in many respects the first nation in Europe; but it was on their army that they prided themselves most. And with reason. They had beaten the Russians and the Austrians, and the Prussians too, in bygone years, and they thought they were invincible. Well do I remember the great review held at Paris by the Emperor Napoleon during the Great Exhibition, and how proud he looked showing off his splendid Guards to the assembled kings and princes. Yet, three years afterwards, the force so long deemed the first in Europe was ignominiously beaten, and the whole army taken prisoners. Such a defeat had never happened before in the world's history; and with this proof before us of the folly of disbelieving in the possibility of disaster merely because it had never fallen upon us, it might have been supposed that we should have the sense to take the lesson to heart. And the country was certainly roused for a time, and a cry was raised that the army ought to be reorganized, and our defences strengthened against the enormous power for sudden attacks which it was seen other nations were able to put forth. And a scheme of army reform was brought forward by the Government. It was a half-and-half affair at best; and, unfortunately, instead of being taken up in Parliament as a national scheme, it was made a party matter of, and so fell through. There was a Radical section of the House, too, whose votes had to be secured by conciliation, and which blindly demanded a reduction of armaments as the price of allegiance. This party always decried military establishments as part of a fixed policy for reducing the influence of the Crown and the aristocracy. They could not understand that the times had altogether changed, that the Crown had really no power, and that the Government merely existed at the pleasure of the House of Commons, and that even Parliament-rule was beginning to give way to mob-law. At any rate, the Ministry, baffled on all sides, gave up by degrees all the strong points of a scheme which they were not heartily in earnest about. It was not that there was any lack of money, if only it had been spent in the right way. The army cost enough, and more than enough, to give us a proper defence, and there were armed men of sorts in plenty and to spare, if only they had been decently organized. It was in organization and forethought that we fell short, because our rulers did not heartily believe in the need for preparation. The fleet and the Channel, they said, were sufficient protection. So army reform was put off to some more convenient season, and the militia and volunteers were left untrained as before, because to call them out for drill would 'interfere with the industry of the country'. We could have given up some of the industry of those days, forsooth, and yet be busier than we are now. But why tell you a tale you have so often heard already? The nation, although uneasy, was misled by the false security its leaders professed to feel; the warning given by the disasters that overtook France was allowed to pass by unheeded. We would not even be at the trouble of putting our arsenals in a safe place, or of guarding the capital against a surprise, although the cost of doing so would not have been so much as missed from the national wealth. The French trusted in their army and its great reputation, we in our fleet; and in each case the result of this blind confidence was disaster, such as our forefathers in their hardest struggles could not have even imagined.

I need hardly tell you how the crash came about. First, the rising in India drew away a part of our small army; then came the difficulty with America, which had been threatening for years, and we sent off ten thousand men to defend Canada—a handful which did not go far to strengthen the real defences of that country, but formed an irresistible temptation to the Americans to try and take them prisoners, especially as the contingent included three battalions of the Guards. Thus the regular army at home was even smaller than usual, and nearly half of it was in Ireland to check the talked-of Fenian invasion fitting out in the West. Worse still—though I do not know it would really have mattered as things turned out—the fleet was scattered abroad: some ships to guard the West Indies, others to check privateering in the China seas, and a large part to try and pro-

4

tect our colonies on the Northern Pacific shore of America, where, with incredible folly, we continued to retain possessions which we could not possibly defend. America was not the great power forty years ago that it is now; but for us to try and hold territory on her shores which could only be reached by sailing round the Horn, was as absurd as if she had attempted to take the Isle of Man before the independence of Ireland. We see this plainly enough now, but we were all blind then.

It was while we were in this state, with our ships all over the world, and our little bit of an army cut up into detachments, that the Secret Treaty was published, and Holland and Denmark were annexed. People say now that we might have escaped the troubles which came on us if we had at any rate kept quiet till our other difficulties were settled; but the English were always an impulsive lot: the whole country was boiling over with indignation, and the Government, egged on by the press, and going with the stream, declared war. We had always got out of scrapes before, and we believed our old luck and pluck would somehow pull us through.

Then, of course, there was bustle and hurry all over the land. Not that the calling up of the army reserves caused much stir, for I think there were only about 5,000 altogether, and a good many of these were not to be found when the time came; but recruiting was going on all over the country, with a tremendous high bounty, 50,000 more men having been voted for the army. Then there was a Ballot Bill passed for adding 55,500 men to the militia; why a round number was not fixed on I don't know, but the Prime Minister said that this was the exact quota wanted to put the defences of the country on a sound footing. Then the shipbuilding that began! Ironclads, despatch-boats, gunboats, monitors—every building-yard in the country got its job, and they were offering ten shillings a-day wages for anybody who could drive a rivet. This didn't improve the recruiting, you may suppose. I remember, too, there was a squabble in the House of Commons about whether artisans should be drawn for the ballot, as they were so much wanted, and I think they got an exemption. This sent numbers to the yards: and if we had had a couple of years to prepare instead of a couple of weeks, I daresay we should have done very well.

It was on a Monday that the declaration of war was announced, and in a few hours we got our first inkling of the sort of preparation the enemy had made for the event which they had really brought about, although the actual declaration was made by us. A pious appeal to the God of battles, whom it was said we had aroused, was telegraphed back; and from that moment all communication with the north of Europe was cut off. Our embassies and legations were packed off at an hour's notice, and it was as if we had suddenly come back to the Middle Ages. The dumb astonishment visible all over London the next morning, when the papers came out void of news, merely hinting at what had happened, was one of the most startling things in this war of surprises. But everything had been arranged beforehand; nor ought we to have been surprised, for we had seen the same Power, only a few months before, move down half a million men on a few days' notice, to conquer the greatest military nation in Europe, with no more fuss than our War Office used to make over the transport of a brigade from Aldershot to Brighton—and this, too, without the allies it had now. What happened now was not a bit more wonderful in reality: but people of this country could not bring themselves to believe that what had never occurred before to England could ever possibly happen. Like our neighbours, we became wise when it was too late.

Of course the papers were not long in getting news—even the mighty organization set at work could not shut out a special correspondent; and in a very few days, although the telegraphs and railways were intercepted right across Europe, the main facts oozed out. An embargo had been laid on all the shipping in every port from the Baltic to Ostend; the fleets of the two great Powers had moved out, and it was supposed were assembled in the great northern harbour, and troops were hurrying on board all the steamers detained in these places, most of which were British vessels. It was clear that invasion was intended. Even then we might have been saved, if the fleet had been ready. The forts which guarded the flotilla were perhaps too strong for shipping to attempt; but an ironclad or two, handled as British sailors knew how to use them, might have destroyed or damaged a part of the transports, and delayed the expedition, giving us what we wanted, time. But then the best part of the fleet had been decoyed down to the Dardanelles, and what remained of the Channel squadron was looking after Fenian filibusters off the west of Ireland; so it was ten days before the fleet was got together, and by that time it was plain the enemy's preparations were too far advanced to be stopped by a *coup-de-main*. Information, which came chiefly through Italy, came slowly, and was more or less vague and uncertain; but this much was known, that at least a couple of hundred thousand men were embarked or ready to be put on board ships, and that the flotilla was guarded by more ironclads than we could then muster. I suppose it was the uncertainty as to the point the enemy would aim at for landing, and the fear lest he should give us the go-by, that kept the fleet for several days in the Downs; but it was not until the Tuesday fortnight after the declaration of war that it weighed anchor and steamed away for the North Sea. Of course you have read about the Queen's visit to the fleet the day before, and how she sailed round the ships in her yacht, and went on board the flag-ship to take leave of the admiral; how, overcome with emotion, she told him that the safety of the country was committed to his keeping. You remember, too, the gallant old officer's reply, and how all the ships' yards were manned, and how lustily the tars cheered as her Majesty was rowed off. The account was of course telegraphed to London, and the high spirits of the fleet infected the whole town. I was outside the Charing Cross station when the Queen's special train from Dover arrived, and from the cheering and shouting which greeted her Majesty as she drove away, you might have supposed we had already won a great victory. The leading journal, which had gone in strongly for the army reduction carried out during the session, and had been nervous and desponding in tone during the past fortnight, suggesting all sorts of compromises as a way of getting out of the war, came out in a very jubilant form next morning. 'Panic-stricken inquirers,' it said, 'ask now, where are the means of meeting the invasion? We reply that the

7

invasion will never take place. A British fleet, manned by British sailors whose courage and enthusiasm are reflected in the people of this country, is already on the way to meet the presumptuous foe. The issue of a contest between British ships and those of any other country, under anything like equal odds, can never be doubtful. England awaits with calm confidence the issue of the impending action.'

Such were the words of the leading article, and so we all felt. It was on Tuesday, the 10th of August, that the fleet sailed from the Downs. It took with it a submarine cable to lay down as it advanced, so that continuous communication was kept up, and the papers were publishing special editions every few minutes with the latest news. This was the first time such a thing had been done, and the feat was accepted as a good omen. Whether it is true that the Admiralty made use of the cable to keep on sending contradictory orders, which took the command out of the admiral's hands, I can't say; but all that the admiral sent in return was a few messages of the briefest kind, which neither the Admiralty nor any one else could have made any use of. Such a ship had gone off reconnoitring; such another had rejoined—fleet was in latitude so and so. This went on till the Thursday morning. I had just come up to town by train as usual, and was walking to my office, when the newsboys began to cry, 'New edition—enemy's fleet in sight!' You may imagine the scene in London! Business still went on at the banks, for bills matured although the independence of the country was being fought out under our own eyes, so to say, and speculators were active enough. But even with the people who were making and losing their fortunes, the interest in the fleet overcame everything else; men who went to pay in or draw out their money stopped to show the last bulletin to the cashier. As for the street, you could hardly get along for the crowd stopping to buy and read the papers; while at every house or office the members sat restlessly in the common room, as if to keep together for company, sending out some one of their number every few minutes to get the latest edition. At least this is what happened at our office; but to sit still was as impossible as to do anything, and most of us went out and wandered about among the crowd, under a sort of feeling that the news was got quicker at in this way. Bad as were the times coming, I think the sickening suspense of that day, and the shock which followed, was almost the worst that we underwent. It was about ten o'clock that the first telegram came; an hour later the wire announced that the admiral had signalled to form line of battle, and shortly afterwards that the order was given to bear down on the enemy and engage. At twelve came the announcement, 'Fleet opened fire about three miles to leeward of us'—that is, the ship with the cable. So far all had been expectancy, then came the first token of calamity. 'An ironclad has been blown up'—'the enemy's torpedoes are doing great damage'—'the flag-ship is laid aboard the enemy'—'the flag-ship appears to be sinking'—'the vice-admiral has signalled to'—there the cable became silent, and, as you know, we heard no more till, two days afterwards, the solitary ironclad which escaped the disaster steamed into Portsmouth.

Then the whole story came out—how our sailors, gallant as ever, had tried to close with the enemy; how the latter evaded the conflict at close quarters, and, sheering off, left behind them the fatal engines which sent our ships, one after the other, to the bottom; how all this happened almost in a few minutes. The Government, it appears, had received warnings of this invention; but to the nation this stunning blow was utterly unexpected. That Thursday I had to go home early for regimental drill, but it was impossible to remain doing nothing, so when that was over I went up to town again, and after waiting in expectation of news which never came, and missing the midnight train, I walked home. It was a hot sultry night, and I did not arrive till near sunrise. The whole town was quite still—the lull before the storm; and as I let myself in with my latch-key, and went softly upstairs to my room to avoid waking the sleeping household, I could not but contrast the peacefulness of the morning—no sound breaking the silence but the singing of the birds in the garden—with the passionate remorse and indignation that would break out with the day. Perhaps the inmates of the rooms were as wakeful as myself; but the house in its stillness was just as it used to be when I came home alone from balls or parties in the happy days gone by. Tired though I was, I could not sleep, so I went down to the river and had a swim; and on returning found the household was assembling for early breakfast. A sorrowful household it was, although the burden pressing on each was partly an unseen one. My father, doubting whether his firm could last through the day; my mother, her distress about my brother, now with his regiment on the coast, already exceeding that which she felt for the public misfortune, had come down, although hardly fit to leave her room. My sister Clara was worst of all, for she could not but try to disguise her special interest in the fleet; and though we had all guessed that her heart was given to the young lieutenant in the flag-ship—the first vessel to go down—a love unclaimed could not be told, nor could we express the sympathy we felt for the poor girl. That breakfast, the last meal we ever had together, was soon ended, and my father and I went up to town by an early train, and got there just as the fatal announcement of the loss of the fleet was telegraphed from Portsmouth.

The panic and excitement of that day—how the funds went down to 35; the run upon the bank and its stoppage; the fall of half the houses in the city; how the Government issued a notification suspending specie payment and the tendering of bills—this last precaution too late for most firms, Graham & Co. among the number, which stopped payment as soon as my father got to the office; the call to arms, and the unanimous response of the country—all this is history which I need not repeat. You wish to hear about my own share in the business of the time. Well, volunteering had increased immensely from the day war was proclaimed, and our regiment went up in a day or two from its usual strength of 600 to nearly 1,000. But the stock of rifles was deficient. We are promised a further supply in a few days, which, however, we never received; and while waiting for them the regiment had to be divided into two parts, the recruits drilling with the rifles in the morning, and we old hands in the evening. The failures and stoppage of work on this black Friday threw an immense number of young men out of employment, and we recruited up to 1,400 strong by the next day; but what was the use of all these men without arms? On the Saturday it was announced that a lot of smooth-bore muskets in store at the Tower would be served out to regiments applying for them, and a regular scramble took place among the volunteers for them, and our people got hold of a couple of hundred. But you might almost as well have tried to learn rifle-drill with a broom-stick as with old brown bess; besides, there was no smooth-bore ammunition in the country. A national subscription was opened for the manufacture of rifles at Birmingham, which ran up to a couple of millions in two days, but, like everything else, this came too late. To return to the volunteers: camps had been formed a fortnight before at Dover, Brighton, Harwich, and other places, of regulars and militia, and the headquarters of most of the volunteer regiments were attached to one or other of them, and the volunteers themselves used to go down for drill from day to day, as they could spare time, and on Friday an order went out that they should be permanently embodied; but the metropolitan volunteers still kept about London as a sort of reserve, till it could be seen at what point the invasion would take place. We were all told off to brigades and divisions. Our brigade consisted of the 4th Royal Surrey Militia, the 1st Surrey Administrative Battalion, as it was called, at Clapham, the 7th Surrey Volunteers at Southwark, and ourselves; but only our battalion and the militia were quartered in the same place, and the whole brigade had merely two or three afternoons together at brigade exercise in Bushey Park before the march took place. Our brigadier belonged to a line regiment in Ireland, and did not join till the very morning the order came. Meanwhile, during the preliminary fortnight, the militia colonel commanded. But though we volunteers were busy with our drill and preparations, those of us who, like myself, belonged to Government offices, had more than enough of office work to do, as you may suppose. The volunteer clerks were allowed to leave office at four o'clock, but the rest were kept hard at the desk far into the night. Orders to the lord-lieutenants, to the magistrates, notifications, all the arrangements for cleaning out the workhouses for hospitals—these and a hundred other things had to be managed in our office, and there was as much bustle indoors as out. Fortunate we were to be so busy—the people to be pitied were those who had nothing to do. And on Sunday (that was the 15th August) work went on just as usual. We had an early parade and drill, and I went up to town by the nine o'clock train in my uniform, taking my rifle with me in case of accidents, and luckily too, as it turned out, a mackintosh overcoat. When I got to Waterloo there were all sorts of rumours afloat. A fleet had been seen off the Downs, and some of the despatch-boats which were hovering about the coasts brought news that there was a large flotilla off Harwich, but nothing could be seen from the shore, as the weather was hazy. The enemy's light ships had taken and sunk all the fishing-boats they could catch, to prevent the news of their whereabouts reaching us; but a few escaped during the night and reported that the Inconstant frigate coming home from North America, without any knowledge of what had taken place, had sailed right into the enemy's fleet and had been captured. In town the troops were all getting ready for a move; the Guards in the Wellington Barracks were under arms, and their baggage-waggons packed and drawn up in the Bird-cage Walk. The usual guard at the Horse Guard had been withdrawn, and orderlies and staff-officers were going to and fro. All this I saw on the way to my office, where I worked away till twelve o'clock, and then feeling hungry after my early breakfast, I went across Parliament Street to my club to get some luncheon. There were about half-a-dozen men in the coffee-room, none of whom I knew; but in a minute or two Danvers of the Treasury entered in a tremendous hurry. From him I got the first bit of authentic news I had had that day. The enemy had landed in force near Harwich, and the metropolitan regiments were ordered down there to reinforce the troops already collected in that neigh-bourhood; his regiment was to parade at one o'clock, and he had come to get something to eat before starting. We bolted a hurried lunch, and were just leaving the club when a messenger from the Treasury came running into the hall.

'Oh, Mr Danvers,' said he, 'I've come to look for you, sir; the secretary says that all the gentlemen are wanted at the office, and that you must please not one of you go with the regiments.'

'The devil!' cried Danvers.

'Do you know if that order extends to all the public offices?' I asked.

'I don't know,' said the man, 'but I believe it do. I know there's messengers gone round to all the clubs and luncheon-bars to look for the gentlemen; the secretary says it's quite impossible any one can be spared just now, there's so much work to do; there's orders just come to send off our records to Birmingham to-night.'

I did not wait to condole with Danvers, but, just glancing up Whitehall to see if any of our messengers were in pursuit, I ran off as hard as I could for Westminster Bridge, and so to the Waterloo station.

The place had quite changed its aspect since the morning. The regular service of trains had ceased, and the station and approaches were full of troops, among them the Guards and artillery. Everything was very orderly: the men had piled arms, and were standing about in groups. There was no sign of high spirits or enthusiasm. Matters had become too serious. Every man's face reflected the general feeling that we had neglected the warnings given us, and that now the danger so long derided as impossible and absurd had really come and found us unprepared. But the soldiers, if grave, looked determined, like men who meant to do their duty whatever might happen. A train full of guardsmen was just starting for Guildford. I was told it would stop at Surbiton, and, with several other volunteers, hurrying like myself to join our regiment, got a place in it. We did not arrive a moment too soon, for the regiment was marching from Kingston down to the station. The destination of our brigade was the east coast. Empty carriages were drawn up in the siding, and our regiment was to go first. A large crowd was assembled to see it off, including the recruits who had joined during the last fortnight, and who formed by far the largest part of our strength. They were to stay behind, and were certainly very much in the way already; for as all the officers and sergeants belonged to the active part, there was no one to keep discipline among them, and they came crowding around us, breaking the ranks and making it difficult to get into the train. Here I saw our new brigadier for the first time. He was a soldier-like man, and no doubt knew his duty, but he appeared new to volunteers, and did not seem to know how to deal with gentlemen privates. I wanted very much to run home and get my greatcoat and knapsack, which I had bought a few days ago, but feared to be left behind; a good-natured recruit volunteered to fetch them for me, but he had not returned before we started, and I began the campaign with a kit consisting of a mackintosh and a small pouch of tobacco.

It was a tremendous squeeze in the train; for, besides the ten men sitting down, there were three or four standing up in every compartment, and the afternoon was close and sultry, and there were so many stoppages on the way that we took nearly an hour and a half crawling up to Waterloo. It was between five and six in the afternoon when we arrived there, and it was nearly seven before we marched up to the Shoreditch station. The whole place was filled up with stores and ammunition, to be sent off to the east, so we piled arms in the street and scattered about to get food and drink, of which most of us stood in need, especially the latter, for some were already feeling the worse for the heat and crush. I was just stepping into a public-house with Travers, when who should drive up but his pretty wife! Most of our friends had paid their adieus at the Surbiton station, but she had driven up by the road in his brougham, bringing their little boy to have a last look at papa. She had also brought his knapsack and greatcoat, and, what was still more acceptable, a basket containing fowls, tongue, bread-and-butter, and biscuits, and a couple of bottles of claret—which priceless luxuries they insisted on my sharing.

Meanwhile the hours went on. The 4th Surrey Militia, which had marched all the way from Kingston, had come up, as well as the other volunteer corps; the station had been partly cleared of the stores that encumbered it; some artillery, two militia regiments, and a battalion of the line, had been despatched, and our turn had come, and long lines of carriages were drawn up ready for us; but still we remained in the street. You may fancy the scene. There seemed to be as many people as ever in London, and we could hardly move for the crowds of spectators—fellows hawking fruits and volunteers' comforts, newsboys and so forth, to say nothing of the cabs and omnibuses; while orderlies and staff-officers were constantly riding up with messages. A good many of the militiamen, and some of our people too, had taken more than enough to drink; perhaps a hot sun had told on empty stomachs; anyhow, they became very noisy. The din, dirt, and heat were indescribable. So the evening wore on, and all the information our officers could get from the brigadier, who appeared to be acting under another general, was, that orders had come to stand fast for the present. Gradually the street became quieter and cooler. The brigadier, who, by way of setting an example, had remained for some hours without leaving his saddle, had got a chair out of a shop, and sat nodding in it; most of the men were lying down or sitting on the pavement—some sleeping, some smoking. In vain had Travers begged his wife to go home. She declared that, having come so far, she would stay and see the last of us. The brougham had been sent away to a by-street, as it blocked up the road; so he sat on a doorstep, she by him on the knapsack. Little Arthur, who had been delighted at the bustle and the uniforms, and in high spirits, became at last very cross, and eventually cried himself to sleep in his father's arms, his golden hair and one little dimpled arm hanging over his shoulder. Thus went on the weary hours, till suddenly the assembly sounded, and we all started up. We were to return to Waterloo. The landing on the east was only a feint—so ran the rumour—the real attack was on the south. Anything seemed better than indecision and delay, and, tired though we were, the march back was gladly hailed. Mrs Travers, who made us take the remains of the luncheon with us, we left to look for her carriage; little Arthur, who was awake again, but very good and quiet, in her arms.

We did not reach Waterloo till nearly midnight, and there was some delay in starting again. Several volunteers and militia regiments had arrived from the north; the station and all its approaches were jammed up with men, and trains were being despatched away as fast as they could be made up. All this time no news had reached us since the first announcement; but the excitement then aroused had now passed away under the influence of fatigue and want of sleep, and most of us dozed off as soon as we got under way. I did, at any rate, and was awoke by the train stopping at Leatherhead. There was an up-train returning to town, and some persons in it were bringing up news from the coast. We could not, from our part of the train, hear what they said, but the rumour was passed up from one carriage to another. The enemy had landed in force at Worthing. Their position had been attacked by the troops from the camp near Brighton, and the action would be renewed in the morning. The volunteers behaved very well. This was all the information we could get. So, then, the invasion had come at last. It was clear, at any rate, from what was said, that the enemy had not been driven back yet, and we should be in time most likely to take a share in the defence. It was sunrise when the train crawled into Dorking, for there had been numerous stop-pages on the way; and here it was pulled up for a long time, and we were told to get out and stretch ourselves—an order gladly responded to, for we had been very closely packed all night. Most of us, too, took the opportunity to make an early breakfast off the food we had brought from Shoreditch. I had the remains of Mrs Travers's fowl and some bread wrapped up in my waterproof, which I shared with one or two less provident comrades. We could see from our halting-place that the line was blocked with trains beyond and behind. It must have been about eight o'clock when we got orders to take our seats again, and the train began to move slowly on towards Horsham. Horsham Junction was the point to be occupied—so the rumour went; but about ten o'clock, when halting at a small station a few miles short of it, the order came to leave the train, and our brigade formed in column on the highroad. Beyond us was some field-artillery; and further on, so we were told by a staff-officer, another brigade, which was to make up a division with ours. After more delays the line began to move, but not forwards; our route was towards the north-west, and a sort of suspicion of the state of affairs flashed across my mind. Horsham was already occupied by the enemy's advanced-guard, and we were to fall back on Leith Common, and take up a position threatening his flank, should he advance either to Guildford or Dorking. This was soon confirmed by what the colonel was told by the brigadier and passed down the ranks; and just now, for the first time, the boom of artillery came up on the light south breeze. In about an hour the firing ceased. What did it mean? We could not tell. Meanwhile our march continued. The day was very close and sultry, and the clouds of dust stirred up by our feet almost suffocated us. I had saved a soda-water-bottleful of yesterday's claret; but this went only a short way, for there were many mouths to share it with, and the thirst soon became as bad as ever. Several of the regiment fell out from faintness, and we made frequent halts to rest and let the stragglers come up. At last we reached the top of Leith Hill. It is a striking spot, being the highest point in the south of England. The view from it is splendid, and most lovely did the country look this summer day, although the grass was brown from the long drought. It was a great relief to get from the dusty road on to the common, and at the top of the hill there was a refreshing breeze. We could see now, for the first time, the whole of our division. Our regiment did not muster more than 500, for it contained a large number of Government office men who had been detained, like Danvers, for duty in town, and others were not much larger; but the militia regiment was very strong, and the whole division, I was told, mustered nearly 5,000 rank and file. We could see other troops also in extension of our division, and could count a couple of field-batteries of Royal Artillery, besides some heavy guns, belonging to the volunteers apparently, drawn by carthorses. The cooler air, the sense of numbers, and the evident strength of the position we held, raised our spirits, which, I am not ashamed to say, had all the morning been depressed. It was not that we were not eager to close with the enemy, but that the counter-marching and halting ominously betokened a vacillation of purpose in those who had the guidance of affairs. Here in two days the invaders had got more than twenty miles inland, and nothing effectual had been done to stop them. And the ignorance in which we volunteers, from the colonel downwards, were kept of their movements, filled us with uneasiness. We could not but depict to ourselves the enemy as carrying out all the while firmly his well-considered scheme of attack, and contrasting it with our own uncertainty of purpose. The very silence with which his advance appeared to be conducted filled us with mysterious awe. Meanwhile the day wore on, and we became faint with hunger, for we had eaten nothing since daybreak. No provisions came up, and there were no signs of any commissariat officers. It seems that when we were at Waterloo station a whole trainful of provisions was drawn up there, and our colonel proposed that one of the trucks should be taken off and attached to our train, so that we might have some food at hand; but the officer in charge, an assistant-controller I think they called him—this control department was a newfangled affair which did us almost as much harm as the enemy in the long-run—said his orders were to keep all the stores together, and that he couldn't issue any without authority from the head of his department. So we had to go without. Those who had tobacco smoked—indeed there is no solace like a pipe under such circumstances. The militia regiment, I heard afterwards, had two days' provisions in their haversacks; it was we volunteers who had no haversacks, and nothing to put in them. All this time, I should tell you, while we were lying on the grass with our arms piled, the General, with the brigadiers and staff, was riding about slowly from point to point of the edge of the common, looking out with his glass towards the south valley. Orderlies and staff-officers were constantly coming, and about three o'clock there arrived up a road that led towards Horsham a small body of lancers and a regiment of yeomanry, who had, it appears, been out in advance, and now drew up a short way in front of us in column facing to the south. Whether they could see anything in their front I could not tell, for we were behind the crest of the hill ourselves, and so could not look into the valley below; but shortly afterwards the assembly sounded. Commanding officers were called out by the General, and received some brief instructions; and the column began to march again towards London, the militia this time coming last in our brigade. A rumour regarding the object of this counter-march soon spread through the ranks. The enemy was not going to attack us here, but was trying to turn the position on both sides, one column pointing to Reigate, the other to Aldershot; and so we must fall back and take up a position at Dorking. The line of the great chalk-range was to be defended. A large force was concentrating at Guildford, another at Reigate, and we should find supports at Dorking. The enemy would be awaited in these positions. Such, so far as we privates could get at the facts, was to be the plan of operations. Down the hill, therefore, we marched. From one or two points we could catch a brief sight of the railway in the valley below running from Dorking to Horsham. Men in red were working upon it here and there. They were the Royal Engineers, someone said, breaking up the line. On we marched. The dust seemed worse than ever. In one village through which we passed—I forget the name now—there was a pump on the green. Here we stopped and had a good drink; and passing by a large farm, the farmer's wife and two or three of her maids stood at the gate and handed us hunches of bread and cheese out of some baskets. I got the share of a bit, but the bottom of the good woman's baskets must soon have been reached. Not a thing else was to be had till we got to Dorking about six o'clock; indeed most of the farm-houses appeared deserted already. On arriving there we were drawn up in the street, and just opposite was a baker's shop. Our fellows asked leave at first by twos and threes to go in and buy some loaves, but soon others began to break off and crowd into the shop, and at last a regular scramble took place. If there had been any order preserved, and a regular distribution arranged, they would no doubt have been steady enough, but hunger makes men selfish; each man felt that his stopping behind would do no good—he would simply lose his share; so it ended by almost the whole regiment joining in the scrimmage, and the shop was cleared out in a couple of minutes; while as for paying, you could not get your hand into your pocket for the crush. The colonel tried in vain to stop the row; some of the officers were as bad as the men. Just then a staff-officer rode by; he could scarcely make way for the crowd, and was pushed against rather rudely, and in a passion he called out to us to behave properly, like soldiers, and not like a parcel of roughs. 'Oh, blow it, governor,' said Dick Wake, 'you aren't agoing to come between a poor cove and his grub.' Wake was an articled attorney, and, as we used to say in those days, a cheeky young chap, although a good-natured fellow enough. At this speech, which was followed by some more remarks of the sort from those about him, the staff-officer became angrier still. 'Orderly,' cried he to the lancer riding behind him, 'take that man to the provost-marshal. As for you, sir,' he said, turning to our colonel, who sat on his horse silent with astonishment, 'if you don't want some of your men shot before their time, you and your precious officers had better keep this rabble in a little better order'; and poor Wick, who looked crestfallen enough, would certainly have been led off at the tail of the sergeant's horse, if the brigadier had not come up and arranged matters, and marched us off to the hill beyond the town. This incident made us both angry and crestfallen. We were annoyed at being so roughly spoken to: at the same time we felt we had deserved it, and were ashamed of the misconduct. Then, too, we had lost confidence in our colonel, after the poor figure he cut in the affair. He was a good fellow, the colonel, and showed himself a brave one next day; but he aimed too much at being popular, and didn't understand a bit how to command.

To resume:—We had scarcely reached the hill above the town, which we were told was to be our bivouac for the night, when the welcome news came that a food-train had arrived at the station; but there were no carts to bring the things up, so a fatigue-party went down and carried back a supply to us in their arms—loaves, a barrel of rum, packets of tea, and joints of meat—abundance for all; but there was not a kettle or a cooking-pot in the regiment, and we could not eat the meat raw. The colonel and officers were no better off. They had arranged to have a regular mess, with crockery, steward, and all complete, but the establishment never turned up, and what had become of it no-one knew. Some of us were sent back into the town to see what we could procure in the way of cooking utensils. We found the street full of artillery, baggage-waggons, and mounted officers, and volunteers shopping like ourselves; and all the houses appeared to be occupied by troops. We succeeded in getting a few kettles and saucepans, and I obtained for myself a leather bag, with a strap to go over the shoulder, which proved very handy afterwards; and thus laden, we trudged back to our camp on the hill, filling the kettles with dirty water from a little stream which runs between the hill and the town, for there was none to be had above. It was nearly a couple of miles each way; and, exhausted as we were with marching and want of rest, we were almost too tired to eat. The cooking was of the roughest, as you may suppose; all we could do was to cut off slices of the meat and boil them in the saucepans, using our fingers for forks. The tea, however, was very refreshing; and, thirsty as we were, we drank it by the gallon. Just before it grew dark, the brigade-major came round, and, with the adjutant, showed our colonel how to set a picket in advance of our line a little way down the face of the hill. It was not necessary to place one, I suppose, because the town in our front was still occupied with troops; but no doubt the practice would be useful. We had also a quarter-guard, and a line of sentries in front and rear of our line, communicating with those of the regiments on our flanks. Firewood was plentiful, for the hill was covered with beautiful wood; but it took some time to collect it, for we had nothing but our pocket-knives to cut down the branches with.

So we lay down to sleep. My company had no duty, and we had the night undisturbed to ourselves; but, tired though I was, the excitement and the novelty of the situation made sleep difficult. And although the night was still and warm, and we were sheltered by the woods, I soon found it chilly with no better covering than my thin dust-coat, the more so as my clothes, saturated with perspiration during the day, had never dried; and before daylight I woke from a short nap, shivering with cold, and was glad to get warm with others by a fire. I then noticed that the opposite hills on the south were dotted with fires; and we thought at first they must belong to the enemy, but we were told that the ground up there was still held by a strong rear-guard of regulars, and that there need be no fear of a surprise.

At the first sign of dawn, the bugles of the regiments sounded the *reveillé*, and we were ordered to fall in, and the roll was called. About twenty men were absent, who had fallen out sick the day before; they had been sent up to London by train during the night, I believe. After standing in column for about half an hour, the brigade-major came down with orders to pile arms and stand easy; and perhaps half an hour afterwards we were told to get breakfast as quickly as possible, and to cook a day's food at the same time. This operation was managed pretty much in the same way as the evening before, except that we had our cooking pots and kettles ready. Meantime there was leisure to look around, and from where we stood there was a commanding view of one of the most beautiful scenes in England. Our regiment was drawn up on the extremity of the ridge which runs from Guildford to Dorking. This is indeed merely a part of the great chalk-range which extends from beyond Aldershot east to the Medway; but there is a gap in the ridge just here where the little stream that runs past Dorking turns suddenly to the north, to find its way to the Thames. We stood on the slope of the hill, as it trends down eastward towards this gap, and had passed our bivouac in what appeared to be a gentleman's park. A little way above us, and to our right, was a very fine country-seat to which the park was attached, now occupied by the headquarters of our division. From this house the hill sloped steeply down southward to the valley below, which runs nearly east and west parallel to the ridge, and carries the railway and the road from Guildford to Reigate; and in which valley, immediately in front of the chateau, and perhaps a mile and a half distant from it, was the little town of Dorking, nestled in the trees, and rising up the foot of the slopes on the other side of the valley which stretched away to Leith Common, the scene of yesterday's march. Thus the main part of the town of Dorking was on our right front, but the suburbs stretched away eastward nearly to our proper front, culminating in a small railway station, from which the grassy slopes of the park rose up dotted with shrubs and trees to where we were standing. Round this railway station was a cluster of villas and one or two mills, of whose gardens we thus had a bird's-eye view, their little ornamental ponds glistening like looking-glasses in the morning sun. Immediately on our left the park sloped steeply down to the gap before mentioned, through which ran the little stream, as well as the railway from Epsom to Brighton, nearly due north and south, meeting the Guildford and Reigate line at right angles. Close to the point of intersection and the little station already mentioned, was the station of the former line where we had stopped the day before. Beyond the gap on the east (our left), and in continuation of our ridge, rose the chalk-hill again. The shoulder of this ridge overlooking the gap is called Box Hill, from the shrubbery of box-wood with which it was covered. Its sides were very steep, and the top of the ridge was covered with troops. The natural strength of our position was manifested at a glance: a high grassy ridge steep to the south, with a stream in front, and but little cover up the sides. It seemed made for a battle-field. The weak point was the gap; the ground at the junction of the railways and the roads immediately at the entrance of the gap formed a little valley, dotted, as I have said, with buildings and gardens. This, in one sense, was the key of the position; for although it would not be tenable while we held the ridge commanding it, the enemy by carrying this point and advancing through the gap would cut our line in two. But you must not suppose I scanned the ground thus critically at the time. Anybody, indeed, might have been struck with the natural advantages of our position; but what, as I remember, most impressed me, was the peaceful beauty of the scene—the little town with the outline of the houses obscured by a blue mist, the massive crispness of the foliage, the outlines of the great trees, lighted up by the sun, and relieved by deep-blue shade. So thick was the timber here, rising up the southern slopes of the valley, that it looked almost as if it might have been a primeval forest. The quiet of the scene was the more impressive because it contrasted in the mind with the scenes we expected to follow; and I can remember, as if it were yesterday, the sensation of bitter regret that it should now be too late to avert this coming desecration of our country, which might so easily have been prevented. A little firmness, a little prevision on the part of own rulers, even a little common-sense, and this great calamity would have been rendered utterly impossible. Too late, alas! We were like the foolish virgins in the parable.

But you must not suppose the scene immediately around was gloomy: the camp was brisk and bustling enough. We had got over the stress of weariness; our stomachs were full; we felt a natural enthusiasm at the prospect of having so soon to take a part as the real defenders of the country, and we were inspirited at the sight of the large force that was now assembled. Along the slopes which trended off to the rear of our ridge, troops came marching up—volunteers, militia, cavalry, and guns; these, I heard, had come down from the north as far as Leatherhead the night before, and had marched over at daybreak. Long trains, too, began to arrive by the rail through the gap, one after the other, containing militia and volunteers, who moved up to the ridge to the right and left, and took up their position, massed for the most part on the slopes which ran up from, and in rear of, where we stood. We now formed part of an army corps, we were told, consisting of three divisions, but what regiments composed the other two divisions I never heard. All this movement we could distinctly see from our position, for we had hurried over our break-fast, expecting every minute that the battle would begin, and now stood or sat about on the ground near our piled arms. Early in the morning, too, we saw a very long train come along the valley from the direction of Guildford, full of redcoats. It halted at the little station at our feet, and the troops alighted. We could soon make out their bear-skins. They were the Guards, coming to reinforce this part of the line. Leaving a detachment of skirmishers to hold the line of the railway embankment, the main body marched up with a springy step and with the band playing, and drew up across the gap on our left, in prolongation of our line. There appeared to be three battalions of them, for they formed up in that number of columns at short intervals.

Shortly after this I was sent over to Box Hill with a message from our colonel to the colonel of a volunteer regiment stationed there, to know whether an ambulance-cart was obtainable, as it was reported this regiment was well supplied with carriage, whereas we were without any: my mission, however, was futile. Crossing the valley, I found a scene of great confusion at the railway station. Trains were still coming in with stores, ammunition, guns, and appliances of all sorts, which were being unloaded as fast as possible; but there were scarcely any means of getting the things off. There were plenty of waggons of all sorts, but hardly any horses to draw them, and the whole place was blocked up; while, to add to the confusion, a regular exodus had taken place of the people from the town, who had been warned that it was likely to be the scene of fighting. Ladies and women of all sorts and ages, and children, some with bundles, some empty-handed, were seeking places in the train, but there appeared no one on the spot authorized to grant them, and these poor creatures were pushing their way up and down, vainly asking for information and permission to get away. In the crowd I observed our surgeon, who likewise was in search of an ambulance of some sort: his whole professional apparatus, he said, consisted of a case of instruments. Also in the crowd I stumbled upon Wood, Travers's old coachman. He had been sent down by his mistress to Guildford, because it was supposed our regiment had gone there, riding the horse, and laden with a supply of things—food, blankets, and, of course, a letter. He had also brought my knapsack; but at Guildford the horse was pressed for artillery work, and a receipt for it given him in exchange, so he had been obliged to leave all the heavy packages there, including my knapsack; but the faithful old man had brought on as many things as he could carry, and hearing that we should be found in this part, had walked over thus laden from Guildford. He said that place was crowded with troops, and that the heights were lined with them the whole way between the two towns; also, that some trains with wounded had passed up from the coast in the night, through Guildford. I led him off to where our regiment was, relieving the old man from part of the load he was staggering under. The food sent was not now so much needed, but the plates, knives, etc., and drinking-vessels, promised to be handy—and Travers, you may be sure, was delighted to get his letter; while a couple of newspapers the old man had brought were eagerly competed for by all, even at this critical moment, for we had heard no authentic news since we left London on Sunday. And even at this distance of time, although I only glanced down the paper, I can remember almost the very words I read there. They were both copies of the same paper: the first, published on Sunday evening, when the news had arrived of the successful landing at three points, was written in a tone of despair. The country must confess that it had been taken by surprise. The conqueror would be satisfied with the humiliation inflicted by a peace dictated on our own shores; it was the clear duty of the Government to accept the best terms obtainable, and to avoid further bloodshed and disaster, and avert the fall of our tottering mercantile credit. The next morning's issue was in quite a different tone. Apparently the enemy had received a check, for we were here exhorted to resistance. An impregnable position was to be taken up along the Downs, a force was concentrating there far outnumbering the rash invaders, who, with an invincible line before them, and the sea behind, had no choice between destruction or surrender. Let there be no pusillanimous talk of negotiation, the fight must be fought out; and there could be but one issue. England, expectant but calm, awaited with confidence the result of the attack on its unconquerable volunteers. The writing appeared to me eloquent, but rather inconsistent. The same paper said the Government had sent off 500 workmen from Woolwich, to open a branch arsenal at Birmingham.

All this time we had nothing to do, except to change our position, which we did every few minutes, now moving up the hill farther to our right, now taking ground lower down to our left, as one order after another was brought down the line; but the staff-officers were galloping about perpetually with orders, while the rumble of the artillery as they moved about from one part of the field to another went on almost incessantly. At last the whole line stood to arms, the bands struck up, and the general commanding our army corps came riding down with his staff. We had seen him several times before, as we had been moving frequently about the position during the morning; but he now made a sort of formal inspection. He was a tall thin man, with long light hair, very well mounted, and as he sat his horse with an erect seat, and came prancing down the line, at a little distance he looked as if he might be five-and-twenty; but I believe he had served more than fifty years, and had been made a peer for services performed when quite an old man. I remember that he had more decorations than there was room for on the breast of his coat, and

26

wore them suspended like a necklace round his neck. Like all the other generals, he was dressed in blue, with a cocked-hat and feathers—a bad plan, I thought, for it made them very conspicuous. The general halted before our battalion, and after looking at us a while, made a short address: We had a post of honour next her Majesty's Guards, and would show ourselves worthy of it, and of the name of Englishmen. It did not need, he said, to be a general to see the strength of our position; it was impregnable, if properly held. Let us wait till the enemy was well pounded, and then the word would be given to go at him. Above everything, we must be steady. He then shook hands with our colonel, we gave him a cheer, and he rode on to where the Guards were drawn up.

Now then, we thought, the battle will begin. But still there were no signs of the enemy; and the air, though hot and sultry, began to be very hazy, so that you could scarcely see the town below, and the hills opposite were merely a confused blur, in which no features could be distinctly made out. After a while, the tension of feeling which followed the general's address relaxed, and we began to feel less as if everything depended on keeping our rifles firmly grasped: we were told to pile arms again, and got leave to go down by tens and twenties to the stream below to drink. This stream, and all the hedges and banks on our side of it, were held by our skirmishers, but the town had been abandoned. The position appeared an excellent one, except that the enemy, when they came, would have almost better cover than our men. While I was down at the brook, a column emerged from the town, making for our position. We thought for a moment it was the enemy, and you could not make out the colour of the uniforms for the dust; but it turned out to be our rear-guard, falling back from the opposite hills which they had occupied the previous night. One battalion, of rifles, halted for a few minutes at the stream to let the men drink, and I had a minute's talk with a couple of the officers. They had formed part of the force which had attacked the enemy on their first landing. They had it all their own way, they said, at first, and could have beaten the enemy back easily if they had been properly supported; but the whole thing was mismanaged. The volunteers came on very pluckily, they said, but they got into confusion, and so did the militia, and the attack failed with serious loss. It was the wounded of this force which had passed through Guildford in the night. The officers asked us eagerly about the arrangements for the battle, and when we said that the Guards were the only regular troops in this part of the field, shook their heads ominously.

While we were talking, a third officer came up; he was a dark man with a smooth face and a curious excited manner. 'You are volunteers, I suppose,' he said, quickly, his eye flashing the while. 'Well, now, look here; mind I don't want to hurt your feelings, or to say anything unpleasant, but I'll tell you what; if all you gentlemen were just to go back, and leave us to fight it out alone, it would be a devilish good thing. We could do it a precious deal better without you, I assure you. We don't want your help, I can tell you. We would much rather be left alone, I assure you. Mind I don't want to say anything rude, but that's a fact.' Having blurted out this passionately, he strode away before any one could reply, or the other officers could stop him. They apologized for his rudeness, saying that his brother, also in the regiment, had been killed on Sunday, and that this, and the sun, and marching, had affected his head. The officers told us that the enemy's advanced-guard was close behind, but that he had apparently been waiting for reinforcements, and would probably not attack in force until noon. It was, however, nearly three o'clock before the battle began. We had almost worn out the feeling of expectancy. For twelve hours had we been waiting for the coming struggle, till at last it seemed almost as if the invasion were but a bad dream, and the enemy, as yet unseen by us, had no real existence. So far things had not been very different, but for the numbers and for what we had been told, from a Volunteer review on Brighton Downs. I remember that these thoughts were passing through my mind as we lay down in groups on the grass, some smoking, some nibbling at their bread, some even asleep, when the listless state we had fallen into was suddenly disturbed by a gunshot fired from the top of the hill on our right, close by the big house. It was the first time I had ever heard a shotted gun fired, and although it is fifty years ago, the angry whistle of the shot as it left the gun is in my ears now. The sound was soon to become common enough. We all jumped up at the report, and fell in almost without the word being given, grasping our rifles tightly, and the leading files peering forward to look for the approaching enemy. This gun was apparently the signal to begin, for now our batteries opened fire all along the line. What they were firing at I could not see, and I am sure the gunners could not see much themselves. I have told you what a haze had come over the air since the morning, and now the smoke from the guns settled like a pall over the hill, and soon we could see little but the men in our ranks, and the outline of some gunners in the battery drawn up next us on the slope on our right. This firing went on, I should think for nearly a couple of hours, and still there was no reply. We could see the gunners—it was a troop of horse-artillery—working away like fury, ramming, loading, and running up with cartridges, the officer in command riding slowly up and down just behind his guns, and peering out with his field-glass into the mist. Once or twice they ceased firing to let their smoke clear away, but this did not do much good. For nearly two hours did this go on, and not a shot came in reply. If a battle is like this, said Dick Wake, who was my next-hand file, it's mild work, to say the least. The words were hardly uttered when a rattle of musketry was heard in front; our skirmishers were at it, and very soon the bullets began to sing over our heads, and some struck the ground at our feet. Up to this time we had been in column; we were now deployed into line on the ground assigned to us. From the valley or gap on our left there ran a lane right up the hill almost due west, or along our front. This lane had a thick bank about four feet high, and the greater part of the regiment was drawn up behind it; but a little way up the hill the lane trended back out of the line, so the right of the regiment here left it and occupied the open grass-land of the park. The bank had been cut away at this point to admit of our going in and out. We had been told in the morning to cut down the bushes on the top of the bank, so as to make the space clear for firing over, but we had no tools to work with; however, a party of sappers had come down and finished the job. My company was on the right, and was thus beyond the shelter of the friendly bank. On our right again was the battery of artillery already mentioned; then came a battalion of the line, then more guns, then a great mass of militia and volunteers and a few line up to the big house. At least this was the order before the firing began; after that I do not know what changes took place.

And now the enemy's artillery began to open; where their guns were posted we could not see, but we began to hear the rush of the shells over our heads, and the bang as they burst just beyond. And now what took place I can really hardly tell you. Sometimes when I try and recall the scene, it seems as if it lasted for only a few minutes; yet I know, as we lay on the ground, I thought the hours would never pass away, as we watched the gunners still plying their task, firing at the invisible enemy, never stopping for a moment except when now and again a dull blow would be heard and a man fall down, then three or four of his comrades would carry him to the rear. The captain no longer rode up and down; what had become of him I do not know. Two of the guns ceased firing for a time; they had got injured in some way, and up rode an artillery general. I think I see him now, a very handsome man, with straight features and a dark moustache, his breast covered with medals. He appeared in a great rage at the guns stopping fire.

'Who commands this battery?' he cried.

'I do, Sir Henry,' said an officer, riding forward, whom I had not noticed before.

The group is before me at this moment, standing out clear against the background of smoke, Sir Henry erect on his splendid charger, his flashing eye, his left arm pointing towards the enemy to enforce something he was going to say, the young officer reining in his horse just beside him, and saluting with his right hand raised to his busby. This for a moment, then a dull thud, and both horses and riders are prostrate on the ground. A round-shot had struck all four at the saddle-line. Some of the gunners ran up to help, but neither officer could have lived many minutes. This was not the first I saw killed. Some time before this, almost immediately on the enemy's artillery opening, as we were lying, I heard something like the sound of metal striking metal, and at the same moment Dick Wake, who was next me in the ranks, leaning on his elbows, sank forward on his face. I looked round and saw what had happened; a shot fired at a high elevation, passing over his head, had struck the ground behind, nearly cutting his thigh off. It must have been the ball striking his sheathed bayonet which made the noise. Three of us carried the poor fellow to the rear, with difficulty for the shattered limb; but he was nearly dead from loss of blood when we got to the doctor, who was waiting in a sheltered hollow about two hundred yards in rear, with two other doctors in plain clothes, who had come up to help. We deposited our burden and returned to the front. Poor Wake was sensible when we left him, but apparently too shaken by the shock to be able to speak. Wood was there helping the doctors. I paid more visits to the rear of the same sort before the evening was over.

All this time we were lying there to be fired at without returning a shot, for our skirmishers were holding the line of walls and enclosures below. However, the bank protected most of us, and the brigadier now ordered our right company, which was in the open, to get behind it also; and there we lay about four deep, the shells crashing and bullets whistling over our heads, but hardly a man being touched. Our colonel was, indeed, the only one exposed, for he rode up and down the lane at a foot-pace as steady as a rock; but he made the major and adjutant dismount, and take shelter behind the hedge, holding their horses. We were all pleased to see him so cool, and it restored our confidence in him, which had been shaken yesterday.

The time seemed interminable while we lay thus inactive. We could not, of course, help peering over the bank to try and see what was going on; but there was nothing to be made out, for now a tremendous thunderstorm, which had been gathering all day, burst on us, and a torrent of almost blinding rain came down, which obscured the view even more than the smoke, while the crashing of the thunder and the glare of the lightning could be heard and seen even above the roar and flashing of the artillery. Once the mist lifted, and I saw for a minute an attack on Box Hill, on the other side of the gap on our left. It was like the scene at a theatre—a curtain of smoke all round and a clear gap in the centre, with a sudden gleam of evening sunshine lighting it up. The steep smooth slope of the hill was crowded with the dark-blue figures of the enemy, whom I now saw for the first time—an irregular outline in front, but very solid in rear: the whole body was moving forward by fits and starts, the men firing and advancing, the officers waving their swords, the columns closing up and gradually making way. Our people were almost concealed by the bushes at the top, whence the smoke and their fire could be seen proceeding: presently from these bushes on the crest came out a red line, and dashed down the brow of the hill, a flame of fire belching out from the front as it advanced. The enemy hesitated, gave way, and finally ran back in a confused crowd down the hill. Then the mist covered the scene, but the glimpse of this splendid charge was inspiriting, and I hoped we should show the same coolness when it came to our turn. It was about this time that our skirmishers fell back, a good many wounded, some limping along by themselves, others helped. The main body retired in very fair order, halting to turn round and fire; we could see a mounted officer of the Guards riding up and down encouraging them to be steady. Now came our turn. For a few minutes we saw nothing, but a rattle of bullets came through the rain and mist, mostly, however, passing over the bank. We began to fire in reply, stepping up against the bank to fire, and stooping down to load; but our brigade-major rode up with an order, and word was passed through the men to reserve our fire. In a very few moments it must have been that, when ordered to stand up, we could see the helmet-spikes and then the figures of the skirmishers as they came on: a lot of them there appeared to be, five or six deep I should say, but in loose order, each man stopping to aim and fire, and then coming forward a little. Just then the brigadier clattered on horseback up the lane. 'Now, then, gentlemen, give it them hot!' he cried; and fire away we did, as fast as ever we were able. A perfect storm of bullets seemed to be flying about us too, and I thought each moment must be the last; escape seemed impossible, but I saw no one fall, for I was too busy, and so were we all, to look to the right or left, but loaded and fired as fast as we could. How long this went on I know not—it could not have been long; neither side could have lasted many minutes under such a fire, but it ended by the enemy gradually falling back, and as soon as we saw this we raised a tremendous shout, and some of us jumped up on the bank to give them our parting shots. Suddenly the order was passed down the line to cease firing, and we soon discovered the cause; a battalion of the Guards was charging obliquely across from our left across our front. It was, I expect, their flank attack as much as our fire which had turned back the enemy; and it was a splendid sight to see their steady line as they advanced slowly across the smooth lawn below us, firing as they went, but as steady as if on parade. We felt a great elation at this moment; it seemed as if the battle was won. Just then somebody called out to look to the wounded, and for the first time I turned to glance down the rank along the line. Then I saw that we had not beaten back the attack without loss. Immediately before me lay Bob Lawford of my office, dead on his back from a bullet through his forehead, his hand still grasping his rifle. At every step was some friend or acquaintance killed or wounded, and a few paces down the lane I found Travers, sitting with his back against the bank. A ball had gone through his lungs, and blood was coming from his mouth. I was lifting him up, but the cry of agony he gave stopped me. I then saw that this was not his only wound; his thigh was smashed by a bullet (which must have hit him when standing on the bank), and the blood streaming down mixed in a muddy puddle with the rain-water under him. Still he could not be left here, so, lifting him up as well as I could, I carried him through the gate which led out of the lane at the back to where our camp hospital was in the rear. The movement must have caused him awful agony, for I could not support the broken thigh, and he could not restrain his groans, brave fellow though he was; but how I carried him at all I cannot make out, for he was a much bigger man than myself; but I had not gone far, one of a stream of our fellows, all on the same errand, when a bandsman and Wood met me, bringing a hurdle as a stretcher, and on this we placed him. Wood had just time to tell me that he had got a cart down in the hollow, and would endeavour to take off his master at once to Kingston, when a staff-officer rode up to call us to the ranks. 'You really must not straggle in this way, gentlemen,' he said, 'pray keep your ranks.' 'But we can't leave our wounded to be trodden down and die,' cried one of our fellows. 'Beat off the enemy first, sir,' he replied. 'Gentlemen, do, pray, join your regiments, or we shall be a regular mob.' And no doubt he did not speak too soon; for besides our fellows straggling to the rear, lots of volunteers from the regiments in reserve were running forward to help, till the whole ground was dotted with groups of men. I hastened back to my post, but I had just time to notice that all the ground in our rear was occupied by a thick mass of troops, much more numerous than in the morning, and a column was moving down to the left of our line, to the ground before held by the Guards. All this time, although the musketry had slackened, the artillery-fire seemed heavier than ever; the shells screamed overhead or burst around; and I confess to feeling quite a relief at getting back to the friendly shelter of the lane. Looking over the bank, I noticed for the first time the frightful execution our fire had created. The space in front was thickly strewed with dead and badly wounded, and beyond the bodies of the fallen enemy could just be seen—for it was now getting dusk—the bear-skins and red coats of our own gallant Guards scattered over the slope, and marking the line of their victorious advance. But hardly a minute could have passed in thus looking over the field, when our brigade-major came moving up the lane on foot (I suppose his horse had been shot), crying, 'Stand to your arms, volunteers! they're coming on again'; and we found ourselves a second time engaged in a hot musketry-fire. How long it went on I cannot now remember, but we could distinguish clearly the thick line of skirmishers, about sixty paces off, and mounted officers among them; and we seemed to be keeping them well in check, for they were quite exposed to our fire, while we were protected nearly up to our shoulders, when—I know not how—I became sensible that something had gone wrong. 'We are taken in the flank!' called out someone; and looking along the left, sure enough there were dark figures jumping over the bank into the lane and firing up along our line. The volunteers in reserve, who had come down to take the place of the

Guards, must have given way at this point; the enemy's skirmishers had got through our line, and turned our left flank. How the next move came about I cannot recollect, or whether it was without orders, but in a short time we found ourselves out of the lane, and drawn up in a straggling line about thirty yards in rear of it—at our end, that is, the other flank had fallen back a good deal more—and the enemy were lining the hedge, and numbers of them passing over and forming up on our side. Beyond our left a confused mass were retreating, firing as they went, followed by the advancing line of the enemy. We stood in this way for a short space, firing at random as fast as we could. Our colonel and major must have been shot, for there was no one to give an order, when somebody on horseback called out from behind—I think it must have been the brigadier—'Now, then, volunteers! give a British cheer, and go at them—charge!' and, with a shout, we rushed at the enemy. Some of them ran, some stopped to meet us, and for a moment it was a real hand-to-hand fight. I felt a sharp sting in my leg, as I drove my bayonet right through the man in front of me. I confess I shut my eyes, for I just got a glimpse of the poor wretch as he fell back, his eyes starting out of his head, and, savage though we were, the sight was almost too horrible to look at. But the struggle was over in a second, and we had cleared the ground again right up to the rear hedge of the lane. Had we gone on, I believe we might have recovered the lane too, but we were now all out of order; there was no one to say what to do; the enemy began to line the hedge and open fire, and they were streaming past our left; and how it came about I know not, but we found ourselves falling back towards our right rear, scarce any semblance of a line remaining, and the volunteers who had given way on our left mixed up with us, and adding to the confusion. It was now nearly dark. On the slopes which we were retreating to was a large mass of reserves drawn up in columns. Some of the leading files of these, mistaking us for the enemy, began firing at us; our fellows, crying out to them to stop, ran towards their ranks, and in a few moments the whole slope of the hill became a scene of confusion that I cannot attempt to describe, regiments and detachments mixed up in hopeless disorder. Most of us, I believe, turned towards the enemy and fired away our few remaining cartridges; but it was too late to take aim, fortunately for us, or the guns which the enemy had brought up through the gap, and were firing point-blank, would have done more damage. As it was, we could see little more than the bright flashes of their fire. In our confusion we had jammed up a line regiment immediately behind us, which I suppose had just arrived on the field, and its colonel and some staff-officers were in vain trying to make a passage for it, and their shouts to us to march to the rear and clear a road could be heard above the roar of the guns and the confused babel of sound. At last a mounted officer pushed his way through, followed by a company in sections, the men brushing past with firm-set faces, as if on a desperate task; and the battalion, when it got clear, appeared to deploy and advance down the slope. I have also a dim recollection of seeing the Life Guards trot past the front, and push on towards the town—a last desperate attempt to save the day—before we left the field. Our adjutant, who had got separated from our flank of the regiment in the confusion, now came up, and managed to lead us, or at any rate some of us, up to the crest of the hill in the rear, to re-form, as he said; but there we met a vast crowd of volunteers, militia, and waggons, all hurrying rearward from the direction of the big house, and we were borne in the stream for a mile at least before it was possible to stop. At last the adjutant led us to an open space a little off the line of fugitives, and there we reformed the remains of the companies. Telling us to halt, he rode off to try and obtain orders, and find out where the rest of our brigade was. From this point, a spur of high ground running off from the main plateau, we looked down through the dim twilight into the battlefield below. Artillery-fire was still going on. We could see the flashes from the guns on both sides, and now and then a stray shell came screaming up and burst near us, but we were beyond the sound of musketry. This halt first gave us time to think about what had happened. The long day of expectancy had been succeeded by the excitement of battle; and when each minute may be your last, you do not think much about other people, nor when you are facing another man with a rifle have you time to consider whether he or you are the invader, or that you are fighting for your home and hearths. All fighting is pretty much alike, I suspect, as to sentiment, when once it begins. But now we had time for reflection; and although we did not yet quite understand how far the day had gone against us, an uneasy feeling of self-condemnation must have come up in the minds of most of us; while, above all, we now began to realize what the loss of this battle meant to the country. Then, too, we knew not what had become of all our wounded comrades. Reaction, too, set in after the fatigue and excitement. For myself, I had found out for the first time that besides the bayonet-wound in my leg, a bullet had gone through my left arm, just below the shoulder, and outside the bone. I remember feeling something like a blow just when we lost the lane, but the wound passed unnoticed till now, when the bleeding had stopped and the shirt was sticking to the wound.

This half-hour seemed an age, and while we stood on this knoll the endless tramp of men and rumbling of carts along the down beside us told their own tale. The whole army was falling back. At last we could discern the adjutant riding up to us out of the dark. The army was to retreat and take up a position on Epsom Downs, he said; we should join in the march, and try and find our brigade in the morning; and so we turned into the throng again, and made our way on as best we could. A few scraps of news he gave us as he rode alongside of our leading section; the army had held its position well for a time, but the enemy had at last broken through the line between us and Guildford, as well as in our front, and had poured his men through the point gained, throwing the line into confusion, and the first army corps near Guildford were also falling back to avoid being outflanked. The regular troops were holding the rear; we were to push on as fast as possible to get out of their way, and allow them to make an orderly retreat in the morning. The gallant old lord commanding our corps had been badly wounded early in the day, he heard, and carried off the field. The Guards had suffered dreadfully; the household cavalry had ridden down the cuirassiers, but had got into broken ground and been awfully cut up. Such were the scraps of news passed down our weary column.

What had become of our wounded no one knew, and no one liked to ask. So we trudged on. It must have been midnight when we reached Leatherhead. Here we left the open ground and took to the road, and the block became greater. We pushed our way painfully along; several trains passed slowly ahead along the railway by the roadside, containing the wounded, we supposed—such of them, at least, as were lucky enough to be picked up. It was daylight when we got to Epsom. The night had been bright and clear after the storm, with a cool air, which, blowing through my soaking clothes, chilled me to the bone. My wounded leg was stiff and sore, and I was ready to drop with exhaustion and hunger. Nor were my comrades in much better case; we had eaten nothing since breakfast the day before, and the bread we had put by had been washed away by the storm: only a little pulp remained at the bottom of my bag. The tobacco was all too wet to smoke. In this plight we were creeping along, when the adjutant guided us into a field by the roadside to rest awhile, and we lay down exhausted on the sloppy grass. The roll was here taken, and only 180 answered out of nearly 500 present on the morning of the battle. How many of these were killed and wounded no one could tell; but it was certain many must have got separated in the confusion of the evening. While resting here, we saw pass by, in the crowd of vehicles and men, a cart laden with commissariat stores, driven by a man in uniform. 'Food!' cried someone, and a dozen volunteers jumped up and surrounded the cart. The driver tried to whip them off; but he was pulled off his seat, and the contents of the cart thrown out in an instant. They were preserved meats in tins, which we tore open with our bayonets. The meat had been cooked before, I think; at any rate we devoured it. Shortly after this a general came by with three or four staff-officers. He stopped and spoke to our adjutant, and then rode into the field. 'My lads,' said he, 'you shall join my division for the present: fall in, and follow the regiment that is now passing.' We rose up, fell in by companies, each about twenty strong, and turned once more into the stream moving along the road—regiments, detachments, single volunteers or militiamen, country people making off, some with bundles, some without, a few in carts, but most on foot; here and there waggons of stores, with men sitting wherever there was room, others crammed with wounded soldiers. Many blocks occurred from horses falling, or carts breaking down and filling up the road. In the town the confusion was even worse, for all the houses seemed full of volunteers and militiamen, wounded or resting, or trying to find food, and the streets were almost choked up. Some officers were in vain trying to restore order, but the task seemed a hopeless one. One or two volunteer regiments which had arrived from the north the previous night, and had been halted here for orders, were drawn up along the roadside steadily enough, and some of the retreating regiments, including ours, may have preserved the semblance of discipline, but for the most part the mass pushing to the rear was a mere mob. The regulars, or what remained of them, were now, I believe, all in the rear, to hold the advancing enemy in check. A few officers among such a crowd could do nothing. To add to the confusion, several houses were being emptied of the wounded brought here the night before, to prevent their falling into the hands of the enemy, some in carts, some being carried to the railway by men. The groans of these poor fellows as they were jostled through the street went to our hearts, selfish though fatigue and suffering had made us. At last, following the guidance of a staff-officer who was standing to show the way, we turned off from the main London road and took that towards Kingston. Here the crush was less, and we managed to move along pretty steadily. The air had been cooled by the storm, and there was no dust. We passed through a village where our new general had seized all the public-houses, and taken possession of the liquor; and each regiment as it came up was halted, and each man got a drink of beer, served out by companies. Whether the owner got paid, I know not, but it was like nectar. It must have been about one o'clock in the afternoon that we came in sight of Kingston. We had been on our legs sixteen hours, and had got over about twelve miles of ground. There is a hill a little south of the Surbiton station, covered then mostly with villas, but open at the western extremity, where there was a clump of trees on the summit. We had diverged from the road towards this, and here the general halted us and disposed the line of the division along his front, facing to the south-west, the right of the line reaching down to the water-works on the Thames, the left extending along the southern slope of the hill, in the direction of the Epsom road by which we had come. We were nearly in the centre, occupying the knoll just in front of the general, who dismounted on the top and tied his horse to a tree. It is not much of a hill, but commands an extensive view over the flat country around; and as we lay wearily on the ground we could see the Thames glisten-ing like a silver field in the bright sunshine, the palace at Hampton Court, the bridge at Kingston, and the old church tower rising above the haze of the town, with the woods of Richmond Park behind it. To most of us the scene could not but call up the associations of happy days of peace—days now ended and peace destroyed through national infatuation. We did not say this to each other, but a deep depression had come upon us, partly due to weakness and fatigue, no doubt, but we saw that another stand was going to be made, and we had no longer any confidence in ourselves. If we could not hold our own when stationary in line, on a good position, but had been broken up into a rabble at the first shock, what chance had we now of manoeuv-ring against a victorious enemy in this open ground? A feeling of desperation came over us, a determination to struggle on against hope; but anxiety for the future of the country, and our friends, and all dear to us, filled our thoughts now that we had time for reflection. We had had no news of any kind since Wood joined us the day before—we knew not what was doing in London, or what the Government was about, or anything else; and exhausted though we were, we felt an intense craving to know what was happening in other parts of the country.

Our general had expected to find a supply of food and ammunition here, but nothing turned up. Most of us had hardly a cartridge left, so he ordered the regiment next to us, which came from the north and had not been engaged, to give us enough to make up twenty rounds a man, and he sent off a fatigue-party to Kingston to try and get pro-visions while a detachment of our fellows was allowed to go foraging among the villas in our rear; and in about an hour they brought back some bread and meat, which gave us a slender meal all round. They said most of the houses were empty, and that many had been stripped of all eatables, and a good deal damaged already.

It must have been between three and four o'clock when the sound of cannonading began to be heard in the front, and we could see the smoke of the guns rising above the woods of Esher and Claremont, and soon afterwards some troops emerged from the fields below us. It was the rear-guard of regular troops. There were some guns also, which were driven up the slope and took up their position round the knoll. There were three batteries, but they only counted eight guns among them. Behind them was posted the line; it was a brigade apparently of four regiments, but the whole did not look to be more than eight or nine hundred men. Our regiment and another had been moved a little to the rear to make way for them, and presently we were ordered down to occupy the railway station on our right rear. My leg was now so stiff I could no longer march with the rest, and my left arm was very swollen and sore, and almost useless; but anything seemed better than being left behind, so I limped after the battalion as best I could down to the station. There was a goods shed a little in advance of it down the line, a strong brick building, and here my company was posted. The rest of our men lined the wall of the enclosure. A staff-officer came with us to arrange the distribution; we should be supported by line troops, he said; and in a few minutes a train full of them came slowly up from Guildford way. It was the last; the men got out, the train passed on, and a party began to tear up the rails, while the rest were distributed among the houses on each side. A sergeant's party joined us in our shed, and an engineer officer with sappers came to knock holes in the walls for us to fire from; but there were only half a dozen of them, so progress was not rapid, and as we had no tools we could not help.

It was while we were watching this job that the adjutant, who was as active as ever, looked in, and told us to muster in the yard. The fatigue-party had come back from Kingston, and a small baker's hand-cart of food was made over to us as our share. It contained loaves, flour, and some joints of meat. The meat and the flour we had time or means to cook. The loaves we devoured; and there was a tap of water in the yard, so we felt refreshed by the meal. I should have liked to wash my wounds, which were becoming very offensive, but I dared not take off my coat, feeling sure I should not be able to get it on again. It was while we were eating our bread that the rumour first reached us of another disaster, even greater than that we had witnessed ourselves. Whence it came I know not; but a whisper went down the ranks that Woolwich had been captured. We all knew that it was our only arsenal, and understood the significance of the blow. No hope, if this were true, of saving the country. Thinking over this, we went back to the shed.

Although this was only our second day of war, I think we were already old soldiers so far that we had come to be careless about fire, and the shot and shell that now began to open on us made no sensation. We felt, indeed, our need of discipline, and we saw plainly enough the slender chance of success coming out of troops so imperfectly trained as we were; but I think we were all determined to fight on as long as we could. Our gallant adjutant gave his spirit to everybody; and the staff-officer commanding was a very cheery fellow, and went about as if we were certain of victory. Just as the firing began he looked in to say that we were as safe as in a church, that we must be sure and pepper the enemy well, and that more cartridges would soon arrive. There were some steps and benches in the shed, and on these a part of our men were standing, to fire through the upper loop-holes, while the line soldiers and others stood on the ground, guarding the second row. I sat on the floor, for I could not now use my rifle, and besides, there were more men than loop-holes. The artillery fire which had opened now on our position was from a longish range; and occupation for the riflemen had hardly begun when there was a crash in the shed, and I was knocked down by a blow on the head. I was almost stunned for a time, and could not make out at first what had happened. A shot or shell had hit the shed without quite penetrating the wall, but the blow had upset the steps resting against it, and the men standing on them, bringing down a cloud of plaster and brickbats, one of which had struck me. I felt now past being of use. I could not use my rifle, and could barely stand; and after a time I thought I would make for my own house, on the chance of finding some one still there. I got up therefore, and staggered homewards. Musketry fire had now commenced, and our side were blazing away from the windows of the houses, and from behind walls, and from the shelter of some trucks still standing in the station. A couple of field-pieces in the yard were firing, and in the open space in rear of the station a reserve was drawn up. There, too, was the staff-officer on horseback, watching the fight through his field-glass. I remember having still enough sense to feel that the position was a hopeless one. That straggling line of houses and gardens would surely be broken through at some point, and then the line must give way like a rope of sand. It was about a mile to our house, and I was thinking how I could possibly drag myself so far when I suddenly recollected that I was passing Travers's house—one of the first of a row of villas then leading from the Surbiton station to Kingston. Had he been brought home, I wonder, as his faithful old servant promised, and was his wife still here? I remember to this day the sensation of shame I felt, when I recollected that I had not once given him—my greatest friend—a thought since I carried him off the field the day before. But war and suffering make men selfish. I would go in now at any rate and rest awhile, and see if I could be of use. The little garden before the house was as trim as ever—I used to pass it every day on my way to the train, and knew every shrub in it—and ablaze with flowers, but the hall-door stood ajar. I stepped in and saw little Arthur standing in the hall. He had been dressed as neatly as ever that day, and as he stood there in his pretty blue frock and white trousers and socks showing his chubby little legs, with his golden locks, fair face, and large dark eyes, the picture of childish beauty, in the quiet hall, just as it used to look—the vases of flowers, the hat and coats hanging up, the familiar pictures on the walls—this vision of peace in the midst of war made me wonder for a moment, faint and giddy as I was, if the pandemonium outside had any real existence, and was not merely a hideous dream. But the roar of the guns making the house shake, and the rushing of the shot, gave a ready answer. The little fellow appeared almost unconscious of the scene around him, and was walking up the stairs holding by the railing, one step at a time, as I had seen him do a hundred times before, but turned round as I came in. My appearance frightened him, and staggering as I did into the hall, my face and clothes covered with blood and dirt, I must have looked an awful object to the child, for he gave a cry and turned to run towards the basement stairs. But he stopped on hearing my voice calling him back to his god-papa, and after a while came timidly up to me. Papa had been to the battle, he said, and was very ill: mamma was with papa: Wood was out: Lucy was in the cellar, and had taken him there, but he wanted to go to mamma. Telling him to stay in the hall for a minute till I called him, I climbed upstairs and opened the bedroom-door. My poor friend lay there, his body resting on the bed, his head supported on his wife's shoulder as she sat by the bedside. He breathed heavily, but the pallor of his face, the closed eyes, the prostrate arms, the clammy foam she was wiping from his mouth, all spoke of approaching death. The good old servant had done his duty, at least— he had brought his master home to die in his wife's arms. The poor woman was too intent on her charge to notice the opening of the door, and as the child would be better away, I closed it gently and went down to the hall to take little Arthur to the shelter below, where the maid was hiding. Too late! He lay at the foot of the stairs on his face, his little arms stretched out, his hair dabbled in blood. I had not noticed the crash among the other noises, but a splinter of shell must have come through the open doorway; it had carried away the back of his head. The poor child's death must have been instantaneous. I tried to lift up the little corpse with my one arm, but even this load was too much for me, and while stooping down I fainted away.

When I came to my sense again it was quite dark, and for some time I could not make out where I was; I lay indeed for some time like one half asleep, feeling no inclination to move. By degrees I became aware that I was on the carpeted floor of a room. All noise of battle had ceased, but there was a sound as of many people close by. At last I sat up and gradually got to my feet. The movement gave me intense pain, for my wounds were now highly inflamed, and my clothes sticking to them made them dreadfully sore. At last I got up and groped my way to the door, and opening it at once saw where I was, for the pain had brought back my senses. I had been lying in Travers's little writing-room at the end of the passage, into which I made my way. There was no gas, and the drawing-room door was closed; but from the open dining-room the glimmer of a candle feebly lighted up the hall, in which half a dozen sleeping figures could be discerned, while the room itself was crowded with men. The table was covered with plates, glasses, and bottles; but most of the men were asleep in the chairs or on the floor, a few were smoking cigars, and one or two with their helmets on were still engaged at supper, occasionally grunting out an observation between the mouthfuls.

'Sind wackere Soldaten, diese Englischen Freiwilligen,' said a broad-shouldered brute, stuffing a great hunch of beef into his mouth with a silver fork, an implement I should think he must have been using for the first time in his life.

'Ja, ja,' replied a comrade, who was lolling back in his chair with a pair of very dirty legs on the table, and one of poor Travers's best cigars in his mouth. 'Sie so gut laufen können.'

'Ja wohl,' responded the first speaker; 'aber sind nicht eben so schnell wie die Französischen Mobloten.'

'Gewiss,' grunted a hulking lout from the floor, leaning on his elbow, and sending out a cloud of smoke from his ugly jaws; 'und da sind hier etwa gute Schützen.'

'Hast recht, lange Peter,' answered number one; 'wenn die Schurken so gut exerciren wie schützen können, so wären wir heute nicht hier!'

'Recht! recht!' said the second; 'das exerciren macht den guten Soldaten.'

What more criticisms on the shortcomings of our unfortunate volunteers might have passed I did not stop to hear, being interrupted by a sound on the stairs. Mrs Travers was standing on the landing-place; I limped up the stairs to meet her. Among the many pictures of those fatal days engraven on my memory, I remember none more

45

clearly than the mournful aspect of my poor friend, widowed and childless within a few moments, as she stood there in her white dress, coming forth like a ghost from the chamber of the dead, the candle she held lighting up her face, and contrasting its pallor with the dark hair that fell disordered round it, its beauty radiant even through features worn with fatigue and sorrow. She was calm and even tearless, though the trembling lip told of the effort to restrain the emotion she felt. 'Dear friend,' she said, taking my hand, 'I was coming to seek you; forgive my selfishness in neglecting you so long; but you will understand'—glancing at the door above—'how occupied I have been.' 'Where,' I began, 'is'—'my boy?' she answered, anticipating my question. 'I have laid him by his father. But now your wounds must be cared for; how pale and faint you look!—rest here a moment' —and, descending to the dining-room, she returned with some wine, which I gratefully drank, and then, making me sit down on the top step of the stairs, she brought water and linen, and, cutting off the sleeve of my coat, bathed and bandaged my wounds. 'Twas I who felt selfish for thus adding to her troubles; but in truth I was too weak to have much will left, and stood in need of the help which she forced me to accept; and the dressing of my wounds afforded indescribable relief. While thus tending me, she explained in broken sentences how matters stood. Every room but her own, and the little parlour into which with Wood's help she had carried me, was full of soldiers. Wood had been taken away to work at repairing the railroad, and Lucy had run off from fright; but the cook had stopped at her post, and had served up supper and opened the cellar for the soldiers' use; she herself did not understand what they said, and they were rough and boorish, but not uncivil. I should now go, she said, when my wounds were dressed, to look after my own home, where I might be wanted; for herself, she wished only to be allowed to remain watching there—glancing at the room where lay the bodies of her husband and child—where she would not be molested. I felt that her advice was good. I could be of no use as protection, and I had an anxious longing to know what had become of my sick mother and sister; besides, some arrangement must be made for the burial. I therefore limped away. There was no need to express thanks on either side, and the grief was too deep to be reached by any outward show of sympathy.

Outside the house there was a good deal of movement and bustle; many carts going along, the waggoners, from Sussex and Surrey, evidently impressed and guarded by soldiers; and although no gas was burning, the road towards Kingston was well lighted by torches held by persons standing at short intervals in line, who had been seized for the duty, some of them the tenants of neighbouring villas. Almost the first of these torchbearers I came to was an old gentleman whose face I was well acquainted with, from having frequently travelled up and down in the same train with him. He was a senior clerk in a Government office, I believe, and was a mild-looking old man with a prim face and a long neck, which he used to wrap in a white double neckcloth, a thing even in those days seldom seen. Even in that moment of bitterness I could not help being amused by the absurd figure this poor old fellow presented, with his solemn face and long cravat doing penance with a torch in front of his own gate, to light up the path of our conquerors. But a more serious object now presented itself, a corporal's guard passing by, with two English volunteers in charge, their hands tied behind their backs. They cast an imploring glance at me, and I stepped into the road to ask the corporal what was the matter, and even ventured, as he was passing on, to lay my hand on his sleeve. 'Aus dem Wege, Spitzbube!' cried the brute, lifting his rifle as if to knock me down. 'Must one prisoners who fire at us let shoot,' he went on to add; and shot the poor fellows would have been, I suppose, if I had not interceded with an officer, who happened to be riding by. 'Herr Hauptmann,' I cried, as loud as I could, 'is this your discipline, to let unarmed prisoners be shot without orders?' The officer, thus appealed to, reined in his horse, and halted the guard till he heard what I had to say. My knowledge of other languages here stood me in good stead, for the prisoners, north-country factory hands apparently, were of course utterly unable to make themselves understood, and did not even know in what they had offended. I therefore interpreted their explanation: they had been left behind while skirmishing near Ditton, in a barn, and coming out of their hiding-place in the midst of a party of the enemy, with their rifles in their hands, the latter thought they were going to fire at them from behind. It was a wonder they were not shot down on the spot. The captain heard the tale, and then told the guard to let them go, and they slunk off at once into a by-road. He was a fine soldier-like man, but nothing could exceed the insolence of his manner, which was perhaps all the greater because it seemed not intentional, but to arise from a sense of immeasurable superiority. Between the lame *Freiwilliger* pleading for his comrades, and the captain of the conquering army, there was, in his view, an infinite gulf. Had the two men been dogs, their fate could not have been decided more contemptuously. They were let go simply because they were not worth keeping as prisoners, and perhaps to kill any living thing without cause went against the *Hauptmann's* sense of justice. By why speak of this insult in particular? Had not every man who lived then his tale to tell of humiliation and degradation? For it was the same story everywhere. After the first stand in line, and when once they had got us on the march, the enemy laughed at us. Our handful of regular troops was sacrificed almost to a man in a vain conflict with numbers; our volunteers and militia, with officers who did not know their work, without ammunition or equipment, or staff to superintend, starving in the midst of plenty, we had soon become a helpless mob, fighting desperately here and there, but with whom, as a manoeuvring army, the disciplined invaders did just what they pleased. Happy those whose bones whitened the fields of Surrey; they at least were spared the disgrace we lived to endure. Even you, who have never known what it is to live otherwise than on sufferance, even your cheeks burn when we talk of these days; think, then, what those endured who, like your grandfather, had been citizens of the proudest nation on earth, which had never known disgrace or defeat, and whose boast it used to be that they bore a flag on which the sun never set! We had heard of generosity in war; we found none: the war was made by us, it was said, and we must take the consequences. London and our only arsenal captured, we were at the mercy of our captors, and right heavily did they tread on our necks. Need I tell you the rest?—of the ransom we had to pay, and the taxes raised to cover it, which keep us paupers to this day?—the brutal frankness that announced we must give place to a new naval Power, and be made harmless for revenge? —the victorious troops living at free quarters, the yoke they put on us made the more gallant that their requisitions had a semblance of method and legality? Better have been robbed at first and by the soldiery themselves, than through our own magistrates made the instruments for extortion. How we lived through the degradation we daily and hourly underwent, I hardly even now understand. And what was there left to us to live for? Stripped of our colonies; Canada and the West Indies gone to America; Australia forced to separate; India lost for ever, after the English there had all been destroyed, vainly trying to hold the country when cut off from aid by their countrymen; Gibraltar and Malta ceded to the new naval Power; Ireland independent and in perpetual anarchy and revolution. When I look at my country as it is now—its trade gone, its factories silent, its harbours empty, a prey to pauperism and decay—when I see all this, and think what Great Britain was in my youth, I ask myself whether I have really a heart or any sense of patriotism that I should have witnessed such degradation and still care to live! France was different. There, too, they had to eat the bread of tribulation under the yoke of the conqueror! Their fall was hardly more sudden or violent than ours; but war could not take away their rich soil; they had no colonies to lose; their broad lands, which made their wealth, remained to them; and they rose again from the blow. But our people could not be got to see how artificial our prosperity was—that it all rested on foreign trade and financial credit; that the course of trade once turned away from us, even for a time, it might never return; and that our credit once shaken might never be restored. To hear men talk in those days, you would have thought that Providence had ordained that our Government should always borrow at three per cent, and that trade came to us because we lived in a foggy little island set in a boisterous sea. They could not be got to see that the wealth heaped up on every side was not created in the country, but in India and China, and other parts of the world; and that it would be quite possible for the people who made money by buying and selling the natural treasures of the earth, to go and live in other places, and take their profits with them. Nor would men believe that there could ever be an end to our coal and iron, or that they would get to be so much dearer than the coal and iron of America that it would no longer be worth while to work them, and that therefore we ought to insure against the loss of our artificial position as the great centre of trade, by making ourselves secure and strong and respected. We thought we were living in a commercial millennium, which must last for a thousand years at least. After all, the bitterest part of our reflection is, that all this misery and decay might have been so easily prevented, and that we brought it about ourselves by our own shortsighted recklessness. There, across the narrow Straits, was the writing on the wall, but we would not choose to read i t. The warnings of the few were drowned in the voice of the multitude. Power was then passing away from the class which had been used to rule, and to face political dangers, and which had brought the nation with honour unsullied through former struggles, into the hands of the lower classes, uneducated, untrained to the use of political rights, and swayed by demagogues; and the few who were wise in their generation were denounced as alarmists, or as aristocrats who sought their own aggrandisement by wasting public money on bloated armaments. The rich were idle and luxurious; the poor grudged the cost of defence. Politics had become a mere bidding for Radical votes, and those who should have led the nation stopped rather to pander to the selfishness of the day, and humoured the popular cry which denounced those who would secure the defence of the nation by enforced arming of its manhood, as interfering with the liberties of the people. Truly the nation was ripe for a fall; but when I reflect how a little firmness and self-denial, or political courage and foresight, might have averted the disaster, I feel that the judgement must have really been deserved. A nation too selfish to defend its liberty, could not have been fit to retain it. To you, my grandchildren, who are now going to seek a new home in a more prosperous land, let not this bitter lesson be lost upon you in the country of your adoption. For me, I am too old to begin life again in a strange country; and hard and evil as have been my days, it is not much to await in solitude the time which cannot now be far off, when my old bones will be laid to rest in the soil I have loved so well, and whose happiness and honour I have so long survived.

Charles Collins

THE COMPENSATION HOUSE

"There's not a looking-glass in all the house, sir. It's some peculiar fancy of my master's. There isn't one in any single room in the house."

It was a dark and gloomy-looking building, and had been purchased by this Company for an enlargement of their Goods Station. The value of the house had been referred to what was popularly called " a compensation jury," and the house was called, in consequence, The Compensation House. It had become the Company's property ; but its tenant still remained in possession, pending the commencement of active building operations. My attention was originally drawn to this house because it stood directly in front of a collection of huge pieces of timber which lay near this part of the Line, and on which I sometimes sat for half an hour at a time, when I was tired by my wanderings about Mugby Junction.

It was square, cold, grey-looking, built of rough-hewn stone, and roofed with thin slabs of the same material. Its windows were few in number, and very small for the size of the building. In the great blank, grey broadside, there were only four windows. The entrance-door was in the middle of the house ; there was a window on either side of it, and there were two more in the single story above. The blinds were all closely drawn, and when the door was shut, the dreary building gave no sign of life or occupation.

But the door was not always shut. Sometimes it was opened from within, with a great jingling of bolts and door-chains, and then a man would come forward and stand upon the doorstep, snuffing the air as one might do who was ordinarily kept on rather a small allowance of that element. He was stout, thickset, and perhaps fifty or sixty years old—a man whose hair was cut exceedingly close, who wore a large bushy beard, and whose eye had a sociable twinkle in it which was prepossessing. He was dressed, whenever I saw him, in a greenish-brown frock-coat made of some material which was not cloth, wore a waistcoat and trousers of light colour, and had a frill to his shirt—an ornament, by the way, which did not seem to go at all well with the beard, which was continually in contact with it. It was the custom of this worthy person, after standing for a short time on the threshold inhaling the air, to come forward into the road, and, after glancing at one of the upper windows in a half mechanical way, to cross over to the logs, and, leaning over the fence which guarded the railway, to look up and down the Line (it passed before the house) with the air of a man accomplishing a self-imposed task of which nothing was expected to come. This done, he would cross the road again, and turning on the threshold to take a final sniff of air, disappeared once more within the house, bolting and chaining the door again as if there were no probability of its being reopened for at least a week. Yet half an hour had not passed before he was out in the road again, sniffing the air and looking up and down the Line as before.

It was not very long before I managed to scrape acquaintance with this restless personage. I soon found out that my friend with the shirt-frill was the confidential servant, butler, valet, factotum, what you will, of a sick gentleman, a Mr. Oswald Strange, who had recently come to inhabit the house opposite, and concerning whose history my new acquaintance, whose name I ascertained was Masey, seemed disposed to be somewhat communicative. His master, it appeared, had come down to this place, partly for the sake of reducing his establishment—not, Mr. Masey was swift to inform me, on economical principles, but because the poor gentleman, for particular reasons, wished to have few dependents about him—partly in order that he might be near his old friend, Dr. Garden, who was established in the neighbourhood, and whose society and advice were necessary to Mr. Strange's life. That life was, it appeared, held by this suffering gentleman on a precarious tenure. It was ebbing away fast with each passing hour. The servant already spoke of his master in the past tense, describing him to me as a young gentleman not more than five-and-thirty years of age, with a young face, as far as the features and build of it went, but with an expression which had nothing of youth about it. This was the great peculiarity of the man. At a distance he looked younger than he was by many years, and strangers, at the time when he had been used to get about, always took him for a man of seven or eight-and-twenty, but they changed their minds on getting nearer to him. Old Masey had a way of his own of summing up the peculiarities of his master, repeating twenty times over : " Sir, he was Strange by name, and Strange by nature, and Strange to look at into the bargain."

It was during my second or third interview with the old fellow that he uttered the words quoted at the beginning of this plain narrative.

"Not such a thing as a looking-glass in all the house," the old man said, standing beside my piece of timber, and looking across reflectively at the house opposite. "Not one."

"In the sitting-rooms, I suppose you mean?"

"No, sir, I mean sitting-rooms and bedrooms both; there isn't so much as a shaving-glass as big as the palm of your hand anywhere."

"But how is it?" I asked. "Why are there no looking-glasses in any of the rooms?"

"Ah, sir!" replied Masey, "that's what none of us can ever tell. There is the mystery. It's just a fancy on the part of my master. He had some strange fancies, and this was one of them. A pleasant gentleman he was to live with, as any servant could desire. A liberal gentleman, and one who gave but little trouble; always ready with a kind word, and a kind deed, too, for the matter of that. There was not a house in all the parish of St..George's (in which we lived before we came down here) where the servants had more holidays or a better table kept; but, for all that, he had his queer ways and his fancies, as I may call them, and this was one of them. And the point he made of it, sir," the old man went on; "the extent to which that regulation was enforced, whenever a new servant was engaged; and the changes in the establishment it occasioned! In hiring a new servant, the very first stipulation made, was that about the looking-glasses. It was one of my duties to explain the thing, as far as it could be explained, before any servant was taken into the house. 'You'll find it an easy place,' I used to say, 'with a liberal table, good wages, and a deal of leisure; but there's one thing you must make up your mind to; you must do without looking-glasses while you're here, for there isn't one in the house, and, what's more, there never will be.'"

"But how did you know there never would be one?" I asked.

"Lor' bless you, sir! If you'd seen and heard all that I'd seen and heard, you could have no doubt about it. Why, only to take one instance :—I remember a particular day when my master had occasion to go into the housekeeper's room, where the cook lived, to see about some alterations that were making, and when a pretty scene took place. The cook—she was a very ugly woman, and awful vain—had left a little bit of a looking-glass, about six inches square, upon the chimney-piece; she had got it *surreptitious*, and kept it always locked up; but she'd left it out, being called away suddenly, while titivating her hair. I had seen the glass, and was making for the chimney-piece as fast as I could; but master came in front of it before I could get there, and it was all over in a moment. He gave one long piercing look into it, turned deadly pale, and seizing the glass, dashed it into a hundred pieces on the floor, and then stamped upon the fragments and ground them into powder with his feet. He shut himself up for the rest of that day in his own room, first ordering me to discharge the cook, then and there, at a moment's notice."

"What an extraordinary thing!" I said, pondering.

"Ah, sir," continued the old man, "it was astonishing what trouble I had with those women-servants. It was difficult to get any that would take the place at all under the circumstances. 'What not so much as a mossul to do one's 'air at?' they would say, and they'd go off, in spite of extra wages. Then those who did consent to come, what lies they would tell, to be sure! They would protest that they didn't want to look in the glass, that they never had been in the habit of looking in the glass, and all the while that very wench would have her looking-glass, of some kind or another, hid away among her clothes upstairs. Sooner or later, she would bring it out too, and leave it about somewhere or other (just like the cook), where it was as likely as not that master might see it. And then—for girls like that have no consciences, sir—when I had caught one of 'em at it, she'd turn round as bold as brass, 'And how am I to know whether my 'air's parted straight?' she'd say, just as if it hadn't been considered in her wages that that was the very thing which she never *was* to know while she lived in our house. A vain lot, sir, and the ugly ones always the vainest. There was no end to their dodges. They'd have looking-glasses in the interiors of their workbox-lids, where it was next to impossible that I could find 'em, or inside the covers of hymn-books, or cookery-books, or in their caddies. I recollect one girl, a sly one she was, and marked with the small-pox terrible, who was always reading her prayer-book at odd times. Sometimes I used to think what a religious mind she'd got, and at other times (depending on the mood I was in) I would conclude that it was the marriage-service she was studying; but one day, when I got behind her to satisfy my doubts—lo and behold! it was the old story: a bit of glass, without a frame, fastened into the kiver with the outside edges of the sheets of postage-stamps. Dodges ! Why they'd keep their looking-glasses in the scullery or the coal-cellar, or leave them in charge of the servants next door, or with the milk-woman round the corner ; but have 'em they would. And I don't mind confessing, sir," said the old man, bringing his long speech to an end, " that it *was* an inconveniency not to have so much as a scrap to shave before. I used to go to the barber's at first, but I soon gave that up, and took to wearing my beard as my master did ; likewise to keeping my hair "—Mr. Masey touched his head as he spoke—" so short, that it didn't require any parting, before or behind."

I sat for some time lost in amazement, and staring at my companion. My curiosity was powerfully stimulated, and the desire to learn more was very strong within me.

" Had your master any personal defect," I inquired, " which might have made it distressing to him to see his own image reflected ? "

" By no means, sir," said the old man. " He was as handsome a gentleman as you would wish to see : a little delicate-looking and care-worn, perhaps, with a very pale face ; but as free from any deformity as you or I, sir. No, sir, no ; it was nothing of that."

" Then what was it ? What is it ? " I asked, desperately. " Is there no one who is, or has been, in your master's confidence ? "

" Yes, sir," said the old fellow, with his eyes turning to that window opposite. " There is one person who knows all my master's secrets, and this secret among the rest."

" And who is that ? "

The old man turned round and looked at me fixedly. " The doctor here," he said. " Dr. Garden. My master's very old friend."

" I should like to speak with this gentleman," I said, involuntarily.

" He is with my master now," answered Masey. " He will be coming out presently, and I think I may say he will answer any question you may like to put to him." As the old man spoke, the door of the house opened, and a middle-aged gentleman, who was tall and thin, but who lost something of his height by a habit of stooping, appeared on the step. Old Masey left me in a moment. He muttered something about taking the doctor's directions, and hastened across the road. The tall gentleman spoke to him for a minute or two very seriously, probably about the patient upstairs, and it then seemed to me from their gestures that I myself was the subject of some further conversation between them. At all events, when old Masey retired into the house, the doctor came across to where I was standing, and addressed me with a very agreeable smile.

" John Masey tells me that you are interested in the case of my poor friend, sir. I am now going back to my house, and if you don't mind the trouble of walking with me, I shall be happy to enlighten you as far as I am able."

I hastened to make my apologies and express my acknowledgments, and we set off together. When we had reached the doctor's house and were seated in his study, I ventured to inquire after the health of this poor gentleman.

" I am afraid there is no amendment, nor any prospect of amendment," said the doctor. " Old Masey has told you something of his strange condition, has he not ? "

" Yes, he has told me something," I answered, " and he says you know all about it."

Dr. Garden looked very grave. " I don't know all about it. I only know what happens when he comes into the presence of a looking-glass. But as to the circumstances which have led to his being haunted in the strangest fashion that I ever heard of, I know no more of them than you do."

" Haunted ? " I repeated. " And in the strangest fashion that you ever heard of ? "

Dr. Garden smiled at my eagerness, seemed to be collecting his thoughts, and presently went on :

" I made the acquaintance of Mr. Oswald Strange in a curious way. It was on board of an Italian steamer, bound from Civita Vecchia to Marseilles. We had been travelling all night. In the morning I was shaving myself in the cabin, when suddenly this man came behind me, glanced for a moment into the small mirror before which I was standing, and then, without a word of warning, tore it from the nail, and dashed it to pieces at my feet. His face was at first livid with passion—it seemed to me rather the passion of fear than of anger—but it changed after a moment, and he seemed ashamed of what he had done. Well," continued the doctor, relapsing for a moment into a smile, " of course I was in a devil of a rage. I was operating on my under-jaw, and the start the thing gave me caused me to cut myself. Besides, altogether it seemed an outrageous and insolent thing, and I gave it to poor Strange in a style of language which I am sorry to think of now, but which, I hope, was excusable at the time. As to the offender himself, his confusion and regret, now that his passion was at an end, disarmed me. He sent for the steward, and paid most liberally for the damage done to the steamboat property, explaining to him, and to some other passengers who were present in the cabin, that what had happened had been accidental. For me, however, he had another explanation. Perhaps he felt that I must know it to have been no accident—perhaps he really wished to confide in someone. At all events, he owned to me that what he had done was done under the influence of an uncontrollable impulse—a seizure which took him, he said, at times—something like a fit. He begged my pardon, and entreated that I would endeavour to disassociate him personally from this action, of which he was heartily ashamed. Then he attempted a sickly joke, poor fellow, about his wearing a beard, and feeling a little spiteful, in consequence, when he saw other people taking the trouble to shave ; but he said nothing about any infirmity or delusion, and shortly after left me.

" In my professional capacity I could not help taking some interest in Mr. Strange. I did not altogether lose sight of him after our sea-journey to Marseilles was over. I found him a pleasant companion up to a certain point ; but I always felt that there was a reserve about him. He was uncommunicative about his past life, and especially would never allude to anything connected with his travels or his residence in Italy, which, however, I could make out had been a long one. He spoke Italian well, and seemed familiar with the country, but disliked to talk about it.

" During the time we spent together there were seasons when he was so little himself, that I, with a pretty large experience, was almost afraid to be with him. His attacks were violent and sudden in the last degree ; and there was one most extraordinary feature connected with them all :—some horrible association of ideas took possession of him whenever he found himself before a looking-glass. And after we had travelled together for a time, I dreaded the sight of a mirror hanging harmlessly against a wall, or a toilet-glass standing on a dressing-table, almost as much as he did.

" Poor Strange was not always affected in the same manner by a looking-glass. Sometimes it seemed to madden him with fury ; at other times, it appeared to turn him to stone : remaining motionless and speechless as if attacked by catalepsy. One night— the worst things always happen at night, and oftener than one would think on stormy nights—we arrived at a small town in the central district of Auvergne : a place but little known, out of the line of railways, and to which we had been drawn, partly by the antiquarian attractions which the place possessed, and partly by the beauty of the scenery. The weather had been rather against us. The day had been dull and murky, the heat stifling, and the sky had threatened mischief since the morning. At sundown, these threats were fulfilled. The thunderstorm, which had been all day coming up—as it seemed to us, against the wind—burst over the place where we were lodged, with very great violence.

" There are some practical-minded persons with strong constitutions, who deny roundly that their fellow-creatures are, or can be, affected, in mind or body, by atmospheric influences. I am not a disciple of that school, simply because I cannot believe that those changes of weather, which have so much effect upon animals, and even on inanimate objects, can fail to have some influence on a piece of machinery so sensitive and intricate as the human frame. I think, then, that it was in part owing to the disturbed state of the atmosphere that, on this particular evening I felt nervous and depressed. When my new friend Strange and I parted for the night, I felt as little disposed to go to rest as I ever did in my life. The thunder was still lingering among the mountains in the midst of which our inn was placed. Sometimes it seemed nearer, and at other times further off ; but it never left off altogether, except for a few minutes at a time. I was quite unable to shake off a succession of painful ideas which persistently besieged my mind.

" It is hardly necessary to add that I thought from time to time of my travelling-companion in the next room. His image was almost continually before me. He had been dull and depressed all the evening, and when we parted for the night there was a look in his eyes which I could not get out of my memory.

" There was a door between our rooms, and the partition dividing them was not very solid ; and yet I had heard no sound since I parted from him which could indicate that he was there at all, much less that he was awake and stirring. I was in a mood, sir, which made this silence terrible to me, and so many foolish fancies —as that he was lying there dead, or in a fit, or what not—took possession of me, that at last I could bear it no longer. I went to the door, and, after listening, very attentively but quite in vain, for any sound, I at last knocked pretty sharply. There was no answer. Feeling that longer suspense would be unendurable, I, without more ceremony, turned the handle and went in.

" It was a great bare room, and so imperfectly lighted by a single candle that it was almost impossible—except when the lightning flashed—to see into its great dark corners. A small rickety bedstead stood against one of the walls, shrouded by yellow cotton curtains, passed through a great iron ring in the ceiling. There was, for all other furniture, an old chest-of-drawers which served also as a washing-stand, having a small basin and ewer and a single towel arranged on the top of it. There were, moreover, two ancient chairs and a dressing-table. On this last, stood a large old-fashioned looking-glass with a carved frame.

" I must have seen all these things, because I remember them so well now, but I do not know how I could have seen them, for it seems to me that, from the moment of my entering that room, the action of my senses and of the faculties of my mind was held fast by the ghastly figure which stood motionless before the looking-glass in the middle of the empty room.

" How terrible it was ! The weak light of one candle standing on the table shone upon Strange's face, lighting it from below, and throwing (as I now remember) his shadow, vast and black, upon the wall behind him and upon the ceiling overhead. He was leaning rather forward, with his hands upon the table supporting him, and gazing into the glass which stood before him with a horrible fixity. The sweat was on his white face ; his rigid features and his pale lips showed in that feeble light were horrible, more than words can tell, to look at. He was so completely stupefied and lost, that the noise I had made in knocking and in entering the room was unobserved by him. Not even when I called him loudly by name did he move or did his face change.

" What a vision of horror that was, in the great dark empty room, in a silence that was something more than negative, that ghastly figure frozen into stone by some unexplained terror ! And the silence and the stillness ! The very thunder had ceased now. My heart stood still with fear. Then, moved by some instinctive feeling, under whose influence I acted mechanically, I crept with slow steps nearer and nearer to the table, and at last, half expecting to see some spectre even more horrible than this which I saw already, I looked over his shoulder into the looking-glass. I happened to touch his arm, though only in the lightest manner. In that one moment the spell which had held him—who knows how long ?—enchained, seemed broken, and he lived in this world again. He turned round upon me, as suddenly as a tiger makes its spring, and seized me by the arm.

" I have told you that even before I entered my friend's room I had felt, all that night, depressed and nervous. The necessity for action at this time was, however, so obvious, and this man's agony made all that I had felt, appear so trifling, that much of my own discomfort seemed to leave me. I felt that I *must* be strong.

" The face before me almost unmanned me. The eyes which looked into mine were so scared with terror, the lips—if I may say so—looked so speechless. The wretched man gazed long into my face, and then, still holding me by the arm, slowly, very slowly, turned his head. I had gently tried to move him away from the looking-glass, but he would not stir, and now he was looking into it as fixedly as ever. I could bear this no longer, and, using such force as was necessary, I drew him gradually away, and got him to one of the chairs at the foot of the bed. ' Come ! ' I said—after the long silence my voice, even to myself, sounded strange and hollow—' come ! You are over-tired, and you feel the weather. Don't you think you ought to be in bed ? Suppose you lie down. Let me try my medical skill in mixing you a composing draught.'

" He held my hand, and looked eagerly into my eyes. ' I am better now,' he said, speaking at last very faintly. Still he looked at me in that wistful way. It seemed as if there were something that he wanted to do or say, but had not sufficient resolution. At length he got up from the chair to which I had led him, and beckoning me to follow him, went across the room to the dressing-table, and stood again before the glass. A violent shudder passed through his frame as he looked into it ; but apparently forcing himself to go through with what he had now begun, he remained where he was, and, without looking away, moved to me with his hand to come and stand beside him. I complied.

" ' Look in there ! ' he said, in an almost inaudible tone. He was supported, as before, by his hands resting on the table, and could only bow with his head towards the glass to intimate what he meant. ' Look in there ! ' he repeated.

" I did as he asked me.

" ' What do you see ? ' he asked next.

" ' See ? ' I repeated, trying to speak as cheerfully as I could, and describing the reflexion of his own face as nearly as I could. ' I see a very, very pale face with sunken cheeks——'

" ' What ? ' he cried, with an alarm in his voice which I could not understand.

" ' With sunken cheeks,' I went on, ' and two hollow eyes with large pupils.'

" I saw the reflexion of my friend's face change, and felt his hand clutch my arm even more tightly than he had done before. I stopped abruptly and looked round at him. He did not turn his head towards me, but, gazing still into the looking-glass, seemed to labour for utterance.

" ' What,' he stammered at last. ' Do—you—see it—too ? '

" ' See what ? ' I asked, quickly.

" ' That face ! ' he cried, in accents of horror. ' That face— which is not mine—and which—I SEE INSTEAD OF MINE—always ! '

" I was struck speechless by the words. In a moment this mystery was explained—but what an explanation ! Worse, a hundred times worse, than anything I had imagined. What ! Had this man lost the power of seeing his own image as it was reflected there before him ? and, in its place, was there the image of another ? Had he changed reflexions with some other man ? The frightfulness of the thought struck me speechless for a time—then I saw how false an impression my silence was conveying.

" ' No, no, no ! ' I cried, as soon as I could speak—' a hundred times, no ! I see you, of course, and only you. It was your face I attempted to describe, and no other.'

" He seemed not to hear me. ' Why, look there ! ' he said, in a low, indistinct voice, pointing to his own image in the glass. ' Whose face do you see there ? '

" ' Why yours, of course.' And then, after a moment, I added, ' Whose do you see ? '

" He answered, like one in a trance, ' His—only his—always his ! ' He stood still a moment, and then, with a loud and terrific scream, repeated those words, ' ALWAYS HIS, ALWAYS HIS,' and fell down in a fit before me.

"I knew what to do now. Here was a thing which, at any rate, I could understand. I had with me my usual small stock of medicines and surgical instruments, and I did what was necessary : first to restore my unhappy patient, and next to procure for him the rest he needed so much. He was very ill—at death's door for some days —and I could not leave him, though there was urgent need that I should be back in London. When he began to mend, I sent over to England for my servant—John Masey—whom I knew I could trust. Acquainting him with the outlines of the case, I left him in charge of my patient, with orders that he should be brought over to this country as soon as he was fit to travel.

"That awful scene was always before me. I saw this devoted man day after day, with the eyes of my imagination, sometimes destroying in his rage the harmless looking-glass, which was the immediate cause of his suffering, sometimes transfixed before the horrid image that turned him to stone. I recollect coming upon him once when we were stopping at a roadside inn, and seeing him stand so by broad daylight. His back was turned towards me, and I waited and watched him for nearly half an hour as he stood there motionless and speechless, and appearing not to breathe. I am not sure but that this apparition seen so by daylight was more ghastly than that apparition seen in the middle of the night, with the thunder rumbling among the hills.

"Back in London in his own house, where he could command in some sort the objects which should surround him, poor Strange was better than he would have been elsewhere. He seldom went out except at night, but once or twice I have walked with him by daylight, and have seen him terribly agitated when we have had to pass a shop in which looking-glasses were exposed for sale.

"It is nearly a year now since my poor friend followed me down to this place, to which I have retired. For some months he has been daily getting weaker and weaker, and a disease of the lungs has become developed in him, which has brought him to his death-bed. I should add, by-the-by, that John Masey has been his constant companion ever since I brought them together, and I have had, consequently, to look after a new servant.

"And now tell me," the doctor added, bringing his tale to an end, "did you ever hear a more miserable history, or was ever man haunted in a more ghastly manner than this man?"

I was about to reply, when we heard a sound of footsteps outside, and before I could speak old Masey entered the room, in haste and disorder.

"I was just telling this gentleman," the doctor said : not at the moment observing old Masey's changed manner : "how you deserted me to go over to your present master."

"Ah ! sir," the man answered, in a troubled voice, " I'm afraid he won't be my master long."

The doctor was on his legs in a moment. "What ! Is he worse?"

" I think, sir, he is dying," said the old man.

" Come with me, sir ; you may be of use if you can keep quiet."
The doctor caught up his hat as he addressed me in those words,
and in a few minutes we had reached The Compensation House.
A few seconds more and we were standing in a darkened room on
the first floor, and I saw lying on a bed before me—pale, emaciated
and, as it seemed, dying—the man whose story I had just heard.

He was lying with closed eyes when we came into the room,
and I had leisure to examine his features. What a tale of misery
they told ! They were regular and symmetrical in their arrangement, and not without beauty—the beauty of exceeding refine-
ment and delicacy. Force there was none, and perhaps it was to
the want of this that the faults—perhaps the crime—which had
made the man's life so miserable were to be attributed. Perhaps
the crime ? Yes, it was not likely that an affliction, lifelong and
terrible, such as this he had endured, would come upon him unless some misdeed had provoked the punishment. What misdeed
we were soon to know.

It sometimes—I think generally—happens that the presence of
anyone who stands and watches beside a sleeping man will wake
him, unless his slumbers are unusually heavy. It was so now. While
we looked at him, the sleeper awoke very suddenly, and fixed his
eyes upon us. He put out his hand and took the doctor's in its
feeble grasp. "Who is that?" he asked next, pointing towards me.

" Do you wish him to go ? The gentleman knows something of
your sufferings, and is powerfully interested in your case ; but he
will leave us, if you wish it," the doctor said.

" No. Let him stay."

Seating myself out of sight, but where I could both see and hear
what passed, I waited for what should follow. Dr. Garden and John
Masey stood beside the bed. There was a moment's pause.

" I want a looking-glass," said Strange, without a word of
preface.

We all started to hear him say those words.

" I am dying," said Strange ; " will you not grant me my
request ? "

Dr. Garden whispered to old Masey ; and the latter left the
room. He was not absent long, having gone no further than the
next house. He held an oval-framed mirror in his hand when he
returned. A shudder passed through the body of the sick man as
he saw it.

" Put it down," he said, faintly—" anywhere—for the present."

No one of us spoke. I do not think, in that moment of suspense, that we *could*, any of us, have spoken if we had tried.

The sick man tried to raise himself a little. " Prop me up," he said. " I speak with difficulty—I have something to say."

They put pillows behind him, so as to raise his head and body.

" I have presently a use for it," he said, indicating the mirror. " I want to see——" He stopped, and seemed to change his mind. He was sparing of his words. " I want to tell you—all about it." Again he was silent. Then he seemed to make a great effort, and spoke once more, beginning very abruptly.

" I loved my wife fondly. I loved her—her name was Lucy. She was English ; but, after we were married, we lived long abroad—in Italy. She liked the country, and I liked what she liked. She liked to draw, too, and I got her a master. He was an Italian. I will not give his name. We always called him ' the Master.' A treacherous insidious man this was, and, under cover of his profession, took advantage of his opportunities, and taught my wife to love him—to love him.

" I am short of breath. I need not enter into details as to how I found them out ; but I *did* find them out. We were away on a sketching expedition when I made my discovery. My rage maddened me, and there was one at hand who fomented my madness. My wife had a maid, who, it seemed, had also loved this man— the Master—and had been ill-treated and deserted by him. She told me all. She had played the part of go-between—had carried letters. When she told me these things, it was night, in a solitary Italian town, among the mountains. ' He is in his room now,' she said, ' writing to her.'

" A frenzy took possession of me as I listened to those words. I am naturally vindictive—remember that—and now my longing for revenge was like a thirst. Travelling in those lonely regions, I was armed, and when the woman said, ' He is writing to your wife,' I laid hold of my pistols, as by an instinct. It has been some comfort to me since, that I took them both. Perhaps, at that moment, I may have meant fairly by him—meant that we should fight. I don't know what I meant, quite. The woman's words, ' He is in his own room now, writing to her,' rung in my ears.

The sick man stopped to take breath. It seemed an hour, though it was probably not more than two minutes, before he spoke again.

" I managed to get into his room unobserved. Indeed, he was

altogether absorbed in what he was doing. He was sitting at the only table in the room, writing at a travelling-desk, by the light of a single candle. It was a rude dressing-table, and—and before him—exactly before him—there was—there was a looking-glass.

" I stole up behind him as he sat and wrote by the light of the candle. I looked over his shoulder at the letter, and I read, ' Dearest Lucy, my love, my darling.' As I read the words, I pulled the trigger of the pistol I held in my right hand, and killed him—killed him—but, before he died, he looked up once—not at me, but at my image before him in the glass, and his face—such a face—has been there—ever since, and mine—my face—is gone ! "

He fell back exhausted, and we all pressed forward thinking that he must be dead, he lay so still.

But he had not yet passed away. He revived under the influence of stimulants. He tried to speak, and muttered indistinctly from time to time words of which we could sometimes make no sense. We understood, however, that he had been tried by an Italian tribunal, and had been found guilty ; but with such extenuating circumstances that his sentence was commuted to imprisonment, during, we thought we made out, two years. But we could not understand what he said about his wife, though we gathered that she was still alive, from something he whispered to the doctor of there being provision made for her in his will.

He lay in a doze for something more than an hour after he had told his tale, and then he woke up quite suddenly, as he had done when we had first entered the room. He looked round uneasily in all directions, until his eye fell on the looking-glass.

" I want it," he said, hastily ; but I noticed that he did not shudder now as it was brought near. When old Masey approached, holding it in his hand, and crying like a child, Dr. Garden came forward and stood between him and his master, taking the hand of poor Strange in his.

" Is this wise ? " he asked. " Is it good, do you think, to revive this misery of your life now, when it is so near its close ? The chastisement of your crime," he added, solemnly, " has been a terrible one. Let us hope in God's mercy that your punishment is over."

The dying man raised himself with a last great effort, and looked up at the doctor with such an expression on his face as none of us had seen on any face, before.

" I do hope so," he said, faintly, " but you must let me have my way in this—for if, now, when I look, I see aright—once more —I shall then hope yet more strongly—for I shall take it as a sign."

The doctor stood aside without another word, when he heard the dying man speak thus, and the old servant drew near, and, stooping over softly, held the looking-glass before his master. Presently afterwards, we, who stood around looking breathlessly at him, saw such a rapture upon his face, as left no doubt upon our minds that the face which had haunted him so long, had, in his last hour, disappeared.

At the Fork of the Roads

ALEISTER CROWLEY

HYPATIA GAY KNOCKED timidly at the door of Count Swanoff's flat. Hers was a curious mission, to serve the envy of the long lank melancholy unwashed poet whom she loved. Will Bute was not only a poetaster but a dabbler in magic, and black jealousy of a younger man and a far finer poet gnawed at his petty heart. He had gained a subtle hypnotic influence over Hypatia, who helped him in his ceremonies, and he had now commissioned her to seek out his rival and pick up some magical link through which he might be destroyed.

The door opened, and the girl passed from the cold stone dusk of the stairs to a palace of rose and gold. The poet's rooms were austere in their elegance. A plain gold-black paper of Japan covered the walls; in the midst hung an ancient silver lamp within which glowed the deep ruby of an electric lamp. The floor was covered with black and gold of leopards' skins; on the walls hung a great crucifix in ivory and ebony. Before the blazing fire lay the poet (who had concealed his royal Celtic descent beneath the pseudonym of Swanoff) reading in a great volume bound with vellum.

He rose to greet her.

'Many days have I expected you,' he exclaimed, 'many days have I wept over you. I see your destiny – how thin a thread links you to that mighty Brotherhood of the Silver Star whose trembling neophyte I am – how twisted and thick are the tentacles of the Black Octopus whom you now serve. Ah! wrench yourself away while you are yet linked with us: I would not that you sank into the Ineffable Slime. Blind and bestial are the worms of the Slime: come to me, and by the Faith of the Star, I will save you.'

The girl put him by with a light laugh. 'I came,' she said, 'but to chatter about clairvoyance – why do you threat me with these strange and awful words?'

'Because I see that today may decide all for you. Will you come with me into the White Temple, while I administer the Vows? Or will you enter the Black Temple, and swear away your soul?'

'Oh, really,' she said, 'you are too silly – but I'll do what you like next time I come here.'

'Today your choice – tomorrow your fate,' answered the young poet.

And the conversation drifted to lighter subjects.

But as she left she managed to scratch his hand with a brooch, and this tiny blood-stain on the pin she bore back in triumph to her master; he would work a strange working therewith!

Swanoff closed his books and went to bed. The streets were deadly silent; he turned his thoughts to the Infinite Silence of the Divine Presence, and fell into a peaceful sleep. No dreams disturbed him; later than usual he awoke.

How strange! The healthy flush of his cheek had faded: the hands were white and thin and wrinkled: he was so weak that he could hardly stagger to the bath. Breakfast refreshed him somewhat; but more than this the expectation of a visit from his master.

The master came. 'Little brother!' he cried aloud as he entered, 'you have disobeyed me. You have been meddling again with the Goetia!'

'I swear to you, master!' He did reverence to the adept.

The newcomer was a dark man with a powerful cleanshaven face almost masked in a mass of jet-black hair.

'Little brother,' he said, 'if that be so, then the Goetia has been meddling with you.'

He lifted up his head and sniffed. 'I smell evil,' he said, 'I smell the dark brothers of iniquity. Have you duly performed the Ritual of the Flaming Star?'

'Thrice daily, according to your word.'

'Then evil has entered in a body of flesh. Who has been here?'

The young poet told him. His eyes flashed. 'Aha!' he said, 'now let us Work!'

The neophyte brought writing materials to his master: the quill of a young gander, snow-white; virgin vellum of a young male lamb; ink of the gall of a certain rare fish; and a mysterious Book.

The master drew a number of incomprehensible signs and letters upon the vellum.

'Sleep with this beneath the pillow,' he said: 'you will awake if you are attacked; and whatever it is that attacks you, kill it! Kill it! Kill it! Then instantly go into your temple and assume the shape and dignity of the god Horus; send back the Thing to its sender by the might of the god that is in you! Come! I will discover unto you the words and the signs and the spells for this working of magic art.'

They disappeared into the little white room lined with mirrors which Swanoff used for a temple.

Hypatia Gay, that same afternoon, took some drawings to a publisher in Bond Street. This man was bloated with disease and drink; his loose lips hung in an eternal leer; his fat eyes shed venom; his cheeks seemed ever on the point of bursting into nameless sores and ulcers.

He bought the young girl's drawings. 'Not so much for their value,' he explained, 'as that I like to help promising young artists – like you, my dear!'

Her steely virginal eyes met his fearlessly and unsuspiciously. The beast cowered, and covered his foulness with a hideous smile of shame.

The night came, and young Swanoff went to his rest without alarm. Yet with that strange wonder that denotes those who expect the unknown and terrible, but have faith to win through.

This night he dreamt – deliciously.

A thousand years he strayed in gardens of spice, by darling streams, beneath delightful trees, in the blue rapture of the wonderful weather. At the end of a long glade of ilex that reached up to a marble palace stood a woman, fairer than all the women of the earth. Imperceptibly they drew together – she was in his arms. He awoke with a start. A woman indeed lay in his arms and showered a rain of burning kisses on his face. She clothed him about with ecstasy; her touch waked the serpent of essential madness in him.

Then, like a flash of lightning, came his master's word to his memory – Kill it! In the dim twilight he could see the lovely face that kissed him with lips of infinite splendour, hear the cooing words of love.

'Kill it! My God! Adonai! Adonai!' He cried aloud, and took her by the throat. Ah God! Her flesh was not the flesh of woman. It was hard as india-rubber to the touch, and his strong young fingers slipped. Also he loved her – loved, as he had never dreamt that love could be.

But he knew now, he knew! And a great loathing mingled with his lust. Long did they struggle; at last he got the upper, and with all his weight above her drove down his fingers in her neck. She gave one gasping cry – a cry of many devils in hell – and died. He was alone.

He had slain the succubus, and absorbed it. Ah! With what force and fire his veins roared! Ah! How he leapt from the bed, and donned the holy robes. How he invoked the God of Vengeance, Horus the mighty, and turned loose the Avengers upon the black soul that had sought his life!

At the end he was calm and happy as a babe; he returned to bed, slept easy, and woke strong and splendid.

Night after night for ten nights this scene was acted and re-acted: always identical. On the eleventh day he received a postcard from Hypatia Gay that she was coming to see him that afternoon.

'It means that the material basis of their working is exhausted,' explained his master. 'She wants another drop of blood. But we must put an end to this.'

They went out into the city, and purchased a certain drug of which the master knew. At the very time that she was calling at the flat, they were at the boarding-house where she lodged, and secretly distributing the drug about the house. Its function was a strange one: hardly had they left the house when from a thousand quarters came a lamentable company of cats, and made the winter hideous with their cries.

'That' (chuckled the master) 'will give her mind something to occupy itself with. She will do no black magic for our friend awhile!'

Indeed the link was broken; Swanoff had peace. 'If she comes again,' ordered the master, 'I leave it to you to punish her.'

A month passed by; then, unannounced, once more Hypatia Gay knocked at the flat. Her virginal eyes still smiled; her purpose was yet deadlier than before.

Swanoff fenced with her awhile. Then she began to tempt him.

'Stay!' he said, 'first you must keep your promise and enter the temple!'

Strong in the trust of her black master, she agreed. The poet opened the little door, and closed it quickly after her, turning the key.

As she passed into the utter darkness that hid behind curtains of black velvet, she caught one glimpse of the presiding god.

It was a skeleton that sat there, and blood stained all its bones. Below it was the evil altar, a round table supported by an ebony figure of a Negro standing upon his hands. Upon the altar smouldered a sickening perfume, and the stench of the slain victims of the god defiled the air. It was a tiny room, and the girl, staggering, came against the skeleton. The bones were not clean; they were hidden by a greasy slime mingling with the blood, as though the hideous worship were about to endow it with a new body of flesh. She wrenched herself back in disgust. Then suddenly she felt it was alive! It was coming towards her! She shrieked once the blasphemy which her vile master had chosen as his mystic name; only a hollow laugh echoed back.

Then she knew all. She knew that to seek the left-hand path may lead one to the power of the blind worms of the Slime – and she resisted. Even then she might have called to the White Brothers; but she did not. A hideous fascination seized her.

And then she felt the horror.

Something – something against which nor clothes nor struggles were any protection – was taking possession of her, eating its way into her . . .

And its embrace was deadly cold . . . Yet the hell-clutch at her heart filled her with a fearful joy. She ran forward; she put her arms round the skeleton; she put her young lips to its bony teeth, and kissed it. Instantly, as at a signal, a drench of the waters of death washed all the human life out of her being, while a rod as of steel smote her even from the base of the spine to the brain. She had passed the gates of the abyss. Shriek after shriek of ineffable agony burst from her tortured mouth; she writhed and howled in that ghastly celebration of the nuptials of the Pit.

Exhaustion took her; she fell with a heavy sob.

When she came to herself she was at home. Still that lamentable crew of cats miauled about the house. She awoke and shuddered. On the table lay two notes.

The first: 'You fool! They are after me; my life is not safe. You have ruined me – Curse you!' This from the loved master, for whom she had sacrificed her soul.

The second a polite note from the publisher, asking for more drawings. Dazed and desperate, she picked up her portfolio, and went round to his office in Bond Street.

He saw the leprous light of utter degradation in her eyes; a dull flush came to his face; he licked his lips.

Lucifer over London

LEWIS SPENCE

Some voices possess a kind of monotonous chant which almost compels one to listen to them. The only two men in the dull and decorous bar-room except the barman and myself were conversing in a semi-confidential manner. One, a squat, little man, spoke incisively with a cockney accent; the other, the very picture of a manservant off duty, was all ears and eyes.

'Shock to the system!' the little man hissed. 'I bin seventeen years on this job now, Frank, and I tell you it's the worst case I ever seen. Something's scared the old fella mortal bad. Raves, he does, all day long, 'cept when he's under O.P.M. Always the same cry: "Asmodeus, Asmodeus!" whoever or whatever that means. Then a lot of whisperin' and chatterin' and groanin' something awful. "Set me free," he yells, "I never signed the bond. Save my soul, save me from the darkness." Enough to give you the fantods, believe me.'

'The old boy's 'aunted,' said the other fellow drearily. 'I know the symptoms. What's the doctor say?'

'Him? Very little. Close sort o' card,' replied the little man. 'Fed up with the case, he is. Well, Frank, I'm not goin' to stay on there any longer. My nerve's fair to good, as you know, but it's not equal to that constant ravin' and mutterin'. Ought to be in a looney-bin, he should. So if that job with the legless officer gent you were speakin' of is still vacant. . . . The 'ouse is being watched, too. What it all means, I can't think. . . .'

'You take my tip, Harry, and git out o' that outfit before yer nerve gives way,' counselled the other. 'They're foreigners, you say. Well, you leave it flat. If I were you, I'd ring up 999 this very night, report the case, and quit. Narsty work, if you asks me. Any talk of Nazis, or that sort o' thing?'

'Funny you should ask that, Frank. When it isn't Asmodeus, it's Hitler. Raves about 'em as if they were one and the same, he does. But Hitler can't do much harm to anybody now, one would think.'

'Well, you got my advice,' snapped the other sententiously, finishing his drink and sliding from his stool. 'I'm off. Shouldn't ha' stayed so long. If you quit, Harry, ring me, and I'll fix you up if I can.'

74

I reflected for a moment. I watched Harry smoking his cigarette until the butt end grew so small that it was impossible to smoke it any more, then I offered him a drink and a cigarette. I told him I was a medical student – which was true – and said that I had overheard his talk. Thus we were able to discuss as fellow 'professionals' the details of his patient's case, in which I pretended to be greatly interested. It was the word 'Asmodeus', however, that had roused my attention. Asmodeus, as I told him, when he asked me, is one of the names of Satan, the Devil, Mephistopheles, Lucifer, the King of Hell, the Prince of Darkness who carries power over the fires of Heaven. Now I had not long left lunching with my uncle, Sir Robin Butler, whose expert knowledge of occult matters was known to students all over the world, but whose habit of expecting all his guests to be equally interested made him a notorious bore. All through luncheon and most of the afternoon I had sat under a lecture on the connection between the deliberate worship of Satan as the god-captain of all evil and the forces which moved the German Nazi leaders. He seemed to believe that devil-worship was still being practised. He had used the word 'Asmodeus' several times – and, damn it all, after yawning over Satan half the day, here was Satan again, under his most rarely used cognomen, being spoken about in a respectable public-house. Devilish odd, you might say, devilish odd.

Well by the time we had had a few more drinks, Harry and I were pals. The more I heard of his patient's ravings about the power and the glory of Lucifer the more I wished my uncle had come along with me. I could have left the two together. What then possessed me to tell Harry that if he did not want the job any longer I would take his place as male nurse to this foreigner? It was because he had mentioned at last who his patient was. The name of Dr Ludwig Lehmann meant nothing to Harry, but to a medical student like myself, whose ambition was to be a great doctor, the name of Lehmann meant everything. Before the war, this Austrian doctor had been a world figure in medicine. To think that he was a refugee, in London, ill, perhaps friendless! I determined to offer my services, especially when Harry, now decidedly tipsy, said he was not going back anyway.

The next morning I called at the address 'Harry' had given me, said I had heard that a male nurse was wanted, and discovered that while the patient was *the* Dr Lehmann, he was by no means friendless. His stepdaughter was keeping house for him and nursing him. She seemed only too glad of my offer, however, and I agreed to look after Dr Lehmann for a week at least. Over lunch she gave me details of the case – persecution in Austria – anxiety – escape – overwork in Switzerland during the war – nervous breakdown. I told her that I was surprised that I had seen no mention of his name anywhere. After all, he was a famous doctor. Since the war ended, she answered, he had dropped everything. What, then, had caused the breakdown? After some hesitation, she said that he had plunged with strange enthusiasm into the study of the Occult. She feared that it had turned his brain. . . .

For some days after I took over, Dr Lehmann was placid. He was a thin, gaunt person of about seventy, Teutonic, bearded, and sallow. The yellow, bloodshot eyes opened occasionally, but otherwise he showed few signs of life. I gave him a thorough examination and found the heart weak and flabby, while it was obvious that the entire nervous system had been subjected not only to long-continued strain, but to a violent shock, or series of shocks, quite recently. And there were signs of diabetic disease.

My time was regularly arranged. I had a break of three hours in the afternoon. But it was part of my duty to sleep in the patient's room. I had my meals alone and scarcely saw the stepdaughter except when she came to take my place after lunch. The almost complete isolation of the house and its consequent silence made my vigil dreary enough.

Nothing happened until the third night, when Dr Lehmann suddenly raised himself in bed. He seemed to be listening. His action roused me, and I was on the alert in a moment. For three or four minutes he remained in this posture. But he suddenly flopped backward, and in a few minutes his regular breathing showed that he was asleep. On the following night, however, he woke about the same time, a little after 2 a.m., and once more raised himself in bed. This time he seemed to be listening more intently than ever. Then he began to talk rapidly in German. So quick and confused was his utterance that at first I was able to distinguish words only here and there. He was praying, in a tone of earnestness, solemn and entreating, with clasped hands and upturned face. Then the utterance grew clearer and even more fervid. He was beseeching someone for mercy, to free him from a vow he had made – I heard the name 'Asmodeus', not once but many times. I did not interrupt, hoping to learn more, but in a little while the voice died away in a moan and, exhausted, he lay back and sank into a coma.

About half an hour later he rose again, this time in such a state of wild excitement that I leapt out of bed and stood by him. This time he seemed to be in angry, even furious, argument with someone. To some policy he had the strongest objection. He solemnly gave warning that 'the Powers' were not in agreement with it, that they would not tolerate it. It would mean ruin, 'final and irrevocable', for all, for 'the cause' as well as for humanity.

The following night passed without disturbance, but on the next, Lehmann suddenly awoke in a shocking state of distraction, calling wildly on 'Asmodeus'. Throwing aside the bedclothes, he flung himself on his knees, and when I went over to him and tried to soothe him, he thrust me aside with what seemed extraordinary vigour for a man of his age. Then, furiously, he turned upon me, brandishing his fists in my face and cursing. He would, he cried angrily, have nothing to do with what was going on at Kempton Park. My god was not his god. His Asmodeus was the true world-spirit, mine merely a German parody, distorted to comply with Germanic aims and ambitions. He, an Austrian, had been a fool to have associated with Germans who construed every cause in terms of Germanic purpose and design. The chapel at Marionville was a travesty, a blasphemy. He washed his hands of the whole affair. He appealed to his god to destroy this profane counterfeit of his holy worship. And so he raved on, until he collapsed in exhaustion.

I gave him an injection, after which he dozed.

I seemed to have stumbled into a grotesque situation. If Lehmann was not lunatic, what the devil was going on in that respectable London suburb known as Kempton Park? After some serious thought, I decided to consult my tedious but knowledgeable uncle. But first it would be amusing to do a little sleuthing. I knew the London district – Kempton Park. I had the name, Marionville, which was probably the name of a house. What about spending the afternoon looking for it? If there were such a house, I should have something firm to go on. It would mean that Lehmann was not merely having a nightmare. Then one would know how to act. Perhaps these Germans were people the police ought to be told about? They would have been 'vetted' before being allowed to settle here – but then the 'vetting' net probably had some holes in it. Lehmann, an anti-Nazi, would surely not have associated with Nazi sympathisers?

The next afternoon I was on my way to Kempton Park, having told the stepdaughter that I might be late getting back. I parked my car in a Hampton Court garage. I mentioned Marionville to the attendant, and he said it seemed familiar to him. He rather thought he had been asked to take his taxi to a house of that name. But it was some time ago. If the name was Marionville, then it was an old house somewhere behind East Molesey.

By the time I had reached East Molesey and had turned into the complex of roads beyond it, it was almost dark. Up and down the quiet, conventional highways I wandered, but my search was unrewarded. At last it occurred to me that it was probably a much older and larger house than any of the dwellings I had passed, so I pushed farther north towards Kempton Park. Traversing a long, silent road which did not seem to contain more than three houses in its entire length, I came to it at last – the kind of house that people built near London about a century ago – square, solid, and flat-roofed, with a semicircular abutment in the centre, and standing in about an acre and a half of garden.

If any place near London could be isolated, it was surely this. I couldn't see a single light in the whole solid façade of the place, which stood back from the road some forty feet or more. Only a new wooden fence separated it from the pathway: I opened the gate, and walked boldly in.

I had made up my mind what to do should I encounter anyone. I would be the hectoring, busy doctor who had been called on an emergency case. Bluff would do the rest. I walked up the path and round to the side of the house. The mass of a large timber building jutted out from its rear. I pushed the door. It opened, and I peeped in. Then I knew my quest had not been in vain. This was 'the chapel at Marionville'.

The interior looked at first like a hall of carved stone, but I soon perceived that it had been panelled with cunningly painted canvas which gave it the appearance of masonry grotesquely carved with the shapes of gods, fiends, and satyrs. The general effect was horrible. At the end of the 'chapel', if one may call it so, was a large tapestry on which a gigantic figure of Lucifer was displayed. Beneath it was an altar which seemed to be littered with the apparatus of infernal worship – black candles, ornaments, incense-burners, and books.

Curtains of sable and scarlet hung on either side of the tapestry, and these were decorated with pentacles, stars, and other goetic symbols.

As I stared at the details of this strange shrine, I heard someone coming along the gravel path. In one corner the canvas which masked the timber of the chapel did not meet completely, and into the gap I quickly dived and found that the painted screen was set on a frame at least a couple of feet from the walls, giving me ample space to hide.

The chapel lights were switched on. Through the chinks in the canvas I could now see quite clearly. Along the aisle a tall, elderly man walked to the altar, genuflected before the image of Lucifer, and raising the black-and-scarlet hangings which flanked the altar, disappeared behind them.

One by one other people entered. Between thirty and forty men and women had at last seated themselves. A bell sounded sharply, and the man who had passed behind the curtains now reappeared, dressed in elaborate robes. A dark-skinned youth with him swung a censer from which steamed thick clouds of incense. The congregation stood.

The priest – or whatever he was – did not look at the worshippers beneath him. He seemed concentrated on his own movements. But I stared hard enough at the 'congregation'. Were all these people Germans? Most of them seemed to be.

The muttered prayers ceased and I began to be nauseated by the fetid incense, which in Satanist shrines is usually compounded of rue, henbane, deadly nightshade, and rotting leaves. The 'host' was carried to the altar. The wafer it contained was torn from its receptacle by the celebrant, who then stamped upon it to the accompaniment of profane cries by the congregation. A chalice of liquor was passed round. As it circulated, I heard distant thunder. The lights were lowered. A vivid flash of lightning illumined the dreadful shrine. In sonorous German the celebrant began to speak.

'Friends and brothers,' he said, 'through the grace and power of our lord Lucifer-Asmodeus, our great cause is about to triumph and the folk of the German Reich to be avenged upon their enemies. We shall destroy our foes by supernatural means. What is an atomic bomb compared to the powers of Lucifer? He bears in his hand the fires of heaven. He can be controlled only by our arch-enemy, the God Jehovah.

'But this condition of inferiority now lies behind us,' he continued. 'The chief obstacle is removed. Our lord Lucifer, the king of light, will now have a new link with mankind. He shall make us the media of his terrible potency. As you know, he cannot wield that frightful power of which he is the source and reservoir without the perfect co-operation of mankind, who are gifted with freewill and who have the right to employ it "for good or evil", as the cant Christian phrase has it. This impediment, I say, has been removed at last. It is now possible to effect a perfect union between our god and us, so that at last we can function as the direct agents of his overwhelming might.

'That great scientist, Dr Lehmann, who now lies stricken, has discovered an essence that heightens the powers of human mental concentration a hundredfold. This temporary extension of human mental potentiality will enable Lucifer to operate through his servants. Once he could do so only through humanity in the mass, an imperfect medium. Now he can act through spiritual concurrence with some few chosen persons. You are that few! You shall be the weapon through which Lucifer shall attack England, Russia, and America, and so avenge imperial Germany, Lucifer's own particular province, and render her once again the greatest power on earth. Through our divine master, the spirit of heavenly fire, of which he is the only begetter, will descend upon this city of London and destroy it. By mental concentration we shall focus our lord's destructive flame upon any place we choose. Nothing will be able to withstand its power. Even stone will melt before the force of the magnified lightning-bolts of our master, Lucifer, and granite crumble under its consuming ray. The first blow will be struck now. As a symbolic gesture, we shall demolish one of the chief national palladia of Britain. By the hour of noon tomorrow, the Nelson Monument in Trafalgar Square will have crumbled into a heap of smouldering lime.'

With a sonorous benediction he concluded and dismissed the congregation. When the place seemed empty, I sneaked out and got safely to the road.

I could hardly believe I had not dreamt it all. It seemed preposterous. But why should this infernal priest make so extraordinary an announcement? Perhaps he and his fellow-conspirators intended to blow up conspicuous London buildings. Their crazy followers would believe it was the work of Lucifer.

Could I go to Scotland Yard with this story? As I drove towards London, I decided I would not go back to my patient that night. I would stay at an hotel and – I felt like a fool – take a careful look at the Nelson Monument in the morning. If I saw anything suspicious, I would call the police.

By eleven next morning I had walked several times round Trafalgar Square and stared so much at the monument that I felt that even the pigeons were wondering what I was up to. I could see nothing and felt more like a fool than ever. But, of course, I hung round till midday – it was only natural – and as noon approached I took care to get as far from the monument as I could without losing sight of it. I stood a little way down Northumberland Avenue. What soon afterwards occurred in Trafalgar Square has been alluded to by scientists as 'one of the most extraordinary meteorological phenomena on record', and as 'quite inexplicable'. It had been a fairly bright morning towards the close of August, with only a very little cloud. But on the stroke of twelve we beheld a volume of vapour approaching the Square the like of which I have never beheld in a clear sky. It was thick, dark, indeed almost black, globular in shape and of considerable bulk, and it advanced with tremendous velocity. But in the heart of this nebulous globe, which emitted a rolling, rattling din of terrific intensity, louder than that made by a large plane flying low, glowed and flashed a heart of vivid flame which gave forth sparks and coruscations, like an immense catherine-wheel. It seemed that something special in the way of a storm was coming.

Within a few moments the sky over the great Square was filled with this strange fiery cloud. People rushed for shelter. I heard someone exclaim that it was a plane on fire and about to crash. I stood staring in the middle of the road as if hypnotised. For just as the heart of this cloud was over the monument it seemed to halt in its course while a man might draw breath. Then it began to roll backward at a speed considerably greater than that with which it had advanced. As it retreated, it gathered momentum until, within a few seconds, it was nothing but a dimly sparkling globe in the sky miles away to the south-west. People in the crowd were explaining the phenomenon as the strangest freak of the weather they had known – quite frightening, in fact, when I heard the distant sound of an explosion. I thought I knew where the awful thing had thundered, and jumping into my car I rushed towards Kempton

Park and the house called Marionville. Of course, I found what I expected. The house had been struck by lightning – and with a flash and a roar so frightful as to scare everybody in the neighbour-hood, Marionville had been almost completely destroyed. As I got there, the fire-brigade were just getting ready to leave. From the crowd I gathered that twelve bodies had been fetched out of the ruins. They had been burnt beyond recognition.

When I got away and went to Dr Lehmann's house I found that he had died peacefully during the night. I said goodbye to his step-daughter. I said nothing to her and nothing to the police. I don't want people to think I'm a lunatic.

The Primate of the Rose

M. P. SHIEL

' "Friends of the Rose?" ' said E. P. Crooks to Smyth one night, at the Savage Club. 'Is it an actual fact that there are secret societies in London?'

And Smyth, with his expression of lazy surprise, replied: 'Why, yes. Ask me another time. Come and dine with us too, if you like.'

It is a wonder that Crichton Smyth ever did invite Crooks. As editor of the *Westminster Magazine,* he had known Crooks as a little story-writer, and had never had any such impulse; but suddenly Englishmen, with their genius for discovery, had discovered that they had a Crooks; proceeded to pay him ninepence for writing 'the'; and then Smyth, with his eyebrows of surprise, muttered: 'Come and dine with us.'

Smyth was of that better aristocracy, the upper middle-class, which gives to England its ladies: slim, clean-looking, old-blooded—not much blood, and thin: but rare, like wine of Yquem.

Of another family was Crooks—a fatty little man, fat-cheeked, with an outsticking moustache that hung. Still, there was something or other in him—something brisk in his glance, in the dash of his hair across his forehead; and if at seventeen he had vended soda-water from door to door, at twenty-six he was a graduate, and at thirty-six a star.

But he was a gay Romeo, Crooks—in a rather vulgar mood; and Smyth had a sister.

If one had prophesied to Smyth that his sister, Minna Smyth of the Smyths, could possible commit follies for E. P. Crooks, or look twice at Crooks, Smyth would hardly have bothered to smile. . . .

However, the human female can be pretty queer and wayward; and her heart is like spittle on the palm that the Tartar slaps—no telling which way it will pitch.

From that first night of the dinner Minna Smyth showed herself amiable to the celebrity—a *chic* dinner of dated wines in a flat in Westminster: for editors are awfully well-to-do people—do you know? The piano there was a mosaiced thing in mother-of-pearl; and, in turning Miss Smyth's music, Crooks's fingers got positive magnetism, hers negative, and they met.

She was a tall, thin girl of twenty-five, very like Smyth, very English in type, pretty, but washed-out and superfine, with light eyes of the colour of quinine-solution which X-rays make 'fluorescent.' Was Crooks genuinely smitten with this? It is doubtful. Besides, he was married. But she was a conquest worth making, and he was a man ever on the *qui vive* to add yet a photo to his packet, and a feather to his cap.

Minna Smyth, for her part, took studiously from that night to feeding her mind on the spiced meat of Crooks's books, who, meanwhile, had retaliated upon Smyth by banqueting him at the National Liberal, and might drive home anon with him from the Savage, Crooks felt that he was patronizing Smyth; and Smyth felt that he was patronizing Crooks: for when one has known a tremendous man in his days of '£2-a-thousand-words,' one has no respect for his tremendousness—especially Smyth, who was the chilliest thing that the Heavens ever invented. At any rate, they became friendly.

During which time Crooks and Minna Smyth had a way of meeting at private views, lectures, concerts—meetings of which Smyth did not know; letters were written which Smyth did not see; and it happened one evening at the flat, at a moment when Smyth was in the next room, that Minna mentioned to Crooks in the course of conversation that on Friday nights her brother was out 'at his secret society,' and never came home till 4 a.m.

On this Crooks, picking up her hand, said to her: 'I'll come on Friday night.'

She looked at him under her eyes, meditating upon him; then moved her face from side to side, while her lips took the shape of 'No.'

'Something to *say*,' said he 'I hope you are inexorable.'

Her lids now veiled her eyes, while her bosom rose and rose, unloaded itself of a sigh, and tumbled back.

'Is it yes?' he whispered.

'*Crichton!*' she breathed, with a sudden expression of shrinking and fright in her eyes.

'Oh, I think that that will be all right about Crichton,' Crooks said.

'You don't *know* him!' she whispered: 'his nose goes white....'

Smyth now came in; and presently, when Minna had gone out, Crooks said to him: 'By the way, how about that wondrous "Friends of the Rose," Smyth, that you are always to tell me of?' He threw himself into roomy red velvet opposite Smyth's red velvet on the other side of a fire—it was December—and drank from a large and fragile glass.

'What can one tell of it, if it is a secret society?' Smyth asked, his eyebrows raised over lazy lids that seemed to strain to be open, for there was an ample valley of country between his eyebrows and his nose-tip.

'I mean to say—is the thing *real*? Is it like *London*?'—from Crooks, who had an inquisitive intellect, and, then, was ever on the quest of 'copy.' He added: 'Years ago I wrote a story about a secret society—you must remember it; but I never for a moment believed that there are such things. Anarchism, yes—Freemasonry —the Irish—'

'Those are mushrooms,' Smyth remarked, his lips giving out a trickle of thick cigar-smoke, languid as himself; while Crooks smoked a briar pipe.

'What! Freemasonry a mushroom?' — from Crooks — 'on the contrary—'

'Comparatively, of course, I meant. And I don't call those secret societies, of whose existence and objects everyone knows. Where's the secrecy? . . . But there are others.'

Crooks bent forward. He knew that Smyth was Cockney, as much a thing of London as was Charles Lamb, sometimes burrowing in some Slav night-club at the docks, or among 'Ye Merrie Men,' when supposed to be at holiday in Homburg: a being deeply initiated into London lore, knowing somewhat more behind those eyebrows of mild surprise than he ever mentioned at table: hence Crooks's interest; and his interest, like his other emotions, was usually shown.

'But in London?' he said. 'Really, now? Why have I never dropped across them? In Paris, yes—'

Smyth answered—his taciturnity sometimes melted when the subject was London—'Paris is to London as a shilling dictionary to the Encyclopaedia Britannica. Everything's in London.'

'Except Paris'—from Crooks.

'Paris is, too: I could take you to the Bal Bullier within half a mile of here. Only, in Paris it has name and fame, in London it is lost.'

'But this "Rose" business—"secret societies"—you assure me they're a fact?'

'I am a member of two; I know of a third; and have suspicions of a fourth.' Smyth laughed a little to himself.

'That's three, say'—Crooks had animated eyes—'now, tell me how I can join them all!'

Smyth chuckled inwardly at this crude enthusiasm; and he said: 'You don't seem quite to realize—they are *secret* societies. There are more multi-millionaires—more experts in Becquerel rays—than members. To become a member of those I know is about as rare a thing as the conjunction of four planets; and requires long preparation. You can't go about "joining them" like that. One of them has consisted of sixteen members since the time of Edward II, another of twenty-three—'

'But what are they *for?*' Crooks fretfully cried. 'What's—what's their *motif*, their *idea?*'

'Different *motifs*. Most are benevolent, I think. All mystic.'

'Then, why on earth are they secret, if they are benevolent?' Crooks peered piercingly into it with the interest of the perplexed busybody: 'The mere fact that they are benevolent—'

'Different reasons for secrecy: some are secret to avoid—hanging sometimes.' Smyth showed his teeth in a silent laugh.

'Then, I don't tumble,' from Crooks. 'Why need they avoid hanging, if they are benevolent?'

'Seems fairly obvious to me,' Smyth remarked, his straining lids half-shut behind his *pince-nez*: 'There are three types of really secret societies—absurd, obscene, and benevolent: and the benevolent ones can only be created for one reason—because Government, so far, is immature and defective. They assist Government by taking the law into their own hands, executing justice, doing good, in cases where Government can't, or won't, yet do it, and calling upon God to witness in a mystic mood.'

'Oho! Is that it? Then, they have my approval. And as to these "Friends of the Rose" tell me the particular—'

'It was a bad day for me,' Smyth interrupted, 'when I mentioned to you "Friends of the Rose," for you have left me no peace since. What business is it of yours? And what can you expect me to tell? Does the great Crooks take it for granted that secrets guarded six centuries will be blabbed to him for the asking? You may be perfectly certain, for instance, that "Friends of the Rose" is not really their name—though it is not unlike that. What can one tell? Perhaps I may tell you that the membership has always been limited to sixteen; or I may tell you that there is a certain apartment somewhere in London of whose existence only one man at a time—occasionally two—has known for five hundred years.

Crooks winked quick, hearing it; then threw his face about, frowning, fretted, almost offended, for he disliked being 'out of' anything. 'Apartment,' he muttered. . . . 'and who is that one man who knows?'

'The Primate of the Society.'

'Primate . . .' Crooks meditated it over the fire; then animatedly looked up to ask: 'Now, where can that apartment be?'

On which Smyth, tickled, let himself go into a sort of laugh, saying: 'What, want to take a lady there? I am sorry I can't tell you, if only because I have no notion myself. But when the Primate dies—he is a very old man—lives in Camden Town—I shall know.

'Oh, *you'll* be Primate then?'

Smyth's lids lay closed. He made no answer.

'I should just like half-an-hour's interview with that "very old man who lives in Camden Town",' Crooks mentioned.

And Smyth answered: 'If you saw him hobbling along Gray's Inn Road, it would not occur to you to glance twice at him. London is like that. We brush shoulders with angels at Charing Cross, little divining the depths that some common-looking type has dived, the oddity of his destiny, his store of lore, his giftedness, or the dignity on his head. I know an old patternmaker in Wapping—'

But at this point Minna came in, and, as Crooks's attention was drawn off, Smyth suddenly stopped.

That was a Wednesday.

Now, on Fridays Smyth invariably left his office an hour earlier, dined at home, locked himself in his book-room for two hours, and then went out dumb, like a monk, not to come back till the morning hours.

Years had seen no break in this routine; but this Friday there was a break: for, for some unknown reason, Smyth was back at home before eleven.

In Victoria Street he glanced up at his windows on the second floor; noticed that the drawing-room light seemed low behind the blinds; and muttered something to himself.

He then went up by the lift, opened the flat-door with his key—and did it noiselessly, though he was *far* from admitting to himself that he did it noiselessly. He now glanced into the kitchen, and his eyebrows went higher because of the fact that it was in darkness. He passed, on padded carpet, to two other rooms — no one there: the servants had perhaps gone to the theatre. He then stepped down a passage to the drawing-room door, and, still without sound, turned the handle. But that door was locked: and his eyebrows went higher still.

Standing there, he seemed to come to a sudden decision: and walked sharply, softly, out of the flat.

87

Down below he stepped into a by-street where there is a Police Ambulance cot; and, standing in the shadow of this, looking toward Victoria Street, he waited.

After half-an-hour he saw Crooks come out of his 'Mansion'; saw him walk away with quite an air of jauntiness; and presently saw his drawing-room lights turned on full.

He slept at the Hotel Victoria that night; and the next morning turned up at Covent House the same cold Smyth as ever—made a jest with the lift-man, going up to his office; and his sub-editor did not dream that day what was in him, nor that its name was Legion.

But in the afternoon his sister Minna, who had spent a day of wonderment and trembling, received a note 'by hand' from him:

> 'Dear Minna,
>   I regret that reasons have arisen which make it impossible for us to live any longer together. Pray write me by tomorrow whether you desire to stay on at the flat, or would rather that I took another for you.
> Yours,
Crichton.'

So they parted.

She, knowing that he was attached to the flat, left it for one in Maida Vale, he settling an income upon her. From that night of the lowered lights he did not see her again—not for an instant. To her prayers for an explanation he made no answer.

But his pain proved more than he had bargained for, and he would have done better to have left those rooms which had known her presence. Though not very visible to others, there was a friendship and link between them extremely sacred and sweet; and he pretty soon discovered that, in sending her away, he had plucked out his right eye. Sometimes for days now he would absent himself from the office; his thin, palish face went pinched and paler; some grey began to mingle with his hair; his taciturnity turned to something like dumbness.

But he never relented; until, after six months, it came to his ears, through a doctor, that she was not well, and in a tragic fix. And then he wrote to her:

> 'Dear Minna,
>   I know everything: and whatever there is to forgive I forgive. Please, dear, come back to my arms.
> Yours,
Crichton.'

She would not at first; but then the wings of love proved stronger than her shrinkings: and she took herself back to the old flat.

But she was not well for she, too, had rued and gnashed, chewing the ashes of the fire of passion; so that daily he saw her vanishing like a shadow from him; and in a month she sighed at him, and died, leaving him a little girl to nurse.

As for Crooks, he was at Naples, and it was three months before he had definite knowledge that a child was born, a mother dead. Then he asserted himself. Since that Friday night of Smyth's earlier return he had had no interview with Smyth, for Minna, as it were on her knees, had ever pleaded with him, 'Please, please, try not to meet Crichton!' But now Crooks asserted himself.

He sought out Smyth one night at the Savage, and, standing before Smyth's chair, said: 'Smyth, I must have the child.'

Smyth looked up from the slightly surprising thing in his *Standard* to the slightly surprising object before him, and said 'No.'

'Then, I have to see her sometimes—fair's fair.'

'If you like,' Smyth muttered. 'She is at my flat. Try not to see her often'—he read again.

So Crooks went and revolved philosophic thoughts over the insignificant stick of womanhood, that one could push into a jug; and she exclaimed on seeing his fat face, with hair stuck on it.

Then twice a month he went; and once, when, on meeting Smyth in Smyth's hall, he put out his hand, Smyth, with his eyebrows on high, let his long fingers be shaken. (Smyth, in fact, never participated in a hand-shake with any child of Adam, simply permitted and witnessed it, with surprise.)

And when this had happened several times in the course of a year, one night found Crooks seated by the fire, the child on his knee, over against Smyth, as of old. Without greatly caring, he had set himself to be friends again with Smyth, doing it in a patronizing mood, and so caring nothing for Smyth's surprise—nor, in truth, could he be sure that Smyth was more surprised than usual, since Smyth was for ever surprised. Moreover, Crooks's fame had lately swelled and mellowed; if he had an opinion on this or that matter, that was put into the newspapers; and he was puffed up, the fact being that the little men of his trade and grain have no essential self, nor impregnable self-estimation, which cannot be raised at all by any applause, nor depressed at all by any dispraise: but when the wind blows they are big, and when the wind lulls they are little. As for Crooks, at this time he felt that his presence honoured inventors and philosophers.

And 'Cluck, cluck,' he went, cantering his chick on his knee with a gee-up cackling; then 'I say, Smyth, did you ever become Primate of the Rose Society?'

'Yes,' Smyth replied with surprise.

'Ah, you did. So *you* have the secret now of that mysterious "Apartment"—'

'Yes,' Smyth replied with surprise.

'Then,' says Crooks to himself, 'I shall *set foot* in that apartment—sooner or later'; and he sat an hour with Smyth.

In this sort of relaxation they co-existed, until the midget Minna, fair and frail like its mother, could crawl, could walk, the months for mourning now long over, though Crichton Smyth still dressed in raiment of the raven—crape never more to leave that sleeve of his. Every Sunday sun-down found him in the Brompton Cemetery moping over a tomb; and most who saw him thought him cold; but some thought not. Meantime, Crooks came fairly regularly to the flat; and he said one night by the fire: 'I shall leave off coming here, Smyth, if you don't talk to me. I have assumed that there can be no resentment left, since you realize that I loved Minna.'

Smyth's lips oozed smoke a minute; then: 'How many others did you love that year?'

'Several perhaps. I consider the question irrelevant—'

'How many have you loved since?'

'Several—many, perhaps. That is quite outside—'

'You are married.'

'Yes, but I am impatient of argument of the subject, Smyth. It simply means that your views on sex-relations are different from mine; and, as mine are the offspring of thought—'

'I am not "arguing",'—from Smyth with sleep-loaded lids: 'it is not a question of anyone's "views." I merely said that you are married, and it is a fact that, if a married man lets himself love a girl of the middle class, he runs a risk of killing her with shame. I do not say that it ought to be so—I am not arguing—I only state, what you know, that it *is* so—at present; and when a death occurs, you get murder. Of course, there is no law against it, but—' He stopped, passing his palm lazily across his raised forehead, his lids closed down, straining to open.

'Men are not exactly angels,' Crooks remarked.

'More like devils, some'—a mutter.

'Not referring to poor me?'

'Your existence seems to do a great deal of harm. I don't know that you do any good.'

'You don't know that my books do good?'

'No, I don't know. I know that men are already getting past "novels" without novelty, and that as soon as women cease to be children the last "novel" will be written. Yours are entertaining, I believe—'

'Not prophetic? Not vital?'

This tickled three of Smyth's ribs on the right side, and he let out on a breath of disdain: 'Lot of Simple-Simons we still are.'

But at this statement the little maid commenced to lament, and Crooks, handing her to her nurse, kissed her head, murmuring: 'I'll go.'

But, half-way to the door, he turned to say: 'What about that "Apartment" of yours, Smyth, that I am to be taken to? You said you'd consider it.'

Smyth's answer was a little singular. With a push of the lips, pettish, yet mixed with a smile, he said: 'Oh, you keep on about that!'

This was the *sixth* time that Crooks had asked—Smyth knew the number. At the first asking a flush of offence had touched Smyth's forehead at the cocky pushfulness that could prick Crooks to make such a request. But since then Smyth had begun to answer with a certain demur, a flirting reluctance, as of a girl who murmurs 'no,' but blushes 'yes.'

'*Oh, you keep on about that. . . .*'

'Where's the harm?' asked Crooks on his next visit. 'Provided you can absolutely rely upon my lifelong silence. My curiosity, of course, is intrinsically *literary*. Energize my imagination with an actual sight of the place, and I tell you what—I'll do a series of mystery-stories, and *The Westminster* shall have 'em.'

And Smyth, his lids closed but for a slit that rested on Crooks, answered: 'Ah, Crooks, don't tempt me.'

It was, then, a question of temptation now? Crooks felt exultation. Had not the sister yielded to his tempting? The brother should be his conquest, too. . . .

But on the next occasion of Smyth's temptation, Smyth said with a laugh: 'You don't apparently care whether you urge me to the breach of a vow of office! And you do it with that same facile callousness with which you break your own marriage-vow.'

'Smyth, you will not do as a conscience—you are too pale,' said Crooks. 'Please leave our evil marriage-customs out of the discussion. As to your "vow of office," did you not yourself tell me that sometimes *two* men have known the alleged "Apartment"?'

'Well, yes, I think I did say so. And you conceive, do you, that *you* have a right to be one of the two? Well, perhaps you have—I'll look into the question. But, if ever I do take you, I hope you are not nervous.'

'Fancy a nervous E. P. Crooks! What is there to see, then?'

'It is a little—lethal.'

'Then, I'm the man. But when?'

'I haven't said yes. Give one time. I have to get the approval of others. . . .'

But only three weeks afterwards Smyth yielded. 'Very well,' he said: 'you shall see it; the thing's settled; your imagination shall be "energized,"' as you call it. But you are not permitted to know *where* the room is: you have to go to it blindfold. And, by the way, you must go disguised: just hang a beard round your ears—that'll do. And be before the Temple Church on Tuesday night, to hear the Law Courts clock strike eleven.'

'*Fiet!*' Crooks cried.

That Tuesday night in October a high wind blew, and by the light of a moon that flew to encounter flying troops of cloud, Crooks stood looking at those eight old tombs, and the circular west-end of the church. The Strand river had thinned now to a trickle of feet: in there in the secrecy of the Inn not a step passed; and Crooks felt upon him the mood of adventure: London was partly Baghdad; this an Arabian night: some time or other he'd make 'copy' of the mood of it. To be disguised, too, was quite novel to him: anon he pawed his false beard with a mock pomposity; then he had the thought: 'But why, after all, the disguise?'; and just then eleven struck.

At its last stroke a step was on the paving, and Crichton Smyth with his crape and raven dress was there. He put finger to lip when Crooks began to say something, beckoned, and Crooks followed out through Hare Court, by Middle Temple Lane, past the under-porter's lodge; when Smyth got into a coupé brougham waiting by the Griffin, Crooks followed in.

'I must blindfold you here,' Smyth said at his ear.

'There remains the inward eye,'—from Crooks—'blindfold away.'

At once Smyth produced two pads of black cotton, and a black ribbon that had two narrower ribbons sewed to its ends; cottons and ribbon he tied over Crooks's eyes and nose: and now it could be seen that the broad ribbon had crimson borders, and three roses embroidered on it.

As soon as it was secured, Smyth, unknown to Crooks, slipped a strip of brass-plate inside the band of Crooks's bowler-hat—a brass-plate on which were etched the words: 'Edgar Crichton Smyth, P.' Whereupon the driver, as if he had waited for all this, went forward without being ordered.

But Crooks understood that they were going eastward. He heard Bennett's Clock quite near above strike the quarter-past. And presently the following words were uttered within that brougham

Crooks: Talk to me. I am lost in darkness. Silence must be awful to the blind.

Smyth: I don't want to talk. This is not a night like every night for you and me.

Crooks: You think something of that 'Apartment' of yours!

Smyth: It is not an Apartment with 'To Let' in the window. It has no window. I hope you have said your prayers.

Crooks: Men of my birth have no need to say prayers, Smyth. Behind and underneath we are essentially religious; and our existence, properly understood, is a prayer.

Smyth: Good thing you are religious behind.

Crooks: Did you not *know* that I am ?

Smyth: No, how was I to know ? You aren't where one sees you.

Crooks: Smyth, you are the most—

Smyth: Don't chatter.

Here Crooks could hear a tram droning somewhere through the humdrum plod-clap, plod-clap, of the brougham-horse's hoofs on asphalt; he thought to himself: 'We must be somewhere in Whitechapel; and presently they spoke again:

Crooks: Is it far now?

Smyth: Ten minutes.

Crooks: I don't like the blindfolding, though—and, by the way, what is the disguise for? I understand the blindfold, but why the disguise?

Smyth: You will soon guess why.

Crooks : Your disguise is a mystery, and your blindfolding a plague. Ah, it must be sad to be blind!

Smyth: What about being dead ?

Crooks: The dead don't know that they are blind, but the blind know that they are dead. Oh, it is a great thing to see the sun! to be alive, and see it. People don't realize, because the universe is not meant for men to see, but for the lords of older orbs than this to cast down their crowns before. Tomorrow morning when I have back my sight, I shall build me an altar.

Smyth: Don't make any vows at it.

Crooks: Certainly, Smyth, you are the most surly and cynical—

Smyth: We get out here.

On this the brougham, without order, stopped; Smyth, having

got out, led out Crooks; and, without order, the brougham rolled away.

As it had made several turnings, Crooks did not know in what district of London he now was—he knew that it was East. But no sound of foot-falls passing here; only, he could hear a rush of machinery going on somewhere.

'Those are alternators driven by steam-turbines,' he said. 'But are we in a street?'

'Sh-h, don't talk.' said Smyth.

Crooks next felt himself led by the hand over what seemed to be cobble-stones, where the feet echoed, and there was a draught, so that he thought he must be under some tunnel, or vault. Then he felt himself in the open again, still going over old cobble-stones; and still the thump and rush of machinery reached the ear from somewhere. As for Smyth, he uttered not a word, and would listen to none.

Then there was a stoppage: Crooks knew that a door was being unlocked. And, hearing now a click at his ear, he could guess that Smyth had switched on the light of a torch.

He was next led over bare boards in some place that had a smell of soap and candles, tar and benzoline; and twice his steps tripped over what seemed to be empty bags. Then he was led slowly down some board steps; at the bottom of which Smyth stooped to unlock something—apparently a trapdoor in the ground.

Through this Crooks was led down, Smyth now saying to him: 'Hold my jacket; these steps are narrow'—and Crooks went down some steep steps of stone, each step a jolt, where he ceased to hear the beat of the machinery.

After this he passed through a passage, apparently of hardened marl, markedly damp and clammy, and uneven to the feet, where even sightless eyes could see and feel the thickness of the darkness; at the far end of which Smyth was again known to open some door—evidently a very heavy one—whose lock gnashed at the key, whose hinges chattered. From which point Crooks was led up steps so narrow, that he could easily feel the wall on either hand, they going now in single file.

To these steps there seemed no end—up and still up; and soon Crooks was afresh conscious of the throb and thresh of steam-machinery, jumbled with the hum of generators making their jew's-harp music: this business and to-do seeming to increase on the ear, and then, as still up they climbed, seeming to die away. Whenever they came to a landing or passage, Crooks, who was fat, and panted, said to himself 'at last'; but several times he had to recommence the climb; and he thought to himself 'Can it be the Tower of London? We are in some tower, within the thickness of the wall'; but he did not say anything: a mood of utter dumbness had come upon him.

At last, in moving along a passage over stone floor, he being then in front of Smyth, he stumbled, apparently in dust or rubbish; the next moment he was stopped, butting upon wall; and 'Hallo,' said he, 'what's this?'

There was no reply. . . .

Waiting against the wall for guidance, Crooks was conscious of a clang behind him, as of a massive portal slammed, and of the croak of a rusty lock being coaxed by a key. Then he was aware of a scraping, as if a ponderous object was being dragged across the corridor; and simultaneously he was aware of an odour under his nose.

'Smyth!' he called out: 'are you there?'

There was no reply. . . .

Now he was aware of a match being struck, then of another, and another. By this time his bones were as cold as the stones that enclosed him.

He suddenly cried out 'Smyth! I am going to take the bandage off!'

Still there was no answer but some moments afterwards there burst upon his startled heart a most bizarre noise, a babbling, or lalling, half-talk, half-song, in some unknown tongue—from Smyth. The next instant Crooks had the bandage snatched from his eyes.

There was light—a pink light—brilliant at first to him; and by it he instantly realized that he was interned. He stood in a room of untooled ashlar some fourteen feet square, with a doorway three feet wide looking down a corridor three feet wide. It was the door of this doorway that had been slammed; but he could still look out, since the door had a hole in its iron—a hole Gothic in shape like the door itself; and outside the door stood an old pricket-candlestick of iron supporting seven candles, all alight, higher than a man's head, occupying all the breadth of the corridor.

Crooks understood that that scraping sound he had heard must have been due to the placing of the candlestick in position, and that the striking of the matches had been for lighting the seven candles, each of which had, before and behind it, a screen of pink porcelain with a pattern of roses—two perpendicular rows of roses—so that, as the candles got lower, they would still glow through a rose.

All this he noticed in some moments; also that there was a handbag open on the floor, out of which he assumed that Smyth had got the sort of linen amice, dotted with roses, which he now wore round his shoulders; moreover, in some moments it had entered his consciousness that the dust and rubbish into which he had stumbled was made of the bones and dust and clothes of men who had ended their days there; moreover, he noticed that, hanging before the hole in the portal, was an old Toledo *puñal* of damascened steel, and he understood that this was mercifully meant for his use against himself, if he so chose. If he had doubted this—if he had cherished a hope—it would have vanished when he saw what was hanging on the shaft of the candlestick—a bit of ebony, or black marble, on which had been scribbled in red pencil:

MINNA AND FOUR OTHERS

But what most froze the current of Crooks's blood was the horrid comedy of Smyth's psalmodying and dancing in his amice a yard beyond the candles, like one putting forth a spell of 'woven paces and of waving hands,' his head cast back, his gaze on Heaven—his pince-nez on his nose! But in what occult Chaldæan was that bleating to Moloch and Baal that his tongue baa'd and bleated? Crooks knew some languages but this recitative had no affinity with any speech of men which he had ever conceived; and then that antic fandango-tangle of writhing palms and twining thighs that went on with the psalming, like some entranced wight steadily treading the treadmill of dance in the land of the tarantula—a piece of witchcraft as antique and aboriginal as torch-lit orgies of Sheba and Egypt . . .

His throat straining out of the hole—his eyes straining out of his head—Crooks sent out to that dread dancer the whisper: '*Smyth, don't do it, Smyth . . .*'

He might as well have whispered to the dust and ashes in which he stood.

After three minutes the ritual ceased; Smyth stood another minute, his brow bowed down, with muttering mouth; then took off and put the amice into a handbag; picked up and put on his hat; and, without speaking, went away, leaving the candles watching there, as for a wake.

"OH, WHISTLE, AND I'LL COME TO YOU, MY LAD"

by M. R. James

"I SUPPOSE you will be getting away pretty soon, now Full term is over, Professor," said a person not in the story to the Professor of Ontography, soon after they had sat down next to each other at a feast in the hospitable hall of St. James's College.

The Professor was young, neat, and precise in speech.

"Yes," he said; "my friends have been making me take up golf this term, and I mean to go to the East Coast – in point of fact to Burnstow (I dare say you know it) – for a week or ten days, to improve my game. I hope to get off tomorrow."

"Oh, Parkins," said his neighbour on the other side, "if you are going to Burnstow, I wish you would look at the site of the Templars' preceptory, and let me know if you think it would be any good to have a dig there in the summer."

It was, as you might suppose, a person of antiquarian pursuits who said this, but, since he merely appears in this prologue, there is no need to give his entitlements.

"Certainly," said Parkins, the Professor: "if you will describe to me whereabouts the site is, I will do my best to give you an idea of the lie of the land when I get back, or I could write to you about it, if you would tell me where you are likely to be."

"Don't trouble to do that, thanks. It's only that I'm thinking of taking my family in that direction in the Long, and it occurred to me that, as very few of the English preceptories have ever been properly planned, I might have an opportunity of doing something useful on off-days."

The Professor rather sniffed at the idea that planning out a preceptory could be described as useful. His neighbour continued :

"The site – I doubt if there is anything showing above ground – must be down quite close to the beach now. The sea has encroached tremendously, as you know, all along that bit of coast. I should think, from the map, that it must be about three-quarters of a mile from the Globe Inn, at the north end of the town. Where are you going to stay?"

"Well, *at* the Globe Inn, as a matter of fact," said Parkins. "I have engaged a room there. I couldn't get in anywhere else; most of the lodging-houses are shut up in winter, it seems; and, as it is, they tell me that the only room of any size I can have is really a double-bedded one, and that they haven't a corner in which to store the other bed, and so on. But I must have a fairly large room, for I am taking some books down, and mean to do a bit of work; and though I don't quite fancy having an empty bed – not to speak of two – in what I may call for the time being my study, I suppose I can manage to rough it for the short time I shall be there."

"Do you call having an extra bed in your room roughing it, Parkins?" said a bluff person opposite. "Look here, I shall come down and occupy it for a bit; it'll be company for you."

The Professor quivered, but managed to laugh in a courteous manner.

"By all means, Rogers; there's nothing I should like better. But I'm afraid you would find it rather dull; you don't play golf, do you?"

"No, thank Heaven!" said rude Mr. Rogers.

"Well, you see, when I'm not writing I shall most likely be out on the links, and that, as I say, would be rather dull for you, I'm afraid."

"Oh, I don't know! There's certain to be somebody I know in the place; but, of course, if you don't want me, speak the word, Parkins; I shan't be offended. Truth, as you always tell us, is never offensive."

Parkins was, indeed, scrupulously polite and strictly truthful. It is to be feared that Mr. Rogers sometimes practised upon his knowledge of these characteristics. In Parkins's breast there was a conflict now raging, which for a moment or two did not allow him to answer. That interval being over, he said :

"Well, if you want the exact truth, Rogers, I was considering whether the room I speak of would really be large enough to accommodate us both comfortably; and also whether (mind, I shouldn't have said this if you hadn't pressed me) you would not constitute something in the nature of a hindrance to my work."

Rogers laughed loudly.

"Well done, Parkins!" he said. "It's all right. I promise not to interrupt your work; don't you disturb yourself about that. No, I won't come if you don't want me; but I thought I should do so nicely to keep the ghosts off." Here he might have been seen to wink and to nudge his next neighbour. Parkins might also have been seen to become pink. "I beg pardon, Parkins," Rogers continued; "I oughtn't to have said that. I forgot you didn't like levity on these topics."

"Well," Parkins said, "as you have mentioned the matter, I freely own that I do *not* like careless talk about what you call ghosts. A man in my position," he went on, raising his voice a little, "cannot, I find, be too careful about appearing to sanction the current beliefs on such subjects. As you know, Rogers, or as you ought to know; for I think I have never concealed my views – "

"No, you certainly have not, old man," put in Rogers *sotto voce.*

" – I hold that any semblance, any appearance of concession to the view that such things might exist is equivalent to a renunciation of all that I hold most sacred. But I'm afraid I have not succeeded in securing your attention."

"Your *undivided* attention, was what Dr. Blimber actually *said*,"[1] Rogers interrupted, with every appearance of an earnest desire for accuracy. "But I beg your pardon, Parkins: I'm stopping you."

"No, not at all," said Parkins. "I don't remember Blimber; perhaps he was before my time. But I needn't go on. I'm sure you know what I mean."

"Yes, yes," said Rogers, rather hastily – "just so. We'll go into it fully at Burnstow, or somewhere."

In repeating the above dialogue I have tried to give the impression which it made on me, that Parkins was something of an old woman – rathen hen-like, perhaps, in his little ways; totally destitute, alas! of the sense of humour, but at the same time dauntless and sincere in his convictions, and a man deserving of the greatest respect. Whether or not the reader has gathered so much, that was the character which Parkins had.

On the following day Parkins did, as he had hoped, succeed in getting away from his college, and in arriving at Burnstow. He was made welcome at the Globe Inn, was safely installed in the large double-bedded room of which we have heard, and was able before retiring to rest to arrange his material for work in apple-pie order upon a commodious table which occupied the outer end of the room, and was surrounded on three sides by windows looking out seaward; that is to say, the central window looked straight out to sea, and those on the left and right com-

[1] Mr. Rogers was wrong, *vide Dombey and Son,* chapter xii.

manded prospects along the shore to the north and south respectively. On the south you saw the village of Burnstow. On the north no houses were to be seen, but only the beach and the low cliff backing it. Immediately in front was a strip – not considerable – of rough grass, dotted with old anchors, capstans, and so forth; then a broad path; then the beach. Whatever may have been the original distance between the Globe Inn and the sea, not more than sixty yards now separated them.

The rest of the population of the inn was, of course, a golfing one, and included few elements that call for a special description. The most conspicuous figure was, perhaps, that of an *ancien militaire*, secretary of a London club, and possessed of a voice of incredible strength, and of view of a pronouncedly Protestant type. These were apt to find utterance after his attendance upon the ministrations of the Vicar, an estimable man with inclinations towards a picturesque ritual, which he gallantly kept down as far as he could out of deference to East Anglian tradition.

Professor Parkins, one of whose principal characteristics was pluck, spent the greater part of the day following his arrival at Burnstow in what he had called improving his game, in company with this Colonel Wilson : and during the afternoon – whether the process of improvement were to blame or not, I am not sure – the Colonel's demeanour assumed a colouring so lurid that even Parkins jibbed at the thought of walking home with him from the links. He determined, after a short and furtive look at that bristling moustache and those incarnadined features, that it would be wiser to allow the influence of tea and tobacco to do what they could with the Colonel before the dinner-hour should render a meeting inevitable.

"I might walk home tonight along the beach," he reflected – "yes, and take a look – there will be light enough for that – at the ruins of which Disney was talking. I don't exactly know where they are, by the way; but I expect I can hardly help stumbling on them."

This he accomplished, I may say, in the most literal sense, for in picking his way from the links to the shingle beach his foot caught, partly in a gorse-root and partly in a biggish stone, and over he went. When he got up and surveyed his surroundings, he found himself in a patch of somewhat broken ground covered with small depressions and mounds. These latter, when he came to examine them, proved to be simply masses of flints embedded in mortar and grown over with turf. He must, he quite rightly concluded, be on the site of the preceptory he had promised to look at. It seemed not unlikely to reward the spade of the explorer; enough of the foundations was probably left at no great depth to throw a good deal of light on the general plan. He remembered vaguely that the Templars, to whom this site had belonged, were in the habit of building round churches, and he thought a particular series of the humps or mounds near him did appear to be arranged in something of a circular form. Few people can resist the temptation to try a little amateur research in a department quite outside their own, if only for the satisfaction of showing how successful they would have been had they only taken it up seriously. Our Professor, however, if he felt something of this mean desire, was also truly anxious to oblige Mr. Disney. So he paced with care the circular area he had noticed, and wrote down its rough dimensions in his pocket-book. Then he proceeded to examine an oblong eminence which lay east of the centre of the circle, and seemed to his thinking likely to be the base of a platform or altar. At one end of it, the northern, a patch of the turf was gone – removed by some boy or other creature *feræ naturæ*. It might, he thought, be as well to probe the soil here for evidences of masonry, and he took out his knife and began scraping away the earth. And now followed another little discovery : a portion of soil fell inward as he scraped, and disclosed a small cavity. He lighted one match after another to help him to see of what nature the hole was, but the wind was too strong for them all. By tapping and scratching the sides with his knife, however, he was able to make out that it must be an artficial hole in masonry. It was rectangular, and the sides, top, and bottom, if not actually plastered, were smooth and regular. Of course it was empty. No! As he withdrew the knife he heard a metallic clink, and when he introduced his hand it met with a cylindrical object lying on the floor of the hole. Naturally enough, he picked it up, and when he brought it into the light, now fast fading, he could see that it, too, was of man's making – a metal tube about four inches long and evidently of some considerable age.

By the time Parkins had made sure that there was nothing else in this odd receptacle, it was too late and too dark for him to think of undertaking any further search. What he had done had proved so unexpectedly interesting that he determined to sacrifice a little more of the daylight on the morrow to archæology. The object which he now had' safe in his pocket was bound to be of some slight value at least, he felt sure.

Bleak and solemn was the view on which he took a last look before starting homeward. A faint yellow light in the west showed the links, on which a few figures moving towards the club-house were still visible, the squat martello tower, the lights of Aldsey village, the pale ribbon of sands intersected at intervals by black wooden groynes, the dim and murmuring sea. The wind was bitter from the north, but was at his back when he set out for the Globe. He quickly rattled and clashed through the shingle and gained the sand, upon which, but for the groynes which had to be got over every few yards, the going was both good and quiet. One last look behind, to measure the distance he had made since leaving the ruined Templars' church, showed him a prospect of company on his walk, in the shape of a rather indistinct personage, who seemed to be making great efforts to catch up with him, but made little, if any, progress. I mean that there was an appearance of running about his movements, but that the distance between him and Parkins did not seem materially to lessen. So, at least, Parkins thought, and decided that he almost certainly did not know him, and that it would be absurd to wait until he came up. For all that, company, he began to think, would really be very welcome on that lonely shore, if only you could choose your companion. In his unenlightened days he had read of meetings in such places which even now would hardly bear thinking of. He went on thinking of them, however, until he reached home, and particularly of one which catches most people's fancy at some time of their childhood. "Now I saw in my dream that Christian had gone but a very little way when he saw a foul fiend coming over the field to meet him." "What should I do now," he thought, "if I looked back and caught sight of a black figure sharply defined against the yellow sky, and saw that it had horns and wings? I wonder whether I should stand or run for it. Luckily, the gentleman behind is not of that kind, and he seems to be about as far off now as when I saw him first. Well, at this rate he won't get his dinner as soon as I shall; and, dear me! it's within a quarter of an hour of the time now. I must run!"

Parkins had, in fact, very little time for dressing. When he met the Colonel at dinner, Peace – or as much of her as that gentleman could manage – reigned once more in the military bosom; nor was she put to flight in the hours of bridge that followed dinner, for Parkins was a more than respectable player. When, therefore, he retired towards twelve o'clock, he felt that he had spent his evening in quite a satisfactory way, and that, even for so long as a fortnight or three weeks, life at the Globe would be supportable under similar conditions – "especially," thought he, "if I go on improving my game."

As he went along the passages he met the boots of the Globe, who stopped and said :

"Beg your pardon, sir, but as I was a-brushing your coat just now there was somethink fell out of the pocket. I put it on your chest of drawers, sir, in your room, sir – a piece of a pipe or somethink of that, sir. Thank you, sir. You'll find it on your chest of drawers, sir – yes, sir. Good night, sir."

The speech served to remind Parkins of his little discovery of that afternoon. It was with some considerable curiosity that he turned it over by the light of his candles. It was of bronze, he now saw, and was shaped very much after the manner of the modern dog-whistle; in fact it was – yes, certainly it was – actually no more nor less than a whistle. He put it to his lips, but it was quite full of a fine, caked-up sand or earth, which would not yield to knocking, but must be loosened with a knife. Tidy as ever in his habits, Parkins cleared out the earth on to a piece of paper, and took the latter to the window to empty it out. The night was clear and bright, as he saw when he had opened the casement, and he stopped for an instant to look at the sea and note a belated wanderer stationed on the shore in front of the inn. Then he shut the window, a little surprised at the late hours people kept at Burnstow, and took his whistle to the light again. Why, surely there were marks on it, and not merely marks, but letters ! A very little rubbing rendered the deeply-cut inscription quite legible, but the Professor had to confess, after some earnest thought, that the meaning of it was as obscure to him as the writing on the wall to Belshazzar. There were legends both on the front and on the back of the whistle. The one read thus :

$$\text{FUR} \quad \begin{matrix} \text{PLA} \\ \text{FLE} \end{matrix} \quad \text{BIS}$$

The other :

$$\text{⚜ QUIS EST ISTE QUI UENIT ⚜}$$

"I ought to be able to make it out," he thought; "but I suppose I am a little rusty in my Latin. When I come to think of it, I don't believe I even know the word for a whistle. The long one does seem simple enough. It ought to mean, 'Who is this who is coming?' Well, the best way to find out is evidently to whistle for him."

He blew tentatively and stopped suddenly, startled and yet pleased at the note he had elicited. It had a quality of infinite distance in it, and, soft as it was, he somehow felt it must be audible for miles round. It was sound, too, that seemed to have the power (which many scents possess) of forming pictures in the brain. He saw quite clearly for a moment a vision of a wide, dark expanse at night, with a fresh wind blowing, and in the midst a lonely figure – how employed, he could not tell. Perhaps he would have seen more had not the picture been broken by the sudden surge of a gust of wind against his casement, so sudden that it made him look up, just in time to see the white glint of a sea-bird's wing somewhere outside the dark panes.

The sound of the whistle had so fascinated him that he could not help trying it once more, this time more boldly. The note was little, if at all, louder than before, and repetition broke the illusion – no picture followed, as he had half hoped it might. "But what is this? Goodness! what force the wind can get up in a few minutes! What a tremendous gust! There! I knew that window-fastening was no use! Ah! I thought so – both candles out. It's enough to tear the room to pieces."

The first thing was to get the window shut. While you might count twenty Parkins was struggling with the small casement, and felt almost as if he were pushing back a sturdy burglar, so strong was the pressure. It slackened all at once, and the window banged to and latched itself. Now to relight the candles and see what damage, if any, had been done. No, nothing seemed amiss; no glass even was broken in the casement. But the noise had evidently roused at least one member of the household : the Colonel was to be heard stumping in his stockinged feet on the floor above, and growling.

Quickly as it had risen, the wind did not fall at once. On it went, moaning and rushing past the house, at times rising to a cry so desolate that, as Parkins disinterestedly said, it might have made fanciful people feel quite uncomfortable; even the unimaginative, he thought after a quarter of an hour, might be happier without it.

Whether it was the wind, or the excitement of golf, or of the researches in the preceptory that kept Parkins awake, he was not sure. Awake he remained, in any case, long enough to fancy (as I am afraid I often do myself under such conditions), that he was the victim of all manner of fatal disorders : he would lie counting the beats of his heart, convinced that it was going to stop work every moment, and would entertain grave suspicions of his lungs, brain, liver, etc. – suspicions which he was sure would be dispelled by the return of daylight, but which until then refused to be put aside. He found a little vicarious comfort in the idea that someone else was in the same boat. A near neighbour (in the darkness it was not easy to tell his direction) was tossing and rustling in his bed, too.

The next stage was that Parkins shut his eyes and determined to give sleep every chance. Here again over-excitement asserted itself in another form – that of making pictures. *Experto crede*, pictures do come to the closed eyes of one trying to sleep, and are often so little to his taste that he must open his eyes and disperse them.

Parkins's experience on this occasion was a very distressing one. He found that the picture which presented itself to him was continuous. When he opened his eyes, of course, it went; but when he shut them once more it framed itself afresh, and acted itself out again, neither quicker nor slower than before. What he saw was this :

A long stretch of shore – shingle edged by sand, and

intersected at short intervals with black groynes running down to the water – a scene, in fact, so like that of his afternoon's walk that, in the absence of any landmark, it could not be distinguished therefrom. The light was obscure, conveying an impression of gathering storm, late winter evening, and slight cold rain. On this bleak stage at first no actor was visible. Then, in the distance, a bobbing black object appeared; a moment more, and it was a man running, jumping, clambering over the groynes, and every few seconds looking eagerly back. The nearer he came the more obvious it was that he was not only anxious, but even terribly frightened, though his face was not to be distinguished. He was, moreover, almost at the end' of his strength. On he came; each successive obstacle seemed to cause him more difficulty than the last. "Will he get over this next one?" thought Parkins; "it seems a little higher than the others." Yes; half climbing, half throwing himself, he did get over, and fell all in a heap on the other side (the side nearest to the spectator). There, as if really unable to get up again, he remained crouching under the groyne, looking up in an attitude of painful anxiety.

So far no cause whatever for the fear of the runner had been shown; but now there began to be seen, far up the shore, a little flicker of something light-coloured moving to and fro with great swiftness and irregularity. Rapidly growing larger, it, too, declared itself as a figure in pale, fluttering draperies, ill-defined. There was something about its motion which made Parkins very unwilling to see it at close quarters. It would stop, raise arms, bow itself towards the sand, then run stooping across the beach to the water-edge and back again; and then, rising upright, once more continue its course forward at a speed that was startling and terrifying. The moment came when the pursuer was hovering about from left to right only a few yards beyond the groyne where the runner lay in hiding. After two or three ineffectual castings hither and thither it came to a stop, stood upright, with arms raised high, and then darted straight forward towards the groyne.

It was at this point that Parkins always failed in his resolution to keep his eyes shut. With many misgivings as to incipient failure of eyesight, over-worked brain, excessive smoking, and so on, he finally resigned himself to light his candle, get out a book, and pass the night waking, rather than be tormented by this persistent panorama, which he saw clearly enough could only be a morbid reflection of his walk and his thoughts on that very day.

The scraping of match on box and the glare of light must have startled some creatures of the night – rats or what not – which he heard scurry across the floor from the side of his bed with much rustling. Dear, dear! the match is out! Fool that it is! But the second one burnt better, and a candle and book were duly procured, over which Parkins pored till sleep of a wholesome kind came upon him, and that in no long space. For about the first time in his orderly and prudent life he forgot to blow out the candle, and when he was called next morning at eight there was still a flicker in the socket and a sad mess of guttered grease on the top of the little table.

After breakfast he was in his room, putting the finishing touches to his golfing costume – fortune had again allotted the Colonel to him for a partner – when one of the maids came in.

"Oh, if you please," she said, "would you like any extra blankets on your bed, sir?"

"Ah! thank you," said Parkins. "Yes, I think I should like one. It seems likely to turn rather colder."

In a very short time the maid was back with the blanket.

"Which bed should I put it on, sir?" she asked.

"What? Why, that one – the one I slept in last night," he said, pointing to it.

"Oh yes! I beg your pardon, sir, but you seemed to have

tried both of 'em; leastways, we had to make 'em both up this morning."

"Really? How very absurd!" said Parkins. "I certainly never touched the other, except to lay some things on it. Did it actually seem to have been slept in?"

"Oh yes, sir!" said the maid. "Why, all the things was crumpled and throwed about all ways, if you'll excuse me, sir – quite as if anyone 'adn't passed but a very poor night, sir."

"Dear me," said Parkins. "Well, I may have disordered it more than I thought when I unpacked my things. I'm very sorry to have given you the extra trouble, I'm sure. I expect a friend of mine soon, by the way – a gentleman from Cambridge – to come and occupy it for a night or two. That will be all right, I suppose, won't it?"

"Oh yes, to be sure, sir. Thank you, sir. It's no trouble, I'm sure," said the maid, and departed to giggle with her colleagues.

Parkins set forth, with a stern determination to improve his game.

I am glad to be able to report that he succeeded so far in this enterprise that the Colonel, who had been rather repining at the prospect of a second day's play in his company, became quite chatty as the morning advanced; and his voice boomed out over the flats, as certainly also of our own minor poets have said, "like some great bourdon in a minster tower".

"Extraordinary wind, that, we had last night," he said. "In my old home we should have said someone had been whistling for it."

"Should you, indeed!" said Parkins. "Is there a superstition of that kind still current in your part of the country?"

"I don't know about superstition," said the Colonel. "They believe in it all over Denmark and Norway, as well as on the Yorkshire coast; and my experience is, mind you, that there's generally something at the bottom of what these country-folk hold to, and have held to for generations. But it's your drive" (or whatever it might have been : the golfing reader will have to imagine appropriate digressions at the proper intervals).

When conversation was resumed, Parkins said, with a slight hesitancy :

"Apropos of what you were saying just now, Colonel, I think I ought to tell you that my own views on such subjects are very strong. I am, in fact, a convinced disbeliever in what is called the 'supernatural'."

"What!" said the Colonel, "do you mean to tell me you don't believe in second-sight, or ghosts, or anything of that kind?"

"In nothing whatever of that kind," returned Parkins firmly.

"Well," said the Colonel, "but it appears to me at that rate, sir, that you must be little better than a Sadducee."

Parkins was on the point of answering that, in his opinion, the Sadducees were the most sensible persons he had ever read of in the Old Testament; but, feeling some doubt as to whether much mention of them was to be found in that work, he preferred to laugh the accusation off.

"Perhaps I am," he said; "but – Here, give me my cleek, boy! – Excuse me one moment, Colonel." A short interval. "Now, as to whistling for the wind, let me give you my theory about it. The laws which govern winds are really not at all perfectly known – to fisher-folk and such, of course, not known at all. A man or woman of eccentric habits, perhaps, or a stranger, is seen repeatedly on the beach at some unusual hour, and is heard whistling. Soon afterwards a violent wind rises; a man who could read the sky perfectly or who possessed a barometer could have foretold that it would. The simple people of a fishing-village have no barometers, and only a few rough rules for prophesying weather. What more natural than that the eccentric personage I postulated should be regarded as having raised the

wind, or that he or she should clutch eagerly at the reputation of being able to do so? Now, take last night's wind :
as it happens, I myself was whistling. I blew a whistle twice,
and the wind seemed to come absolutely in answer to my
call. If anyone had seen me – "

The audience had been a little restive under this
harangue, and Parkins had, I fear, fallen somewhat into
the tone of a lecturer; but at the last sentence the Colonel
stopped.

"Whistling, were you?" he said. "And what sort of whistle
did you use? Play this stroke first." Interval.

"About that whistle you were asking, Colonel. It's rather
a curious one. I have it in my – No; I see I've left it in my
room. As a matter of fact, I found it yesterday."

And then Parkins narrated the manner of his discovery of
the whistle, upon hearing which the Colonel grunted, and
opined that, in Parkins's place, he should himself be careful
about using a thing that had belonged to a set of Papists,
of whom, speaking generally, it might be affirmed that you
never knew what they might not have been up to. From
this topic he diverged to the enormities of the Vicar, who
had given notice on the previous Sunday that Friday would
be the Feast of St. Thomas the Apostle, and that there
would be service at eleven o'clock in the church. This and
other similar proceedings constituted in the Colonel's view
a strong presumption that the Vicar was a concealed Papist,
if not a Jesuit; and Parkins, who could not very readily
follow the Colonel in this region, did not disagree with him.
In fact, they got on so well together in the morning that
there was no talk on either side of their separating after
lunch.

Both continued to play well during the afternoon, or, at
least, well enough to make them forget everything else
until the light began to fail them. Not until then did
Parkins remember that he had meant to do some more
investigating at the preceptory; but it was of no great

importance, he reflected. One day was as good as another; he might as well go home with the Colonel.

As they turned the corner of the house, the Colonel was almost knocked down by a boy who rushed into him at the very top of his speed, and then, instead of running away, remained hanging on to him and panting. The first words of the warrior were naturally those of reproof and objurgation, but he very quickly discerned that the boy was almost speechless with fright. Inquiries were useless at first. When the boy got his breath he began to howl, and still clung to the Colonel's legs. He was at last detached, but continued to howl.

"What in the world *is* the matter with you? What have you been up to? What have you seen?" said the two men.

"Ow, I seen it wive at me out of the winder," wailed the boy, "and I don't like it."

"What window?" said the irritated Colonel. "Come, pull yourself together, my boy."

"The front winder it was, at the 'otel," said the boy.

At this point Parkins was in favour of sending the boy home, but the Colonel refused; he wanted to get to the bottom of it, he said; it was most dangerous to give a boy such a fright as this one had had, and if it turned out that people had been playing jokes, they should suffer for it in some way. And by a series of questions he made out this story: The boy had been playing about on the grass in front of the Globe with some others; then they had gone home to their teas, and he was just going, when he happened to look up at the front winder and see it a-wiving at him. *It* seemed to be a figure of some sort, in white as far as he knew – couldn't see its face; but it wived at him, and it warn't a right thing – not to say not a right person. Was there a light in the room? No, he didn't think to look if there was a light. Which was the window? Was it the top one or the second one? The seckind one it was – the big winder what got two little uns at the sides.

"Very well, my boy," said the Colonel, after a few more questions. "You run away home now. I expect it was some person trying to give you a start. Another time, like a brave English boy, you just throw a stone – well, no, not that exactly, but you go and speak to the waiter, or to Mr. Simpson, the landlord, and – yes – and say that I advised you to do so."

The boy's face expressed some of the doubt he felt as to the likelihood of Mr. Simpson's lending a favourable ear to his complaint, but the Colonel did not appear to perceive this, and went on :

"And here's a sixpence – no, I see it's a shilling – and you be off home, and don't think any more about it."

The youth hurried off with agitated thanks, and the Colonel and Parkins went round to the front of the Globe and reconnoitred. There was only one window answering to the description they had been hearing.

"Well, that's curious," said Parkins; "it's evidently my window the lad was talking about. Will you come up for a moment, Colonel Wilson? We ought to be able to see if anyone has been taking liberties in my room."

They were soon in the passage, and Parkins made as if to open the door. Then he stopped and felt in his pockets.

"This is more serious than I thought," was his next remark. "I remember now that before I started this morning I locked the door. It is locked now, and, what is more, here is the key." And he held it up. "Now," he went on, "if the servants are in the habit of going into one's room during the day when one is away, I can only say that – well, that I don't approve of it at all." Conscious of a somewhat weak climax, he busied himself in opening the door (which was indeed locked) and in lighting candles. "No," he said, "nothing seems disturbed."

"Except your bed," put in the Colonel.

"Excuse me, that isn't my bed," said Parkins. "I don't

use that one. But it does look as if someone had been playing tricks with it."

It certainly did : the clothes were bundled up and twisted together in a most tortuous confusion. Parkins pondered.

"That must be it," he said at last : "I disordered the clothes last night in unpacking, and they haven't made it since. Perhaps they came in to make it, and that boy saw them through the window; and then they were called away and locked the door after them. Yes, I think that must be it."

"Well, ring and ask," said the Colonel, and this appealed to Parkins as practical.

, The maid appeared, and, to make a long story, short, deposed that she had made the bed in the morning when the gentleman was in the room, and hadn't been there since. No, she hadn't no other key. Mr. Simpson he kep' the keys; he'd be able to tell the gentleman if, anyone had been up.

This was a puzzle. Investigation showed that nothing of value had been taken, and Parkins remembered the disposition of the small objects on tables and so forth well enough to be pretty sure that no pranks had been played with them. Mr. and Mrs. Simpson furthermore agreed that neither of them had given the duplicate key of the room to any person whatever during the day. Nor could Parkins, fairminded man as he was, detect anything in the demeanour of master, mistress, or maid that indicated guilt. He was much more inclined to think that the boy had been imposing on the Colonel.

The latter was unwontedly silent and pensive at dinner and throughout the evening. When he bade good night to Parkins, he murmured in a gruff undertone :

"You know where I am if you want me during the night."

"Why, yes, thank you, Colonel Wilson, I think I do; but there isn't much prospect of my disturbing you, I hope. By the way," he added, "did I show you that old whistle I spoke of? I think not. Well, here it is."

The Colonel turned it over gingerly in the light of the candle.

"Can you make anything of the inscription?" asked Parkins, as he took it back.

"No, not in this light. What do you mean to do with it?"

"Oh, well, when I get back to Cambridge I shall submit it to some of the archæologists there, and see what they think of it; and very likely, if they consider it worth having, I may present it to one of the museums."

" 'M !" said the Colonel. "Well, you may be right. All I know is that, if it were mine, I should chuck it straight into the sea. It's no use talking, I'm well aware, but I expect that with you it's a case of live and learn. I hope so, I'm sure, and I wish you a good night."

He turned away, leaving Parkins in act to speak at the bottom of the stair, and soon each was in his own bedroom.

By some unfortunate accident, there were neither blinds nor curtains to the windows of the Professor's room. The previous night he had thought little of this, but tonight there seemed every prospect of a bright moon rising to shine directly on his bed, and probably wake him later on. When he noticed this he was a good deal annoyed, but, with an ingenuity which I can only envy, he succeeded in rigging up, with the help of a railway-rug, some safety-pins, and a stick and umbrella, a screen which, if it only held together, would completely keep the moonlight off his bed. And shortly afterwards he was comfortably in that bed. When he had read a somewhat solid work long enough to produce a decided wish for sleep, he cast a drowsy glance round the room, blew out the candle, and fell back upon the pillow.

He must have slept soundly for an hour or more, when a sudden clatter shook him up in a most unwelcome manner. In a moment he realized what had happened : his carefully-constructed screen had given way, and a very bright frosty moon was shining directly on his face. This was highly annoying. Could he possibly get up and reconstruct the screen? or could he manage to sleep if he did not?

For some minutes he lay and pondered over the possibilities; then he turned over sharply, and with all his eyes open lay breathlessly listening. There had been a movement, he was sure, in the empty bed on the opposite side of the room. Tomorrow he would have it moved, for there must be rats or something playing about in it. It was quiet now. No! the commotion began again. There was a rustling and shaking : surely more than any rat could cause.

I can figure to myself something of the Professor's bewilderment and horror, for I have in a dream thirty years back seen the same thing happen; but the reader will hardly, perhaps, imagine how dreadful it was to him to see a figure suddenly sit up in what he had known was an empty bed. He was out of his own bed in one bound, and made a dash towards the window, where lay his only weapon, the stick with which he had propped his screen. This was, as it turned out, the worst thing he could have done, because the personage in the empty bed, with a sudden smooth motion, slipped from the bed and took up a position, with outspread arms, between the two beds, and in front of the door. Parkins watched it in a horrid perplexity. Somehow, the idea of getting past it and escaping through the door was intolerable to him; he could not have borne – he didn't know why – to touch it; and as for its touching him, he would sooner dash himself through the window than have that happen. It stood for the moment in a band of dark shadow, and he had not seen what its face was like. Now it began to move, in a stooping posture, and all at once the spectator realized, with some horror and some relief, that it must be blind, for it seemed to feel about it with its muffled arms in a groping and random fashion. Turning half away from him, it became suddenly conscious of the bed he had just left, and darted towards it, and bent over and felt the pillows in a way which made Parkins shudder as he had never in his life thought it possible. In a very few moments it seemed to know that the bed was empty, and then, moving forward into the area of light and facing the window, it showed for the first time what manner of thing it was.

Parkins, who very much dislikes being questioned about it, did once describe something of it in my hearing, and I gathered that what he chiefly remembers about it is a horrible, an intensely horrible, face *of crumpled linen.* What expression he read upon it he could not or would not tell, but that the fear of it went nigh to maddening him is certain.

But he was not at leisure to watch it for long. With formidable quickness it moved into the middle of the room, and, as it groped and waved, one corner of its draperies swept across Parkins's face. He could not – though he knew how perilous a sound was – he could not keep back a cry of disgust, and this gave the searcher an instant clue. It leapt towards him upon the instant, and the next moment he was half-way through the window backwards, uttering cry upon cry at the utmost pitch of his voice, and the linen face was thrust close into his own. At this, almost the last possible second, deliverance came, as you will have guessed : the Colonel burst the door open, and was just in time to see the dreadful group at the window. When he reached the figures only one was left. Parkins sank forward into the room in a faint, and before him on the floor lay a tumbled heap of bedclothes.

Colonel Wilson asked no questions, but busied himself in keeping everyone else out of the room and in getting Parkins back to his bed; and himself, wrapped in a rug, occupied the other bed for the rest of the night. Early on the next day Rogers arrived, more welcome than he would have been a day before, and the three of them held a very long consultation in the Professor's room. At the end of it the Colonel left the hotel door carrying a small object between his finger and thumb, which he cast as far into the sea as a very brawny arm could send it. Later on the smoke of a burning ascended from the back premises of the Globe.

Exactly what explanation was patched up for the staff and visitors at the hotel I must confess I do not recollect. The Professor was somehow cleared of the ready suspicion of delirium tremens, and the hotel of the reputation of a troubled house.

There is not much question as to what would have happened to Parkins if the Colonel had not intervened when he did. He would either have fallen out of the window or else lost his wits. But it is not so evident what more the creature that came in answer to the whistle could have done than frighten. There seemed to be absolutely nothing material about it save the bedclothes of which it had made itself a body. The Colonel, who remembered a not very dissimilar occurrence in India, was of opinion that if Parkins had closed with it it could really have done very little, and that its one power was that of frightening. The whole thing, he said, served to confirm his opinion of the Church of Rome.

There is really nothing more to tell, but, as you may imagine, the Professor's views on certain points are less clear cut than they used to be. His nerves, too, have suffered : he cannot even now see a surplice hanging on a door quite unmoved, and the spectacle of a scarecrow in a field late on a winter afternoon has cost him more than one sleepless night.

A Kind of Madness

ANTHONY BOUCHER

IN 1888 LONDON was terrified, as no city has been before or since, by Jack the Ripper, who from April through November killed and dissected at least seven prostitutes, without leaving a single clue to his identity. The chain of murders snapped abruptly. After 1888 Jack never ripped again. Because on 12th July, 1889 . . .

He paused on the steps of University College, surrounded by young ladies prattling the questions that were supposed to prove they had paid careful attention to his lecture-demonstration.

The young ladies were, he knew as a biologist, human females; dissection would establish the fact beyond question. But for him womankind was divided into three classes: angels and devils and students. He had never quite forgiven the college for admitting women nine years ago. That these female creatures should irrelevantly possess the same terrible organs that were the arsenal of the devils, the same organs through which the devils could strike lethally at the angels, the very organs which he . . .

He answered the young ladies without hearing either their questions or his answers, detached himself from the bevy, and strolled towards the Euston Road.

For eight months now he had seen neither angel nor devil. The events of 1888 seemed infinitely remote, like a fever remembered after convalescence. It had indeed been a sort of fever of the brain, perhaps even – he smiled gently – a kind of madness. But after his own angel had died of that unspeakable infection which the devil had planted in him – which had affected him so lightly but had penetrated so fatally to those dread organs which render angels vulnerable to devils . . .

He observed, clinically, that he was breathing heavily and that his hand was groping in his pocket – a foolish gesture, since he had not carried the scalpel for eight months. Deliberately he slowed his pace and his breathing. The fever was spent – though surely no sane man could see anything but good in an effort to rid London of its devils.

'Pardon, m'sieur.'

The woman was young, no older than his students, but no one would mistake her for a female of University College. Even to his untutored eye her clothes spoke of elegance and chic and, in a word, Paris. Her delicate scent seemed no man-made otto but pure *essence de femme*. Her golden hair framed a piquant face, the nose slightly tilted, the upper lip a trifle full – irregular, but delightful.

'Ma'm'selle?' he replied, with courtesy and approbation.

'If m'sieur would be so kind as to help a stranger in your great city . . . I seek an establishment of baggages.'

He tried to suppress his smile, but she noticed it, and a response sparkled in her eyes. 'Do I say something improper?' she asked almost hopefully.

'Oh, no. Your phrase is quite correct. Most Englishmen, however, would say "a luggage shop".'

'Ah, *c'est ca*. "A luggage shop" – I shall remember me. I am on my first voyage to England, though I have known Englishmen at Paris. I feel like a small child in a world of adults who talk strangely. Though I know' – his gaze was resting on what the French politely call the throat – 'I am not shaped like one.'

An angel, he was thinking. Beyond doubt an angel, and a delectable one. And this innocently provocative way of speaking made her seem only the more angelic.

He took from her gloved fingers the slip of paper on which was written the address of the 'establishment of baggages'.

'You are at the wrong end of the Euston Road,' he explained. 'Permit me to hail a cab for you; it is too far to walk on such a hot day.'

'Ah, yes, this is a July of Julys, is it not? One has told me that in England it is never hot, but behold I sweat!'

He frowned.

'Oh, do I again say something beastly? But it is true: I do sweat.' Tiny moist beads outlined her all but invisible blonde moustache.

He relaxed. 'As a professor of biology I should be willing to acknowledge the fact that the human female is equipped with sweat glands, even though proper English usage would have it otherwise, Forgive me, my dear child, for frowning at your innocent impropriety.'

She hesitated, imitating his frown. Then she looked up, laughed softly, and put her small plump hand on his arm. 'As a token of for-giveness, m'sieur, you may buy me an ice before hailing my cab. My name,' she added, 'is Gaby.'

He felt infinitely refreshed. He had been wrong, he saw it now, to abstain so completely from the company of women once his fever had run its course. There was a delight, a solace, in the presence of a woman. Not a student, or a devil, but the true woman: an angel.

Gaby daintily dabbed ice and sweat from her full upper lip and rose from the table. 'M'sieur has been most courteous to the stranger within his gates. And now I must seek my luggage shop.'

'Mademoiselle Gaby—'

'Hein? Speak up, m'sieur le professeur. Is it that you wish to ask if we shall find each other again?'

'I should indeed be honoured if while you are in London—'

'Merde alors!' She winked at him, and he hoped that he had mis-understood her French. 'Do we need such fine phrases? I think we understand ourselves, no? There is a small bistro — a pub, you call it? — near my lodgings. If you wish to meet me there tomorrow evening . . .' She gave him instructions. Speechless, he noted them down.

'You will not be sorry, m'sieur. I think well you will enjoy your little tour of France after your dull English diet.'

She held his arm while he hailed a cab. He did not speak except to the cabman. She extended her ungloved hand and he automatically took it. Her fingers dabbled deftly in his palm while her pink tongue peered out for a moment between her lips. Then she was gone.

'And I thought her an angel,' he groaned.

His hand fumbled again in his empty pocket.

The shiny new extra large trunk dominated the bedroom.

Gabrielle Bompart stripped to the skin as soon as the porter had left (more pleased with her wink than with her tip) and perched on the trunk. The metal trim felt refreshingly cold against her flesh.

Michel Eyraud looked up lazily from the bed where he was sprawled. 'I never get tired of looking at you, Gaby.'

'When you are content just to look,' Gaby grinned, 'I cut your throat.'

'It's hot,' said Eyraud.

'I know, and you are an old man. You are old enough to be my father. You are a very wicked lecherous old man, but for old men it is often hot.'

Eyraud sprang off the bed, strode over to the trunk, and seized her by her naked shoulders. She laughed in his face. 'I was teasing you. It is too hot. Even for me. Go lie down and tell me about your day. You got everything?'

Eyraud waved an indolent hand at the table. A coil of rope, a block and tackle, screws, screwdriver . . .

Gaby smiled approvingly. 'And I have the trunk, such a nice big one, and this.' She reached for her handbag, drew out a red-and-white girdle. 'It goes well with my dressing gown. And it is strong.' She stretched it and tugged at it, grunting enthusiastically.

Eyraud looked from the girdle to the rope to the pulley to the top of the door leading to the sitting-room, then back to the trunk. He nodded.

Gaby stood by the full-length mirror contemplating herself. 'That silly bailiff, that Gouffé. Why does he dare to think that Gaby should be interested in him? This Gaby, such as you behold her . . .' She smiled at the mirror and nodded approval.

'I met a man,' she said. 'An Englishman. Oh, so very stiff and proper. He looks like Phileas Fogg in Jules Verne's *Le Tour du Monde*. He wants me.'

'Fogg had money,' said Eyraud. 'Lots of it.'

'So does my professor . . . Michi?'

'Yes?'

Gabrielle pirouetted before the mirror. 'Am I an actress?'

'All women are actresses.'

'Michi, do not try to be clever. It is not becoming to you. Am I an actress?'

Eyraud lit a French cigarette and tossed the blue pack to Gaby. 'You're a performer, and entertainer. You have better legs than any actress in Paris. And if you made old Gouffé think you love him for his fat self . . . Yes, I guess you're an actress.'

'Then I know what I want.' Gaby's eyelids were half closed. 'Michi, I want a rehearsal.'

Eyraud looked at the trunk and the block and tackle and the red-and-white girdle. He laughed, heartily and happily.

He found her waiting for him in the pub. The blonde hair picked up the light and gave it back, to form a mocking halo around the pert devil's face.

His fingers reassured him that the scalpel was back where it belonged. He had been so foolish to call 'a fever' what was simply his natural rightful temperature. It was his mission in life to rid the world of devils. That was the simple truth. And not all devils had cockney accents and lived in Whitechapel.

'Be welcome, m'sieur le professeur.' She curtseyed with impish grace. 'You have thirst?'

'No,' he grunted.

'Ah, you mean you do not have thirst in the throat. It lies lower, hein?' She giggled, and he wondered how long she had been waiting in the pub. She laid her hand on his arm. The animal heat seared through his sleeve. 'I go upstairs. You understand, it is more chic when you do not see me make myself ready. You ascend in a dozen of minutes. It is on the first floor, at the left to the rear.'

He left the pub and waited on the street. The night was cool and the fog was beginning to settle down. On just such a night in last August . . . What was her name? He had read it later in *The Times*. Martha Tabor? Tabby? Tabbypussydevil.

He had nicked his finger on the scalpel. As he sucked the blood he heard a clock strike. He had been waiting almost half hour; where had the time gone? The devil would be impatient.

The sitting-room was dark, but subdued lamplight gleamed from the bedroom. The bed was turned down. Beside it stood a huge trunk.

The devil was wearing a white dressing-gown and a red-and white girdle that emphasized its improbably slender waist. It came towards him and stroked his face with hot fingers and touched its tongue like a branding iron to his chin and ears and at last his lips. His hands closed around its waist.

'Ouf!' gasped the devil, 'You may crush me, I assure you M'sieur. I love that. But please to spare my pretty new girdle. Perhaps if I debarrass myself of it . . .' It unclasped the girdle and the dressing-gown fell open.

His hand took a firm grip on the scalpel.

The devil moved him towards the door between the two rooms. It festooned the girdle around his neck. 'Like that,' it said gleefully. 'There – doesn't that make you a pretty red-and-white cravat?'

Hand and scalpel came out of his pocket.

And Michel Eyraud, standing in the dark sitting-room fastened the ends of the girdle to the rope running through the block and tackle and gave a powerful jerk.

The rope sprang to the ceiling, the girdle followed it, and the professor's thin neck snapped. The scalpel fell from his dead hand.

The rehearsal had been a complete success.

Just as they planned to do with the bailiff Gouffé, they stripped the body and plundered the wallet. 'Not bad,' said Eyraud. 'Do actresses get paid for rehearsing?'

'This one does,' said Gaby. And they dumped the body in the trunk.

Later the clothes would be disposed of in dustbins, the body carried by trunk to some quiet countryside where it might decompose in naked namelessness.

Gaby swore when she stepped on the scalpel. 'What the hell is this?' She picked it up. 'It's sharp. Do you suppose he was one of those types who like a little blood to heighten their pleasures? I've heard of them but never met one.'

Gaby stood pondering, her dressing-gown open . . .

The first night, to the misfortune of the bailiff Gouffé, went off as smoothly as the rehearsal. But the performers reckoned without the patience and determination and génie policier of Marie-Francois Goron, Chief of the Paris Sûreté.

The upshot was, as all aficionados of true crime know, that Eyraud was guillotined, nineteen months after the rehearsal, and Gaby, who kept grinning at the jury, was sentenced to twenty years of hard labour.

When Goron was in London before the trial, he paid his usual courtesy call at Scotland Yard and chatted at length with Inspector Frederick G. Abberline.

'Had one rather like yours recently ourselves,' said Abberline. 'Naked man, broken neck, left to rot in the countryside. Haven't succeeded in identifying him yet. You were luckier there.'

'It is notorious,' Goron observed, 'that the laboratories of the French police are the best in the world.'

'We do very well, thank you,' said Abberline distantly.

'Of course.' The French visitor was all politeness: 'As you did last year in that series of Whitechapel murders.'

'I don't know if you're being sarcastic, Mr Goron, but no police force in the world could have done more than we did in the Ripper case. It was a nightmare with no possible resolution. And unless he strikes again, it's going to go down as one of the greatest unsolved cases in history. Jack the Ripper will never hang.'

'Not,' said M. Goron, 'so long as he confines his attention to the women of London.' He hurried to catch the boat train thinking of Gabrielle Bompard and feeling a certain regret that such a woman was also such a devil.

A True Story of a Vampire

COUNT ERIC STENBOCK

                    *   *   *

Vampire stories are generally located in Styria; mine is also. Styria is
by no means the romantic kind of place described by those who
have certainly never been there. It is a flat, uninteresting country, only
celebrated for its turkeys, its capons, and the stupidity of its
inhabitants. Vampires generally arrive at night, in carriages drawn by
two black horses.

Our Vampire arrived by the commonplace means of the railway
train, and in the afternoon. You must think I am joking, or perhaps
that by the word 'Vampire' I mean a financial vampire. No, I am quite
serious. The Vampire of whom I am speaking, who laid waste to our
hearth and home, was a *real* vampire.

Vampires are generally described as dark, sinister-looking, and
singularly handsome. Our Vampire was, on the contrary, rather fair,
and certainly was not at first sight sinister-looking, and though
decidedly attractive in appearance, not what one would call singularly
handsome.

Yes, he desolated our home, killed my brother – the one object of my adoration – also my dear father. Yet, at the same time, I must say that I myself came under the spell of his fascination, and, in spite of all, have no ill-will towards him now.

Doubtless you have read in the papers *passim* of 'the Baroness and her beasts'. It is to tell how I came to spend most of my useless wealth on an asylum for stray animals that I am writing this.

I am old now; what happened then was when I was a little girl of about thirteen. I will begin by describing our household. We were Poles; our name was Wronski: we lived in Styria, where we had a castle. Our household was very limited. It consisted, with the exclusion of domestics, of only my father, our governess – a worthy Belgian named Mademoiselle Vonnaert – my brother, and myself. Let me begin with my father: he was old and both my brother and I were children of his old age. Of my mother I remember nothing: she died in giving birth to my brother, who was only one year, or not as much, younger than myself. Our father was studious, continually occupied in reading books, chiefly on recondite subjects and in all kinds of unknown languages. He had a long white beard, and wore habitually a black velvet skull-cap.

How kind he was to us! It was more than I could tell. Still it was not I who was the favourite. His whole heart went out to Gabriel – Gabryel as we spelt it in Polish. He was always called by the Russian abbreviation – Gavril – I mean, of course, my brother, who had a resemblance to the only portrait of my mother, a slight chalk sketch which hung in my father's study. But I was by no means jealous: my brother was and has been the only love of my life. It is for his sake that I am now keeping in Westbourne Park a home for stray cats and dogs.

I was at that time, as I said before, a little girl; my name was Carmela. My long tangled hair was always all over the place, and never would be combed straight. I was not pretty – at least, looking at a photograph of me at that time, I do not think I could describe myself as such. Yet at the same time, when I look at the photograph, I think my expression may have been pleasing to some people: irregular features, large mouth, and large wild eyes.

I was by way of being naughty – not so naughty as Gabriel in the opinion of Mlle Vonnaert. Mlle Vonnaert, I may intercalate, was a wholly excellent person, middle-aged, who really did speak good French, although she was a Belgian, and could also make herself understood in German, which, as you may or may not know, is the current language of Styria.

I find it difficult to describe my brother Gabriel; there was something about him strange and superhuman, or perhaps I should rather say praeterhuman, something between the animal and the divine. Perhaps the Greek idea of the Faun might illustrate what I mean; but that will not do either. He had large, wild, gazelle-like eyes: his hair, like mine, was in a perpetual tangle – that point he had in common with me, and indeed, as I afterwards heard, our mother having been of gipsy race, it will account for much of the innate wildness there was in our natures. I was wild enough, but Gabriel was much wilder. Nothing would induce him to put on shoes and stockings, except on Sundays – when he also allowed his hair to be combed, but only by me. How shall I describe the grace of that lovely mouth, shaped verily 'en arc d'amour'. I always think of the text in the Psalm, 'Grace is shed forth on thy lips, therefore has God blessed thee eternally' – lips that seemed to exhale the very breath of life. Then that beautiful, lithe, living, elastic form!

He could run faster than any deer: spring like a squirrel to the topmost branch of a tree: he might have stood for the sign and symbol of vitality itself. But seldom could he be induced by Mlle Vonnaert to learn lessons; but when he did so, he learnt with extraordinary quickness. He would play upon every conceivable instrument, holding a violin here, there, and everywhere except the right place: manufacturing instruments for himself out of reeds – even sticks. Mlle Vonnaert made futile efforts to induce him to learn to play the piano. I suppose he was what was called spoilt, though merely in the superficial sense of the word. Our father allowed him to indulge in every caprice.

One of his peculiarities, when quite a little child, was horror at the sight of meat. Nothing on earth would induce him to taste it. Another thing which was particularly remarkable about him was his extraordinary power over animals. Everything seemed to come tame to his hand. Birds would sit on his shoulder. Then sometimes Mlle Vonnaert and I would lose him in the woods – he would suddenly dart away. Then we would find him singing softly or whistling to himself, with all manner of woodland creatures around him – hedgehogs, little foxes, wild rabbits, marmots, squirrels, and such like. He would frequently bring these things home with him and insist on keeping them. This strange menagerie was the terror of poor Mlle Vonnaert's heart. He chose to live in a little room at the top of a turret; but which, instead of going upstairs, he chose to reach by means of a very tall chestnut-tree, through the window. But in contradiction of all this, it was his custom to serve every Sunday Mass in the parish church, with hair nicely combed and with white surplice and red cassock. He looked as demure and tamed as possible. Then came the element of the divine. What an expression of ecstasy there was in those glorious eyes!

Thus far I have not been speaking about the Vampire. However, let me begin with my narrative at last. One day my father had to go to the neighbouring town – as he frequently had. This time he returned accompanied by a guest. The gentleman, he said, had missed his train, through the late arrival of another at our station, which was a junction, and he would therefore, as trains were not frequent in our parts, have had to wait there all night. He had joined in conversation with my father in the too-late-arriving train from the town: and had consequently accepted my father's invitation to stay the night at our house. But of course, you know, in those out-of-the-way parts we are almost partriarchal in our hospitality.

He was announced under the name of Count Vardalek – the name being Hungarian. But he spoke German well enough: not with the monotonous accentuation of Hungarians, but rather, if anything, with a slight Slavonic intonation. His voice was peculiarly soft and insinuating. We soon afterwards found out he could talk Polish, and Mlle Vonnaert vouched for his good French. Indeed he seemed to know all languages. But let me give my first impressions. He was rather tall with fair wavy hair, rather long, which accentuated a certain effeminacy about his smooth face. His figure had something – I cannot say what – serpentine about it. The features were refined; and he had long, slender, subtle, magnetic-looking hands, a somewhat long sinuous nose, a graceful mouth, and an attractive smile, which belied the intense sadness of the expression of the eyes. When he arrived his eyes were half closed – indeed they were habitually so – so that I could not decide their colour. He looked worn and wearied. I could not possibly guess his age.

Suddenly Gabriel burst into the room: a yellow butterfly was clinging to his hair. He was carrying in his arms a little squirrel. Of course he was bare-legged as usual. The stranger looked up at his approach; then I noticed his eyes. They were green: they seemed to dilate and grow larger. Gabriel stood stock-still, with a startled look, like that of a bird fascinated by a serpent. But nevertheless he held out his hand to the newcomer. Vardalek, taking his hand – I don't know why I noticed this trivial thing – pressed the pulse with his forefinger. Suddenly Gabriel darted from the room and rushed upstairs, going to his turret-room this time by the staircase instead of the tree. I was in terror what the Count might think of him. Great was my relief when he came down in his velvet Sunday suit, and shoes and stockings. I combed his hair, and set him generally right.

When the stranger came down to dinner his appearance had somewhat altered; he looked much younger. There was an elasticity of the skin, combined with a delicate complexion, rarely to be found in a man. Before, he had struck me as being very pale.

Well, at dinner we were all charmed with him, especially my father. He seemed to be thoroughly acquainted with all my father's particular hobbies. Once, when my father was relating some of his military experiences, he said something about a drummer-boy who was wounded in battle. His eyes opened completely again and dilated: this time with a particularly disagreeable expression, dull and dead, yet at the same time animated by some horrible excitement. But this was only momentary.

The chief subject of his conversation with my father was about certain curious mystical books which my father had just lately picked up, and which he could not make out, but Vardalek seemed completely to understand. At dessert-time my father asked him if he were in a great hurry to reach his destination: if not, would he not stay with us a little while: though our place was out of the way, he would find much that would interest him in his library.

He answered, 'I am in no hurry. I have no particular reason for going to that place at all, and if I can be of service to you in deciphering these books, I shall be only too glad.' He added with a smile which was bitter, very very bitter: 'You see I am a cosmopolitan, a wanderer on the face of the earth.'

After dinner my father asked him if he played the piano. He said, 'Yes, I can a little,' and he sat down at the piano. Then he played a Hungarian csardas – wild, rhapsodic, wonderful.

That is the music which makes men mad. He went on in the same strain.

Gabriel stood stock-still by the piano, his eyes dilated and fixed, his form quivering. At last he said very slowly, at one particular motive – for want of a better word you may call it the relâche of a csardas, by which I mean that point where the original quasi-slow movement begins again – 'Yes, I think I could play that.'

Then he quickly fetched his fiddle and self-made xylophone, and did, actually alternating the instruments, render the same very well indeed.

Vardalek looked at him, and said in a very sad voice, 'Poor child! you have the soul of music within you.'

I could not understand why he should seem to commiserate instead of congratulate Gabriel on what certainly showed an extraordinary talent.

Gabriel was shy even as the wild animals who were tame to him. Never before had he taken to a stranger. Indeed, as a rule, if any stranger came to the house by any chance, he would hide himself, and I had to bring him up his food to the turret chamber. You may imagine what was my surprise when I saw him walking about hand in hand with Vardalek the next morning, in the garden, talking livelily with him, and showing his collection of pet animals, which he had gathered from the woods, and for which we had had to fit up a regular zoological gardens. He seemed utterly under the domination of Vardalek. What surprised us was (for otherwise we liked the stranger, especially for being kind to him) that he seemed, though not noticeably at first – except perhaps to me, who noticed everything with regard to him – to be gradually losing his general health and vitality. He did not become pale as yet; but there was a certain languor about his movements which certainly there was by no means before.

My father got more and more devoted to Count Vardalek. He helped him in his studies: and my father would hardly allow him to go away, which he did sometimes – to Trieste, he said: he always came back, bringing us presents of strange Oriental jewellery or textures.

I knew all kinds of people came to Trieste, Orientals included. Still, there was a strangeness and magnificence about these things which I was sure even then could not possibly have come from such a place as Trieste, memorable to me chiefly for its necktie shops.

When Vardalek was away, Gabriel was continually asking for him and talking about him. Then at the same time he seemed to regain his old vitality and spirits. Vardalek always returned looking much older, wan, and weary. Gabriel would rush to meet him, and kiss him on the mouth. Then he gave a slight shiver: and after a while began to look quite young again.

Things continued like this for some time. My father would not hear of Vardalek's going away permanently. He came to be an inmate of our house. I indeed, and Mlle Vonnaert also, could not help noticing what a difference there was altogether about Gabriel. But my father seemed totally blind to it.

One night I had gone downstairs to fetch something which I had left in the drawing-room. As I was going up again I passed Vardalek's room. He was playing on a piano, which had been specially put there for him, one of Chopin's nocturnes, very beautifully: I stopped, leaning on the banisters to listen.

Something white appeared on the dark staircase. We believed in ghosts in our part. I was transfixed with terror, and clung to the banisters. What was my astonishment to see Gabriel walking slowly down the staircase, his eyes fixed as though in a trance! This terrified me even more than a ghost would. Could I believe my senses? Could that be Gabriel?

I simply could not move. Gabriel, clad in his long white night-shirt, came downstairs and opened the door. He left it open. Vardalek still continued playing, but talked as he played.

He said – this time speaking in Polish – *Nie umiem wyrazic jak ciechi kocham* – 'My darling, I fain would spare thee; but thy life is my life, and I must live, I who would rather die. Will God not have any mercy on me? Oh! Oh! life; oh, the torture of life!' Here he struck one agonized and strange chord, then continued playing softly, 'O Gabriel, my beloved! my life, yes *life* – oh, why life? I am sure this is but a little that I demand of thee. Surely thy superabundance of life can spare a little to one who is already dead. No, stay,' he said now almost harshly, 'what must be, must be!'

Gabriel stood there quite still, with the same fixed vacant expression, in the room. He was evidently walking in his sleep. Vardalek played on: then said, 'Ah!' with a sign of terrible agony. Then very gently, 'Go now, Gabriel; it is enough.' And Gabriel went out of the room and ascended the staircase at the same slow pace, with the same unconscious stare. Vardalek struck the piano, and although he did not play loudly, it seemed as though the strings would break. You never heard music so strange and so heart-rending!

I only know I was found by Mlle Vonnaert in the morning, in an unconscious state, at the foot of the stairs. Was it a dream after all? I am sure now that it was not. I thought then it might be, and said nothing to anyone about it. Indeed, what could I say?

Well, to let me cut a long story short, Gabriel, who had never known a moment's sickness in his life, grew ill: and we had to send to Gratz for a doctor, who could give no explanation of Gabriel's strange illness. Gradual wasting away, he said: absolutely no organic complaint. What could this mean?

My father at last became conscious of the fact that Gabriel was ill. His anxiety was fearful. The last trace of grey faded from his hair, and it became quite white. We sent to Vienna for doctors. But all with the same result.

Gabriel was generally unconscious, and when conscious, only seemed to recognize Vardalek, who sat continually by his bedside, nursing him with the utmost tenderness.

One day I was alone in the room: and Vardalek cried suddenly, almost fiercely, 'Send for a priest at once, at once,' he repeated. 'It is now almost too late!'

Gabriel stretched out his arms spasmodically, and put them round Vardalek's neck. This was the only movement he had made for some time. Vardalek bent down and kissed him on the lips. I rushed downstairs: and the priest was sent for. When I came back Vardalek was not there. The priest administered extreme unction. I think Gabriel was already dead, although we did not think so at the time.

Vardalek had utterly disappeared; and when we looked for him he was nowhere to be found; nor have I seen or heard of him since.

My father died very soon afterwards: suddenly aged, and bent down with grief. And so the whole of the Wronski property came into my sole possession. And here I am, an old woman, generally laughed at for keeping, in memory of Gabriel, an asylum for stray animals – and – people do not, as a rule, believe in Vampires!

'And No Bird Sings'

E. F. BENSON

THE red chimneys of the house for which I was bound were visible from just outside the station at which I had alighted, and, so the chauffeur told me, the distance was not more than a mile's walk if I took the path across the fields. It ran straight till it came to the edge of that wood yonder, which belonged to my host, and above which his chimneys were visible. I should find a gate in the paling of this wood, and a track traversing it, which debouched close to his garden. So, in this adorable afternoon of early May, it seemed a waste of time to do other than walk through the meadows and woods, and I set off on foot, while the motor carried my traps.

It was one of those golden days which every now and again leak out of Paradise and drip to earth. Spring had been late in coming, but now it was here with a burst, and the whole world was boiling with the sap of life. Never have I seen such a wealth of spring flowers, or such vividness of green, or heard such melodious business among the birds in the hedgerows; this walk through the meadows was a jubilee of festal ecstasy. And best of all, so I promised myself, would be the passage through the wood newly fledged with milky green that lay just ahead. There was the gate, just facing me, and I passed through it into the dappled lights and shadows of the grass-grown track.

Coming out of the brilliant sunshine was like entering a dim tunnel; one had the sense of being suddenly withdrawn from the brightness of the spring into some subaqueous cavern. The tree-tops formed a green roof overhead, excluding the light to a remarkable degree; I moved in a world of shifting obscurity. Presently, as the trees grew more scattered, their place was taken by a thick growth of hazels, which met over the path, and then, the ground sloping downwards, I came upon an open clearing, covered with bracken and heather and studded with birches. But though I now walked once more beneath the luminous sky, with the sunlight pouring down, it seemed to have lost its effulgence. The brightness – was it some odd optical illusion? – was veiled as if it came through crêpe. Yet there was the sun still well above the tree-tops in an unclouded heaven, but for all that the light was that of a stormy winter's day, without warmth or brilliance. It was oddly silent, too; I had thought that the bushes and trees would be ringing with the song of mating birds, but listening, I could hear no note of any sort, neither the fluting of thrush or blackbird, nor the cheerful whirr of the chaffinch, nor the cooing wood-pigeon, nor the strident clamour of the jay. I paused to verify this odd silence; there was no doubt about it. It was rather eerie, rather uncanny, but I supposed the birds knew their own business best, and if they were too busy to sing it was their affair.

As I went on it struck me also that since entering the wood I had not seen a bird of any kind; and now, as I crossed the clearing, I kept my eyes alert for them, but fruitlessly, and soon I entered the further belt of thick trees which surrounded it. Most of them I noticed were beeches, growing very close to each other, and the ground beneath them was bare but for the carpet of fallen leaves, and a few thin bramble-bushes. In this curious dimness and thickness of the trees, it was impossible to see far to right or left of the path, and now, for the first time since I had left the open, I heard some sound of life. There came the rustle of leaves from not far away, and I thought to myself that a rabbit, anyhow, was moving. But somehow it lacked the staccato patter of a small animal; there was a certain stealthy heaviness about it, as if something much larger were stealing along and desirous of not being heard. I paused again to see what might emerge, but instantly the sound ceased. Simultaneously I was conscious of some faint but very foul odour reaching me, a smell choking and corrupt, yet somehow pungent, more like the odour of something alive rather than rotting. It was peculiarly sickening, and not wanting to get any closer to its source I went on my way.

Before long I came to the edge of the wood; straight in front of me was a strip of meadow-land, and beyond an iron gate between two brick walls, through which I had a glimpse of lawn and flower-beds. To the left stood the house, and over house and garden there poured the amazing brightness of the declining afternoon.

Hugh Granger and his wife were sitting out on the lawn, with the usual pack of assorted dogs: a Welsh collie, a yellow retriever, a fox-terrier, and a Pekinese. Their protest at my intrusion gave way to the welcome of recognition, and I was admitted into the circle. There was much to say, for I had been out of England for the last three months, during which time Hugh had settled into this little estate left him by a recluse uncle, and he and Daisy had been busy during the Easter vacation with getting into the house. Certainly it was a most attractive legacy; the house, through which I was presently taken, was a delightful little Queen Anne manor, and its situation on the edge of this heather-clad Surrey ridge quite superb. We had tea in a small panelled parlour overlooking the garden, and soon the wider topics narrowed down to those of the day and the hour. I had walked, had I, asked Daisy, from the station: did I go through the wood, or follow the path outside it?

The question she thus put to me was given trivially enough; there was no hint in her voice that it mattered a straw to her which way I had come. But it was quite clearly borne in upon me that not only she but Hugh also listened intently for my reply. He had just lit a match for his cigarette, but held it unapplied till he heard my answer. Yes, I had gone through the wood; but now, though I had received some odd impressions in the wood, it seemed quite ridiculous to mention what they were. I could not soberly say that the sunshine there was of very poor quality, and that at one point in my traverse I had smelt a most iniquitous odour. I had walked through the wood; that was all I had to tell them.

I had known both my host and hostess for a tale of many years, and now, when I felt that there was nothing except purely fanciful stuff that I could volunteer about my experiences there, I noticed that they exchanged a swift glance, and could easily interpret it. Each of them signalled to the other an expression of relief; they told each other (so I construed their glance) that I, at any rate, had found nothing unusual in the wood, and they were pleased at that. But then, before any real pause had succeeded to my answer that I had gone through the wood, I remembered that strange absence of bird-song and birds, and as that seemed an innocuous observation in natural history, I thought I might as well mention it.

'One odd thing struck me,' I began (and instantly I saw the attention of both riveted again), 'I didn't see a single bird or hear one from the time I entered the wood to when I left it.'

Hugh lit his cigarette.

'I've noticed that too,' he said, 'and it's rather puzzling. The wood is certainly a bit of primeval forest, and one would have thought that hosts of birds would have nested in it from time immemorial. But, like you, I've never heard or seen one in it. And I've never seen a rabbit there either.'

'I thought I heard one this afternoon,' said I. 'Something was moving in the fallen beech leaves.'

'Did you see it?' he asked.

I recollected that I had decided that the noise was not quite the patter of a rabbit.

'No, I didn't see it,' I said, 'and perhaps it wasn't one. It sounded, I remember, more like something larger.'

Once again and unmistakingly a glance passed between Hugh and his wife, and she rose.

'I must be off,' she said. 'Post goes out at seven, and I lazed all morning. What are you two going to do?'

'Something out of doors, please,' said I. 'I want to see the domain.'

Hugh and I accordingly strolled out again with the cohort of dogs. The domain was certainly very charming; a small lake lay beyond the garden, with a reed bed vocal with warblers, and a tufted margin into which coots and moorhens scudded at our approach. Rising from the end of that was a high heathery knoll full of rabbit holes, which the dogs nosed at with joyful expectations, and there we sat for a while overlooking the wood which covered the rest of the estate. Even now in the blaze of the sun near to its setting, it seemed to be in shadow, though like the rest of the view it should have basked in brilliance, for not a cloud flecked the sky and the level rays enveloped the world in a crimson splendour. But the wood was grey and darkling. Hugh, also, I was aware, had been looking at it, and now, with an air of breaking into a disagreeable topic, he turned to me.

'Tell me,' he said, 'does anything strike you about that wood?'

'Yes: it seems to lie in shadow.'

He frowned.

'But it can't, you know,' he said. 'Where does the shadow come from? Not from outside, for sky and land are on fire.'

'From inside, then?' I asked.

He was silent a moment.

'There's something queer about it,' he said at length. 'There's something there, and I don't know what it is. Daisy feels it too; she won't ever go into the wood, and it appears that birds won't either. Is it just the fact that, for some unexplained reason, there are no birds in it that has set all our imaginations at work?'

I jumped up.

'Oh, it's all rubbish,' I said. 'Let's go through it now and find a bird. I bet you I find a bird.'

'Sixpence for every bird you see,' said Hugh.

We went down the hillside and walked round the wood till we came to the gate where I had entered that afternoon. I held it open after I had gone in for the dogs to follow. But there they stood, a yard or so away, and none of them moved.

'Come on, dogs,' I said, and Fifi, the fox-terrier, came a step nearer and then with a little whine retreated again.

'They always do that,' said Hugh, 'not one of them will set foot inside the wood. Look!'

He whistled and called, he cajoled and scolded, but it was no use. There the dogs remained, with little apologetic grins and signallings of tails, but quite determined not to come.

'But why?' I asked.

'Same reason as the birds, I suppose, whatever that happens to be. There's Fifi, for instance, the sweetest-tempered little lady; once I tried to pick her up and carry her in, and she snapped at me. They'll have nothing to do with the wood; they'll trot round outside it and go home.'

We left them there, and in the sunset light which was now beginning to fade began the passage. Usually the sense of eeriness disappears if one has a companion, but now to me, even with Hugh walking by my side, the place seemed even more uncanny than it had done that afternoon, and a sense of intolerable uneasiness, that grew into a sort of waking nightmare, obsessed me. I had thought before that the silence and loneliness of it had played tricks with my nerves; but with Hugh here it could not be that, and indeed I felt that it was not any such notion that lay at the root of this fear, but rather the conviction that there was some presence lurking there, invisible as yet, but permeating the gathered gloom. I could not form the slightest idea of what it might be, or whether it was material or ghostly; all I could diagnose of it from my own sensations was that it was evil and antique.

As we came to the open ground in the middle of the wood, Hugh stopped, and though the evening was cool I noticed that he mopped his forehead.

'Pretty nasty,' he said. 'No wonder the dogs don't like it. How do you feel about it?'

Before I could answer, he shot out his hand, pointing to the belt of trees that lay beyond.

'What's that?' he said in a whisper.

I followed his finger, and for one half-second thought I saw against the black of the wood some vague flicker, grey or faintly luminous. It waved as if it had been the head and forepart of some huge snake rearing itself, but it instantly disappeared, and my glimpse had been so momentary that I could not trust my impression.

'It's gone,' said Hugh, still looking in the direction he had pointed; and as we stood there, I heard again what I had heard that afternoon, a rustle among the fallen beech-leaves. But there was no wind nor breath of breeze astir.

He turned to me.

'What on earth was it?' he said. 'It looked like some enormous slug standing up. Did you see it?'

'I'm not sure whether I did or not,' I said. 'I think I just caught sight of what you saw.'

'But what was it?' he said again. 'Was it a real material creature, or was it——'

'Something ghostly, do you mean?' I asked.

'Something halfway between the two,' he said. 'I'll tell you what I mean afterwards, when we've got out of this place.'

The thing, whatever it was, had vanished among the trees to the left of where our path lay, and in silence we walked across the open till we came to where it entered tunnel-like among the trees. Frankly I hated and feared the thought of plunging into that darkness with the knowledge that not so far off there was something the nature of which I could not ever so faintly conjecture, but which, I now made no doubt, was that which filled the wood with some nameless terror. Was it material, was it ghostly, or was it (and now some inkling of what Hugh meant began to form itself into my mind) some being that lay on the borderline between the two? Of all the sinister possibilities that appeared the most terrifying.

As we entered the trees again I perceived that reek, alive and yet corrupt, which I had smelt before, but now it was far more potent, and we hurried on, choking with the odour that I now guessed to be not the putrescence of decay, but the living substance of that which crawled and reared itself in the darkness of the wood where no bird would shelter. Somewhere among those trees lurked the reptilian thing that defied and yet compelled credence.

It was a blessed relief to get out of that dim tunnel into the wholesome air of the open and the clear light of evening. Within doors, when we returned, windows were curtained and lamps lit. There was a hint of frost, and Hugh put a match to the fire in his room, where the dogs, still a little apologetic, hailed us with thumpings of drowsy tails.

'And now we've got to talk,' said he, 'and lay our plans, for whatever it is that is in the wood, we've got to make an end of it. And, if you want to know what I think it is, I'll tell you.'

'Go ahead,' said I.

'You may laugh at me, if you like,' he said, 'but I believe it's an elemental. That's what I meant when I said it was a being halfway between the material and the ghostly. I never caught a glimpse of it till this afternoon; I only felt there was something horrible there. But now I've seen it, and it's like what spiritualists and that sort of folk describe as an elemental. A huge phosphorescent slug is what they tell us of it, which at will can surround itself with darkness.'

Somehow, now safe within doors, in the cheerful light and warmth of the room, the suggestion appeared merely grotesque. Out there in the darkness of that uncomfortable wood something within me had quaked, and I was prepared to believe any horror, but now commonsense revolted.

'But you don't mean to tell me you believe in such rubbish?' I said. 'You might as well say it was a unicorn. What *is* an elemental, anyway? Who has ever seen one except the people who listen to raps in the darkness and say they are made by their aunts?'

'What is it then?' he asked.

'I should think it is chiefly our own nerves,' I said. 'I frankly acknowledge I got the creeps when I went through the wood first, and I got them much worse when I went through it with you. But it was just nerves; we are frightening ourselves and each other.'

'And are the dogs frightening themselves and each other?' he asked. 'And the birds?'

That was rather harder to answer; in fact I gave it up.

Hugh continued.

'Well, just for the moment we'll suppose that something else, not ourselves, frightened us and the dogs and the birds,' he said, 'and that we did see something like a huge phosphorescent slug. I won't call it an elemental, if you object to that; I'll call it It. There's another thing, too, which the existence of It would explain.'

'What's that?' I asked.

'Well, It is supposed to be some incarnation of evil; it is a corporeal form of the devil. It is not only spiritual, it is material to this extent that it can be seen bodily in form, and heard, and, as you noticed, smelt, and, God forbid, handled. It has to be kept alive by nourishment. And that explains perhaps why, every day since I have been here, I've found on that knoll we went up some half-dozen dead rabbits.'

'Stoats and weasels,' said I.

'No, not stoats and weasels. Stoats kill their prey and eat it. These rabbits have not been eaten; they've been drunk.'

'What on earth do you mean?' I asked.

'I examined several of them. There was just a small hole in their throats, and they were drained of blood. Just skin and bones, and a sort of grey mash of fibre, like, like the fibre of an orange which has been sucked. Also there was a horrible smell lingering on them. And was the thing you had a glimpse of like a stoat or a weasel?'

There came a rattle at the handle of the door.

'Not a word to Daisy,' said Hugh as she entered.

'I heard you come in,' she said. 'Where did you go?'

'All round the place,' said I, 'and came back through the wood. It is odd; not a bird did we see, but that is partly accounted for because it was dark.'

I saw her eyes search Hugh's, but she found no communication there. I guessed that he was planning some attack on It next day, and he did not wish her to know that anything was afoot.

'The wood's unpopular,' he said. 'Birds won't go there, dogs won't go there, and Daisy won't go there. I'm bound to say I share the feeling too, but having braved its terrors in the dark I've broken the spell.'

'All quiet, was it?' asked she.

'Quiet wasn't the word for it. The smallest pin could have been heard dropping half a mile off.'

We talked over our plans that night after she had gone up to bed. Hugh's story about the sucked rabbits was rather horrible, and though there was no certain connection between those empty rinds of animals and what we had seen, there seemed a certain reasonableness about it. But anything, as he pointed out, which could feed like that was clearly not without its material side – ghosts did not have dinner, and if it was material it was vulnerable.

Our plans, therefore, were very simple; we were going to tramp through the wood, as one walks up partridges in a field of turnips, each with a shot-gun and a supply of cartridges. I cannot say that I looked forward to the expedition, for I hated the thought of getting into closer quarters with that mysterious denizen of the woods; but there was a certain excitement about it, sufficient to keep me awake a long time, and when I got to sleep to cause very vivid and awful dreams.

The morning failed to fulfil the promise of the clear sunset; the sky was lowering and cloudy and a fine rain was falling. Daisy had shopping-errands which took her into the little town, and as soon as she had set off we started on our business. The yellow retriever, mad with joy at the sight of guns, came bounding with us across the garden, but on our entering the wood he slunk back home again.

The wood was roughly circular in shape, with a diameter perhaps of half a mile. In the centre, as I have said, there was an open clearing about a quarter of a mile across, which was thus surrounded by a belt of thick trees and copse a couple of hundred yards in breadth. Our plan was first to walk together up the path which led through the wood, with all possible stealth, hoping to hear some movement on the part of what we had come to seek. Failing that, we had settled to tramp through the wood at the distance of some fifty yards from each other in a circular track; two or three of these circuits would cover the whole ground pretty thoroughly. Of the nature of our quarry, whether it would try to steal away from us, or possibly attack, we had no idea; it seemed, however, yesterday to have avoided us.

Rain had been falling steadily for an hour when we entered to wood; it hissed a little in the tree-tops overhead; but so thick was the cover that the ground below was still not more than damp. It was a dark morning outside; here you would say that the sun had already set and that night was falling. Very quietly we moved up the grassy path, where our footfalls were noiseless, and once we caught a whiff of that odour of live corruption; but though we stayed and listened not a sound of anything stirred except the sibilant rain over our heads. We went across the clearing and through to the far gate, and still there was no sign.

'We'll be getting into the trees then,' said Hugh. 'We had better start where we got that whiff of it.'

We went back to the place, which was towards the middle of the encompassing trees. The odour still lingered on the windless air.

'Go on about fifty yards,' he said, 'and then we'll go in. If either of us comes on the track of it we'll shout to each other.'

I walked on down the path till I had gone the right distance, signalled to him, and we stepped in among the trees.

I have never known the sensation of such utter loneliness. I knew that Hugh was walking parallel with me, only fifty yards away, and if I hung on my step I could faintly hear his tread among the beech leaves. But I felt as if I was quite sundered in this dim place from all companionship of man; the only live thing that lurked here was that monstrous mysterious creature of evil. So thick were the trees that I could not see more than a dozen yards in any direction; all places outside the wood seemed infinitely remote, and infinitely remote also everything that had occurred to me in normal human life. I had been whisked out of all wholesome experiences into this antique and evil place. The rain had ceased, it whispered no longer in the tree-tops, testifying that there did exist a world and a sky outside, and only a few drops from above pattered on the beech leaves.

Suddenly I heard the report of Hugh's gun, followed by his shouting voice.

'I've missed it,' he shouted, 'it's coming in your direction.'

I heard him running towards me, the beech-leaves rustling, and no doubt his footsteps drowned a stealthier noise that was close to me. All that happened now, until once more I heard the report of Hugh's gun, happened, I suppose, in less than a minute. If it had taken much longer I do not imagine I should be telling it today.

I stood there then, having heard Hugh's shout, with my gun cocked, and ready to put to my shoulder, and I listened to his running footsteps. But still I saw nothing to shoot at and heard nothing. Then between two beech trees, quite close to me, I saw what I can only describe as a ball of darkness. It rolled very swiftly towards me over the few yards that separated me from it, and then, too late, I heard the dead beech-leaves rustling below it. Just before it reached me, my brain realised what it was, or what it might be, but before I could raise my gun to shoot at that nothingness, it was upon me. My gun was twitched out of my hand, and I was enveloped in this blackness, which was the very essence of corruption. It knocked me off my feet, and I sprawled flat on my back, and upon me, as I lay there, I felt the weight of this invisible assailant.

I groped wildly with my hands and they clutched something cold and slimy and hairy. They slipped off it, and next moment there was laid across my shoulder and neck something which felt like an india-rubber tube. The end of it fastened on to my neck like a snake, and I felt the skin rise beneath it. Again, with clutching hands, I tried to tear that obscene strength away from me, and as I struggled with it, I heard Hugh's footsteps close to me through this layer of darkness that hid everything.

My mouth was free, and I shouted at him.

'Here, here!' I yelled. 'Close to you, where it is darkest.'

I felt his hands on mine, and that added strength detached from my neck that sucker that pulled at it. The coil that lay heavy on my legs and chest writhed and struggled and relaxed. Whatever it was that our four hands held, slipped out of them and I saw Hugh standing close to me. A yard or two off, vanishing among the beech trunks, was that darkness which had poured over me. Hugh put up his gun, and with his second barrel fired at it.

The blackness dispersed, and there, wriggling and twisting like a huge worm lay what we had come to find. It was alive still, and I picked up my gun which lay by my side and fired two more barrels into it. The writhings dwindled into mere shudderings and shakings, and then it lay still.

With Hugh's help I got to my feet, and we both reloaded before going nearer. On the ground there lay a monstrous thing, half slug, half worm. There was no head to it; it ended in a blunt point with an orifice. In colour it was grey covered with sparse black hairs; its length I suppose was some four feet, its thickness at the broadest part was that of a man's thigh, tapering towards each end. It was shattered by shot at its middle. There were stray pellets which had hit it elsewhere, and from the holes they had made there oozed not blood, but some grey viscous matter.

As we stood there some swift process of disintegration and decay began. It lost outline, it melted, it liquefied, and in a minute more we were looking at a mass of stained and coagulated beech leaves. Again and quickly that liquor of corruption faded, and there lay at our feet no trace of what had been there. The overpowering odour passed away, and there came from the ground just the sweet savour of wet earth in springtime, and from above the glint of a sunbeam piercing the clouds. Then a sudden pattering among the dead leaves sent my heart into my mouth again, and I cocked my gun. But it was only Hugh's yellow retriever who had joined us.

We looked at each other.

'You're not hurt?' he said.

I held my chin up.

'Not a bit,' I said. 'The skin's not broken, is it?'

'No; only a round red mark. My God, what was it? What happened?'

'Your turn first,' said I. 'Begin at the beginning.'

'I came upon it quite suddenly,' he said. 'It was lying coiled like a sleeping dog behind a big beech. Before I could fire, it slithered off in the direction where I knew you were. I got a snap shot at it among the trees, but I must have missed, for I heard it rustling away. I shouted to you and ran after it. There was a circle of absolute darkness on the ground, and your voice came from the middle of it. I couldn't see you at all, but I clutched at the blackness and my hands met yours. They met something else, too.'

We got back to the house and had put the guns away before Daisy came home from her shopping. We had also scrubbed and brushed and washed. She came into the smoking-room.

'You lazy folk,' she said. 'It has cleared up, and why are you still indoors? Let's go out at once.'

I got up.

'Hugh has told me you've got a dislike of the wood,' I said, 'and it's a lovely wood. Come and see; he and I will walk on each side of you and hold your hands. The dogs shall protect you as well.'

'But not one of them will go a yard into the wood,' said she.

'Oh yes, they will. At least we'll try them. You must promise to come if they do.'

Hugh whistled them up, and down we went to the gate. They sat panting for it to be opened, and scuttled into the thickets in pursuit of interesting smells.

'And who says there are no birds in it?' said Daisy. 'Look at that robin! Why, there are two of them. Evidently house-hunting.'

A Silent Witness

by RICHARD MARSH

1. THE LIVING DEATH

I doubt if a more terrible thing ever happened to any man than that which happened to me in the autumn of 1883. The memory of it all is with me now as though it were but yesterday. And sometimes I wake shrieking in my dreams, and lie awake all night, oppressed with a great agony of fear.

I was a clerk in Burton's Bank at Exeter. For some days I had been queer and out of sorts. More than once I had been conscious of what seemed to me a sudden numbness of the limbs. For instance, on two separate occasions I had been incapable of rising from my office-stool. My wife and fellow-clerks noticed that I did not seem to be in my usual health, and my wife in particular had been urgent in entreating me to take my annual holiday without delay. But I had some complicated accounts to balance which I was unwilling to leave undone. And that more especially since they had given me an infinitude of trouble, the sought-for balance being exactly the thing I could not get.

It was the evening of 14 September. It was a Friday. I had decided at the last moment to remain at the bank after the rest had gone, for I had arranged that if I could get the accounts all right I would start for Penzance on the following morning with my wife. God alone knows how I yearned for a sight of the sea!

It had been a hot day, that Friday – a terribly hot day – and all day long I had been conscious not only of a curious unwillingness, but of an absolute incapacity, to move. In some extraordinary way my limbs seemed in a measure to have passed from my control. I suppose it was past six o'clock. I was all alone in the bank; the rest of the establishment had left a good hour ago. I was leaning forward on my desk, racking my brains to think where the error could be, when – shall I ever forget it? – in an instant – in a flash of lightning – I became conscious of a singular sensation which was stealing over me. It was just as though some malevolent spirit had woven a spell and deprived me of the power of motion. I was spellbound, rooted to my seat, as helpless as though I had been struck by the hand of death.

The strangest part of it was that while in that sudden, awful visitation I had lost the use of my limbs, I had preserved my faculties intact. I could see – straight in front, that is – for not only could I not turn my head a hair's-breadth to either side, not only could I not even close my eyes, but I could not even change the direction of my glance. I could only look straight in front of me with what I felt instinctively must be a fixed, horrible, glassy stare. But what there was in front of me, that I could plainly see. And I could hear. Indeed, my hearing seemed to be unnaturally keen. For instance, Burton's Bank is in the Cathedral Yard. Not only could I hear every footstep which passed even on the other side of the Cathedral – no slight distance for the sound of a foot to travel – but I could hear the traffic that went up and down Fore Street Hill, and over the bridge, right away to St Thomas's on the other side. And worse – for God knows that in the horror of all that followed it was of a surety the worst of all! – I could think. My brain, like my hearing, seemed to have become phenomenally clear. Instantaneously I knew what had come upon me. It was catalepsy. I was in a cataleptic fit!

I felt no pain – physical pain, at least. In that sense I was like a man whose physical side is dead, but whose mind still lives. And as I sat there hour after hour, dead, my agony of mind rose to such a climax that I cannot but think that it transcended whatever agony of body the most morbid imagination has at any time described.

It became dark – so dark that my eyes became useless for any purposes of sight, and yet they would not shut. It became silent, too – the intense silence of the night. But all at once, when the night was stillest, a sound struck on my ears – a peculiar sound, as of someone who walked with muffled steps. And then – could it be? Yes! A window was being opened close at hand.

I cannot doubt but that the only thing which had kept me from promptly falling on to the floor when the fit had first taken me, was the fact that I was leaning so forward that the greater part of my weight was on my desk. So, leaning forward on the desk, I stayed. Just in front of me was a glass partition, on the other side of which the safe was kept. It was the window of this inner office which was being opened now. By what I cannot but suppose was a providential accident, since I could not alter the direction of my glance, the safe was right in my line of sight; and so, although I could not immediately see who it was that entered, directly the mysterious intruder came between myself and the safe I could see him plainly.

At first all was dark. Then a light was struck, and someone, bearing a shaded lantern in his hand, appeared in my line of sight.

It was Philip Morris, our head cashier, and practically the manager of the bank!

I shall never forget my unutterable amazement when I perceived that it was he. What could bring him there at such an hour, in such a way? He wore a light dust coat which was unbuttoned down the front, so that I could see his dress clothes beneath and the diamonds gleaming in his shirt.

He carried a small leather bag in his hand. He took a bunch of keys from his pocket; with these he unlocked the safe. From it he took a quantity of notes – I could hear them rustle – and several bags of gold, which jingled as he dropped them in his bag. Then he turned right round, so that I saw him full in the face.

'If Wheeler could only see me now!' – I should mention that my name is Wheeler – Richard Wheeler. The allusion was to me. 'I guess he would soon unriddle the mystery of his accounts. Well, the game is up, I suppose; I have had my fling, even if the result is penal servitude for life. I flatter myself that few men would have had the dexterity to carry it on so long.'

He came a few steps forward, the lantern in his hand, and suddenly stopped short. His eyes were fixed on the glass partition. On his face there was an expression of the most awful ghastly fear. His lips seemed parched; he gasped for breath. For a moment I thought he would be seized with a convulsion, but he had sufficient control over himself to ward off that. He spoke at last, and his voice was like the voice of a strangled man.

'Wheeler! Wheeler! Is it you? For God's sake don't look like that! Your eyes are horrible!'

He covered his own eyes with his hand; I could see him shudder. Then he looked again; his mood was changed. With quick, firm steps he advanced to the partition door, and entered the office in which I was.

'I suppose you think you have caught me?' he cried. 'I congratulate you upon your cleverness; but perhaps, my friend, you have caught more than you think.'

Suddenly he seemed struck by my immobility. He came a step nearer.

'Why do you sit there like a wooden block, you hypocritical old fool? Do you hear? Can't you speak? You think you have trapped me very neatly, eh?'

He paused, he came a step nearer.

'Can't you speak, you fool? Wheeler! Wheeler!'

He laid his hand upon my shoulder; he shone the lantern in my face. Suddenly he gave the most dreadful shriek that ever yet I heard.

'My God!' he cried. 'He's dead!'

In his sudden fear the lantern fell from his hand with a crash. He gave me a push which sent me flying head-foremost to the floor. And where I fell, there, like a dead man I lay.

II. THE CONSCIOUS CORPSE

I lay on my own bed in my own room. Oh! what had I ever done to deserve the agony which I endured then? There was my wife on her knees beside the bed; there was a candle which flickered on the chest of drawers, although daylight already streamed into the room; and there was I, wrapped in the garments which enfold the dead. How my wife wept! How she mourned in the sudden anguish of her woe! Now she called on God for mercy and for strength, and now she got upon the bed and pillowed her head upon my breast, or bedewed my face with her kisses and her tears.

'Richard!' she cried. 'Richard! After all these years! My own! My dear!'

And then she wept as though her heart would break. Who shall conceive my agony as I lay there?

A little later there was this scene. Five men came into the room. There was Dr Leverson, my old medical attendant; Wilfred Burton, the banker, whom, man and boy, I had served for thirty years; Mr Fellowes, the lawyer to the bank; Philip Morris, that accursed thief; and Captain Philipson, the chief of the county police.

It was Mr Burton who spoke first. His voice was dry and cold – very different from the kindly, pleasant voice I knew so well.

'Before we go any further, I suppose, Dr Leverson, there is no doubt that this wretched man is dead? That you certify? No autopsy necessary, or anything of that sort?'

Dr Leverson smiled a superior smile.

'Richard Wheeler is certainly dead. I have the certificate of death in my pocket. The funeral is already arranged. He died from valvular disease of the heart – a disease of whose presence I have long been aware.' My brain reeled as I listened to the glib announcement. 'Doubtless his death was accelerated at the last by a sudden shock.'

'God,' said Mr Burton, with a solemnity the unconscious irony of which was hideous, 'saw fit to strike down the criminal at the moment of the crime.'

I wondered what Philip Morris looked like as he heard the words. This time he was out of my sight.

'And now,' continued Mr Burton, 'to proceed to the business which has brought us here. I need not point out to you, Dr Leverson, that all that passes here is in the strictest confidence.' I presume that the doctor bowed his head. 'The bank has been a victim of—' The speaker's voice trembled, and I felt that my wife covered her face with her hands. '—of the most terrible dishonesty. To what extent the affair has gone I have not yet had time to ascertain, but I fear that we have been robbed to the extent of at least a hundred thousand pounds.'

A hundred thousand pounds! My God! No wonder I could not get the accounts to balance! That villain had robbed us of a hundred thousand pounds at least, and I lay speechless there.

'Mr Morris will repeat the statement which he has already made to me. You, Mr Fellowes, will kindly take it down, and we will have it attested in the presence of Captain Philipson. Mrs Wheeler, you need not stop; it will only be painful to your feelings. Indeed, I think you had better go away.'

'Sir,' said my dear wife – oh, how her dear voice rang through my brain! – 'whatever Mr Morris may have to say, I never shall believe that my dear husband was a thief. I have known him to be a true husband and a God-fearing man for nearly thirty years.'

'Ah, Mrs Wheeler, how appearances may deceive. I had to the full as much confidence in him as you. Before you think that I misjudge him, hear what Mr Morris has to say.'

Philip Morris began his tale. It flashed upon me in an instant that he availed himself of my supposed decease to fasten his guilt upon my head. But I had never imagined that anyone in his circumstances could have carried the matter through with so easy an air. There was even an affectation of pathos in his tones as he filled in the details of his horrid lie.

'I had been spending the evening at Mr Fisher's' – Mr Fisher was one of the minor canons, a bachelor, who was reputed to have a taste for whist and for hours which were, perhaps, a little uncanonical. 'I was returning home, when, on passing the bank, I noticed that there seemed to be a light in the office in which the safe is kept. The window, as you know, is but a few feet from the ground. I have often pointed out how easy it would be for a thief to get in that way.'

'I know you have! I know you have!' said Mr Burton.

The hypocrite went on:

'To my surprise I found it was unlatched. I opened it. Whoever was within was too much absorbed in his occupation to notice what I did. I looked through the open window and saw that someone was in the inner office, but who it was I could not at first perceive. I climbed through the window and went in. Directly I entered the man looked up; it was Richard Wheeler. When he saw me he gave the most awful scream I think I ever heard, and fell down – dead. So soon as I had recovered from my bewilderment, I went to the window and called for help. A constable who heard me came to my assistance. Together we examined the room. That is all I have to say. I only wish that I had not to say so much.'

'But there is more that must be said,' Mr Burton took up the strain. 'In the grate were found the half-consumed fragments of the accounts, which, if they had been suffered to continue in existence, would inevitably have betrayed the dead man's crime. The safe was found wide open – it is still a mystery how he contrived to open it – ransacked of all the chief valuables it contained. On his desk was found a bag containing five hundred pounds in gold, and in his pockets notes for a thousand pounds. But notes and gold to the value of ten thousand pounds, and securities to a very large amount, are gone. We have still to find out where. I am sorry to tell you, Mrs Wheeler, that to search this house is one of the purposes which has brought us here.'

'Sir,' said my dear wife, 'you need make no apology. You are welcome to search the house from attic to basement. You will find nothing that was not righteously my dear husband's own.'

III. THE COFFIN BREAKS

For five days I lay there – dead. Words cannot describe the agony I endured. Conceive it if you can. Picture yourself in my position; conceive what you would suffer then. Far better had I indeed been dead.

On the second day they came and measured me for my coffin. Think of it – a living man! On the fourth day they brought it home, and I was placed within. There were two of them that brought it, and as they placed me in the narrow box they cracked their little jest.

'A tight fit, isn't he?' said one.

'Ah,' replied his fellow, 'they'd have given him as tight a fit if he had lived; four good strong walls for life.'

'Who'd ever have thought old Dick Wheeler would have done a bit upon the cross?'

'Well,' again replied his fellow – how I loathed that man! – 'I would for one. I never knew a psalm-singer yet that wasn't a robber and a thief.'

When that choice pair had gone, my wife came in and looked at me as I lay in my last bed. She had a wreath in her hand, which she placed upon my breast, and a white rose, which betokened innocence, which she placed within the wreath. She stooped and kissed me on the brow; and as she did so she burst into a flood of tears.

'Oh, God!' she cried, 'show that my dear husband was not a thief!'

The next day, the fifth, they came and screwed me down. Imagine that! I learnt from what they said that they feared that if, in that hot weather, I was left for a longer time exposed, decomposition would set in. When they had already placed the lid upon my coffin, my wife came running in. I learnt that they had come in her absence to shut me for ever from her sight. They imagined that if she were there she might object to what they did. Her appearance disconcerted them. She made them immediately remove the lid, and bade them withdraw from the room, so that she might have final solitary communion with her dead.

She knelt down by the side of my coffin and prayed. She expressed the most profound belief in the innocence of the man who had been her husband for nearly thirty years, and she besought the Most High that He would expound that innocence, and make it clear to man. Then she stood up and kissed me on the lips – kissed me a last good-bye!

Then she left me, to the full as broken-hearted as she herself, and the undertaker's men returned and screwed me down. They put the lid upon my coffin, and shut from me the blessed light; for no one had closed my eyes. They had tried to, but the lids would not come down. I could hear the traffickers in death laughing and jesting as they drove the screws well home. When they had done their work, and gone, I was a prisoner indeed.

How long I remained in that box screwed down I never knew. It seemed to me a hundred years. A dreadful thought came to me, not once but again and again, with recurring force. Suppose that I indeed was dead? Who knows the mysteries of death? Is it not conceivable that when the body dies, the mind, which has such a mysterious affinity with the soul, may live? If I were dead, and my shame should live! Was it possible that through the long cycle of the years, the aeons, which were still to come, my mind should be alive and I be dead? . . . It is not strange that my pen should tremble as I recall the thoughts which racked me then.

Racked me with such intensity that, even in my state of death, I feared I should go mad. And then? What then? Mad through the aeons in the womb of time! Even dead, I thought my brain would burst. I tried to scream. I struggled as with the issues of life and death for the power to give expression to the great agony of my fear and pain.

And then? What happened then? To this hour I cannot precisely say. I know that while, mentally, I struggled with inconceivable eager-ness to cry out, I suddenly awoke. I know no other word to use. I knew I was alive. Alive, and prisoned in that box! And I do believe that for the first few moments of my resurrection – what was it else?– I actually was mad. I had a madman's strength, at any rate. I struggled to be free – and with such strength that I burst the box, forced the coffin's sides, and was a prisoner no more.

I stood upon my feet. As I did so I discovered that my display of strength must have been a sort of frenzy, for indeed I was so weak that at first I could not stand. I sank back upon the bed. But only for a moment. There was that within me which gave me strength. I was filled with an overmastering desire to proclaim my innocence and bring home to the criminal his crime. Wholly regardless of the clothes I wore, forgetful of them even, I went down the stairs into the street, and ran to Mr Burton's as certainly I never ran before.

I must have cut a pretty figure as I ran, but Mr Burton's great house was within a couple of hundred yards of my more modest residence, the hour was late, and I never met a creature on the way. I was well acquainted both with the banker's habits and his house. I knew that often, when the rest of the household was fast asleep, Mr Burton would sit for hours writing in his study which opened on to the lawn at the back. To this room I hastened. It was as I supposed. There was a bright light within. I turned the handle of the French window; it yielded to my touch. Without pausing for an instant to reflect on what the consequences of my act might be, I burst into the room.

As I entered, Mr Burton was sitting writing at a table. He looked up. When he saw me he rose from his seat. He clutched the edge of the table. He gazed at me, speechless, unable to believe that what he saw was real.

'Wheeler!' he gasped at last; 'Richard Wheeler!'

'Yes, sir, 'tis I! Not dead, but living! This is no ghost you gaze upon, but a creature of flesh and blood, to whom God has given strength to declare his innocence and expose another's crime.'

I poured out my tale. He was too bewildered at first to grasp the meaning of my words. It was all so unexpected and so strange that he was unable to realise that he was not the victim of some dreadful dream. But it became plain to him at last. It was painful to see his agitation as he began to grasp the purport of my revelation.

'You had a cataleptic fit!'

'If it was not catalepsy, I know not what it was. I am no doctor, sir.'

'And you were within an ace of being buried alive! The thought is terrible.'

'It was terrible to me.'

'And you saw – you actually saw – Philip Morris rob the safe?'

'I was a silent witness of his crime. It was only when he supposed that I was dead that it occurred to him to place the guilt upon my shoulders.'

'What a villain the man must be! It seems incredible! But the whole story seems incredible for the matter of that, and the most incredible part of it is your presence here. But even supposing what you say is true – and God forbid, after what you have told me, that I should deny it – how are you going to prove his villainy?'

'Mr Burton, I am but newly come from the chambers of death.'

'For heaven's sake, don't talk like that! You make my blood run cold.'

'But the fact is so; and things are revealed to me which to you are hidden.' I rose up, still in my grave-clothes, trembling like a leaf. 'At this instant the thief is at his work again, and tampers with the safe. Mr Burton, I entreat you to come with me to the bank; his villainy shall be proved tonight.'

'Come with you – to the bank – at this hour of the night!'

But I had my way. The banker lent me some of his own clothes, and a cloak was thrown over my shoulders. The coachman was roused; a carriage was ordered out. Within a very few minutes we were seated in it, and were being driven swiftly towards the bank, through the silent streets, to catch the criminal in the very moment of his crime.

The carriage was drawn up some little distance from the bank. We got out. Mr Burton had the key of the private door. We approached swiftly, yet silently as well. Our chief object was not to give the slightest alarm.

On the very threshold Mr Burton paused.

'I am afraid that this is a wild-goose chase that you have brought me on. Some folks would even call it by a stronger name.'

'Can you not hear him? Hark! He rustles a bundle of notes! They are those notes which were missing, and which you searched my house to find.'

'Hear him, Wheeler? Are you mad? When he is in the private office – if he is anywhere at all – and we are out in the street!'

'I can hear him, if you can't. Give me the key, or open the door. Every moment which we waste increases the chances of escape.'

Hesitatingly – I believe he doubted my sanity even then – Mr Burton put the key into the lock. Noiselessly it turned. Without a sound the door swung open on its well-oiled hinges. We stood inside. It was pitch dark.

'Hadn't we better have a light? I cannot see my hand before my face. We shall be falling over something if we don't take care.'

'I need no light. Remember my eyes have grown accustomed to the dark. You, sir, have only to keep close to me.'

I led the way. He followed close upon my heels. Suddenly I paused.

'See! There is a light!'

Sure enough there was, in the inner room – in that inner room in which the safe was kept. I caught Mr Burton by the arm. 'Sir, come a little farther, and you shall see it all. You shall see the criminal detected in his crime.'

I did not tremble then; I had become quite cool and calm.

I knew my hour was at hand. With unfaltering fingers I unloosed the cloak from about my shoulders and stood revealed in my cerements, as though I had new-risen from the grave. And then—

Then I stole by the outer door into the office in which I had been overtaken by that strange mockery of death. Through the glass partition, sure enough, I saw at a glance that Philip Morris, lantern in hand, was at his old work, busied with the contents of the safe. I leaned right forward on the desk, and tapped with my fingers against the glass. He caught the sound at once, but for a moment did not perceive from whence it rose. He approached the partition; I saw him trembling as he came. I saw his face was ghastly white.

When he was quite close, in my grave-clothes I rose straight up, and, looking him straight in the face – his pallid, panic-stricken face –, I raised my arm above my head, and in a loud voice cried out –

'Thou thief!'

A wild shriek rang through the night; and sometimes in my ears I seem to hear it still!

When Mr Burton and I ran in we found him, stricken by a sudden agony of conscience-stricken fear, a bundle of bank notes in the frenzied grip of his right hand, lying in a fit upon the floor.

The Mirror of Cagliostro

ROBERT ARTHUR

London, 1910.

The girl's eyes were open. Her face, which had been so softly young, flushed with champagne and excitement, was a thing of horror now. Twisted with shock, contorted with the final spasm of life ejected from the body it had tenanted, her face was a mask of terror, frozen so until the rigor of sudden death should release its hold. Only then would her muscles relax and death be allowed to wipe away the transformation he had wrought.

Charles, Duke of Burchester, wiped his fingers delicately on a silk handkerchief. For a moment, looking down at the girl, Molly Blanchard, his eyes lighted with interest. Was it truly possible that in death the eyes photographed, as he had been told, the last object that sight registered?

He bent over the girl huddled on the crimson carpet of the small private dining-room of Chubb's Restaurant, and stared into the blue eyes that seemed to start from the contorted face. Then he sighed and straightened. It was, after all, a fairy tale. If the story had been true, her dead eyes should have mirrored two tiny, grinning skulls, one in each—for a skull had been the last thing she had seen in life. *His* skull.

But the blue eyes were cold and blank. He had seen in them reflection from one of the tapers that burned upon the table, still set with snowy linen and silver dishes from which they had dined.

He amended the thought. From which Molly had dined. Dined as she, poor lovely creature from some obscure group of actors, had never dined before. He had dined afterwards. She had dined upon food, but he had dined upon life.

He felt replete now. It was a pity he had not been able to restrain his impulse to kill. London was a city of infinite interest

162

in this, the twentieth century. He should have planned on a prolonged stay, to explore it fully, but temptation had been too great, after so long an abstinence.

He moved swiftly now. The cheap necklace of glass beads, which the girl's mind had seen as rare diamonds, he allowed to remain about the throat where they glistened against the blue marks of strangling fingers. But he took his cloak from a hook and threw it over his shoulders. He retrieved his hat and let himself out of the door without a backward glance for the empty husk that lay upon the rug.

A waiter in red livery was coming down the hall, past the series of closed doors that led to the famous—and infamous—private dining-rooms of Chubb's. Charles stopped him.

'I leave,' he said. 'My friend—' he nodded toward the closed door—'wishes to be undisturbed so that she may compose herself. Please see to it.'

A coin slipped from one hand to the other, and the servitor nodded.

'Very good, Sir,' he said. No titles and no names were used at Chubb's. They were, however, well known to both the proprietor and all the help. A pity.

Charles walked down the long corridor, down the steps which led to the street without imposing upon one the necessity of exposing himself to the view of the crowd in the dining-rooms below. As he let himself out, the eight-foot tall doorman, cloaked in crimson with a black shako upon his head—a sight more goggled at in these days by tourists from puritanical America than even Windsor Castle—raised a hand. A hansom cab arrived in place precisely on the moment that his steps carried him to the kerb.

Without looking back, Charles tossed a coin over his shoulder. The giant doorman casually retrieved it from the air as a dozen beggars and street loungers leaped futilely for it.

'Burchester House,' Charles said to the coachman.

He settled back to stare with hungry eyes upon this, the new London of which he had seen so little—and could have seen so much if he had not let himself be carried away by the soft sweet temptation of Molly Blanchard's life so that.....

But it was futile to dwell upon it. There would be other occasions. As they rolled through the dark streets he let himself relive the moment when he had placed the necklace about Molly's throat, telling her to look deep into his eyes. The heady delight of the instant when her trusting eyes had seen behind the mask of flesh which he now wore. The almost intolerable joy of her struggles.

He realized that the hansom had stopped. For how long had he been living again those delights, unaware? There was not, after, all, infinity ahead of him yet. Pursuit would be hot after him soon, and he was as vulnerable now as a new-hatched chick.

He stepped from the cab and flung the driver money. Charles, still with the down of youth upon his pink and white cheeks, strolled with the gait of a man much older and more experienced into the great, three-storied stone mansion which was the London residence of the Burchesters.

Inside, someone came scurrying out of the shadows of the almost dark parlour.

'Charles, my son,' his mother began, in a voice that trembled.

'Later, mother,' he said sharply, and brushed past her. 'I am going to my studio. I will be occupied for some time.' He started up the stairs toward the tower room where he kept his paints and canvases. Behind him he heard his mother whimpering. He paid no heed. As he reached the second floor he increased his pace. It would not do to be late in getting back to his sanctuary.

An hour later, with his mother weeping outside his door and the men from Scotland Yard hammering on it, Charles, Duke of Burchester, flung himself from the casement window and jellied himself on the cobblestones below.

Paris, 1963.

The Musée des Antiquités Historiques was a small brick building, twisted out of shape by the pressure of time and its neighbours. It stood at the end of one of Paris's many obscure streets, so narrow and twisting that no driver of even the smallest car, entering one, could be sure of finding room enough to turn around to get out again.

Beyond the Musée flowed the Seine, and if the waters of the Seine gave off any glint of light this overcast day, the glint was wholly lost in passing through the grime that darkly frosted the windows of the office of the curator, Professor Henri Thibaut.

Thibaut himself was ancient enough to seem one of the museum's exhibits, rather than its curator. But his eyes still snapped, and he spoke with a swift crispness that strained Harry Langham's otherwise excellent understanding of French.

'Cagliostro?' Thibaut said, and the word seemed to uncoil from his lips like a tiny serpent of sound. 'Count Alexander Cagliostro, self-styled. Born in 1743, died in 1795. A man of great controversy.

By some denounced as a fraud. By others acclaimed as a miracle worker—a veritable magician. Ah yes, my young colleague from America, I have studied his life. Your information is entirely correct.'

'Good,' Harry Langham said. He smiled. At thirty-five he still seemed younger than his age, although a carefully acquired professorial manner helped counterbalance his youthful aspect.

'Frankly, sir,' he added, 'I had just about given up hope of getting any decent information about Cagliostro to make my summer in Europe worth while. I'm an associate professor of history at Boston College—my period is the 18th century—and I am working for my doctorate, you see. I have chosen Count Cagliostro as the subject for my thesis. This is my last day in France. Only last night I heard of you—heard that you yourself had once written a thesis on the life of Cagliostro. I'm here, hoping you will assist me.'

'Ah.' Thibaut took a cigarette from an ivory box and lit it. 'And from what viewpoint do you approach your subject? Do you propose to expose him as one of history's great frauds? Or will you credit him with powers bordering on the magical?'

'That's my problem,' Harry Langham said frankly. 'To play it safe I ought to call him a mountebank, a faker, a great charlatan. But I can't. I started thinking that, and now—now I believe that he may really have had mystic powers. His life is wrapped in such mystery—'

'And you wish to clarify the mystery?' Thibaut said, his tone sardonic. 'You will write your thesis about Cagliostro. You will win an advanced degree. You will get a promotion. You will make more salary. You will marry some attractive woman. All from the dusty remains of Cagliostro. N'est-ce pas?'

'Well—yes.' Harry Langham laughed, a bit uneasily. 'Cagliostro—thesis—promotion—money—marriage. Almost like an equation, isn't it?'

'It is indeed.' With a sudden motion, Thibaut ground out his cigarette. 'Except that the answer is wrong.'

'How do you mean?'

'Cagliostro can bring you only grief. Go back to America and erase the name of Cagliostro from your memory!'

'But Professor!' Harry reflected that the French became excited easily, and the thought made his tone amused. 'You yourself wrote a thesis about the man.'

'And destroyed it.' Thibaut sank back into his chair. 'Some things our world will not accept. The truth about Count Cagliostro is one of them.'

'But he's been dead for nearly two hundred years!'

'M'sieu Langham,' Thibaut said, reaching again for the cigarettes in the ivory box, 'Evil never dies. No, no. Do not answer. There is little I can do to help you. I destroyed my thesis and all my notes. However, if you should go to London—'

'I go there tomorrow,' Harry told him. 'I sail from Southampton in a week. I hope to find some material on Cagliostro in the British Museum.'

'You will find little of value,' the Frenchman said. 'To the British, Cagliostro was a charlatan. But attend. Seek in the old furniture shops for a plain desk with a hinged lid, the letter 'C' carved into it in ornate scrolls. Once it belonged to Cagliostro. Later it was acquired by one of the Dukes of Burchester. I have reason to believe that certain of Cagliostro's papers were hidden in a secret drawer in this desk and may possibly still be there.'

'A plain desk with a hinged lid, the letter "C" carved into it.' Harry Langham's expression was eager. 'That would be a find indeed. I certainly thank you, Professor Thibaut.'

The older man eyed him sadly.

'I still repeat my advice—tear up your thesis, forget the name. But you are young, you will not do it. Very well, I shall make one more suggestion. 'Go—now, today—to the Church of St. Martin.'

'St. Martin ?'

'I will give you the address. Find the caretaker, give him ten new francs. Tell him you wish to see the tomb of Yvette Dulaine.'

'Yvette Dulaine?'

'She was buried there in 1780.'

'But I don't understand—I mean, what point is there in seeing the tomb of a girl who died in 1780 ?'

'I said she was buried then.' Thibaut's gaze was inscrutable. 'Insist that the caretaker open the tomb for you. Then do whatever you must do. Au revoir, my young friend.'

In the age-wracked Museum of Historic Antiquities, it had been easy to smile at the melodramatic earnestness of the French. Here, with the streets of Paris Lord alone knew how many feet above his head, moving down a narrow stone passageway slippery with seepage of water, holding aloft his own candle and following the flickering flame borne by the rheumatic old man in front of him, Harry found it less easy to smile.

They had gone down endless steps, along corridors that turned a dozen times. How old was this church anyway, and how far into the bowels of the earth did its subterranean crypts go? The whole thing was too much like an old movie for Harry Langham's taste. Except that the smell of damp corruption in the air, the shuffle of the old man's shoes on the rock flooring, and the scamper of rats in the darkness carried their own conviction.

They passed another room opening off the corridor, a room into which the bobbing candle flames sent just enough light to show old, elaborately carved stone tombs in close-joined ranks.

'Is this it?' Harry asked impatiently, as his guide paused. 'We must be there by now. We have had time enough to travel half-way across Paris.'

'Patience, my son.' The caretaker's tone was unhurried. 'Those who lie here cannot come to us. We must go to them.'

'Then let's hurry it up. This is my last day in Paris. I have a thousand things to tend to.'

They went on, around another turning, down some stairs and came into a low-ceilinged room dug from solid rock. The tombs here were simpler. Many had only a name and a date. In the light from the two candles, they lay like sleeping monsters of stone, jealously hiding within them the bones of the humans they had swallowed.

'Are we there at last?' Harry Langham's tone was ironic. 'Thank heaven for that! Now which of these dandy little one-room apartments belongs to Miss Yvette Dulaine? I've come this far. I'll see it, but then I'm heading back for fresh air.'

'None of these,' the caretaker said quietly. 'She lies over here, la pauvre petite. Come.'

He skirted the outer row of tombs and paused, lifting his candle high. In a crude niche in the stone a tomb apart from the others had been placed. It could have been no plainer—stone sides, a stone slab on top, the date 1780 cut into the top, no other inscription.

'She is here. It is only the second time in this century that she has been disturbed.'

Harry stared sceptically at the simple tomb. His shoes were damp and he felt chilled as well as somehow disappointed.

'Well?' he asked. 'What am I supposed to do? Say ooh and aah? Why isn't her name on it—just the date? How do I know this is even Yvette Dulaine's tomb?'

The caretaker straightened painfully. He held his candle up and stared into Harry's face.

'You are American,' he said. 'When this tomb was closed, your nation had but begun its destiny. You have much to learn.'

'Look,' Harry said, controlling his impatience with an effort. 'I agree we have a lot to learn. But I can't see I'm learning much here, looking at some chunks of stone that hide a lady who died one hundred and eighty-odd years ago.'

'Ah.' The other spoke gently. 'If she had but died.'

'If she had but—' Harry stared at him. 'What are you talking about? They don't bury you unless you're dead. Believe me, I know.'

'M'sieu's knowledge is no doubt formidable.' The other's tone was gentle, the sarcasm in his words. 'Let us now disturb the peace of Mlle Dulaine for but one moment more. We shall open her tomb.'

'Now really, that's hardly necessary—' Harry began, but stopped when the caretaker handed him his candle and grasped the bottom end of the slab top. He tugged; inch by inch the heavy stone moved, screeching its protest. Harry had no special desire to see some mouldering bones. He had avoided such a tourist attraction as the catacombs of Paris, just because he didn't care for morbid reminders of man's mortality. He liked his life—and death—in the pages of books. Both life and death were neat and tidy there and could be studied without emotion. He did not look into the open tomb until the caretaker straightened and motioned with his hand.

'Perceive,' he said. 'Look well upon the contents of this tomb, which the good fathers left nameless so that the poor one inside would not disturb the thoughts of the living.'

Still holding the candles, Harry bent over. As he did so, the flames flickered wildly, as if buffeted by drafts from all sides, though no breath of air stirred there. And the shadows they created made the girl in the tomb seem to smile, as if she would open her eyes and speak.

Her face was madonna-like in its perfection of ivory beauty. Heavy black tresses, unbound, flowed down upon her breast. Her hands, small and exquisite, were crossed upon her bosom. She wore something white and simple which exposed her wrists and arms. As he bent over her Harry's hand shook and one of the candles dropped a blob of molten wax upon her wrist. He so completely expected her to move, to cry out at the pain, that when she did not he felt a sudden wild rage. At her, for seeming so alive, so beautiful and so desirable. At Thibaut for sending him here on a fool's errand. At the shrivelled gnome of a caretaker for wasting his time on so childish a deception.

'Damn you!' he cried. 'She's a wax figure! What kind of tomfoolery is this?'

With surprising strength, the caretaker thrust the stone lid back into place. Harry had one last glimpse of the young and lovely face with the lips that seemed about to speak, and then it was gone. And he could not explain why he felt doubly cheated, doubly angered.

'So!' he shouted. 'You didn't want me to get another look! You knew I was going to touch her and see that she really was wax. Admit it and tell me why you bothered with this nonsense. Or is this a standard tourist attraction that you've rigged up to bring in a little income from gullible Americans?'

The Frenchman faced him with dignity, reaching for and taking back his candle.

'M'sieu,' he said. 'As I remarked, you are young, you have much to learn. Once, Mlle Dulaine attracted the attention of a certain Count Cagliostro. She refused him. He persisted. She rejected him utterly. One night she vanished from her home. The next day, servants of Count Cagliostro found her lying in his rooms, at the base of a great mirror as if she had been admiring herself. The Count was held blameless; he was far from Paris at the time.

'Mlle Dulaine seemed asleep, but did not waken. There was no mark on her. Yet she did not breathe and her heart did not beat. A week passed. A month. She remained unchanged. She did not begin that return to dust which is the fate of us all. So her sorrowing parents consigned her to the good fathers of the church, and they placed her here. She has remained as you see her, since the year 1780.'

'That's idiotic,' Harry said, shakily. 'Such things aren't possible. She's a wax figure. She's certainly not dead.'

'No, m'sieu. She is not dead. Yet she is not alive. She exists in some dark dimension it is not well to think of. The Count Cagliostro took his revenge upon her. She will sleep thus, until the very stones of Paris become dust around her. Now let us go. As you reminded me, you have many things to do.'

'Wait a minute. I want to see that girl—that figure—again.'

Harry's breathing was harsh in the silence; he felt his pulse pounding—with fury? with bafflement?—he couldn't tell what emotion he felt. But the caretaker was already moving toward the stairs.

In a moment he would be gone. Harry wanted to tear the stone slab off that tomb and satisfy himself. But to linger even a moment would mean to be lost in those Stygian depths without a guide.

Furious, he followed the flickering candle that was already becoming small in the darkness.

It was easy, in the daylight above, to regain his composure and laugh at himself for being tricked. It was easy, next day in London, when he met Bart Phillips, his closest friend at the university, who had spent the summer in London working toward his doctorate in chemistry, to entertain him with an elaborate account of the mummery he had gone through. It was easy to erase the lingering doubt that the girl had indeed been a wax figure.

Easy—until he found the mirror.

He found it in a dingy second-hand shop in Soho, called Bob's Odds and Ends. The desk he was seeking he had traced to an auction house which had suffered a fire. Presumably the desk had burned with many other rare pieces. But Bob's Odds and Ends had been mentioned in connection with the sale of the furnishings of Burchester House, residence of a ducal line now extinct.

Bob himself, five feet tall and four feet around the waist, did not bother to remove the toothpick from between his unusually bad teeth when Harry, with Bart in protesting tow, asked about the desk.

'No, guv'nor,' the untidy fat man said. 'No such article 'ere. Probably Murchison's got it, them wot 'ad the fire.'

'Come on, Harry,' Bart said. 'One last day in London and still you're dragging me to junk shops. Let's go get something to drink and see if we can't make a date with those girls from Charlestown we met.'

'Don't 'urry off, gents,' Bob said plaintively, unhooking fat thumbs from a greasy vest. 'Got somethin' pretty near as good. 'Ow would you like to buy th' mirror wot killed th' Duke of Burchester 'imself?'

'Mirror?' Harry asked, the word tugging at his memory.

'Come on, Harry!' Bart exploded, but Harry was already following the fat man toward the dark recesses of the shop.

The mirror was a tall, oval pier glass, hinged so that it could be adjusted. It stood in a corner. As the fat man swung it out, it rolled on a sloping stretch of floor, toppled sideways, and would have crashed down upon him if he had not sidestepped nimbly. The mirror fell to the floor with a violence that should have sent flying glass for a dozen feet.

The proprietor looked at it calmly, then heaved it upright.

'That's 'ow it killed th' duke,' he observed. 'Fell on 'im. And 'im with an 'atchet in his 'and, like he was trying to smash it. But this glass can't smash. Unbreakable, it is.'

'What's unbreakable?' Bart asked, following them.

'This mirror, according to the man,' Harry said.

'Nonsense. Glass can't be made unbreakable,' Bart said. 'Good Lord, it's all painted over with black paint. It's no earthly use to anyone. Come on, I'm dying of thirst.'

'But, gents, it's a rare mirror, it is,' the fat man said sadly. 'Without that paint, it'd be worth a pretty sum. Besides, it's an 'aunted mirror. It killed th' duke 'isself, and it stood in a closet for almost fifty years before that. Ever since th' duke's brother, wot was th' duke then, murdered a girl in Chubb's Restaurant back in 1910, then jumped out th' window into th' courtyard an' broke his neck when the bobbies came for 'im.'

'Come on, Harry,' Bart groaned. But Harry, on the verge of turning away, saw the faint glint of glass near the bottom where something sharp had scratched a few square inches of the black paint which covered the mirror's surface. It seemed to him the bit of glass reflected light, and he stooped to look into it.

He stared for a long minute, until Bart became alarmed and grabbed him by the shoulder.

'Harry!' he said. 'My God, man, you're the colour of putty. Are you sick?'

Harry Langham looked at him without seeing him.

'Bart,' he said, 'Bart—I saw a face in that mirror.'

'Of course you did. Your own.'

'No. I saw the face of that girl, Yvette Dulaine, who lies beneath St. Martin's Church in Paris. She was holding a candle, and looking out at me, and she tried to speak to me. I could read her lips. She said, "Sauvez-moi!" Save me!'

'What in God's name has happened to Harry Langham?' Bart Phillips demanded, and ran his fingers through bristling red hair. 'He's missed his classes two days in a row. Mrs. Graham, is he sick?'

The middle-aged woman, who might have stepped from one of the stiff portraits on the walls of the rundown Beacon Street house, compressed her lips.

'I don't know what has happened to him, Professor Phillips,' she said. 'He hasn't been himself for a week, not since he received word that mirror was due to be landed. Then since they delivered it two days ago he has not left his room. He makes me leave his meals outside the door. I have always considered Professor Langham a very fine lodger, but if this goes on—Well!'

She uttered the final exclamation to Bart Phillips's back as he took the broad, curving stairs of the once elegant house two at a time.

At the top, Bart hesitated outside Harry's door. Some dirty dishes sat on the floor just beside it. He tested the knob, found the door unlocked, and quietly pushed it open.

In the centre of the big, old-fashioned room, Harry was on his knees before the oval pier glass, laboriously scraping away at the black paint which covered its surface. From time to time he paused to wet a rag in turpentine, rub down the surface he had scraped, and then begin again.

The younger man walked quietly up behind him. The glass, he saw, was now nearly free of obscuring paint. It shone with an unusual clarity, giving the effect of a great depth. Then Harry saw his reflection and leaped up.

'Bart!' he shouted. 'What are you doing here? Why have you broken into my room?'

'Easy, boy, easy,' Bart said, putting a hand on his shoulder. 'What's the matter, are you in training for a nervous breakdown? I've been coming in your room without knocking for years.'

'Yes—yes, of course.'

Harry Langham rubbed his forehead wearily. 'Sorry, Bart, I'm edgy. Not enough sleep, I guess.'

Bart looked at the flecks of paint on the floor, and rapped the mirror with his knuckle. Harry started to protest, and subsided.

'At a guess,' Bart said, 'you have been working on this old look-ing-glass since it got here. Now honestly, Harry, aren't you being—well, illogical? I mean, you think you saw a girl's face mysteriously looking out at you from this mirror, back in London. You've been on pins and needles ever since waiting for it to arrive—you've hardly been over to see us, and I must say that Sis is hurt, since she kind of got the idea you planned to propose. Tell me the truth—are you expecting that girl is going to appear in this mirror again ? Is that what you've had all along in the back of your mind ?'

'I don't know.' Harry dropped into a chair and stared at himself in the mirror. 'I tell you, Bart—I just don't know. I feel I *have* to get this mirror clean again. Then—well, I don't know what. But I have to get it clean.'

'In other words, a neurotic compulsion,' Bart told him. 'Under an old church in Paris you saw a wax figure. Later your imagina-tion played a trick on you—'

'It wasn't imagination!' Harry Langham leaped to his feet with a fury that astonished them both. 'I saw her. I tell you I saw her!'

He stopped, breathing harshly. His friend had fallen back a step in surprise.

'I—I'm sorry, Bart. Look, maybe I am being — unreasonable. Just let me get this mirror cleaned, and some sleep, and I'll be myself. And I'll come to dinner tomorrow night with you and Laura. How's that?'

'Well—all right,' Bart said. 'And you'll go to your classes Monday? I officially announced you had a virus, but I can't cover for you any more.'

'I'll be at my classes. And thanks, Bart.'

When Bart had left, Harry dropped into the chair again and stared at the gleaming mirror. It seemed to shine with a light which was not reflection, yet he could discover no source for it.

'Yvette!' he said. 'Yvette? Are you there? If you are—show yourself.'

He knew he was acting ridiculously. Yet he did not care. He wanted to see her face again—the face he had seen in a tomb in Paris, the face he had seen in a bit of mirror in London, the face he saw in his dreams now.

Nothing happened. After a long moment, he got to work again with scraper, turpentine and steel wool.

The paint stuck doggedly. Twilight had dimmed the room to semi-darkness by the time the glass finally showed no trace of black remaining.

Exhausted, Harry sank back into his chair and stared at it. It was curious how brilliant a reflection it gave. Even in the twilight it showed every detail of his room. His studio couch, his bookshelves, his pictures, his hi-fi set—they seemed three dimensional.

He sighed with fatigue and his vision blurred. The reflection in the mirror clouded like wind-rippled water. He rubbed his eyes and once again the image was clear. The handsome black-and-white striped wallpaper, the crystal chandelier for candles, the old rosewood harpsichord, the enormous Oriental rug on the floor, the hunting-scene tapestry on one wall—

Harry Langham sat up abruptly. The room in the mirror was a place he had never seen in his life. It bore no more resemblance to his own room than—than—

And then she entered.

She wore something simple—he had never had an eye for clothes, he only knew it was elegant and expensive and of a style two centuries old. Her black hair was bound up in coiled tiers. She carried a candle, and as she came towards him from one of the doorways that showed in the shadowy sides of the room, she paused to light the candelabra atop the harpsichord. Then she turned towards the man who was watching, his breathing quick and shallow, his pulse hammering. It was she. Yvette Dulaine, whose body lay buried beneath St. Martin's Church.

He thought she was going to step into the room with him. But she stopped as if at an invisible barrier, and gave him a glance of infinite beseechment. Her lips moved. He could hear no sound, but he could read the words.

'Sauvez moi! M'sieu, je vous implore. Sauvez-moi!'

173

'How?' he cried. 'Tell me how—'

She made a gesture of helpless distress. A ripple swept across the mirror and she was gone. Harry Langham sprang to his feet.

'Come back!' he shouted. 'Yvette, come back!'

Behind him the door opened. He turned in a fury, to see Mrs. Graham bearing a tray of food.

'What are you doing?' he shouted at her. 'Why did you break in? You sent her away! You frightened her!'

The woman drew herself up in starchy dignity.

'I am not accustomed to being spoken to that way, Professor Langham,' she said. 'I knocked, and heard you say "Come." I have brought your dinner. I would prefer that you arrange to lodge elsewhere as soon as this month is up.'

She set down the tray and marched like a grenadier out of the room.

Harry passed a hand hopelessly over his forehead. The sight of the food on the tray revolted him. He thrust it away and turned back to the mirror, which now was dull and lifeless in the almost darkened room.

'Yvette,' he whispered. 'Please! Please come back. Tell me how I can help you.'

The mirror did not change. He flung himself into the chair and stared at it as if the very intensity of his willing would make it light again, would reveal the strange and elegant room it had shown before. The room darkened, until he could no longer see the mirror. Then his fingers, gripping the arms of the chair, relaxed. Exhaustion overcame his willpower, and he slept.

It was the booming of a clock that woke him. Or was it a voice, speaking insistently in his ear? Or a sound as of a thousand tinkling chimes intermingled? Or all three? He opened his eyes, and saw before him the mirror, light emanating from it. Once again it showed the strange room. The candles in the crystal chandelier glittered. And an elegantly dressed gentleman, who leaned against the harpsichord and watched, smiled.

'You are awake, m'sieu,' he said, and now Harry heard the words clearly. 'That is good. I have been waiting to speak to you.'

Harry Langham rubbed his eyes, and sat up.

'Who are you?' he asked. 'Where is she? Yvette, I mean.'

'I am Count Lafontaine, at your service.' The man bowed. 'And Mademoiselle Dulaine will be here. She is waiting for you to join us. To save us.'

'Save you?'

'We are both victims of an evil done long ago, before even your great-grandfather was born. The evil of the most evil of living men, Count Alexander Cagliostro. But with your help, that evil can be undone.'

'How?' Harry demanded.

'In a moment I shall tell you. But here comes Mlle Dulaine. Will you not join us?'

Harry rose to his feet, feeling strangely light, disembodied.

'Join you?' he asked. And even as he spoke he was aware that his senses were dulled, his mind sleepy. 'Is it possible?'

'Just step forward.' The Count held out his hand. 'I will assist you.'

Beyond the man, Harry saw the girl come slowly into the room. She came toward him, slowly, on her face a look of infinite appeal.

'Yvette!' he cried. 'Yvette!' He took two steps forward, and felt his hand grasped by the cold, inhuman fingers of the man within the mirror. The pull but assisted his unthinking impulse. For a moment he felt like a swimmer breasting icy water, shoulder deep. Then the sensation was gone and he was within the room in the mirror.

He looked with exultation into the eyes of the girl.

'Yvette!' he said. 'I'm here. I'm here to save you.'

'Alas, m'sieu,' she said. 'Now you too have been trapped. Look.'

He turned. The Count Lafontaine bowed to him, formally.

'A thousand thanks, my young friend,' he said. 'It is half a century since last I left the world of the mirror. I am hungry for the taste of life again—very hungry.'

He kissed the tips of his fingers and flung the kiss to them.

'Adieu, mes enfants,' he said. 'Console each other in my absence.'

He strode confidently forward, and beyond him Harry saw, as through a window, his own room, dimly lit. The Frenchman stepped into the room and approached the chair where Harry had been seated, and now the shadowed figure in the chair, which he had not noticed before, was suddenly clear and vivid.

'That's me!' he gasped. 'Yvette—that's me—asleep in the chair.'

She stood beside him, her coiled dark hair coming to his shoulders, and infinite regret tinged her voice.

'Your body, M'sieu Langham. You are here, in the world of the mirror, this dark dimension which is not life and is not death and yet partakes of both. In your sleep he spoke the words of his spell and evoked your spirit forth from your body without your awareness. Now he will inhabit your body—for an hour, a day, a decade, I do not know.'

'He?' Harry shook his head, fighting the sense of languor and oppression. 'But who is he? He said—'

'He is the Count Alexander Cagliostro, m'sieu. And see—he lives again, in your body.'

As they spoke, the figure that had emerged from the mirror world turned to smile at them with sardonic triumph. Then it settled down upon Harry's sleeping body, blended with it, vanished—and Harry saw himself rise, stretch and yawn and smile.

'Ah, it's good to be alive again, with a young body, a strong body.' It was his voice speaking and in English—his voice subtly accented.

'Now, au revoir. The night is still young.'

'No!' Harry flung himself forward—and was stopped by an impalpable barrier. The glass of the mirror—yet it did not feel like glass. It felt like an icy net which for an instant yielded, then gathered resistance and threw him back. 'You can't!' he cried. 'Come back!'

'But I can,' said Count Cagliostro reasonably, in Harry's own voice. 'And I shall come back when it pleases me. Meanwhile, it is best that none save myself should be able to see you.'

He raised his hand in the air and drew it downward, speaking a dozen words in rolling Latin. And Harry faced only darkness—an empty darkness that stretched beyond him, for an infinitude of time and space.

He lunged into it, and found himself spinning dizzily in a black void where there was neither substance nor direction. There was only a cube of light, from the mirror room, swiftly dwindling into a tiny gleam.

'Come back! You will be lost forever, m'sieu. I pray you, return!'

The words, faint and faraway, steadied his whirling senses. He saw the light, focused his thoughts on the room it represented, on the girl, and once more he stood beside her, with the candles flickering warmly above them and the hungry blackness behind him.

'Mon Dieu, I feared you were gone!' Her voice was unsteady. 'M'sieu, we are alone here together. Even the consolation of death and the sweet sleep of eternity is denied us. At least, let us keep each other company and take what comfort we may from that.'

'Yes, you're right.' Harry passed a trembling hand over his face. 'And maybe we'd better start with you telling me what in God's name has happened to us.'

It did not require many words, Harry thought dully, half stretched out upon a tapestried couch as he listened to the soft tone of Yvette's voice. She had rejected Cagliostro—and with a smile he had promised her that she would have all eternity in which to regret her decision. Then one night in her sleep a strange compulsion had taken her will, and she had gone to his home, admitted herself, and gone up to his empty room—to find him smiling at her from within the mirror. He had spoken—She had left her body behind crumpled on the floor—and she had joined him in the world of the mirror. Then he—his own body many miles away—had left her alone there until the time came for him to take final refuge himself in the world between life and death of which the mirror was a door that he had opened.

'But he died in 1795 in prison,' Harry protested.

'No, m'sieu. They but said he had died. His body is buried somewhere, as is mine, and like mine, it does not change. His spirit sought refuge here, in this sanctuary he planned long in advance. And from time to time he found means to escape, as he has now, in your body. Over the years, the crimes committed by various hands, yet all animated by the spirit of Cagliostro, would fill a library of horrors. One has heard of the Marquis de Sade. Yet the Marquis was but a man interested in things magical—until he encountered the mirror and met the gaze of Cagliostro. Then, m'sieu, the name of de Sade became synonymous with evil.

'Later, given but little choice, he assumed the flesh of a drunken servant who had entrée only to the lowest of London's dives. It was then he acquired a nickname which you will know. Jacques.'

'Jacques?'

'Jacques, the Ripper. Never was he caught, this Jacques. He froze to death in a gutter one winter night—but only after the spirit of Cagliostro had safely quitted his mortal flesh.

'And then young Charles, Duke of Burchester, acquired a desk and the mirror for his studio. And so fell into Cagliostro's power. But the evil Count was too greedy. The first night he killed a girl almost in public and must flee back to this, his place of safety. Charles, himself again, tried to break the mirror. When he could not, when the men of the police came for him, he covered the mirror with black paint, and then he threw himself from his window and was dashed to death on the stones below.

'Now, m'sieu—' her gaze was compassionate—'he is free again in your body. And the hunger is strong within him. I would speak words of consolation, but unfortunately I cannot.'

'But what is he doing?' Harry started to his feet. 'My God, Yvette, isn't there any way to know what he is up to and to stop him?'

'It is possible to know what he is doing,' she said at last, 'for the spirit still is connected with the body, though but faintly. But he cannot be stopped. He is the master, we are his prisoners. And it is not wise to know what your body does at his orders.'

'I must know, I have to know!' Harry declared feverishly.

'Then lie back, stare at the burning candles, and let your mind empty itself. . . .'

He was in a bar somewhere. A crowded, noisy, smoky dive. Impression of laughter, of voices. Of a face looking up into his. A hungry face, over-painted, yet still with some youthful sweetness in it not quite destroyed. They were moving. They were outdoors. They were strolling down a narrow street toward the waterfront, and light and sound here left behind.

The girl was petulant. She did not want to go. But he laughed, and with a hand on her elbow, urged her onward. They came to a railing, with the dark water swirling below, and a mist curling around them.

'No, I'll show you what I promised you,' he was saying. 'But first we must remove these.'

He deftly removed from her ears the cheap, dangling crystal earrings, dropped them into his pocket.

'Why did you do that?' Her voice was shrill, angry. 'You can't treat me like that.'

'Your beauty should be unadorned. Look into my eyes.'

She looked and her gaze grew fixed. In his eyes she saw the black void of eternity, and rising from it the grinning skull-face of Death. She did not struggle, did not scream as his hungry fingers closed around her throat. Only when it was too late did she fight, so deliciously, so rewardingly. When he dropped her over into the rolling waters below and saw them suck her down with hungry swiftness, he felt again deliciously warm and full. . . .

'M'sieu! M'sieu!'

He opened his eyes. Yvette was shaking him, her face concerned.

'M'sieu, you looked so distressed! I told you it was not wise—'

'I'm a murderer,' Harry groaned. 'I killed her—killed that girl for the sheer lust of killing. . . .'

'Comfort yourself, m'sieu. You did not. It was he, Cagliostro, slaking his hunger for life. It is thus his spirit feeds, grows strong—on the life of those he sacrifices.'

'But it was my hands that choked her—Oh, my God, what are we going to do?'

He stood up, his hands clenched. 'Can't we do *anything* ?'

'Nothing, alas. He lives—in your body. We are shadows of the spirit trapped between life and death. Someday he will return and you will once more regain your body—'

'To be accused of all the infamous crimes he committed!' Harry cried. 'To pay for them. But first, I'll break this mirror. That's one thing I won't fail to do.'

Her gaze was wistful.

'If only that could be. Then I could at last die and be at rest. But you will not do what you think. Others have tried and failed. This mirror cannot be broken by human hand—only he himself, Cagliostro, can break it. No—do not ask. I cannot answer how or why these things are. He has the knowledge. I have not. Now, you must distract yourself. Come—let me show you this world.'

He let her take his hand, and numbly followed as she led.

There were doorways to the great room, several of them. She led him through one and he found himself in a small, book-lined library, where alchemical apparatus crowded tables, and a small, white-globed lamp burned with a bright fierceness. A book lay open, revealing mystic symbols. A giant spider squatted upon it and stared at them with glistening pinpoint eyes.

'His library,' Yvette said. 'Once the mirror stood in this room in the world of reality. Everything in the mirror reflected since it was made exists in this dark and fathomless dimension, if only it was reflected long enough; and his arts can call it into being.'

'Like a time exposure being developed,' Harry muttered to himself.

'Pardon?'

'I was just thinking. What lies beyond?'

'There are many rooms and a garden and even a pond. I will show you.'

There were indeed other rooms, but Harry viewed them without interest. There was a garden where fruit trees bloomed, and a pool that reflected the sunlight of a sun not seen for two centuries. But when he would have gone on, through other doors, Yvette held him back.

'No, m'sieu. Beyond there is nothing. Darkness. Emptiness. Where one can become lost and wander until the end of time. And in the darkness there are—creatures.'

She shivered as she spoke the word. But Harry persisted in his exploration. He opened a closed door—and there beyond it did indeed lie abysmal darkness. There were sounds in the darkness . . . flutings and wailings like no sounds he had ever heard before. And something darker than darkness itself drifted past as they watched, accompanied by the sound of a myriad of tiny bells. Swiftly Yvette slammed the door.

'Please, m'sieu,' she panted. 'Promise me. Never go into the darkness. Even Cagliostro knows not what it is or what creatures inhabit it.'

'All right, Yvette,' Harry agreed. 'I promise. Let's go back. Maybe Cagliostro has returned. Maybe he'll be ready to give up my body now.'

They returned through rooms of a dozen different sorts, one of them plainly the cabin of a ship. In the room of the mirror, the candles still burned as they had before, unconsumed and eternal. The wall of blackness which was the mirror remained in place. But even as they entered it, it dissolved, became a window beyond which was Harry's study where Cagliostro sat at a table, eating breakfast and reading a newspaper.

He smiled smugly at them.

'I hope you have become well acquainted, mes enfants. I have waited for your return. M'sieu Langham, this body you have loaned me is a splendid one, so strong, so handsome, so indefatigable. I shall enjoy its use for a long time, I think. This time I make no foolish mistakes. I have begged the most humble pardon of Mrs. Graham, your good landlady, and she has forgiven me. This evening I dine with your friend, Bart, and his sister Laura, with whom I gather you have — what is the word ? — an understanding. I must make amends to them for your behaviour.

'Ah, my good friend, this Boston of yours is a most interesting city. Cold and reserved in appearance, yet it has its undercurrent of wickedness quite as naughty as London or Paris. I enjoyed myself last night. I was rash, perhaps, but fortunately I escaped detection. And now my motto is to be—discretion.'

He rose and tossed down his napkin.

'Now, I shall rest,' he said, and yawned. 'Last night was—fatiguing. Tonight may be the same. Au 'voir.'

He swept his hand downward with a roll of unknown words, and blackness sprang into place.

Wretchedly, Harry turned to the girl.

'How long were we?' he asked. 'A dozen hours have passed since last night, but it seemed like only a few minutes—half an hour, perhaps.'

'There is no time here,' Yvette told him. 'An hour may seem a day, a day an hour. You will become used to it, M'sieu Harry. Compose yourself—think not of Cagliostro.'

She seated herself at the harpsichord and begun to play a light, tinkling tune to which she sang in a sweet soprano. Harry flung himself down on the tapestried couch and listened. Gradually he relaxed. His mind ceased to throb and burn with turbulent thoughts. But as it did, other images, other sounds and sensations entered it.

Voices. Bart and Laura. Laughter. Wine.

'It's good to see you acting normal again, Harry. You had us worried.'

'I don't wonder, old man. That mirror delusion—you brought me to my senses. Guess I worked too hard in Paris.'

'Then there wasn't any girl in the mirror?' Laura's voice. Laura's smile. Laura's hand lightly on his arm as her eyes begged for assurance.

'If there was, she looked like me and needed a shave.' Laughter. 'Besides, what good would a girl in a mirror be?' More laughter. 'You'll see for yourself. When we set up house-keeping.'

'Goodness. Is that a proposal? Or a proposition?' Wide, hopeful eyes, lips that hide a trembling eagerness.

'Look, you two—while you debate the question, I have to see a graduate student of mine who's working on an interesting line of experiment.' Bart, rising, leaving. 'I won't be back until late.'

'Tactful Bart.'

'A nice brother. I like him. Harry—'

'Yes?'

'Whether it was a proposal or a proposition, it's a little sudden. Since you got back from Europe, I've hardly seen you. Why, I think you've kissed me once.'

'An oversight I plead guilty to. I can only say I'm prepared to make amends. Like this.'

Warm lips. Tremulous response becoming breathtless excitement.

'Harry! What *kind* of overwork did you do in Paris? What research were you engaged in, anyway?'

'Can not we go elsewhere ? . . . This is better. My dear . . .'

Breathless excitement becoming recklessness.

'Harry! You mustn't!'

'Oh, yes, my dear I must.'

'And I thought you were so prim and proper—even though I liked you.'

'And I thought you the same. How wrong we can be about people! Now. . . .'

'Stop!' Harry leaped to his feet, pressing his fists to his forehead, shutting out the damnable sensations from his distant body.

'M'sieu Harry.' Yvette rose and came to him. Gently she touched his forehead. 'It is Cagliostro again. You must not try to know what it is he does.'

'I can't help it.' Harry groaned. 'My God, I never thought that Laura—'

'Do not speak of it. Shall I read to you? Shall we walk in the garden?'

'No, no . . . Yvette.'

'Yes?'

'Cagliostro controls whether or not we can see the world outside the mirror—and whether it can see us.'

'That is true. He has charms that control it. If he speaks but the words, we can see and be seen but not heard. Or hear, but not be seen. And the greatest charm, that of drawing the spirit from the body and transporting it within the mirror. Alas, m'sieu, I crave your pardon.'

'For what?'

'It was I—I who enticed you here. I could not help myself. Cagliostro worked magic that brought you to that shop in London where the mirror lay—he had waited long for the right moment. It was he who enabled you to see me. It was his doing that you determined you must own the mirror, must see me.'

'I did feel—possessed,' Harry admitted. 'But don't blame yourself, Yvette. Even without Cagliostro you would have attracted me.'

'You are gallant. I thank you.'

'But what I started to say, if Cagliostro has charms, we can learn. We are not entirely helpless.'

'Learn them? It is true, his books, his philtres, his mystic objects are within his study—'

But in the study, where the white-globed lamp burned with an undying brilliance, Harry groaned and pushed away the strange books, the ancient parchments, after he had leafed through them.

'I can't read them. They're not Latin. Maybe Sanskrit. Maybe Sumerian. Maybe some language that died before history began.'

'It is true,' the girl told him, 'Cagliostro has said that his magic is older than history, that it comes from a race so ancient no trace is left.'

'And I don't believe in magic. That's one trouble. I belong to the twentieth century. Even here—even a victim of it—I still can't believe in magic!'

'Oui,' Yvette agreed, 'belief is necessary. Without belief, the magic does not work. But then one must have faith in God, as well as in evil, m'sieu.'

'Yes, of course!' His eyes lighted. 'And what is magic to one age is mere science to another. So why shouldn't science to one age be magic to another? Yvette, help me work this out.'

'Anything I can do, anything,' she said. 'Sometimes Cagliostro had me help him. He said that in things mystic the female principal helps. Wait.'

She took pins from her hair, let her tresses tumble down over her shoulder. From a drawer beneath the bookselves she withdrew an odious object—the dried and shrunken head of a man who once had had flaming red hair and a red beard. She sat facing him, the head upon her lap.

'Now, m'sieu,' she said. 'This head—Cagliostro swore it was the head of one of the thieves crucified with the true Christ. Perhaps. But now I look like a sorceress. I will sit in silence, and you shall study.'

'Good girl!' He plunged anew into an effort to make sense of the books, the cabbalistic symbols. In his mind he thought of them as simply equations which produced certain results. So categorized, he was able to believe in them. After all, this mirror world—was it so much more than a photograph caught on celluloid, or a motion picture electronically impressed upon magnetic tape? Perhaps the people in pictures felt and thought!

And wasn't it Asimov, right here in Boston, who had said that some day the entire personality of a man could be put on tape, to remain forever, to be reproduced again whenever and as often as desired? What would existence inside a magnetized tape be? What thoughts would the man there think?

Perhaps his analogies were faulty, but they helped give him confidence. Yvette sat in silence as he worked, with feverish imtensity. He deciphered a word, a sentence, for Cagliostro had translated into a doggerel of Italian, French and Latin the older, unknown language—which might, after all, be the scientific language of a long dead race.

As Yvette had said, there was no time in this place. At intervals he paused and put his fingers to throbbing temples. Then he was aware of sensations from the world of life. His classrooms. Students listening with rapt intensity they had never paid before. Himself speaking with brilliant detail of life in London, in Paris, in the eighteenth century. A girl in the back row, blonde, with a face as soft as a camelia. A girl who paused after class at his request.

'Miss Lee, you are very silent. Yet I think you are hiding a genuine intelligence. Are you afraid of me?'

'Afraid of you? Oh professor, I couldn't ever be that.'

'You need confidence. You need—awareness. I would like to talk to you about yourself. Tonight?'

'Why—why, yes, professor.'

. . . Night. His car. Driving. Lights. Stopping.

'Professor. What—what are you doing?'

'Look into my eyes, child. You are not afraid of me?'

'I—I—no, I trust you. I trust you forever and always.'

'That is good. Now come.'

He forced his thoughts back to the books before him. He translated, worked out probable sequences, guessed where he had to. Still the awareness crept into his mind whenever he relaxed.

'Harry—I haven't seen you for so long.'

'Working on my new thesis, Laura. That fraud Cagliostro—I've torn him up. The new one is to be a comparison of social life in London and Paris in the eighteenth century.'

'It sounds quite exciting.'

'It will be masterly. But I must make up for my neglect. My darling—'

'Harry! But—'

'No buts. Did you know that among the Romans—'

Doggedly he resumed work. But the outside impressions pressed in more strongly.

An alley. Blare of music. A girl, provocative in a red dress. She smiled into his eyes. . . . And lay cold, moments later, in a shadowed corner. . . . Another girl. Walking home from a bus. A scream. A struggle, sweet in its intensity. . . .

'No,' he groaned. 'No, Yvette! The things he is doing! The things *I* am doing! Even if I conquer him—I can't live. Not with what I have done.'

'Poor M'sieu Harry,' she said. 'But can you conquer him? Suppose you force him to return here and give back your body, what then? This mirror—it too is under a spell. It can be broken only by Cagliostro.'

'Maybe,' Harry said grimly. 'But it hasn't been tested in an atomic explosion. In any case I'm pretty sure that, bathed in hydrofluoric acid, it would dissolve. Or dropped into molten glass it too would melt.'

'But then—' Horror touched her features. 'But then I would be lost forever in the darkness that lies outside, lost among the beings whose nature I know not. Only if the glass is broken is the spell broken. Only then can spirit and body reunite and blessedly find eternal sleep together.'

'I see. But Cagliostro must be removed from the world. If the mirror were dropped into the ocean where it is a mile deep. . . .'

She shuddered. But nodded.

'He must be removed, oui,' she said. 'What happens to me—it is not important. Continue, m'sieu.'

'I think I'm on the track.' He pronounced some words, crudely. "Does that sound familiar?"

'Yes!' her face lighted. 'It is what he speaks when he wishes to hear but not be seen. But it sounds like this—' She corrected his pronunciation. He repeated after her, the strange, rolling syllables.

'And this?' He spoke again, making a motion with his hand.

'When he wishes to see and be seen. Like this.' She corrected once more. 'And his hands—I'm not sure—there is a certain movement . . .'

He tried, but did no better. Then he stiffened. They heard voices. Real voices. For the first time.

'Yvette!' he whispered. 'We've won the first round. We can hear. Come, the other room. He is there, speaking to someone.'

They moved swiftly back to the great room where one wall of seething darkness represented the mirror. And words came through it.

'Professor Langham?'

'Associate Professor only, I'm afraid.'

'I'm Sergeant Burke, Homicide.'

'So Mrs Graham said. Homicide. Intriguing. What can I do for you, Sergeant?'

'Where were you at three this morning?'

'Here in my room. Working on my thesis. May I ask why you are interested?'

'A girl was strangled outside the Fishnet Bar last night.'

'I don't believe I've heard of the place.'

'One of your students was there. He believes he saw you with the girl who was killed.'

'I am a very ordinary type, Sergeant. And one of my students—in a bar at three in the morning? No wonder they learn so little—academically speaking, of course.'

'He described you pretty closely.'

'Perhaps because he has seen me in class for weeks. Let me assure you, Sergeant, based on their classwork, the powers of recognition and description of my students are limited.'

'Maybe so. Do you know a girl named Elsie Lou Lee?'

'Of course. One of my students. A shy thing.'

'She committed suicide last night. Cut her throat with a razor blade. Her last words were, "He said he wished I was dead and out of the way, so I'm going to die!"'

'A suggestible type, may I remark?'

'Her landlady describes you as the man who sometimes called for her.'

'Believe me, Sergeant, my description would fit twenty thousand men in Boston. I assure you I am too discreet to—fraternize—with a female student.'

'Yeah, I suppose so. But frankly—well, we've had eight women killed in this city in four months. Eight! All young, all without motive. I have to check out everybody.'

'Quite understandable.'

'So—I haven't any warrant—but if you'd be willing to come down and make a statement at Headquarters. . . .'

'With the greatest of pleasure. Let us go.'

Footsteps. A door closing. Silence.

'If only we'd had the rest of the charm,' Harry groaned. 'So that the Sergeant could have seen us! Then we'd have had him for sure.'

'He would have returned to the mirror,' Yvette said sadly. 'It is you who would have paid.'

'Even so—Let's keep trying. Tell me again what he said and how he moved his hands.'

Repetition. Endless. Timeless. Then abruptly the curtain of black vanished and they saw, through the window of the mirror, into his room. In time to see the door open and Laura enter.

She looked distraught and haggard. She advanced swiftly, calling in case Harry might be in the bedroom.

'Harry! Harry, are you here? I must talk to you!'

'Laura!' Harry cried. 'Here. Here!'

She did not turn. She crossed the room, looked into the bedroom, then came and sat back on the studio couch, nervously pulling off her gloves.

'She does not hear,' Yvette said. 'There yet remains some part of the charm incorrect.'

'Laura!' Harry groaned. 'Please, for God's sake, look this way!'

She did not immediately look toward the mirror. But as she sat, nervously playing with her gloves, her gaze swept the room—and finally stopped upon the mirror. And then she saw them.

Slowly, unbelievingly, she rose to her feet and approached them. 'Harry?' she whispered. 'Harry?'

'Yes,' he said, then realized she could not hear. He nodded instead. 'Call the police!' He mouthed the words carefully but she stared at him with numb incomprehension. He turned to Yvette. 'Quickly!' he said. 'Paper and pen!'

Yvette ran. But before she returned, Harry saw himself enter the room. Cagliostro, as himself. And Laura, turning, stared from the man in the doorway to the image in the mirror with mounting disbelief and horror.

'Ah,' said Cagliostro, approaching her. 'Our friends have learned some tricks. I underestimated M'sieu Langham. Now you know.'

'Know what?' Laura asked huskily. 'Harry, I don't understand.'

'You will, my dear. Alas. My plans were so well made. Marriage, a long and honourable career on the faculty. Unlimited opportunities to indulge my little hobby unsuspected—all professors seem so harmless. Now it must end. But perhaps there is still a chance—'

'Laura, look out!' Harry shouted, futilely, Cagliostro approached her—and then his hands were around her throat, throwing her back across the bed, controlling her struggles until she lay still. Breathing hard, he rose. He looked into the mirror.

'Blame yourself, M'sieu Langham,' he said. 'But then, I was growing tired of her. A possessive type. If I can but get her to the river, it is possible I may yet bluff your stupid police into believing in my innocence.'

He turned and was drawing a blanket over Laura when the door burst open and Bart exploded into the room.

'Harry!' he shouted. 'Where's Laura? Mrs. Graham said she came up here. My God, man, don't you know you were seen with that Lee girl only last night before she—'

Abruptly he was silent, staring at the still figure only half concealed.

'Laura fainted, Bart,' Cagliostro said soothingly. 'If you will go for a doctor—'

'Murderer!' The words were a strangled sob as Bart flung himself at the other man. Cagliostro stepped aside and Bart sprawled on the bed atop his sister's body. Before he recovered, Cagliostro held a needle-sharp paperknife he had snatched from the desk.

'My young friend,' he said suavely, 'usually I kill only women. But in your case I will make an exception.'

With the litheness of a fencer he came forward, the point extended. But he was unacquainted with the game called football. The younger man lunged low, caught him around the knees, and flung him backwards. His body stopped only because it came into contact with the face of the mirror. And a myriad of cracks streaked the glass to its every corner.

'The glass!' Yvette said in fervent joy, as she and Harry saw Cagliostro crumple forward, with the paperknife still in his hand. 'Cagliostro himself has broken it!'

Bart Phillips saw the cracked glass, and for just an instant he was aware of the two figures within the glass, figures already twisting and distorting as the glass came loose. A shower of a thousand sharp fragments fell across the prone man on the floor. In one fragment, Bart saw a single eye staring out at him. In another, a pair of lips murmured, 'Merci.'

Then the reflections were gone and the man on the floor groaned and with difficulty rolled over.

The paperknife emerged from his ribcase beside the heart, and dark blood stained his shirt and coat.

'Harry!' Bart dropped to his knee. 'Harry, *why, why?*'

'I am not your doltish friend Harry, m'sieu,' the dying man said. 'He is lost in some strange dimension where there is neither light, nor time, nor space.' His English now was accented. His features flowed, firmed. They became hook-nosed, sharp-jawed, the features of a man of middle age who has seen far too much of life.

'I am Count Alexander Cagliostro.' The words came with difficulty and were punctuated with blood issuing from the mouth. 'And I go now, his body mine, to meet the death which has awaited me patiently for almost two hundred years.'

He fell back, limp, and in a space of seconds his skin became a loathsome corruption, his hair powdered, and the white bone showed through. The corruption became horror, the horror dried, became dust, and the very bones beneath it melted like wax, falling in upon themselves. A moment later and there were but fragments mixed with dust.

Sax Rohmer

THE MYSTERIOUS MUMMY

[I]

It was about five o'clock on a hot August afternoon, that a tall,
thin man, wearing a weedy beard, and made conspicuous by
an ill-fitting frock-coat and an almost napless silk hat, walked

into the entrance hall of the Great Portland Square Museum. He carried no stick, and, looking about him, as though unfamiliar with the building, he ultimately mounted the principal staircase, walking with a pronounced stoop, and at intervals coughing with a hollow sound.

His gaunt figure attracted the attention of several people, among them the attendant in the Egyptian room. Hardened though he was to the eccentric in humanity, the man who hung so eagerly over the mummies of departed kings, and coughed so frequently, nevertheless secured his instant attention. Visitors of the regulation type were rapidly thinning out, so that the gaunt man, during the whole of the time he remained in the room, was kept under close surveillance by the vigilant official. Seeing him go in the direction of the stairs the attendant supposed the strange visitor to be about to leave the museum. But that he did not immediately do so was shown by subsequent testimony.

The day's business being concluded, the staff of police who patrol nightly the Great Portland Square Museum duly filed into the building. A man is placed in each room, it being his duty to thoroughly examine every nook and cranny: having done which, all doors of communication are closed, the officer on guard in one room being unable to leave his post or to enter another. Every hour the inspector, a sergeant, and a fireman make a round of the entire building; from which it will be seen that a person having designs on any of the numerous treasures of the place would require more than average ingenuity to bring his plans to a successful issue.

In recording this very singular case, the only incident of the night to demand attention is that of the mummy in the Etruscan room.

Persons familiar with the Great Portland Square Museum will know that certain of the tombs in the Etruscan room are used as receptacles for Egyptian mummies that have, for various reasons, never been put upon exhibition. Anyone who has peered under the partially raised lid of a huge sarcophagus and found within the rigid form of a mummy, will appreciate the feelings of the man on night duty amid surroundings so lugubrious. The electric light, it should be mentioned, is not extinguished until the various apartments have been examined, and its extinction immediately precedes the locking of the door.

The constable in the Etruscan room glanced into the various sarcophagi and cast the rays of his bull's-eye lantern into the shadows of the great stone tombs. Satisfied that no one lurked there, he mounted the steps leading up to the Roman gallery, turning out the lights in the room below from the switch at the top. The light was still burning on the ground floor, and the sergeant had not yet arrived with the keys. It was whilst the man stood awaiting his coming that a singular thing occurred.

From somewhere within the darkened chamber beneath, there came the sound of a hollow cough!

By no means deficient in courage, the constable went down the steps in three bounds, his lantern throwing discs of light on stately statues and gloomy tombs. The sound was not repeated and having nothing to guide him to its source, he commenced a second methodical search of the sarcophagi, as offering the most likely hiding-places. When all save one had been examined, the constable began to believe that the coughing had existed only in his imagination. It was upon casting the rays of his bull's-eye into the last sarcophagus that he experienced a sudden sensation of fear. It was empty; yet he distinctly remembered from his previous examination, that a mummy had lain there!

At the moment of making this weird discovery, he realised that he would have done better, before commencing his search for the man with the cough, to first turn on the light: for it must be remembered that he had extinguished the electric lamps. Determined to do so before pursuing his investigations further, he ran up the steps – to find the Roman gallery in darkness. The bright disc of a lantern was approaching from the upper end, and the man ran forward.

'Who turned off the lights here?' came the voice of the sergeant.

'That's what I want to know! Somebody did it while I was downstairs!' said the constable, and gave a hurried account of the mysterious coughing and of the missing mummy.

'How long has there been a mummy in this tomb?' asked the sergeant.

'There was one there a month back, but they took it

upstairs. They may have brought it down again last week, though, or it may have been a fresh one. You see, the other lot were on duty up to last night.'

This was quite true, as the sergeant was aware. Three bodies of picked men share the night duties at the Great Portland Square Museum, and those on duty upon this particular occasion had not been in the place during the previous two weeks.

'Very strange!' muttered the sergeant; and a moment later his whistle was sounding.

From all over the building men came running, for none of the doors had yet been locked.

'There seems to be someone concealed in the museum: search all the rooms again!' was the brief order.

The constables disappeared, and the sergeant, accompanied by the inspector, went down to examine the Etruscan room. Nothing was found there; nor were any of the other searchers more successful. There was no trace anywhere of a man in hiding. Beyond leaving open the door between the Roman gallery and the steps of the Etruscan room, no more could be done in the matter. The gallery communicates with the entrance hall, where the inspector, together with the sergeant and fireman, spends the night, and the idea of the former was to keep in touch with the scene of these singular happenings. His action was perfectly natural; but these precautions were subsequently proved to be absolutely useless.

The night passed without any disturbing event, and the mystery of the vanishing mummy and the ghostly cough seemed likely to remain a mystery. The night police filed out in the early morning, and the inspector, with the sergeant, returned, as soon as possible, to the museum, to make further inquiries concerning the missing occupant of the sarcophagus.

'A mummy in the end tomb!' exclaimed the curator of Etruscan antiquities: 'my dear sir, there has been no mummy there for nearly a month!'

'But my man states that he saw one there last night!' declared the inspector.

The curator looked puzzled. Turning to an attendant, he said: 'Who was in charge of the Etruscan room immediately before six last night?'

'I was, sir!'

'Were there any visitors?'

'No one came in between five-forty and six.'

'And before that?'

'I was away at tea, sir!'

'Who was in charge then?'

'Mr Robins.'

'Call Robins.'

The commissionaire in question arrived.

'How long were you in the Etruscan room last night?'

'About half an hour, sir.'

'Are you sure that no one concealed himself?'

The man looked startled. 'Well, sir,' he said hesitatingly. 'I'm sorry I didn't report it before; but when Mr Barton called me at about twenty-five minutes to six there *was* someone there, a gent in a seedy frock-coat and a high hat, and I don't remember seeing him come out.'

'Did you search the room?'

'Yes, sir; but there was no one to be seen!'

'You should have reported the matter at once. I must see Barton.'

Barton, the head attendant, remembered speaking to Robins at the top of the steps leading to the Etruscan room. He saw no one come out, but it was just possible for a person to have done so and yet be seen by neither himself nor Robins.

'Let three of you thoroughly overhaul the room for any sign of a man having hidden there,' directed the curator briskly.

He turned to the sergeant and inspector with a smile. 'I rather fancy it will prove to be a mare's nest!' he said. 'We have had these mysteries before.'

The words had but just left his lips when a museum official, a well-known antiquarian expert, ran up in a perfect frenzy of excitement. 'Good heavens, Peters!' he gasped. 'The Rienzi Vase has gone!'

'*What!*' came an incredulous chorus.

'The circular top of the case has been completely cut out and ingeniously replaced, and a plausible imitation of the vase substituted!'

They waited for no more, but hurried upstairs to the Vase room, which, in the Great Portland Square Museum, is really only a part of the Egyptian room. The Rienzi Vase, though no larger than an ordinary breakfast cup, all the world knows to be of fabulous value. It seemed inconceivable that anyone could have stolen it. Yet there, in the midst of a knot of excited officials, stood the empty case, whilst the imitation antique was being passed from hand to hand.

Never before nor since has such a scene been witnessed in the museum. The staff, to a man, had lost their wits. What is to be done? was the general inquiry. In less than half an hour the doors would have to be opened to the public, and the absence of the famous vase would inevitably be noticed. It was at this juncture, and whilst everybody was speaking at once, that one of the party, standing close to a wall-cabinet, suddenly held up a warning finger. 'Hush!' he said: 'listen!'

A sudden silence fell upon the room so that people running about in other apartments could be plainly heard. And presently, from somewhere behind the glass doors surrounding the place, came a low moan, electrifying the already excited listeners. The keys were promptly forthcoming, and then was made the second astounding discovery of the eventful morning.

A man, gagged and bound, was imprisoned behind a great mummy case!

Eager hands set to work to release him, and restoratives were applied, as he seemed to be in a very weak condition. He was but partially dressed, and breathed heavily through his nose, like a man in a drunken slumber. All waited breathlessly for his return to consciousness: for certainly he, if anyone, should be in a position to furnish some clue to this deep mystery.

On regaining his senses, he had disappointingly little to tell. He was Constable Smith, who had been on night-duty in the Egyptian room. Sometime during the first hour, and not long after the alarm in the basement, he had been mysteriously pinioned as he paraded the apartment. He caught no glimpse of his opponent, who held him from behind in such a manner that he was totally unable to defend himself. Some sweet-smelling drug had been applied to his nostrils, and he remembered no more until regaining partial consciousness in the mummy case! That was the whole of his testimony.

In setting out the particulars of this remarkable affair, a third and final discovery must be noted. The three men who had been directed to examine the Etruscan room brought to light a bundle of old garments, containing an ancient opera-hat, a faded frock-coat, a pair of shiny trousers, and a pair of elastic-sided boots. They were wedged high up at the back of a tall statue, where they had evidently escaped the eyes of all previous searchers.

That constituted the entire data on which investigations had to be based. The Egyptian room was closed indefinitely, 'for repairs'. No further useful evidence could be obtained from anyone. Several witnesses furnished consistent descriptions of the shabby stranger with the hollow cough; but it may here be mentioned that not one of them ever set eyes upon him again. The inspector, the sergeant, and the fireman solemnly swore to having visited the Egyptian room at the end of each hour throughout the night, and to having found the constable on duty as usual! Smith swore, with equal solemnity, that he had been drugged during the first hour and subsequently confined in the mummy case.

The matter was carefully kept out of the papers, although the museum, throughout many following days, positively bristled with detectives. As the second week drew to a close and the Egyptian room still remained locked, well-informed persons began to whisper that a scandal could no longer be avoided. There can be no doubt that, in many quarters, Constable Smith's share in the proceedings was regarded with grave suspicion. It was at this critical juncture, when it seemed inevitable that the loss of the world-famous Rienzi Vase must be made known to an unsympathetic public, that certain high authorities gave out that the vase had been recovered, and that none of the night staff were in any way implicated in its disappearance!

On this announcement being made, several strange theories were mooted. Some stated that the vase had never left the museum! Others averred that it had been pawned to a foreign government!

Whatever the real explanation, and the secret was jealously guarded by the highly placed officials who alone knew the truth, suffice it that the Egyptian room was again thrown open and the Rienzi Vase shown to be reposing in its usual position.

[II]

Now that it again stands in its place for all to see, there can be no objection to my relating how I once held the famous Rienzi Vase in my possession for twelve days. If there be any objection ... I am sorry. You must understand that I am no common thief – no footpad; I am a person of keenly observant character, and my business is to detect vital weaknesses in great institutions and to charge a moderately high fee for my services. Thus I discovered that a certain famous tiara in a French museum was inadequately protected, and accordingly removed it, replacing it by a substitute. The authorities refused me my fee, and all the world knows that my clever forgery was detected by the experts. That brought them to their senses; it is the genuine tiara that reposes in their cabinet now!

In the same way I removed a world-renowned, historical mummy from its resting place in Cairo, and two days later they grew suspicious of my imitation – it was the handiwork of a clever Birmingham artist – and the department was closed. The bulky character of the mummy nearly brought about my downfall, and it was only by abandoning it that I succeeded in leaving Cairo. I am not proud of that case; I was clumsy. But of the case of the Rienzi Vase I have every reason to be highly proud. That you may judge of the neatness and dispatch with which I acted, I will relate how the whole business was conducted.

You must know, then, that the first flaw I discovered in the arrangements at the Great Portland Square Museum was this: The wall-cases were badly guarded. I learnt this interesting fact one afternoon as I strolled about the Egyptian room. A certain gentleman – I will not name him – was showing a party of ladies round the apartment. He had unlocked a wall-case, and was standing with a handsome bead-necklet in his hand, explaining where and when it was found. He was only a few yards away, but with his back towards the case. Enough! The key, with others attached, was in the glass door. You will admit that this was exceedingly careless: but the presence of four charming American ladies ... one can excuse him!

I regret to have to confess that I was somewhat awkward – the keys rattled. The whole party looked in my direction. But the immaculate man-about-town, with his cultivated manner and his very considerable knowledge of Egyptology – how should they suspect? I apologised; I had brushed against them in passing; I made myself agreeable, and the uncomfortable incident was forgotten, by them – not by me. I had a beautiful wax impression to keep my memory fresh!

The scheme formed then. I knew that a body of picked police promenaded the museum at night, and that each of the rooms was usually in charge of the same man. I learnt, later, that there were three bodies of men, so that the same police were in the museum but one week in every three. I made the acquaintance of seven constables and frequented eight different public-houses before I met the man of whom I was in search.

The first policeman I found, who paraded the Egyptian room at night, was short and thickset, and I gave him up as a bad job. I learnt from him, however, who was to occupy the post during the coming week, and presently I unearthed the private bar which this latter officer, his name was Smith, used. Eureka! he was tall and thin. Incidentally, he was also surly. But the winning ways of the jovial master-plumber, who was so free with his money, ultimately thawed him.

Every night throughout the rest of the week I spent in this constable's company, studying his somewhat colourless personality. Then, one afternoon I entered the museum. My weedy beard, my gaunt expression, and my hollow cough – they were all in the part! I went up to the Egyptian room to assure myself that a certain mummy case had not been removed, and having found it to occupy its usual place. I descended to the Etruscan basement.

For half an hour I occupied myself there, but the commissionaire never budged from his seat. I knew that this particular man was only in temporary charge whilst another was at tea, for I was well posted, and wondered if his companion were ever coming back. Luckily, an incident occurred to serve my purpose. The chief attendant appeared at the head of the steps. 'Robins!' he called.

Robins ran briskly upstairs at his command, and then in fifteen seconds my transformation was complete. Gone were the weedy grey beard and moustache – gone the seedy, black garments and the elastic-sided boots – gone the old opera-hat – and, behold I was Constable Smith, attired in mummy wrappings!

An acrobatic spring, and the bundle of aged garments was wedged behind a tall statue, where nothing but a most minute search could reveal it. Down again, not a second to spare! Into the empty sarcophagus at the further end of the room; and, lastly, a hideous rubber mask slipped over the ruddy features of Constable Smith and attached behind the ears, my arms stiffened and my hands concealed in the wrappings, and I was a long-dead mummy – with a neat leather case hidden beneath my arched back!

Brisk work, I assure you: but one grows accustomed to it in time. The commissionaire entered the room very shortly afterwards. He had not seen me go out, but, as I expected, neither was he absolutely sure that I had not done so. He peered about suspiciously, but I did not mind. The real ordeal came a couple of hours later, when a police officer flashed his lantern into all the tombs.

For a moment my heart seemed to cease beating as the light shone on my rubber countenance. But he was satisfied, this stupid policeman, and I heard his footsteps retreating to the door. I allowed him time to get to the top, and extinguish the light in the Etruscan room, and then . . . I was out of my tomb and hidden in the little niche immediately beside the foot of the stairs. I coughed loudly. Heavens! He came back down the steps with such velocity that he was carried halfway along the room. He began to flash his lantern into the tombs again: but, before he had examined the first of them, I was upstairs in the Roman gallery!

Without the electric light it was quite dark in the Etruscan room, which is in the basement: but, being a bright night, I knew I could find what I required in the Roman gallery without the aid of artificial light; besides, I had now to act in the open – someone might arrive too soon. So, thoroughly well posted as to the situation of the switches, I extinguished the lamps, and dodged in among the Roman stonework to the foot of a great pillar, towering almost to the lofty roof and surmounted by an ornate capital.

I had planned all this beforehand, you see; but I must confess it was an awful scramble to the top. I had only just curled up on the summit, the handle of my invaluable leather case held fast in my teeth, when a sergeant came running down the gallery, almost into the arms of the constable who was running up the steps from the Etruscan room.

A moment's hurried conversation, and then the lights turned on and the sound of a whistle. It was foolish, of course; but I had expected it. From all over the building the police arrived, and, fatigued as I was with my climb, yet another acrobatic feat was before me.

The top of my pillar was no great distance from the stone balustrade of the first-floor landing, on which the Egyptian room opens, and a narrow ledge, perhaps of eleven inches, runs all round the wall of the Roman gallery some four feet below the ceiling. I cautiously stepped from the pillar to the ledge – I was invisible from the other end of the place – and, pressing my body close against the wall, reached the balustrade. Before Constable Smith – who had left his post and descended to the lower gallery on hearing the sergeant's whistle – re-entered the Egyptian room, my bright, new key had found the lock of a certain cabinet, and I was secure behind a mummy case – whilst a little steel pin prevented the spring of the lock from shutting me in.

Poor Constable Smith! I was sorry to have to act so; but, ten minutes after the closing of the doors of communication, I came on him from behind, having silently crept from the case as he passed me, and followed him down the darkened room, the thin, linen wrappings that covered my feet making no sound upon the wooden floor. I had a pad ready in my hand, saturated with the contents of a small phial that had reposed in my mummy garments.

I thrust my knee in his spine and seized his hands by a trick which you may learn for a peseta any day in the purlieus of Tangier. A muscular man, he tried hard to cope with his unseen opponent; but the pad never left his mouth and nostrils, and the few muffled cries that escaped him were luckily unheard. He soon became unconscious, and I had to work hard lest the inspector should make his round before I was ready for him. The mummy case had to be lowered on to the floor, and the heavy body tightly bound and lifted into it, then stood up again and securely locked behind the glass doors. It was hot work, and I had but just accomplished the task and climbed into the constable's uniform, when the inspector's key sounded in the door. Ah! it is an exciting profession!

The rest was easy. Wrapped up in my yellow mummy linen were the various appliances I required, and in the leather box was the imitation Rienzi Vase. The circular glass top of the case gave some trouble. So hard and thick was it that I had to desist five times and conceal my tools, owing to the hourly visits of the inspector. Poor Constable Smith began to groan toward six o'clock, and a second dose of medicine was necessary to keep him quiet for another hour or so.

I filed out with the other police in the morning, the Rienzi Vase inside my helmet. As to the sequel, it is brief. Of course the detectives tried their hands at the affair; but, pooh! I am too old a bird to leave 'clues'! It is only amateurs that do that!

My fee, and the conditions to be observed in paying it, I conveyed to the authorities privately. They thought they had a 'clue' though and delayed another week. They actually detained my unhappy agent, a most guileless and upright person, who knew positively nothing. Oh! it was too funny! But, realising that only by the vase being returned to its place could a scandal be avoided, they met me in the matter.

The Hollow Man

by Thomas Burke

He came up one of the narrow streets which lead from the docks, and turned into a road whose farther end was gay with the light of London. At the end of this road he went deep into the lights of London, and sometimes into its shadows, farther and farther away from the river, and did not pause until he reached a poor quarter near the centre.

He was a tall, spare figure, wearing a black macintosh. Below this could be seen brown dungaree trousers. A peaked cap hid most of his face; the little that was exposed was white and sharp. In the autumn mist that filled the lighted streets as well as the dark he seemed a wraith, and some of those who passed him looked again, not sure whether they had indeed seen a living man. One or two of them moved their shoulders, as though shrinking from something.

His legs were long, but he walked with the short, deliberate steps of a blind man, though he was not blind. His eyes were open, and he stared straight ahead; but he seemed to see nothing and hear nothing.

Neither the mournful hooting of sirens across the black

water of the river, nor the genial windows of the shops in the big streets near the centre drew his head to right or left. He walked as though he had no destination in mind, yet constantly, at this corner or that, he turned. It seemed that an unseen hand was guiding him to a given point of whose location he was himself ignorant.

He was searching for a friend of fifteen years ago, and the unseen hand, or some dog-instinct, had led him from Africa to London, and was now leading him, along the last mile of his search, to a certain little eating-house. He did not know that he was going to the eating-house of his friend Nameless, but he did know, from the time he left Africa, that he was journeying towards Nameless, and he now knew that he was very near to Nameless.

Nameless didn't know that his old friend was anywhere near *him*, though, had he observed conditions that evening, he might have wondered why he was sitting up an hour later than usual. He was seated in one of the pews of his prosperous little workmen's dining-rooms – a little gold-mine his wife's relations called it – and he was smoking and looking at nothing.

He had added up the till and written the copies of the bill of fare for next day, and there was nothing to keep him out of bed after his fifteen hours' attention to business. Had he been asked why he was sitting up later than usual, he would first have answered that he didn't know that he was, and would then have explained, in default of any other explanation, that it was for the purpose of having a last pipe. He was quite unaware that he was sitting up and keeping the door unlatched because a long-parted friend from Africa was seeking him and slowly approaching him, and needed his services.

He was quite unaware that he had left the door unlatched at that late hour – half past eleven – to admit pain and woe.

But even as many bells sent dolefully across the night from their steeples their disagreement as to the point of half-past eleven, pain and woe were but two streets away from him. The macintosh and dungarees and the sharp white face were coming nearer every moment.

There was silence in the house and in the streets; a heavy silence, broken, or sometimes stressed, by the occasional night-noises – motor horns, back-firing of lorries, shunting at a distant terminus. That silence seemed to envelop the house, but he did not notice it. He did not notice the bells, and he did not even notice the lagging step that approached his shop, and passed – and returned – and passed again – and halted. He was aware of nothing save that he was smoking a last pipe, and he was sitting in that state of hazy reverie which he called thinking, deaf and blind to anything not in his immediate neighbourhood.

But when a hand was laid on the latch, and the latch was lifted, he did hear that, and he looked up. And he saw the door open, and got up and went to it. And there, just within the door, he came face to face with the thin figure of pain and woe.

To kill a fellow-creature is a frightful thing. At the time the act is committed the murderer may have sound and convincing reasons (to him) for his act. But time and reflection may bring regret; even remorse; and this may live with him for many years. Examined in wakeful hours of the night or early morning, the reasons for the act may shed their cold logic, and may cease to be reasons and become mere excuses.

And these naked excuses may strip the murderer and show him to himself as he is. They begin to hunt his soul, and to run into every little corner of his mind and every little nerve, in search of it.

And if to kill a fellow-creature and to suffer the recurrent regret for an act of heated blood is a frightful thing, it is still more frightful to kill a fellow-creature and bury his body deep in an African jungle, and then, fifteen years later, at about midnight, to see the latch of your door lifted by the hand you had stilled and to see the man, looking much as he did fifteen years ago, walk into your home and claim your hospitality.

When the man in macintosh and dungarees walked into the dining-rooms Nameless stood still; stared; staggered against a table; supported himself by a hand, and said 'Oh!'

The other man said 'Nameless!'

Then they looked at each other; Nameless with head thrust forward, mouth dropped, eyes wide; the visitor with a dull, glazed expression. If Nameless had not been the man he was – thick, bovine and costive – he would have flung up his arms and screamed. At that moment he felt the need of some such outlet, but he did not know how to find it. The only dramatic expression he gave to the situation was to whisper instead of speak.

Twenty emotions came to life in his head and spine, and wrestled there. But they showed themselves only in his staring eyes and his whisper. His first thought, or rather, spasm, was Ghosts-Indigestion-Nervous-Breakdown. His second, when he saw that the figure was substantial and real, was Impersonation. But a slight movement of the part of the visitor dismissed that.

It was a little habitual movement which belonged only to that man; an unconscious twitching of the third finger of the left hand. He knew then that it was Gopak. Gopak, a little changed, but still, miraculously, thirty-two. Gopak, alive, breathing and real. No ghost. No phantom of the stomach. He was as certain of that as he was that fifteen years ago he had killed Gopak stone-dead and buried him.

The Blackness of the moment was lightened by Gopak. In thin, flat tones he asked.'May I sit down? I'm tired.' He sat down, and said: 'So tired. So tired.'

Nameless still held the table. He whispered: 'Gopak . . . Gopak . . . But I – I *killed* you. I killed you in the jungle. You were dead. I know you were.

Gopak passed his hand across his face. He seemed about to cry. 'I know you did. I know. That's all I can remember –

about this earth. You killed me.' The voice became thinner and flatter. 'And I was so comforable. So comfortable. It was – such a rest. Such a rest as you don't know. And then they came and – disturbed me. They woke me up. And brought me back.' He sat with shoulders sagged, arms drooping, hands hanging between his knees. After the first recognition he did not look at Nameless; he looked at the floor.

'Came and disturbed you?' Nameless leaned forward and whispered the words. 'Woke you up? Who?'

'The Leopard Men.'

'The what?'

'The Leopard Men.' The watery voice said it as casually as if it were saying 'the night watchman.'

'The Leopard Men?' Nameless stared, and his fat face crinkled in an effort to take in the situation of a midnight visitation from a dead man, and the dead man talking nonsense. He felt his blood moving out of its course. He looked at his own hand to see if it was his own hand. He looked at the table to see if it was his table. The hand and the table were facts, and if the dead man was a fact – and he was – his story might be a fact! It seemed anyway as sensible as the dead man's presence. He gave a heavy sigh from the stomach. 'A-ah . . . The Leopard Men . . . Yes, I· heard about them out there. Tales!'

Gopak slowly wagged his head. 'Not tales. They're real. If they weren't real – I wouldn't be here. Would I? I'd be at rest.'

Nameless had to admit this. He had heard many tales 'out there' about the Leopard Men, and had dismissed them as jungle yarns. But now, it seemed, jungle yarns had become commonplace fact in a little London shop.

The watery voice went on. 'They do it. I saw them. I came back in the middle of a circle of them. They killed a black man to put his life into me. They wanted a white man – for their farm. So they brought me back. You may not believe it. You wouldn't *want* to believe it. You wouldn't want to – see or know anything like them. And I wouldn't want any man to. But it's true. That's how I'm here.'

'But I left you absolutely dead. I made every test. It was three days before I buried you. And buried you deep.'

'I know. But that wouldn't make any difference to them. It was a long time after when they came and brought me back. And I'm still dead, you know. It's only my body they brought back.' The voice trailed into a thread. 'And I'm so tired. So tired. I want to go back – to rest.'

Sitting in his prosperous eating-house, Nameless was in the presence of an achieved miracle, but the everyday, solid appointments of the eating-house wouldn't let him fully comprehend it. Foolishly, as he realised when he had spoken, he asked Gopak to explain what had happened. Asked a man who couldn't really be alive to explain how he came to be alive. It was like asking Nothing to explain Everything.

Constantly, as he talked, he felt his grasp on his own mind slipping. The surprise of a sudden visitor at a late hour; the shock of the arrival of a long-dead man; and the realisation that this long-dead man was not a wraith, were too much for him.

During the next half-hour he found himself talking to Gopak as to the Gopak he had known seventeen years ago when they were partners. Then he would be halted by the freezing knowledge that he was talking to a dead man, and that a dead man was faintly answering him. He felt that the thing couldn't really have happened, but in the interchange of talk he kept forgetting the improbable side of it, and accepting it. With each recollection of the truth, his mind would clear and settle in one thought – 'I've got to get rid of him. How am I going to get rid of him?'

'But how did you get here?'

'I escaped.' The words came slowly and thinly, and out of the body rather than the mouth.

'How.'

'I don't – know. I don't remember anything – except our quarrel. And being at rest.'

'But why come all the way here? Why didn't you stay on the coast?'

'I don't – know. But you're the only man I know. The only man I can remember.'

'But how did you find me?'

'I don't know. But I had to – find you. You're the only man – who can help me.'

'But how can I help you?'

The head turned weakly from side to side. 'I don't – know. But nobody else – can.'

Nameless stared through the window, looking on to the lamplit street and seeing nothing of it. The everyday being which had been his half an hour ago had been annihilated; the everyday beliefs and disbeliefs shattered and mixed together. But some shred of his old sense and his old standard remained. He must handle this situation. 'Well – what do you want to do? What are you going to do? I don't see how I can help you. And you can't stay here, obviously.' A demon of perversity sent a facetious notion into his head – introducing Gopak to his wife – 'This is my dead friend.'

But on his last spoken remark Gopak made the effort of raising his head and staring with the glazed eyes at Nameless. 'But I *must* stay here. There's nowhere else I can stay. I must stay here. That's why I came. You got to help me.'

'But you can't stay here. I got no room. All occupied. Nowhere for you to sleep.'

The wan voice said: 'That doesn't matter. I *don't* sleep.'

'Eh?'

'I *don't* sleep. I haven't slept since they brought me back. I can sit here – till you can think of some way of helping me.'

'But how *can* I?'

He again forgot the background of the situation, and began to get angry at the vision of a dead man sitting about the place waiting for him to think of something. 'How *can* I if you don't tell me how?'

'I don't – know. But you got to. You killed me. And I was dead – and comfortable. As it all came from you – killing me – you're responsible for me being – like this. So, you got to – help me. That's why I – came to you.'

'But what do you want me to do?'

'I don't – know. I can't – think. But nobody but you can help me. I had to come to you. Something brought me – straight to you. That means that you're the one – that can help me. Now I'm with you, something will – happen to help me. I feel it will. In time you'll – think of something.'

Nameless found his legs suddenly weak. He sat down and stared with a sick scowl at the hideous and the incomprehensible. Here was a dead man in his house – a man he had murdered in a moment of black temper – and he knew in his heart that he couldn't turn the man out. For one thing, he would have been afraid to touch him; he couldn't see himself touching him. For another, faced with the miracle of the presence of a fifteen-years-dead man, he doubted whether physical force or any material agency would be effectual in moving the man.

His soul shivered, as all men's souls shiver at the demonstration of forces outside their mental or spiritual horizon. He had murdered this man, and often, in fifteen years, he had repented the act. If the man's appalling story were true, then he had some sort of right to turn to Nameless. Nameless recognised that, and knew that whatever happened he couldn't turn him out. His hot-tempered sin had literally come home to him.

The wan voice broke into his nightmare. 'You go to rest, Nameless. I'll sit here. You go to rest.' He put his face down to his hands and uttered a little moan. 'Oh, why can't I rest? Why can't I go back to my beautiful rest?'

Nameless came down early next morning with a half-hope that Gopak would not be there. But he was there, seated where Nameless had left him last night. Nameless made some tea, and showed him where he might wash. He washed listlessly, and crawled back to his seat, and listlessly drank the tea which Nameless brought to him.

To his wife and the kitchen helpers Nameless mentioned him as an old friend who had had a bit of a shock. 'Shipwrecked and knocked on the head. But quite harmless, and he won't be staying long. He's waiting for admission to a home. A good pal to me in the past, and it's the least I can do to let him stay here a few days. Suffers from sleeplessness and prefers to sit up at night. Quite harmless.'

But Gopak stayed more than a few days. He outstayed everybody. Even when the customers had gone Gopak was still there.

On the first morning of his visit when the regular customers came in at mid-day, they looked at the odd, white figure sitting vacantly in the first pew, then stared, then moved away.

All avoided the pew in which he sat. Nameless explained him to them, but his explanation did not seem to relieve the slight tension which settled on the dining-room. The atmosphere was not so brisk and chatty as usual. Even those who had their backs to the stranger seemed to be affected by his presence.

At the end of the first day Nameless, noticing this, told him that he had arranged a nice corner of the front room upstairs, where he could sit by the window and took his arm to take him upstairs. But Gopak feebly shook the hand away, and sat where he was. 'No. I don't want to go. I'll stay here. I'll stay here. I don't want to move.'

And he wouldn't move. After a few more pleadings Nameless realised with dismay that his refusal was definite; that it would be futile to press him or force him; that he was going to sit in that dining-room for ever. He was as weak as a child and as firm as a rock.

He continued to sit in that first pew, and the customers continued to avoid it, and to give queer glances at it. It seemed that they half-recognised that he was something more than a fellow who had had a shock.

During the second week of his stay three of the regular customers were missing, and more than one of those that remained made acidly facetious suggestions to Nameless that he park his lively friend somewhere else. He made things too exciting for them; all that whoopee took them off their work, and interfered with digestion. Nameless told them he would be staying only a day or so longer, but they found that this was untrue, and at the end of the second week eight of the regulars had found another place.

Each day, when the dinner-hour came, Nameless tried to get him to take a little walk, but always he refused.

He would go out only at night, and then never more than two hundred yards from the shop. For the rest, he sat in his pew, sometimes dozing in the afternoon, at other times staring at the floor. He took his food abstactedly, and never knew whether he had had food or not. He spoke only when questioned, and the burden of his talk was 'I'm so tired. So tired.'

One thing only seemed to arouse any light of interest in him; one thing only drew his eyes from the floor. That was the seventeen-year-old daughter of his host, who was known as Bubbles, and who helped with the waiting. And Bubbles seemed to be the only member of the shop and its customers who did not shrink from him.

She knew nothing of the truth about him, but she seemed to understand him, and the only response he ever gave to anything was to her childish sympathy. She sat and chatted foolish chatter to him – 'bringing him out of himself' she called it – and sometimes he would be brought out to the extent of a watery smile. He came to recognise her step and would look up before she entered the room. Once or twice in the evening, when the shop was empty, and Nameless was sitting miserably with him, he would ask, without lifting his eyes, 'Where's Bubbles?' and would be told that Bubbles had gone to the pictures or was out at a dance, and would relapse into deeper vacancy.

Nameless didn't like this. He was already visited by a

curse which, in four weeks, had destroyed most of his business. Regular customers had dropped off two by two, and no new customers came to take their place. Strangers who dropped in once for a meal did not come again; they could not keep their eyes or their minds off the forbidding, white-faced figure sitting motionless in the first pew. At mid-day, when the place had been crowded and late-comers had to wait for a seat, it was now two-thirds empty; only a few of the most thick-skinned remained faithful.

And on top of this there was the interest of the dead man in his daughter, an interest which seemed to be having an unpleasant effect. Nameless hadn't noticed it, but his wife had. 'Bubbles don't seem as bright and lively as she was. You noticed it lately? She's getting quiet – and a bit slack. Sits about a lot. Paler than she used to be.'

'Her age, perhaps.'

'No. She's not one of these thin dark sort. No – it's something else. Just the last week or two I've noticed it. Off her food. Sits about doing nothing. No interest. May be nothing; just out of sorts, perhaps ... How much longer's that horrible friend of yours going to stay?'

The horrible friend stayed some weeks longer – ten weeks in all – while Nameless watched his business drop to nothing and his daughter get pale and peevish. He knew the cause of it. There was no home in all England like his: no home that had a dead man sitting in it for ten weeks. A dead man brought, after a long time, from the grave, to sit and disturb his customers and take the vitality from his daughter. He couldn't tell this to anybody. Nobody would believe such nonsense.

But he *knew* that he was entertaining a dead man, and, knowing that a long-dead man was walking the earth, he could believe in any result of that fact. He could believe almost anything that he would have derided ten weeks ago. His customers had abandoned his shop, not because of the presence of a silent, white-faced man, but because of the presence of a dead-living man.

Their minds might not know it, but their blood knew it. And, as his business had been destroyed, so, he believed, would his daughter be destroyed. Her blood was not warming her; her blood told her only that this was a long-ago friend of her father's, and she was drawn to him.

It was at this point that Nameless, having no work to do, began to drink. And it was well that he did so. For out of the drink came an idea, and with that idea he freed himself from the curse upon him and his house.

The shop now served scarcely half a dozen customers at midday. It had become ill-kempt and dusty, and the service and the food were bad. Nameless took no trouble to be civil to his few customers. Often, when he was notably under drink, he went to the trouble of being very rude to them. They talked about this. They talked about the decline of his business and the dustiness of the shop and the bad food. They talked about his drinking, and, of course, exaggerated it.

And they talked about the queer fellow who sat there day after day and gave everybody the creeps. A few outsiders, hearing the gossip, came to the dining-rooms to see the queer fellow and the always-tight proprietor; but they did not come again, and there were not enough of the curious to keep the place busy. It went down until it served scarcely two customers a day. And Nameless went down with it into drink.

Then, one evening, out of the drink he fished an inspiration.

He took it downstairs to Gopak, who was sitting in his usual seat, hands hanging, eyes on the floor. 'Gopak – listen. You came here because I was the only man who could help you in your trouble. You listening?'

A faint 'Yes' was his answer.

'Well, now. You told me I'd got to think of something. I've thought of something. . . . Listen. You say I'm responsible for your condition and got to get you out of it, because I killed you. I did. We had a row. You made me wild. You dared me. And what with that sun and the jungle and the insects, I wasn't meself. I killed you. The moment it was done I could a-cut me hand off. Because you and me were pals. I could a-cut me right hand off.'

'I know. I felt that directly it was over. I knew you were suffering.'

'Ah! . . . I have suffered. And I'm suffering now. Well, this is what I've thought. All your present trouble comes from me killing you in that jungle and burying you. An idea came to me. Do you think it would help you – do you think it would put you back to rest if I – if I – if I – killed you again?'

For some seconds Gopak continued to stare at the floor. Then his shoulders moved. Then, while Nameless watched every little response to his idea, the watery voice began. 'Yes. Yes. That's it. That's what I was waiting for. That's why I came here. I can see now. That's why I had to get here. Nobody else could kill me. Only you. I've got to be killed again. Yes, I see. But nobody else – would be able – to kill me. Only the man who first killed me. . . . Yes, you've found – what we're both – waiting for. Anybody else could shoot me – stab me – hang me – but they couldn't kill me. Only you. That's why I managed to get here and find you.'

The watery voice rose to a thin strength. 'That's it. And you must do it. Do it now. You don't want to, I know. But you must. You *must*.'

His head drooped and he stared at the floor. Nameless, too, stared at the floor. He was seeing things. He had murdered a man and had escaped all punishment save that of his own mind, which had been terrible enough. But now he was going to murder him again – not in a jungle but in a city; and he saw the slow points of the result.

He saw the arrest. He saw the first hearing. He saw the trial. He saw the cell. He saw the rope. He shuddered.

Then he saw the alternative – the breakdown of his life –

a ruined business, poverty, the poorhouse, a daughter robbed of her health and perhaps dying, and always the curse of the dead-living man, who might follow him to the poorhouse. Better to end it all, he thought. Rid himself of the curse which Gopak had brought upon him and his family, and then rid his family of himself with a revolver. Better to follow up his idea.

He got stiffly to his feet. The hour was late evening – half-past ten – and the streets were quiet. He had pulled down the shop-blinds and locked the door. The room was lit by one light at the further end. He moved about uncertainly and looked at Gopak. 'Er – how would you – how shall I – '

Gopak said, 'You did it with a knife. Just under the heart. You must do it that way again.'

Nameless stood and looked at him for some seconds. Then, with an air of resolve, he shook himself. He walked quickly to the kitchen.

Three minutes later his wife and daughter heard a crash, as though a table had been overturned. They called but got no answer. When they came down they found him sitting in one of the pews, wiping sweat from his forehead. He was white and shaking, and appeared to be recovering from a faint.

'Whatever's the matter? You all right?'

He waved them away. 'Yes, I'm all right. Touch of giddiness. Smoking too much, I think.'

'Mmmm. Or drinking. . . . Where's your friend? out for a walk?'

'No. He's gone off. Said he wouldn't impose any longer, had to go and find an infirmary.' He spoke weakly and found trouble in picking words. 'Didn't you hear that bang – when he shut the door?'

'I thought that was you fell down.'

'No. It was him when he went. I couldn't stop him.'

'Mmmm. Just as well, I think.' She looked about her. 'Things seem to a-gone wrong since he's been here.'

There was a general air of dustiness about the place. The

table-cloths were dirty, not from use but from disuse. The windows were dim. A long knife, very dusty, was lying on the table under the window. In a corner by the door leading to the kitchen, unseen by her, lay a dusty mackintosh and dungaree, which appeared to have been tossed there. But it was over by the main door, near the first pew, that the dust was thickest – a long trail of it – greyish-white dust.

'Reely this place gets more and more slapdash. Why can't you attend to business? You didn't use to be like this. No wonder it's gone down, letting the place get into this state. Why don't you pull yourself together. Just *look* at that dust by the door. Looks as though somebody's been spilling ashes all over the place.'

Nameless looked at it, and his hands shook a little. But he answered, more firmly than before: 'Yes, I know. I'll have a proper clean-up to-morrow. I'll put it all to rights to-morrow. I been getting a bit slack.'

For the first time in ten weeks he smiled at them; a thin, haggard smile, but a smile.

The Waxwork

A. M. Burrage

While the uniformed attendants of Marriner's Waxworks were ushering the last stragglers through the great glass-panelled double doors, the manager sat in his office interviewing Raymond Hewson.

The manager was a youngish man, stout, blond and of medium height. He wore his clothes well and contrived to look extremely smart without appearing over-dressed. Raymond Hewson looked neither. His clothes, which had been good when new and which were still carefully brushed and pressed, were beginning to show signs of their owner's losing battle with the world. He was a small, spare, pale man, with lank, errant brown hair, and although he spoke plausibly and even forcibly he had the defensive and somewhat furtive air of a man who was used to rebuffs. He looked what he was, a man gifted somewhat above the ordinary who was a failure through his lack of self-assertion.

The manager was speaking.

"There is nothing new in your request," he said. "In fact we refuse it to different people – mostly young bloods who have tried to make bets – about three times a week. We have nothing to gain and something to lose by letting people spend the night in our Murderers' Den. If I allowed it, and some young idiot lost his senses, what would be my position? But your being a journalist somewhat alters the case."

Hewson smiled.

"I suppose you mean that journalists have no senses to lose."

"No, no," laughed the manager, "but one imagines them to be reasonable people. Besides, here we have something to gain; publicity and advertisement."

"Exactly," said Hewson, "and there I thought we might come to terms."

The manager laughed again.

"Oh," he exclaimed, "I know what's coming. You want to be paid twice, do you? It used to be said years ago that Madame Tussaud's would give a man a hundred pounds for sleeping alone in the Chamber of Horrors. I hope you don't think that we have made any such offer. Er – what is your paper, Mr Hewson?"

"I am freelancing at present," Hewson confessed, "working on space for several papers. However, I should find no difficulty in getting the story printed. The *Morning Echo* would use it like a shot. 'A night with Marriner's Murderers.' No live paper could turn it down."

The manager rubbed his chin.

"Ah! And how do you propose to treat it?"

"I shall make it gruesome, of course; gruesome with just a saving touch of humour."

The other nodded and offered Hewson his cigarette-case.

"Very well, Mr. Hewson," he said. "Get your story printed in the *Morning Echo*, and there will be a five-pound note waiting for you here when you care to come and call for it. But first of all, it's no small ordeal that you're proposing to undertake. I'd like to be quite sure about you, and I'd like you to be quite sure about yourself. I own I shouldn't care to take it on. I've seen those figures dressed and undressed, I know all about the process of their manufacture, I can walk about in company downstairs as unmoved as if I were walking among so many skittles, but I should hate having to sleep down there alone among them."

"Why?" asked Hewson.

"I don't know. There isn't any reason. I don't believe in ghosts. If I did I should expect them to haunt the scene of their crimes or the spot where their bodies were laid, instead of a cellar which happens to contain their waxwork effigies. It's just that I couldn't sit alone among them at night, with their seeming to stare at me the way they do. After all, they represent the lowest and most appalling types of humanity, and – although I would not own it publicly – the people who come to see them are not generally charged with the very highest motives. The whole atmosphere of the place is unpleasant, and if you are susceptible to atmosphere I warn you that you are in for a very uncomfortable night."

Hewson had known that from the moment when the idea had first occurred to him. His soul sickened at the prospect, even while he smiled casually upon the manager. But he had a wife and family to keep, and for the past month he had been living on paragraphs, eked out by his rapidly dwindling store of savings.

Here was a chance not to be missed – the price of a special story in the *Morning Echo*, with a five-pound note to add to it. It meant comparative wealth and luxury for a week, and freedom from the worst anxieties for a fortnight. Besides, if he wrote the story well, it might lead to an offer of regular employment.

"The way of transgressors – and newspaper men – is hard," he said. "I have already promised myself an uncomfortable night because your Murderers' Den is obviously not fitted up as an hotel bedroom. But I don't think your wax-works will worry me much."

"You're not superstitious?"

"Not a bit," Hewson laughed.

"But you're a journalist; you must have a strong imagination."

"The news editors for whom I've worked have always complained that I haven't any. Plain facts are not considered sufficient in our trade, and the papers don't like offering their readers unbuttered bread."

The manager smiled and rose.

"Right," he said. "I think the last of the people have gone. Wait a moment. I'll give orders for the figures downstairs not to be draped, and let the night people know that you'll be here. Then I'll take you down and show you round."

He picked up the receiver of a house telephone, spoke into it and presently replaced it.

"One condition I'm afraid I must impose on you," he remarked. "I must ask you not to smoke. We had a fire scare down in the Murderers' Den this evening. I don't know who gave the alarm, but whoever it was it was a false one. Fortunately there were very few people down there at the time, or there might have been a panic. And now, if you're ready, we'll make a move."

Hewson followed the manager through half a dozen rooms where attendants were busy shrouding the kings and queens of England, the generals and prominent statesmen of this and other generations, all the mixed herd of humanity whose fame or notoriety had rendered them eligible for this kind of immortality. The manager stopped once and spoke to a man in uniform, saying something about an arm-chair in the Murderers' Den.

"It's the best we can do for you, I'm afraid," he said to Hewson. "I hope you'll be able to get some sleep."

He led the way through an open barrier and down ill-lit stone stairs which conveyed a sinister impression of giving access to a dungeon. In a passage at the bottom were a few preliminary horrors, such as relics of the Inquisition, a rack taken from a mediaeval castle, branding irons, thumbscrews, and other mementoes of man's one-time cruelty to man. Beyond the passage was the Murderers' Den.

It was a room of irregular shape with vaulted roof, and dimly lit by electric lights burning behind inverted bowls of frosted glass. It was, by design, an eerie and uncomfortable chamber – a chamber whose atmosphere invited its visitors to speak in whispers. There was something of the air of a chapel about it, but a chapel no longer devoted to the practice of piety and given over now for base and impious worship.

The waxwork murderers stood on low pedestals with numbered tickets at their feet. Seeing them elsewhere, and without knowing whom they represented, one would have thought them a dull-looking crew, chiefly remarkable for the shabbiness of their clothes, and as evidence of the changes of fashion even among the unfashionable.

Recent notorieties rubbed dusty shoulders with the old "favourites". Thurtell, the murderer of Weir, stood as if frozen in the act of making a shop-window gesture to young Bywaters. There was Lefroy the poor half-baked little snob who killed for gain so that he might ape the gentleman. Within five yards of him sat Mrs. Thompson, that erotic romanticist, hanged to propitiate British middle-class matronhood. Charles Peace, the only member of that vile company who looked uncompromisingly and entirely evil, sneered across a gangway at Norman Thorne. Browne and Kennedy, the two most recent additions stood between Mrs. Dyer and Patrick Mahon.

The manager, walking around with Hewson, pointed out several of the more interesting of these unholy notabilities.

"That's Crippen; I expect you recognise him. Insignificant little beast who looks as if he couldn't tread on a worm. That's

Armstrong. Looks like a decent, harmless country gentleman, doesn't he? There's old Vaquier; you can't miss him because of his beard. And of course this—"

"Who's that?" Hewson interrupted in a whisper, pointing.

"Oh, I was coming to him," said the manager in a light undertone. "Come and have a good look at him. This is our star turn. He's the only one of the bunch that hasn't been hanged."

The figure which Hewson had indicated was that of a small, slight man not much more than five feet in height. It wore little waxed moustaches, large spectacles, and a caped coat. There was something so exaggeratedly French in its appearance that it reminded Hewson of a stage caricature. He could not have said precisely why the mild-looking face seemed to him so repellent, but he had already recoiled a step and, even in the manager's company, it cost him an effort to look again.

"But who is he?" he asked.

"That," said the manager, "is Dr. Bourdette."

Hewson shook his head doubtfully.

"I think I've heard the name," he said, "but I forget in connection with what."

The manager smiled.

"You'd remember better if you were a Frenchman," he said. "For some long while that man was the terror of Paris. He carried on his work of healing by day, and of throat-cutting by night, when the fit was on him. He killed for the sheer devilish pleasure it gave him to kill, and always in the same way – with a razor. After his last crime he left a clue behind him which set the police upon his track. One clue led to another, and before very long they knew that they were on the track of the Parisian equivalent of our Jack the Ripper, and had enough evidence to send him to the mad-house or the guillotine on a dozen capital charges.

"But even then our friend here was too clever for them. When he realised that the toils were closing about him he mysteriously disappeared and ever since the police of every civilised country have been looking for him. There is no doubt that he managed to make away with himself, and by some means which has prevented his body coming to light. One or two crimes of a similar nature have taken place since his disappearance, but he is believed almost for certain to be dead, and the experts believe these recrude-scences to be the work of an imitator. It's queer, isn't it, how every notorious murderer has imitators?"

Hewson shuddered and fidgetted with his feet.

"I don't like him at all," he confessed. "Ugh! What eyes he's got!"

"Yes, this figure's a little masterpiece. You find the eyes bite into you? Well, that's excellent realism, then, for Bourdette practised mesmerism, and was supposed to mesmerise his victims before dispatching them. Indeed, had he not done so, it is impossible to see how so small a man could have done his ghastly work. There was never any signs of a struggle."

"I thought I saw him move," said Hewson with a catch in his voice.

The manager smiled.

"You'll have more than one optical illusion before the night's out, I expect. You shan't be locked in. You can come upstairs when you've had enough of it. There are watchmen on the premises, so you'll find company. Don't be alarmed if you hear them moving about. I'm sorry I can't give you any more light, because all the lights are on. For obvious reasons we keep this place as gloomy as possible. And now I think you had better return with me to the office and have a tot of whisky before beginning your night's vigil."

The member of the night staff who placed the arm-chair for Hewson was inclined to be facetious.

"Where will you have it, sir?" he asked, grinning. "Just 'ere, so as you can 'ave a little talk with Crippen when you're tired of sitting still? Or there's old Mother Dyer over there, making eyes and looking as if she could do with a bit of company. Say where, sir."

Hewson smiled. The man's chaff pleased him if only because, for the moment at least, it lent the proceedings a much-desired air of the commonplace.

"I'll place it myself, thanks," he said. "I'll find out where the draughts come from first."

"You won't find any down here. Well, good night, sir. I'm upstairs if you want me. Don't let 'em sneak up be'ind you and touch your neck with their cold and clammy 'ands. And you look out for that old Mrs. Dyer; I b'lieve she's taken a fancy to you."

Hewson laughed and wished the man good-night. It was easier than he had expected. He wheeled the arm-chair – a heavy one upholstered in plush – a little way down the central gangway, and deliberately turned it so that its back was towards the effigy of Dr. Bourdette. For some undefined reason he liked Dr. Bourdette a great deal less than his companions. Busying himself with arranging the chair he was almost light-hearted, but when the attendant's footfalls had died away and a deep hush stole over the chamber he realised that he had no slight ordeal before him.

The dim unwavering light fell on the rows of figures which were so uncannily like human beings that the silence and the stillness seemed unnatural and even ghastly. He missed the sound of breathing, the rustling of clothes, the hundred and one minute noises one hears when even the deepest silence has fallen upon a crowd. But the air was as stagnant as water at the bottom of a standing pond. There was not a breath in the chamber to stir a curtain or rustle a hanging drapery or start a shadow. His own shadow, moving in response to a shifted arm or leg, was all that could be coaxed into motion. All was still to the gaze and silent to the ear. "It must be like this at the bottom of the sea," he thought and wondered how to work the phrase into his story on the morrow.

He faced the sinister figures boldly enough. They were only waxworks. So long as he let that thought dominate all others he promised himself that all would be well. It did not, however, save him long from the discomfort occasioned by the waxen stare of Dr. Bourdette, which, he knew, was directed upon him from behind. The eyes of the little Frenchman's effigy haunted and tormented him, and he itched with the desire to turn and look.

"Come!" he thought, "my nerves have started already. If I turn and look at that dressed-up dummy it will be an admission of funk."

And then another voice in his brain spoke to him.

"It's because you're afraid that you won't turn and look at him."

The two voices quarrelled silently for a moment or two, and at last Hewson slewed his chair round a little and looked behind him.

Among the many figures standing in stiff, unnatural poses, the effigy of the dreadful little doctor stood out with a queer prominence, perhaps because a steady beam of light beat straight down upon it. Hewson flinched before the parody of mildness which some fiendishly skilled craftsman had managed to convey in wax, met the eyes for one agonised second, and turned again to face the other direction.

"He's only a waxwork like the rest of you," Hewson muttered defiantly. "You're all only waxworks."

They were only waxworks, yes, but waxworks don't move. Not that he had seen the least movement anywhere, but it struck him that, in the moment or two while he had looked behind him, there had been the least subtle change in the grouping of the figures in front. Crippen, for instance, seemed to have turned at least one degree to the left. Or, thought Hewson, perhaps the illusion was due to the fact that he had not slewed his chair back into its exact original position. And there were Field and Grey, too; surely one of them had moved his hands. Hewson held his breath for a moment, and then drew his courage back to him as a man lifts a weight. He remembered the words of more than one news editor and laughed savagely to himself.

"And they tell me I've no imagination!" he said beneath his breath.

He took a notebook from his pocket and wrote quickly.

"Deathly silence and unearthly stillness of figures. Like being bottom of sea. Hypnotic eyes of Dr. Bourdette. Figures seem to move when not being watched."

He closed the book suddenly over his fingers and looked round quickly and awfully over his right shoulder. He had neither seen nor heard a movement, but it was as if some sixth sense had made him aware of one. He looked straight into the vapid countenance of Lefroy which smiled vacantly back as if to say, "It wasn't I!"

Of course it wasn't he, or any of them; it was his own nerves. Or was it? Hadn't Crippen moved again during that moment when his attention was directed elsewhere. You couldn't trust that little man! Once you took your eyes off him he took advantage of it to shift his position. That was what they were all doing, if he only knew it, he told himself; and half rose out of his chair. This was not quite good enough! He was going. He wasn't going to spend the night with a lot of waxworks which moved while he wasn't looking.

Hewson sat down again. This was very cowardly and very absurd. They *were* only waxworks, and they *couldn't* move; let him hold that thought and all would yet be well. Then why all that silent unrest about him? – a subtle something in the air which did not quite break the silence and happened, whichever way he looked, just beyond the boundaries of his vision.

He swung round quickly to encounter the mild but baleful stare of Dr. Bourdette. Then, without warning, he jerked his head back to stare straight at Crippen. Ha! He'd nearly caught Crippen that time! "You'd better be careful, Crippen – and all the rest of you! If I do see one of you move I'll smash you to pieces! Do you hear?"

He ought to go, he told himself. Already he had experienced enough to write his story, or ten stories, for the matter of that. Well, then, why not go? The *Morning Echo* would be none the wiser as to how long he had stayed, nor would it care so long as his story was a good one. Yes, but that night-watchman upstairs would chaff him. And the manager – one never knew – perhaps the manager would quibble over that five-pound note which he needed so badly. He wondered if Rose were asleep or if she were lying awake and thinking of him. She'd laugh when he told her that he had imagined . . .

This was a little too much. It was bad enough that the waxwork effigies of murderers should move when they weren't being watched, but it was intolerable that they should *breathe*. Somebody was breathing. Or was it his own breath which sounded to him as if it came from a distance? He sat rigid, listening and straining until he exhaled with a long sigh. His own breath after all, or – if not, something had divined that he was listening and had ceased breathing simultaneously.

Hewson jerked his head swiftly around and looked all about him out of haggard and hunted eyes. Everywhere his gaze encountered the vacant waxen faces, and everywhere he felt that by just some least fraction of a second had he missed seeing a movement of hand or foot, a silent opening or compression of lips, a flicker of eyelids, a look of human intelligence now smoothed out. They were like naughty children in a class, whispering, fidgeting and laughing behind their teacher's back, but blandly innocent when his gaze was turned upon them.

This would not do! This distinctly would not do! He must clutch at something, grip with his mind upon something which belonged essentially to the workaday world, to the daylight London streets. He was Raymond Hewson, an unsuccessful journalist, a living and breathing man, and these figures grouped around him were only dummies, so they could neither move nor whisper. What did it matter if they were supposed to be lifelike effigies of murderers? They were only made of wax and sawdust, and stood there for the entertainment of morbid sightseers and orange-sucking trippers. That was better! Now what was that funny story which somebody had told him in the Falstaff yesterday . . .?

He recalled part of it, but not all, for the gaze of Dr. Bourdette, urged, challenged, and finally compelled him to turn.

Hewson half-turned, and then swung his chair so as to bring him face to face with the wearer of those dreadful hypnotic eyes. His own eyes were dilated, and his mouth, at first set in a grin of terror, lifted at the corners in a snarl. Then Hewson spoke and woke a hundred sinister echoes.

"You moved, damn you!" he cried. "Yes, you did, damn you! I saw you!"

Then he sat quite still, staring straight before him, like a man frozen in the Arctic snows.

Dr. Bourdette's movements were leisurely. He stepped off his pedestal with the mincing care of a lady alighting from a bus. The platform stood about two feet from the ground, and above the edge of it a plush-covered rope hung in arclike curves. Dr. Bourdette lifted up the rope until it formed an arch for him to pass under, stepped off the platform and sat down on the edge facing Hewson. Then he nodded and smiled and said, "Good evening."

"I need hardly tell you," he continued in perfect English in which was traceable only the least foreign accent, "that not until I overheard the conversation between you and the worthy manager of this establishment, did I suspect that I should have the pleasure of a companion here for the night. You cannot move or speak without my bidding, but you can hear me perfectly well. Something tells me that you are – shall I say nervous? My dear sir, have no illusions. I am not one of these contemptible effigies miraculously come to life: I am Dr. Bourdette himself."

He paused, coughed and shifted his legs.

"Pardon me," he resumed, "but I am a little stiff. And let me explain. Circumstances with which I need not fatigue you, have made it desirable that I should live in England. I was close to this building this evening when I saw a policeman regarding me a thought too curiously. I guessed that he intended to follow and perhaps ask me embarrassing questions, so I mingled with the crowd and came in here. An extra coin bought my admission to the chamber in which we now meet, and an inspiration showed me a certain means of escape.

"I raised a cry of fire, and when all the fools had rushed to the stairs I stripped my effigy of the caped coat which you behold me wearing, donned it, hid my effigy under the platform at the back, and took its place on the pedestal.

"I own that I have since spent a very fatiguing evening, but fortunately I was not always being watched and had opportunities to draw an occasional deep breath and ease the rigidity of my pose. One small boy screamed and exclaimed that he saw me moving. I understood that he was to be whipped and put straight to bed on his return home, and I can only hope that the threat has been executed to the letter.

"The manager's description of me, which I had the embarrass-ment of being compelled to overhear, was biased but not altogether inaccurate. Clearly I am not dead, although it is as well that the world thinks otherwise. His account of my hobby, which I have indulged for years, although, through necessity, less frequently of late, was in the main true although not intelligently expressed. The world is divided between collectors and non-collectors. With the non-collectors we are not concerned. The collectors collect anything, according to their individual tastes, from money to cigarette cards, from moths to match boxes. I collect throats."

He paused again and regarded Hewson's throat with interest mingled with disfavour.

"I am obliged to the chance which brought us together tonight," he continued, "and perhaps it would seem ungrateful to complain. From motives of personal safety my activities have been somewhat curtailed of late years, and I am glad of this opportunity of gratifying my somewhat unusual whim. But you have a skinny neck, sir, if you will overlook a personal remark. I should never have selected you from choice. I like men with thick necks . . . thick red necks. . . ."

He fumbled in an inside pocket and took out something which he tested against a wet forefinger and then proceeded to pass gently to and fro across the palm of his left hand.

"This is a little French razor," he remarked blandly. "They are not much used in England, but perhaps you know them? One strops them on wood. The blade, you will observe, is very narrow. They do not cut very deep, but deep enough. In just one little moment you shall see for yourself. I shall ask you the little civil question of all the polite barbers: 'Does the razor suit you, sir?' "

He rose up, a diminutive but menacing figure of evil, and approached Hewson with the silent furtive step of a hunting panther.

"You will have the goodness," he said, "to raise your chin a little. Thank you, and a little more. Just a little more. Ah, thank you! . . . *Merci, m'sieur . . . Ah, merci . . . merci. . . .*"

Over one end of the chamber was a thick skylight of frosted glass which, by day, let in a few sickly and filtered rays from the floor above. After sunrise these began to mingle with the subdued light from the electric bulbs, and this mingled illumination added a certain ghastliness to the scene which needed no additional touch of horror.

The waxwork figures stood apathetically in their places, waiting to be admired or execrated by the crowds who would presently wander fearfully among them. In their midst, in the centre gangway, Hewson sat still, leaning far back in his arm-chair. His chin was uptilted as if he were waiting to receive attention from a barber, and although there was not a scratch upon his throat, nor anywhere upon his body, he was cold and dead. His previous employers were wrong in having him credited with no imagination.

Dr. Bourdette on his pedestal watched the dead man unemotionally. He did not move, nor was he capable of motion. But then, after all, he was only a waxwork.

The Old House in Vauxhall Walk

Charlotte Riddell

I

"Houseless – homeless – hopeless!"

Many a one who had before him trodden that same street must

have uttered the same words – the weary, the desolate, the hungry, the forsaken, the waifs and strays of struggling humanity that are always coming and going, cold, starving and miserable, over the pavements of Lambeth Parish; but it is open to question whether they were ever previously spoken with a more thorough conviction of their truth, or with a feeling of keener self-pity, than by the young man who hurried along Vauxhall Walk one rainy winter's night, with no overcoat on his shoulders and no hat on his head.

A strange sentence for one-and-twenty to give expression to – and it was stranger still to come from the lips of a person who looked like and who was a gentleman. He did not appear either to have sunk very far down in the good graces of Fortune. There was no sign or token which would have induced a passer-by to imagine he had been worsted after a long fight with calamity. His boots were not worn down at the heels or broken at the toes, as many, many boots were which dragged and shuffled and scraped along the pavement. His clothes were good and fashionably cut, and innocent of the rents and patches and tatters that slunk wretchedly by, crouched in doorways, and held out a hand mutely appealing for charity. His face was not pinched with famine or lined with wicked wrinkles, or brutalised by drink and debauchery, and yet he said and thought he was hopeless, and almost in his young despair spoke the words aloud.

It was a bad night to be about with such a feeling in one's heart. The rain was cold, pitiless and increasing. A damp, keen wind blew down the cross streets leading from the river. The fumes of the gas works seemed to fall with the rain. The roadway was muddy; the pavement greasy; the lamps burned dimly; and that dreary district of London looked its very gloomiest and worst.

Certainly not an evening to be abroad without a home to go to, or a sixpence in one's pocket, yet this was the position of the young gentleman who, without a hat, strode along Vauxhall Walk, the rain beating on his unprotected head.

Upon the houses, so large and good – once inhabited by well-to-do citizens, now let out for the most part in floors to weekly tenants – he looked enviously. He would have given much to have had a room, or even part of one. He had been walking for a long time, ever since dark in fact, and dark falls soon in December. He was tired and cold and hungry, and he saw no prospect save of pacing the streets all night.

As he passed one of the lamps, the light falling on his face revealed handsome young features, a mobile, sensitive mouth, and that particular formation of the eyebrows – not a frown exactly, but a certain draw of the brows – often considered to bespeak genius, but which more surely accompanies an impulsive organisation easily pleased, easily depressed, capable of suffering very keenly or of enjoying fully. In his short life he had not enjoyed much, and he had suffered a good deal. That night when he walked bareheaded through the rain, affairs had come to a crisis. So far as he in his despair felt able to see or reason, the best thing he could do was to die. The world did not want him; he would be better out of it.

The door of one of the houses stood open, and he could see in the dimly lighted hall some few articles of furniture waiting to be removed. A van stood beside the curb, and two men were lifting a table into it as he, for a second, paused.

"Ah," he thought, "even those poor people have some place to go to, some shelter provided, while I have not a roof to cover my head, or a shilling to get a night's lodging." And he went on fast, as if memory were spurring him, so fast that a man running after had some trouble to overtake him.

"Master Graham! Master Graham!" this man exclaimed, breathlessly; and, thus addressed, the young fellow stopped as if he had been shot.

"Who are you that know me?" he asked, facing round.

"I'm William; don't you remember William, Master Graham? And, Lord's sake, sir, what are you doing out a night like this without your hat?"

"I forgot it," was the answer, "and I did not care to go back and fetch it."

"Then why don't you buy another, sir? You'll catch your death of cold; and besides, you'll excuse me, sir, but it does look odd."

"I know that," said Master Graham grimly, "but I haven't a halfpenny in the world."

"Have you and the Master, then –" began the man, but there he hesitated and stopped.

"Had a quarrel? Yes, and one that will last us our lives," finished the other, with a bitter laugh.

"And where are you going now?"

"Going! Nowhere, except to seek out the softest paving stone, or the shelter of an arch."

"You are joking, sir."

"I don't feel much in a mood for jesting either."

"Will you come back with me, Master Graham? We are just at the last of our moving, but there is a spark of fire still in the grate, and it would be better talking out of this rain. Will you come, sir?"

"Come! Of course I will come," said the young fellow, and, turning, they retraced their steps to the house he had looked into as he passed along.

An old, old house, with long, wide hall, stairs low, easy of ascent, with deep cornices to the ceilings, and oak floorings, and mahogany doors, which still spoke mutely of the wealth and stability of the original owner, who lived before the Tradescants and Ashmoles were thought of, and had been sleeping for longer than they, in St. Mary's churchyard, hard by the archbishop's palace.

"Step upstairs, sir," entreated the departing tenant; "it's cold down here, with the door standing wide."

"Had you the whole house, then, William?" asked Graham Coulton, in some surprise.

"The whole of it, and right sorry I, for one, am to leave it; but nothing else would serve my wife. This room, sir," and with a little conscious pride, William, doing the honours of his late residence, asked his guest into a spacious apartment occupying the full width of the house on the first floor.

Tired though he was, the young man could not repress an exclamation of astonishment.

"Why, we have nothing so large as this at home, William," he said.

"It's a fine house," answered William, raking the embers

together as he spoke and throwing some wood upon them; "but, like many a good family, it has come down in the world."

There were four windows in the room, shuttered close; they had deep, low seats, suggestive of pleasant days gone by; when, well-curtained and well-cushioned, they formed snug retreats for the children, and sometimes for adults also; there was no furniture left, unless an oaken settle beside the hearth, and a large mirror let into the panelling at the opposite end of the apartment, with a black marble console table beneath it, could be so considered; but the very absence of chairs and tables enabled the magnificent proportions of the chamber to be seen to full advantage, and there was nothing to distract the attention from the ornamented ceiling, the panelled walls, the old-world chimney-piece so quaintly carved, and the fire-place lined with tiles, each one of which contained a picture of some scriptural or allegorical subject.

"Had you been staying on here, William," said Coulton, flinging himself wearily on the settee, "I'd have asked you to let me stop where I am for the night."

"If you can make shift, sir, there is nothing as I am aware of to prevent you stopping," answered the man, fanning the wood into a flame. "I shan't take the key back to the landlord till to-morrow, and this would be better for you than the cold streets at any rate."

"Do you really mean what you say?" asked the other eagerly. "I should be thankful to lie here; I feel dead beat."

"Then stay, Master Graham, and welcome. I'll fetch a basket of coals I was going to put in the van, and make up a good fire, so that you can warm yourself; then I must run round to the other house for a minute or two, but it's not far, and I'll be back as soon as ever I can."

"Thank you, William; you were always good to me," said the young man gratefully. "This is delightful," and he stretched his numbed hands over the blazing wood, and looked round the room with a satisfied smile.

"I did not expect to get into such quarters," he remarked, as his friend in need reappeared, carrying a half-bushel basket full of coals, with which he proceeded to make up a roaring fire. "I am sure the last thing I could have imagined was meeting with anyone I knew in Vauxhall Walk."

"Where were you coming from, Master Graham?" asked William curiously.

"From old Melfield's. I was at his school once, you know, and he has now retired, and is living upon the proceeds of years of robbery in Kennington Oval. I thought, perhaps he would lend me a pound, or offer me a night's lodging, or even a glass of wine; but, oh dear, no. He took the moral tone, and observed he could have nothing to say to a son who defied his father's authority. He gave me plenty of advice, but nothing else, and showed me out into the rain with a bland courtesy, for which I could have struck him."

William muttered something under his breath which was not a blessing, and added aloud:

"You are better here, sir, I think, at any rate. I'll be back in less than half an hour."

Left to himself, young Coulton took off his coat, and shifting the settle a little, hung it over the end to dry. With his hand-kerchief he rubbed some of the wet out of his hair; then, perfectly exhausted, he lay down before the fire and, pillowing his head on his arm, fell fast asleep.

He was awakened nearly an hour afterwards by the sound of someone gently stirring the fire and moving quietly about the room. Starting into a sitting posture, he looked around him, bewildered for a moment, and then, recognising his humble friend, said laughingly:

"I had lost myself; I could not imagine where I was."

"I am sorry to see you here, sir," was the reply; "but still this is better than being out of doors. It has come on a nasty night. I brought a rug round with me that, perhaps, you would wrap yourself in."

"I wish, at the same time, you had brought me something to eat," said the young man, laughing.

"Are you hungry, then, sir?" asked William, in a tone of concern.

"Yes; I have had nothing to eat since breakfast. The governor and I commenced rowing the minute we sat down to luncheon, and I rose and left the table. But hunger does not signify; I am dry and warm, and can forget the other matter in sleep."

"And it's too late now to buy anything," soliloquised the man; "the shops are all shut long ago. Do you think, sir," he added, brightening, "you could manage some bread and cheese?"

"Do I think – I should call it a perfect feast," answered Graham Coulton. "But never mind about food to-night, William; you have had trouble enough, and to spare, already."

William's only answer was to dart to the door and run downstairs. Presently he reappeared, carrying in one hand bread and cheese wrapped up in paper, and in the other a pewter measure full of beer.

"It's the best I could do, sir," he said apologetically. "I had to beg this from the landlady."

"Here's to her good health!" exclaimed the young fellow gaily, taking a long pull at the tankard. "That tastes better than champagne in my father's house."

"Won't he be uneasy about you?" ventured William, who, having by this time emptied the coals, was now seated on the inverted basket, looking wistfully at the relish with which the son of the former master was eating his bread and cheese.

"No," was the decided answer. "When he hears it pouring cats and dogs he will only hope I am out in the deluge, and say a good drenching will cool my pride."

"I do not think you are right there," remarked the man.

"But I am sure I am. My father always hated me, as he hated my mother."

"Begging your pardon, sir; he was over fond of your mother."

"If you had heard what he said about her to-day, you might find reason to alter your opinion. He told me I resembled her in mind as well as body; that I was a coward, a simpleton, and a hypocrite."

"He did not mean it, sir."

"He did, every word. He does think I am a coward, because I– I –" and the young fellow broke into a passion of hysterical tears.

"I don't half like leaving you here alone," said William,

glancing round the room with a quick trouble in his eyes; "but I have no place fit to ask you to stop, and I am forced to go myself, because I am night watchman, and must be on at twelve o'clock."

"I shall be right enough," was the answer. "Only I mustn't talk any more of my father. Tell me about yourself, William. How did you manage to get such a big house, and why are you leaving it?"

"The landlord put me in charge, sir; and it was my wife's fancy not to like it.".

"Why did she not like it?"

"She felt desolate alone with the children at night," answered William, turning away his head; then added, next minute; "Now, sir, if you think I can do no more for you, I had best be off. Time's getting on. I'll look round to-morrow morning."

"Good night," said the young fellow, stretching out his hand, which the other took as freely and frankly as it was offered. "What should I have done this evening if I had not chanced to meet you?"

"I don't think there is much chance in the world, Master Graham," was the quiet answer. "I do hope you will rest well, and not be the worse for your wetting."

"No fear of that," was the rejoinder, and the next minute the young man found himself all alone in the Old House in Vauxhall Walk.

II

Lying on the settle, with the fire burnt out, and the room in total darkness, Graham Coulton dreamed a curious dream. He thought he awoke from deep slumber to find a log smouldering away upon the hearth, and the mirror at the end of the apartment reflecting fitful gleams of light. He could not understand how it came to pass that, far away as he was from the glass, he was able to see everything in it; but he resigned himself to the difficulty without astonishment, as people generally do in dreams.

Neither did he feel surprised when he beheld the outline of a female figure seated beside the fire, engaged in picking something out of her lap and dropping it with a despairing gesture.

He heard the mellow sound of gold, and knew she was lifting and dropping sovereigns. He turned a little so as to see the person engaged in such a singular and meaningless manner, and found that, where there had been no chair on the previous night, there was a chair now, on which was seated an old, wrinkled hag, her clothes poor and ragged, a mob cap barely covering her scant white hair, her cheeks sunken, her nose hooked, her fingers more like talons than aught else as they dived down into the heap of gold, portions of which they lifted but to scatter mournfully.

"Oh! my lost life," she moaned, in a voice of the bitterest anguish. "Oh! my lost life – for one day, for one hour of it again!"

Out of the darkness – out of the corner of the room where the shadows lay deepest – out from the gloom abiding near the door – out from the dreary night, with their sodden feet and the wet dripping from their heads, came the old men and the young children, the worn women and the weary hearts, whose misery that gold might have relieved, but whose wretchedness it mocked.

Round that miser, who once sat gloating as she now sat lamenting, they crowded – all those pale, sad shapes – the aged of days, the infant of hours, the sobbing outcast, honest poverty, repentant vice; but one low cry proceeded from those pale lips – a cry for help she might have given, but which she withheld.

They closed about her, all together, as they had done singly in life; they prayed, they sobbed, they entreated; with haggard eyes the figure regarded the poor she had repulsed, the children against whose cry she had closed her ears, the old people she had suffered to starve and die for want of what would have been the merest trifle to her; then, with a terrible scream, she raised her lean arms above her head, and sank down – down – the gold scattering as it fell out of her lap, and rolling along the floor, till its gleam was lost in the outer darkness beyond.

Then Graham Coulton awoke in good earnest, with the perspiration oozing from every pore, with a fear and an agony upon him such as he had never before felt in all his existence, and with the sound of the heart-rending cry – "Oh! my lost life" – still ringing in his ears.

Mingled with all, too, there seemed to have been some lesson for him which he had forgotten, that, try as he would, eluded his memory, and which, in the very act of waking, glided away.

He lay for a little thinking about all this, and then, still heavy with sleep, retraced his way into dreamland once more.

It was natural, perhaps, that, mingling with the strange fantasies which follow in the train of night and darkness, the former vision should recur, and the young man ere long found himself toiling through scene after scene wherein the figure of the woman he had seen seated beside a dying fire held principal place.

He saw her walking slowly across the floor munching a dry crust – she who could have purchased all the luxuries wealth can command; on the hearth, contemplating her, stood a man of commanding presence, dressed in the fashion of long ago. In his eyes there was a dark look of anger, on his lips a curling smile of disgust, and somehow, even in his sleep, the dreamer understood it was the ancestor to the descendant he beheld – that the house put to mean uses in which he lay had never so far descended from its high estate, as the woman possessed of so pitiful a soul, contaminated with the most despicable and insidious vice poor humanity knows, for all other vices seem to have connection with the flesh, but the greed of the miser eats into the very soul.

Filthy of person, repulsive to look at, hard of heart as she was, he yet beheld another phantom, which, coming into the room, met her almost on the threshold, taking her by the hand, and pleading, as it seemed, for assistance. He could not hear all that passed, but a word now and then fell upon his car. Some talk of former days; some mention of a fair young mother – an appeal, as it seemed, to a time when they were tiny brother and sister, and the accursed greed for gold had not divided them. All in vain; the hag only answered him as she had answered the children, and the young girls, and the old people in his former vision. Her heart was as invulnerable to natural affection as it had proved to human sympathy. He begged, as it appeared, for aid to avert some bitter misfortune or terrible disgrace, and adamant might have been found more yielding to his prayer. Then the figure standing on the hearth changed to an angel, which folded its wings mournfully over its face, and the man, with bowed head, slowly left the room.

Even as he did so the scene changed again; it was night once more, and the miser wended her way upstairs. From below, Graham Coulton fancied he watched her toiling wearily from step to step. She had aged strangely since the previous scenes. She moved with difficulty; it seemed the greatest exertion for her to creep from step to step, her skinny hand traversing the balusters with slow and painful deliberateness. Fascinated, the young man's eyes followed the progress of that feeble, decrepit woman. She was solitary in a desolate house, with a deeper blackness than the darkness of night waiting to engulf her.

It seemed to Graham Coulton that after that he lay for a time in a still, dreamless sleep, upon awakening from which he found himself entering a chamber as sordid and unclean in its appointments as the woman of his previous vision had been in her person. The poorest labourer's wife would have gathered more comforts around her than that room contained. A four-poster bedstead without hangings of any kind – a blind drawn up awry – an old carpet covered with dust, and dirt on the floor – a rickety washstand with all the paint worn off it – an ancient mahogany dressing table, and a cracked glass spotted all over – were all the objects he could at first discern, looking at the room through that dim light which oftentimes obtains in dreams.

By degrees, however, he perceived the outline of someone lying huddled on the bed. Drawing nearer, he found it was that of the person whose dreadful presence seemed to pervade the house. What a terrible sight she looked, with her thin white locks scattered over the pillow, with what were mere remnants of blankets gathered about her shoulders, with her claw-like fingers clutching the clothes, as though even in sleep she was guarding her gold!

An awful and a repulsive spectacle, but not with half the terror in it of that which followed. Even as the young man looked he heard stealthy footsteps on the stairs. Then he saw first one man and then his fellow steal cautiously into the room. Another second, and the pair stood beside the bed, murder in their eyes.

Graham Coulton tried to shout – tried to move, but the

deterrent power which exists in dreams only tied his tongue and paralysed his limbs. He could but hear and look, and what he heard and saw was this: aroused suddenly from sleep, the woman started, only to receive a blow from one of the ruffians, whose fellow followed his lead by plunging a knife into her breast.

Then, with a gurgling scream, she fell back on the bed, and at the same moment, with a cry, Graham Coulton again awoke, to thank heaven it was but an illusion.

III

"I hope you slept well, sir." It was William, who, coming into the hall with the sunlight of a fine bright morning streaming after him, asked this question: "Had you a good night's rest?"

Graham Coulton laughed, and answered:

"Why, faith, I was somewhat in the case of Paddy, 'who could not slape for dhraming'. I slept well enough, I suppose, but whether it was in consequence of the row with my dad, or the hard bed, or the cheese – most likely the bread and cheese so late at night – I dreamt all the night long, the most extraordinary dreams. Some old woman kept cropping up, and I saw her murdered."

"You don't say that, sir?" said William nervously.

"I do, indeed," was the reply. "However, that is all gone and past. I have been down in the kitchen and had a good wash, and I am as fresh as a daisy, and as hungry as a hunter; and, oh, William, can you get me any breakfast?"

"Certainly, Master Graham, I have brought round a kettle, and I will make the water boil immediately. I suppose, sir" – this tentatively – "you'll be going home to-day?"

"Home!" repeated the young man. "Decidedly not. I'll never go home again till I return with some medal hung to my coat, or a leg or arm cut off. I've thought it all out, William. I'll go and enlist. There's a talk of war; and, living or dead, my father shall have reason to retract his opinion about my being a coward."

"I am sure the admiral never thought you anything of the sort, sir," said William. "Why, you have the pluck of ten!"

"Not before him," answered the young fellow sadly.

"You'll do nothing rash, Master Graham; you won't go 'listing, or aught of that sort, in your anger?"

"If I do not, what is to become of me?" asked the other. "I cannot dig – to beg I am ashamed. Why, but for you, I should not have had a roof over my head last night."

"Not much of a roof, I am afraid, sir."

"Not much of a roof!" repeated the young man. "Why, who could desire a better? What a capital room this is," he went on, looking around the apartment, where William was now kindling a fire; "one might dine twenty people here easily!"

"If you think so well of the place, Master Graham, you might stay here for a while, till you have made up your mind what you are going to do. The landlord won't make any objection, I am very sure."

"Oh! nonsense; he would want a long rent for a house like this."

"I daresay; *if he could get it*," was William's significant answer.

"What do you mean? Won't the place let?"

"No, sir. I did not tell you last night, but there was a murder done here, and people are shy of the house ever since."

"A murder! What sort of a murder? Who was murdered?"

"A woman, Master Graham – the landlord's sister; she lived here all alone, and was supposed to have money. Whether she had or not, she was found dead from a stab in her breast, and if there ever was any money, it must have been taken at the same time, for none ever was found in the house from that day to this."

"Was that the reason your wife would not stop here?" asked the young man, leaning against the mantelshelf, and looking thoughtfully down on William.

"Yes, sir. She could not stand it any longer; she got that thin and nervous no one would have believed it possible; she never saw anything, but she said she heard footsteps and voices, and then when she walked through the hall, or up the staircase, someone always seemed to be following her. We put the children to sleep in that big room you had last night, and they declared they often saw an old woman sitting by the hearth. Nothing ever came my way," finished William, with a laugh; "I was always ready to go to sleep the minute my head touched the pillow."

"Were not the murderers discovered?" asked Graham Coulton.

"No, sir; the landlord, Miss Tynan's brother, had always lain under the suspicion of it – quite wrongfully, I am very sure – but he will never clear himself now. It was known he came and asked her for help a day or two before the murder, and it was also known he was able within a week or two to weather whatever trouble had been harassing him. Then, you see, the money was never found; and, altogether, people scarce knew what to think."

"Humph!" ejaculated Graham Coulton, and he took a few turns up and down the apartment. "Could I go and see this landlord?"

"Surely, sir, if you had a hat," answered William, with such a serious decorum that the young man burst out laughing.

"That is an obstacle, certainly," he remarked, "and I must make a note do instead. I have a pencil in my pocket, so here goes."

Within half an hour from the dispatch of that note William was back again with a sovereign; the landlord's compliments, and he would be much obliged if Mr. Coulton could "step round."

"You'll do nothing rash, sir," entreated William.

"Why, man," answered the young fellow, "one may as well be picked off by a ghost as a bullet. What is there to be afraid of?"

William only shook his head. He did not think his young master was made of the stuff likely to remain alone in a haunted house and solve the mystery it assuredly contained by dint of his own unassisted endeavours. And yet when Graham Coulton came out of the landlord's house he looked more bright and gay than usual, and walked up the Lambeth road to the place where Wiliam awaited his return, humming an air as he paced along.

"We have settled the matter," he said. "And now if the dad wants his son for Christmas, it will trouble him to find him."

"Don't say that, Master Graham, don't," entreated the man, with a shiver; "maybe after all it would have been better if you had never happened to chance upon Vauxhall Walk."

"Don't croak, William," answered the young man; "if it was not the best day's work I ever did for myself I'm a Dutchman."

During the whole of that afternoon, Graham Coulton searched diligently for the missing treasure Mr. Tynan assured him had never been discovered. Youth is confident, and self-opinionated, and this fresh explorer felt satisfied that, though others had failed, he would be successful. On the second floor he found one door locked, but he did not pay much attention to that at the moment, as he believed if there was anything concealed it was more likely to be found in the lower than the upper part of the house. Late into the evening he pursued his researches in the kitchen and cellars and old-fashioned cupboards, of which the basement had an abundance.

It was nearly eleven, when, engaged in poking about amongst the empty bins of a wine cellar as large as a family vault, he suddenly felt a rush of cold air at his back. Moving, his candle was instantly extinguished, and in the very moment of being left in darkness he saw, standing in the doorway, a woman, resembling her who had haunted his dreams overnight.

He rushed with outstretched hands to seize her, but clutched only air. He relit his candle, and closely examined the basement, shutting off communication with the ground floor ere doing so. All in vain. Not a trace could he find of living creature – not a window was open – not a door unbolted.

"It is very odd," he thought, as, after securely fastening the door at the top of the staircase, he searched the whole upper portion of the house, with the exception of the one room mentioned.

"I must get the key of that to-morrow," he decided, standing gloomily with his back to the fire and his eyes wandering about the drawing-room, where he had once again taken up his abode.

Even as the thought passed through his mind, he saw standing in the open doorway a woman with white dishevelled hair, clad in mean garments, ragged and dirty. She lifted her hand and shook it at him with a menacing gesture, and then, just as he was darting towards her, a wonderful thing occurred.

From behind the great mirror there glided a second female

figure, at the sight of which the first turned and fled, uttering piercing shrieks as the other followed her from storey to storey.

Sick almost with terror, Graham Coulton watched the dreadful pair as they fled upstairs past the locked room to the top of the house.

It was a few minutes before he recovered his self-possession. When he did so, and searched the upper apartments, he found them totally empty.

That night, ere lying down before the fire, he carefully locked and bolted the drawing-room door; before he did more he drew the heavy settle in front of it, so that if the lock were forced no entrance could be effected without considerable noise.

For some time he lay awake, then dropped into a deep sleep, from which he was awakened suddenly by a noise as if of something scuffling stealthily behind the wainscot. He raised himself on his elbow and listened, and, to his consternation, beheld seated at the opposite side of the hearth the same woman he had seen before in his dreams, lamenting over her gold.

The fire was not quite out, and at the moment shot up a last tongue of flame. By the light, transient as it was, he saw that the figure pressed a ghostly finger to its lips, and by the turn of his head and the attitude of its body seemed to be listening.

He listened also – indeed, he was too much frightened to do aught else; more and more distinct grew the sounds which had aroused him, a stealthy rustling coming nearer and nearer – up and up it seemed, behind the wainscot.

"It is rats," thought the young man, though, indeed, his teeth were almost chattering in his head with fear. But then in a moment he saw what disabused him of that idea – *the gleam of a candle or lamp through a crack in the panelling*. He tried to rise, he strove to shout – all in vain; and, sinking down, remembered nothing more till he awoke to find the grey light of an early morning stealing through one of the shutters he had left partially unclosed.

For hours after his breakfast, which he scarcely touched, long after William had left him at mid-day, Graham Coulton, having in the morning made a long and close survey of the house, sat thinking before the fire, then, apparently having made up his mind, he put on the hat he had bought, and went out.

When he returned the evening shadows were darkening down, but the pavements were full of people going marketing, for it was Christmas Eve, and all who had money to spend seemed bent on shopping.

It was terribly dreary inside the old house that night. Through the deserted rooms Graham could feel that ghostly semblance was wandering mournfully. When he turned his back he knew she was flitting from the mirror to the fire, from the fire to the mirror; but he was not afraid of her now – he was far more afraid of another matter he had taken in hand that day.

The horror of the silent house grew and grew upon him. He could hear the beating of his own heart in the dead quietude which reigned from garret to cellar.

At last William came; but the young man said nothing to him of what was in his mind. He talked to him cheerfully and hopefully enough – wondered where his father would think he had got to, and hoped Mr. Tynan might send him some Christmas pudding. Then the man said it was time for him to go, and, when Mr. Coulton went downstairs to the hall-door, remarked the key was not in it.

"No," was the answer, "I took it out to-day, to oil it."

"It wanted oiling," agreed William, "for it worked terribly stiff." Having uttered which truism he departed.

Very slowly the young man retraced his way to the drawing-room, where he only paused to lock the door on the outside; then taking off his boots he went up to the top of the house, where, entering the front attic, he waited patiently in darkness and in silence.

It was a long time, or at least it seemed long to him, before he heard the same sound which had aroused him on the previous night – a stealthy rustling – then a rush of cold air – then cautious footsteps – then the quiet opening of a door below.

It did not take as long in action as it has required to tell. In a moment the young man was out on the landing and had closed a portion of the panelling on the wall which stood open; noiselessly he crept back to the attic window, unlatched it, and sprung a rattle, the sound of which echoed far and near through the deserted streets, then rushing down the stairs, he encountered a man who, darting past him, made for the landing above; but perceiving that way of escape closed, fled down again, to find Graham struggling desperately with his fellow.

"Give him the knife – come along," he said savagely; and next instant Graham felt something like a hot iron through his shoulder, and then heard a thud, as one of the men, tripping in his rapid flight, fell from the top of the stairs to the bottom.

At the same moment there came a crash, as if the house was falling, and faint, sick, and bleeding, young Coulton lay insensible on the threshold of the room where Miss Tynan had been murdered.

When he recovered he was in the dining-room, and a doctor was examining his wound.

Near the door a policeman stiffly kept guard. The hall was full of people; all the misery and vagabondism the streets contain at that hour was crowding in to see what had happened.

Through the midst two men were being conveyed to the station-house; one, with his head dreadfully injured, on a stretcher, the other handcuffed, uttering frightful imprecations as he went.

After a time the house was cleared of the rabble, the police took possession of it, and Mr. Tynan was sent for.

"What was that dreadful noise?" asked Graham feebly, now seated on the floor, with his back resting against the wall.

'I do not know. Was there a noise?" said Mr. Tynan, humouring his fancy, as he thought.

"Yes, in the drawing-room, I think; the key is in my pocket."

Still humouring the wounded lad, Mr. Tynan took the key and ran upstairs.

When he unlocked the door, what a sight met his eyes! The mirror had fallen – it was lying all over the floor shivered into a thousand pieces; the console table had been borne down by its weight, and the marble slab was shattered as well. But this was not what chained his attention. Hundreds, thousands of gold pieces were scattered about, and an aperture behind the glass contained boxes filled with securities and deeds and bonds, the possession of which had cost his sister her life.

"Well, Graham, and what do you want?" asked Admiral Coulton that evening as his eldest born appeared before him, looking somewhat pale but otherwise unchanged.

"I want nothing," was the answer, 'but to ask your forgiveness. William has told me all the story I never knew before; and, if you let me, I will try to make it up to you for the trouble you have had. I am provided for," went on the young fellow, with a nervous laugh; 'I have made my fortune since I left you, and another man's fortune as well."

"I think you are out of your senses," said the Admiral shortly.

"No, sir, I have found them," was the answer; "and I mean to strive and make a better thing of my life than I should ever have done had I not gone to the Old House in Vauxhall Walk."

"Vauxhall Walk! What is the lad talking about?"

'I will tell you, sir, if I may sit down," was Graham Coulton's answer, and then he told this story.

The Toll-House

W. W. Jacobs

"It's all nonsense," said Jack Barnes. "Of course people have died in the house; people die in every house. As for the noises –

wind in the chimney and rats in the wainscot are very convincing to a nervous man. Give me another cup of tea, Meagle."

"Lester and White are first," said Meagle, who was presiding at the tea-table of the Three Feathers Inn. "You've had two."

Lester and White finished their cups with irritating slowness, pausing between sips to sniff the aroma, and to discover the sex and dates of arrival of the "strangers" which floated in some numbers in the beverage. Mr. Meagle served them to the brim, and then, turning to the grimly expectant Mr. Barnes, blandly requested him to ring for hot water.

"We'll try and keep your nerves in their present healthy condition," he remarked. "For my part I have a sort of half-and-half belief in the supernatural."

"All sensible people have," said Lester. "An aunt of mine saw a ghost once."

White nodded.

"I had an uncle that saw one," he said.

"It always is somebody else that sees them," said Barnes.

"Well, there is the house," said Meagle, "a large house at an absurdly low rent, and nobody will take it. It has taken toll of at least one life of every family that has lived there – however short the time – and since it has stood empty caretaker after caretaker has died there. The last caretaker died fifteen years ago."

"Exactly," said Barnes. "Long enough ago for legends to accumulate."

"I'll bet you a sovereign you won't spend the night there alone, for all your talk," said White suddenly.

"And I," said Lester.

"No," said Barnes slowly. "I don't believe in ghosts nor in any supernatural things whatever; all the same, I admit that I should not care to pass a night there alone."

"But why not?" inquired White.

"Wind in the chimney," said Meagle, with a grin.

"Rats in the wainscot," chimed in Lester.

"As you like," said Barnes, colouring.

"Suppose we all go?" said Meagle. "Start after supper, and get there about eleven? We have been walking for ten days now without an adventure – except Barnes's discovery that ditch-water smells longest. It will be a novelty, at any rate, and, if we break the spell by all surviving, the grateful owner ought to come down handsome."

"Let's see what the landlord has to say about it first," said Lester. "There is no fun in passing a night in an ordinary empty house. Let us make sure that it is haunted."

He rang the bell, and, sending for the landlord, appealed to him in the name of our common humanity not to let them waste a night watching in a house in which spectres and hobgoblins had no part. The reply was more than reassuring, and the landlord, after describing with considerable art the exact appearance of a head which had been seen hanging out of a window in the moonlight, wound up with a polite but urgent request that they would settle his bill before they went.

"It's all very well for you young gentlemen to have your fun," he said indulgently; "but, supposing as how you are all found dead in the morning, what about me? It ain't called the Toll-House for nothing, you know."

"Who died there last?" inquired Barnes, with an air of polite derision.

"A tramp," was the reply. "He went there for the sake of half-a-crown, and they found him next morning hanging from the balusters, dead."

"Suicide," said Barnes. "Unsound mind."

The landlord nodded. "That's what the jury brought it in," he said slowly; "but his mind was sound enough when he went in there. I'd known him, off and on, for years. I'm a poor man, but I wouldn't spend the night in that house for a hundred pounds."

He repeated this remark as they started on their expedition a few hours later. They left as the inn was closing for the night; bolts shot noisily behind them, and, as the regular customers trudged slowly homewards, they set off at a brisk pace in the direction of the house. Most of the cottages were already in darkness, and lights in others went out as they passed.

"It seems rather hard that we have got to lose a night's rest in order to convince Barnes of the existence of ghosts," said White.

"It's in a good cause," said Meagle. "A most worthy object; and something seems to tell me that we shall succeed. You didn't forget the candles, Lester?"

"I have brought two," was the reply; "all the old man could spare."

There was but little moon, and the night was cloudy. The road between high hedges was dark, and in one place, where it ran through a wood, so black that they twice stumbled in the uneven ground at the side of it.

"Fancy leaving our comfortable beds for this!" said White again. "Let me see; this desirable residential sepulchre lies to the right, doesn't it?"

"Farther on," said Meagle.

They walked on for some time in silence, broken only by White's tribute to the softness, the cleanliness, and the comfort of the bed which was receding farther and farther into the distance. Under Meagle's guidance they turned off at last to the right, and, after a walk of a quarter of a mile, saw the gates of the house before them.

The lodge was almost hidden by over-grown shrubs and the drive was choked with rank growths. Meagle leading, they pushed through it until the dark pile of the house loomed above them.

"There is a window at the back where we can get in, so the landlord says," said Lester, as they stood before the hall door.

"Window?" said Meagle. "Nonsense. Let's do the thing properly. Where's the knocker?"

He felt for it in the darkness and gave a thundering rat-tat-tat at the door.

"Don't play the fool," said Barnes crossly.

"Ghostly servants are all asleep," said Meagle gravely, "but *I'll* wake them up before I've done with them. It's scandalous keeping us out here in the dark."

He plied the knocker again, and the noise volleyed in the emptiness beyond. Then with a sudden exclamation he put out his hands and stumbled forward.

"Why, it was open all the time," he said, with an odd catch in his voice. "Come on."

"I don't believe it was open," said Lester, hanging back. "Somebody is playing us a trick."

"Nonsense," said Meagle sharply. "Give me a candle. Thanks. Who's got a match?"

Barnes produced a box and struck one, and Meagle, shielding the candle with his hand, led the way forward to the foot of the stairs. "Shut the door, somebody," he said; "there's too much draught."

"It is shut," said White, glancing behind him.

Meagle fingered his chin. "Who shut it?" he inquired, looking from one to the other. "Who came in last?"

"I did," said Lester, "but I don't remember shutting it – perhaps I did, though."

Meagle, about to speak, thought better of it, and, still carefully guarding the flame, began to explore the house, with the others close behind. Shadows danced on the walls and lurked in the corners as they proceeded. At the end of the passage they found a second staircase, and ascending it slowly gained the first floor.

"Careful!" said Meagle, as they gained the landing.

He held the candle forward and showed where the balusters had broken away. Then he peered curiously into the void beneath.

"This is where the tramp hanged himself, I suppose," he said thoughtfully.

"You've got an unwholesome mind," said White, as they walked on. "This place is quite creepy enough without you remembering that. Now let's find a comfortable room and have a little nip of whisky apiece and a pipe. How will this do?"

He opened a door at the end of the passage and revealed a small square room. Meagle led the way with the candle, and, first melting a drop or two of tallow, stuck it on the mantelpiece. The others seated themselves on the floor and watched pleasantly as White drew from his pocket a small bottle of whisky and a tin cup.

"H'm! I've forgotten the water," he exclaimed.

"I'll soon get some," said Meagle.

He tugged violently at the bell-handle, and the rusty jangling of a bell sounded from a distant kitchen. He rang again.

"Don't play the fool," said Barnes roughly.

Meagle laughed. "I only wanted to convince you," he said kindly. "There ought to be, at any rate, one ghost in the servants' hall."

Barnes held up his hand for silence.

"Yes?" said Meagle, with a grin at the other two. "Is anybody coming?"

"Suppose we drop this game and go back," said Barnes suddenly. "I don't believe in spirits, but nerves are outside anybody's command. You may laugh as you like, but it really seemed to me that I heard a door open below and steps on the stairs."

His voice was drowned in a roar of laughter.

"He is coming round," said Meagle, with a smirk. "By the time I have done with him he will be a confirmed believer. Well, who will go and get some water? Will, you, Barnes?"

"No," was the reply.

"If there is any it might not be safe to drink after all these years," said Lester. "We must do without it."

Meagle nodded, and taking a seat on the floor held out his hand for the cup. Pipes were lit, and the clean, wholesome smell of tobacco filled the room. White produced a pack of cards; talk and laughter rang through the room and died away reluctantly in distant corridors.

"Empty rooms always delude me into the belief that I possess a deep voice," said Meagle. "To-morrow I—"

He started up with a smothered exclamation as the light went out suddenly and something struck him on the head. The others sprang to their feet. Then Meagle laughed.

"It's the candle," he exclaimed. "I didn't stick it enough."

Barnes struck a match, and re-lighting the candle, stuck it on the mantelpiece, and sitting down took up his cards again.

"What was I going to say?" said Meagle. "Oh, I know; to-morrow I—"

"Listen!" said White, laying his hand on the other's sleeve. "Upon my word I really thought I heard a laugh."

"Look here!" said Barnes. "What do you say to going back?

I've had enough of this. I keep fancying that I hear things too; sounds of something moving about in the passage outside. I know it's only fancy, but it's uncomfortable."

"You go if you want to," said Meagle, "and we will play dummy. Or you might ask the tramp to take your hand for you, as you go downstairs."

Barnes shivered and exclaimed angrily. He got up, and, walking to the half-closed door, listened.

"Go outside," said Meagle, winking at the other two. "I'll dare you to go down to the hall door and back by yourself."

Barnes came back, and, bending forward, lit his pipe at the candle.

"I am nervous, but rational," he said, blowing out a thin cloud of smoke. "My nerves tell me that there is something prowling up and down the long passage outside; my reason tells me that that is all nonsense. Where are my cards?"

He sat down again, and, taking up his hand, looked through it carefully and led.

"Your play, White," he said, after a pause.

White made no sign.

"Why, he is asleep," said Meagle. "Wake up, old man. Wake up and play."

Lester, who was sitting next to him, took the sleeping man by the arm and shook him, gently at first and then with some roughness; but White, with his back against the wall and his head bowed, made no sign. Meagle bawled in his ear, and then turned a puzzled face to the others.

"He sleeps like the dead," he said, grimacing. "Well, there are still three of us to keep each other company."

"Yes," said Lester, nodding. "Unless—Good Lord! sup-pose—"

He broke off, and eyed them, trembling.

"Suppose what?" inquired Meagle.

"Nothing," stammered Lester. "Let's wake him. Try him again. *White*! WHITE!"

"It's no good," said Meagle seriously; "there's something wrong about that sleep."

"That's what I meant," said Lester; "and if *he* goes to sleep like that, why shouldn't—"

Meagle sprang to his feet. "Nonsense," he said roughly. "He's tired out; that's all. Still, let's take him up and clear out. You take his legs and Barnes will lead the way with the candle. *Yes? Who's that?*"

He looked up quickly towards the door.

"Thought I heard somebody tap," he said, with a shamefaced laugh. "Now, Lester, up with him. One, two – *Lester! Lester!*"

He sprang forward too late; Lester, with his face buried in his arms, had rolled over on the floor fast asleep, and his utmost efforts failed to awake him.

"He – is – asleep," he stammered. "Asleep!"

Barnes, who had taken the candle from the mantelpiece, stood peering at the sleepers in silence and dropping tallow over the floor.

"We must get out of this," said Meagle. "Quick!"

Barnes hesitated. "We can't leave them here—" he began.

"We must," said Meagle, in strident tones. "If you go to sleep I shall go – Quick! Come!"

He seized the other by the arm and strove to drag him to the door. Barnes shook him off, and, putting the candle back on the mantelpiece, tried again to arouse the sleepers.

"It's no good," he said at last, and, turning from them, watched Meagle. "Don't you go to sleep," he said anxiously.

Meagle shook his head, and they stood for some time in uneasy silence. "May as well shut the door," said Barnes at last.

He crossed over and closed it gently. Then at a scuffling noise behind him he turned and saw Meagle in a heap on the hearthstone.

With a sharp catch in his breath he stood motionless. Inside the room the candle, fluttering in the draught, showed dimly the grotesque attitudes of the sleepers. Beyond the door there seemed to his overwrought imagination a strange and stealthy unrest. He tried to whistle, but his lips were parched, and in a mechanical fashion he stooped, and began to pick up the cards which littered the floor.

He stopped once or twice and stood with bent head listening. The unrest outside seemed to increase; a loud creaking sounded from the stairs.

"Who is there?" he cried loudly.

The creaking ceased. He crossed to the door, and, flinging it open, strode out into the corridor. As he walked his fears left him suddenly.

"Come on!" he cried, with a low laugh. "All of you! All of you! Show your faces – your infernal ugly faces! Don't skulk!"

He laughed again and walked on; and the heap in the fireplace put out its head tortoise fashion and listened in horror to the retreating footsteps. Not until they had become inaudible in the distance did the listener's features relax.

"Good Lord, Lester, we've driven him mad," he said, in a frightened whisper. "We must go after him."

There was no reply. Meagle sprang to his feet.

"Do you hear?" he cried. "Stop your fooling now; this is serious. *White! Lester!* Do you hear?"

He bent and surveyed them in angry bewilderment. "All right," he said, in a trembling voice. "You won't frighten me, you know."

He turned away and walked with exaggerated carelessness in the direction of the door. He even went outside and peeped through the crack, but the sleepers did not stir. He glanced into the blackness behind, and then came hastily into the room again.

He stood for a few seconds regarding them. The stillness in the house was horrible; he could not even hear them breathe. With a sudden resolution he snatched the candle from the mantelpiece and held the flame to White's finger. Then as he reeled back stupefied, the footsteps again became audible.

He stood with the candle in his shaking hand, listening. He heard them ascending the farther staircase, but they stopped suddenly as he went to the door. He walked a little way along the passage, and they went scurrying down the stairs and then at a jog-trot along the corridor below. He went back to the main staircase, and they ceased again.

For a time he hung over the balusters, listening and trying to pierce the blackness below; then slowly, step by step, he made his way downstairs, and, holding the candle above his head, peered about him.

"Barnes!" he called. "Where are you?"

Shaking with fright, he made his way along the passage, and summoning up all his courage, pushed open doors and gazed fearfully into empty rooms. Then, quite suddenly, he heard the footsteps in front of him.

He followed slowly for fear of extinguishing the candle, until they led him at last into a vast bare kitchen, with damp walls and a broken floor. In front of him a door leading into an inside room had just closed. He ran towards it and flung it open, and a cold air blew out the candle. He stood aghast.

"Barnes!" he cried again. "Don't be afraid! It is I – Meagle!"

There was no answer. He stood gazing into the darkness, and all the time the idea of something close at hand watching was upon him. Then suddenly the steps broke out overhead again.

He drew back hastily, and passing through the kitchen groped his way along the narrow passages. He could now see better in the darkness, and finding himself at last at the foot of the staircase, began to ascend it noiselessly. He reached the landing just in time to see a figure disappear round the angle of a wall. Still careful to make no noise, he followed the sound of the steps until they led him to the top floor, and he cornered the chase at the end of a short passage.

"Barnes!" he whispered. "Barnes!"

Something stirred in the darkness. A small circular window at the end of the passage just softened the blackness and revealed the dim outlines of a motionless figure. Meagle, in place of advancing, stood almost as still as a sudden horrible doubt took possession of him. With his eyes fixed on the shape in front he fell back slowly, and, as it advanced upon him, burst into a terrible cry.

"Barnes! For God's sake! Is it *you?*"

The echoes of his voice left the air quivering, but the figure before him paid no heed. For a moment he tried to brace his courage up to endure its approach, then with a smothered cry he turned and fled.

The passages wound like a maze, and he threaded them blindly in a vain search for the stairs. If he could get down and open the hall door –

He caught his breath in a sob; the steps had begun again. At a lumbering trot they clattered up and down the bare passages, in and out, up and down, as though in search of him. He stood appalled, and then as they drew near entered a small room and stood behind the door as they rushed by. He came out and ran swiftly and noiselessly in the other direction, and in a moment the steps were after him. He found the long corridor and raced along it at top speed. The stairs he knew were at the end, and with the steps close behind he descended them in blind haste. The steps gained on him, and he shrank to the side to let them pass, still continuing his headlong flight. Then suddenly he seemed to slip off the earth into space.

Lester awoke in the morning to find the sunshine streaming into the room, and White sitting up and regarding with some perplexity a badly-blistered finger.

"Where are the others?" inquired Lester.

"Gone, I suppose," said White. "We must have been asleep."

Lester arose, and stretching his stiffened limbs, dusted his clothes with his hands and went out into the corridor. White followed. At the noise of their approach a figure which had been lying asleep at the other end sat up and revealed the face of Barnes. "Why, I've been asleep," he said, in surprise. "I don't remember coming here. How did I get here?"

'Nice place to come for a nap," said Lester severely, as he pointed to the gap in the balusters. "Look there! Another yard and where would you have been?"

He walked carelessly to the edge and looked over. In response to his startled cry the others drew near, and all three stood staring at the dead man below.

The Haunted House

I

THE MORTALS IN THE HOUSE

Under none of the accredited ghostly circumstances, and environed by none of the conventional ghostly surroundings, did I first make acquaintance with the house which is the subject of this Christmas piece. I saw it in the daylight, with the sun upon it. There was no wind, no rain, no lightning, no thunder, no awful or unwonted circumstance, of any kind, to heighten its effect. More than that: I had come to it direct from a railway station: it was not more than a mile distant from the railway station; and as I stood outside the house, looking back upon the way I had come, I could see the goods train running smoothly along the embankment in the valley. I will not say that everything was utterly commonplace, because I doubt if anything can be that, except to utterly commonplace people—and there my vanity steps in; but, I will take it on myself to say that anybody might see the house as I saw it, any fine autumn morning.

The manner of my lighting on it was this.

I was travelling towards London out of the North, intending to stop by the way, to look at the house. My health required a temporary residence in the country; and a friend of mine who knew that, and who had happened to drive past the house, had written to me to suggest it as a likely place. I had got into the train at midnight, and had fallen asleep, and had woke up and had sat looking out of window at the brilliant Northern Lights in the sky, and had fallen asleep again, and had woke up again to find the night gone, with the usual discontented conviction on me that I hadn't been to sleep at

all;—upon which question, in the first imbecility of that condition, I am ashamed to believe that I would have done wager
by battle with the man who sat opposite me. That opposite
man had had, through the night—as that opposite man always
has—several legs too many, and all of them too long. In addition to this unreasonable conduct (which was only to be expected of him), he had had a pencil and a pocket-book, and
had been perpetually listening and taking notes. It had appeared to me that these aggravating notes related to the jolts
and bumps of the carriage, and I should have resigned myself
to his taking them, under a general supposition that he was in
the civil-engineering way of life, if he had not sat staring
straight over my head whenever he listened. He was a
goggle-eyed gentleman of a perplexed aspect, and his demeanour became unbearable.

It was a cold, dead morning (the sun not being up yet), and
when I had out-watched the paling light of the fires of the
iron country, and the curtain of heavy smoke that hung at
once between me and the stars and between me and the day,
I turned to my fellow-traveller and said:

"I *beg* your pardon, Sir, but do you observe anything particular in me?" For, really, he appeared to be taking down, either my travelling-cap or my hair, with a minuteness that was
a liberty.

The goggle-eyed gentleman withdrew his eyes from behind
me, as if the back of the carriage were a hundred miles off,
and said, with a lofty look of compassion for my insignifi-
cance:

"In you, Sir?—B."

"B, Sir?" said I, growing warm.

"I have nothing to do with you, Sir," returned the gentleman; "pray let me listen—O."

He enunciated this vowel after a pause, and noted it down.

At first I was alarmed, for an Express lunatic and no communication with the guard, is a serious position. The thought
came to my relief that the gentleman might be what is popularly called a Rapper: one of a sect for (some of) whom I
have the highest respect, but whom I don't believe in. I was

going to ask him the question, when he took the bread out of my mouth.

"You will excuse me," said the gentleman contemptuously, "if I am too much in advance of common humanity to trouble myself at all about it. I have passed the night—as indeed I pass the whole of my time now—in spiritual intercourse."

"O!" said I, something snappishly.

"The conferences of the night began," continued the gentleman, turning several leaves of his note-book, "with the message: 'Evil communications corrupt good manners.' "

"Sound," said I; "but, absolutely new?"

"New from spirits," returned the gentleman.

I could only repeat my rather snappish "O!" and ask if I might be favoured with the last communication.

" 'A bird in the hand,' " said the gentleman, reading his last entry with great solemnity, " 'is worth two in the Bosh.' "

"Truly I am of the same opinion," said I; "but shouldn't it be Bush?"

"It came to me, Bosh," returned the gentleman.

The gentleman then informed me that the spirit of Socrates had delivered this special revelation in the course of the night. "My friend, I hope you are pretty well. There are two in this railway carriage. How do you do? There are seventeen thousand four hundred and seventy-nine spirits here, but you cannot see them. Pythagoras is here. He is not at liberty to mention it, but hopes you like travelling." Galileo likewise had dropped in, with this scientific intelligence. "I am glad to see you, *amico. Come sta?* Water will freeze when it is cold enough. *Addio!*" In the course of the night, also, the following phenomena had occurred. Bishop Butler had insisted on spelling his name, "Bubler," for which offence against orthography and good manners he had been dismissed as out of temper. John Milton (suspected of wilful mystification) had repudiated the authorship of Paradise Lost, and had introduced, as joint authors of that poem, two Unknown gentlemen, respectively named Grungers and Scadgingtone. And Prince Arthur, nephew of King John of England, had described himself as tolerably comfortable in the seventh circle, where he was learning to paint on velvet, under the direction of Mrs. Trimmer and Mary Queen of Scots.

If this should meet the eye of the gentleman who favoured me with these disclosures, I trust he will excuse my confessing that the sight of the rising sun, and the contemplation of the magnificent Order of the vast Universe, made me impatient of them. In a word, I was so impatient of them, that I was mightily glad to get out at the next station, and to exchange these clouds and vapours for the free air of Heaven.

By that time it was a beautiful morning. As I walked away among such leaves as had already fallen from the golden, brown, and russet trees; and as I looked around me on the wonders of Creation, and thought of the steady, unchanging, and harmonious laws by which they are sustained; the gentleman's spiritual intercourse seemed to me as poor a piece of journey-work as ever this world saw. In which heathen state of mind, I came within view of the house, and stopped to examine it attentively.

It was a solitary house, standing in a sadly neglected garden: a pretty even square of some two acres. It was a house of about the time of George the Second; as stiff, as cold, as formal, and in as bad taste, as could possibly be desired by the most loyal admirer of the whole quarter of Georges. It was uninhabited, but had, within a year or two, been cheaply repaired to render it habitable; I say cheaply, because the work had been done in a surface manner, and was already decaying as to the paint and plaster, though the colours were fresh. A lop-sided board drooped over the garden wall, announcing that it was "to let on very reasonable terms, well furnished." It was much too closely and heavily shadowed by trees, and, in particular, there were six tall poplars before the front windows, which were excessively melancholy, and the site of which had been extremely ill chosen.

It was easy to see that it was an avoided house—a house that was shunned by the village, to which my eye was guided by a church spire some half a mile off—a house that nobody would take. And the natural inference was, that it had the reputation of being a haunted house.

No period within the four-and-twenty hours of day and

night is so solemn to me, as the early morning. In the summer time, I often rise very early, and repair to my room to do a day's work before breakfast, and I am always on those occasions deeply impressed by the stillness and solitude around me. Besides that there is something awful in the being surrounded by familiar faces asleep—in the knowledge that those who are dearest to us and to whom we are dearest, are profoundly unconscious of us, in an impassive state, anticipative of that mysterious condition to which we are all tending—the stopped life, the broken threads of yesterday, the deserted seat, the closed book, the unfinished but abandoned occupation, all are images of Death. The tranquillity of the hour is the tranquillity of Death. The colour and the chill have the same association. Even a certain air that familiar household objects take upon them when they first emerge from the shadows of the night into the morning, of being newer, and as they used to be long ago, has its counterpart in the subsidence of the worn face of maturity or age, in death, into the old youthful look. Moreover, I once saw the apparition of my father, at this hour. He was alive and well, and nothing ever came of it, but I saw him in the daylight, sitting with his back towards me, on a seat that stood beside my bed. His head was resting on his hand, and whether he was slumbering or grieving, I could not discern. Amazed to see him there, I sat up, moved my position, leaned out of bed, and watched him. As he did not move, I spoke to him more than once. As he did not move then, I became alarmed and laid my hand upon his shoulder, as I thought—and there was no such thing.

For all these reasons, and for others less easily and briefly statable, I find the early morning to be my most ghostly time. Any house would be more or less haunted, to me, in the early morning; and a haunted house could scarcely address me to greater advantage than then.

I walked on into the village, with the desertion of this house upon my mind, and I found the landlord of the little inn, sanding his doorstep. I bespoke breakfast, and broached the subject of the house.

"Is it haunted?" I asked.

The landlord looked at me, shook his head, and answered, "I say nothing."

"Then it *is* haunted?"

"Well!" cried the landlord, in an outburst of frankness that had the appearance of desperation—"I wouldn't sleep in it."

"Why not?"

"If I wanted to have all the bells in a house ring, with nobody to ring 'em; and all the doors in a house bang, with nobody to bang 'em; and all sorts of feet treading about, with no feet there; why, then," said the landlord, "I'd sleep in that house."

"Is anything seen there?"

The landlord looked at me again, and then, with his former appearance of desperation, called down his stable-yard for "Ikey!"

The call produced a high-shouldered young fellow, with a round red face, a short crop of sandy hair, a very broad humorous mouth, a turned-up nose, and a great sleeved waistcoat of purple bars, with mother-of-pearl buttons, that seemed to be growing upon him, and to be in a fair way—if it were not pruned—of covering his head and overrunning his boots.

"This gentleman wants to know," said the landlord, "if anything's seen at the Poplars."

"'Ooded woman with a howl," said Ikey, in a state of great freshness.

"Do you mean a cry?"

"I mean a bird, Sir."

"A hooded woman with an owl. Dear me! Did you ever see her?"

"I seen the howl."

"Never the woman?"

"Not so plain as the howl, but they always keeps together."

"Has anybody ever seen the woman as plainly as the owl?"

"Lord bless you, Sir! Lots."

"Who?"

"Lord bless you, Sir! Lots."

"The general-dealer opposite, for instance, who is opening his shop?"

"Perkins? Bless you, Perkins wouldn't go a-nigh the place.

No!" observed the young man, with considerable feeling; "he an't overwise, an't Perkins, but he an't such a fool as *that*."

(Here, the landlord murmured his confidence in Perkins's knowing better.)

"Who is—or who was—the hooded woman with the owl? Do you know?"

"Well!" said Ikey, holding up his cap with one hand while he scratched his head with the other, "they say, in general, that she was murdered, and the howl he 'ooted the while."

This very concise summary of the facts was all I could learn, except that a young man, as hearty and likely a young man as ever I see, had been took with fits and held down in 'em, after seeing the hooded woman. Also, that a personage, dimly described as "a hold chap, a sort of one-eyed tramp, answering to the name of Joby, unless you challenged him as Greenwood, and then he said, 'Why not? and even if so, mind your own business,' had encountered the hooded woman, a matter of five or six times. But, I was not materially assisted by these witnesses: inasmuch as the first was in California, and the last was, as Ikey said (and he was confirmed by the landlord), Anywheres.

Now, although I regard with a hushed and solemn fear, the mysteries, between which and this state of existence is interposed the barrier of the great trial and change that fall on all the things that live; and although I have not the audacity to pretend that I know anything of them; I can no more reconcile the mere banging of doors, ringing of bells, creaking of boards, and such-like insignificances, with the majestic beauty and pervading analogy of all the Divine rules that I am permitted to understand, than I had been able, a little while before, to yoke the spiritual intercourse of my fellow-traveller to the chariot of the rising sun. Moreover, I had lived in two haunted houses—both abroad. In one of these, an old Italian palace, which bore the reputation of being very badly haunted indeed, and which had recently been twice abandoned on that account, I lived eight months, most tranquilly and pleasantly; notwithstanding that the house had a score of mysterious bedrooms, which were never used, and possessed, in one large room in which I sat reading, times out of number at all hours, and next to which I slept, a haunted chamber of the first pretensions. I gently hinted these considerations to the landlord. And as to this particular house having a bad name, I reasoned with him, Why, how many things had bad names undeservedly, and how easy it was to give bad names, and did he not think that he and I were persistently to whisper in the village that any weird-looking old drunken tinker of the neighbourhood had sold himself to the Devil, he would come in time to be suspected of that commercial venture! All this wise talk was perfectly ineffective with the landlord, I am bound to confess, and was as dead a failure as ever I made in my life.

To cut this part of the story short, I was piqued about the haunted house, and was already half resolved to take it. So, after breakfast, I got the keys from Perkins's brother-in-law (a whip and harness maker, who keeps the Post Office, and is under submission to a most rigorous wife of the Doubly Seceding Little Emmanuel persuasion), and went up to the house, attended by my landlord and by Ikey.

Within, I found it, as I had expected, transcendently dismal. The slowly changing shadows waved on it from the heavy trees, were doleful-in the last degree; the house was ill-placed, ill-built, ill-planned, and ill-fitted. It was damp, it was not free from dry rot, there was a flavour of rats in it, and it was the gloomy victim of that indescribable decay which settles on all the work of man's hands whenever it is not turned to man's account. The kitchens and offices were too large, and too remote from each other. Above stairs and below, waste tracts of passage intervened between patches of fertility represented by room; and there was a mouldy old well with a green growth upon it, hiding like a murderous trap, near the bottom of the backstairs, under the double row of bells. One of these bells was labelled, on a black ground in faded white letters, MASTER B. This, they told me, was the bell that rang the most.

"Who was Master B?" I asked. "Is it known what he did while the owl hooted?"

"Rang the bell," said Ikey.

I was rather struck by the prompt dexterity with which this

young man pitched his fur cap at the bell, and rang it himself. It was a loud, unpleasant bell, and made a very disagreeable sound. The other bells were inscribed according to the names of the rooms to which their wires were conducted: as "Picture Room," "Double Room," "Clock Room," and the like. Following Master B's bell to its source, I found that young gentleman to have had but indifferent third-class accommodation in a triangular cabin under the cock-loft, with a corner fireplace which Master B must have been exceedingly small if he were ever able to warm himself at, and a corner chimney-piece like a pyramidal staircase to the ceiling for Tom Thumb. The papering of one side of the room had dropped down bodily, with fragments of plaster adhering to it, and almost blocked up the door. It appeared that Master B, in his spiritual condition, always made a point of pulling the paper down. Neither the landlord nor Ikey could suggest why he made such a fool of himself.

Except that the house had an immensely large rambling loft at top, I made no other discoveries. It was moderately well furnished, but sparely. Some of the furniture—say, a third—was as old as the house; the rest was of various periods within the last half-century. I was referred to a corn-chandler in the market-place of the county town to treat for the house. I went that day, and I took it for six months.

It was just the middle of October when I moved in with my maiden sister (I venture to call her eight-and-thirty, she is so very handsome, sensible, and engaging). We took with us, a deaf stable-man, my bloodhound Turk, two women servants, and a young person called an Odd Girl. I have reason to record of the attendant last enumerated, who was one of the Saint Lawrence's Union Female Orphans, that she was a fatal mistake and a disastrous engagement.

The year was dying early, the leaves were falling fast, it was a raw cold day when we took possession, and the gloom of the house was most depressing. The cook (an amiable woman, but of a weak turn of intellect) burst into tears on beholding the kitchen, and requested that her silver watch might be delivered over to her sister (2 Tuppintock's Gardens, Ligg's Walk, Clapham Rise), in the event of anything happening to her from the damp. Streaker, the housemaid, feigned cheerfulness, but was the greater martyr. The Odd Girl, who had never been in the country, alone was pleased, and made arrangements for sowing an acorn in the garden outside the scullery window, and rearing an oak.

We went, before dark, through all the natural—as opposed to supernatural—miseries incidental to our state. Dispiriting reports ascended (like the smoke) from the basement in volumes and descended from the upper rooms. There was no rolling-pin, there was no salamander (which failed to surprise me, for I don't know what it is), there was nothing in the house, what there was, was broken, the last people must have lived like pigs, what could the meaning of the landlord be? Through these distresses, the Odd Girl was cheerful and exemplary. But within four hours after dark we had got into a supernatural groove, and the Odd Girl had seen "Eyes," and was in hysterics.

My sister and I had agreed to keep the haunting strictly to ourselves, and my impression was, and still is, that I had not left Ikey, when he helped to unload the cart, alone with the women, or any one of them, for one minute. Nevertheless, as I say, the Odd Girl had "seen Eyes" (no other explanation could ever be drawn from her), before nine, and by ten o'clock had had as much vinegar applied to her as would pickle a handsome salmon.

I leave a discerning public to judge of my feelings, when, under these untoward circumstances, at about half-past ten o'clock Master B's bell began to ring in a most infuriated manner, and Turk howled until the house resounded with his lamentations!

I hope I may never again be in a state of mind so unchristian as the mental frame in which I lived for some weeks, respecting the memory of Master B. Whether his bell was rung by rats, or mice, or bats, or wind, or what other accidental vibration, or sometimes by one cause, sometimes another, and sometimes by collusion, I don't know; but, certain it is, that it did ring two nights out of three, until I conceived the happy idea of twisting Master B's neck—in other words, breaking his bell short off—and silencing that young gentleman, as to my experience and belief, for ever.

But, by that time, the Odd Girl had developed such improving powers of catalepsy, that she had become a shining example of that very inconvenient disorder. She would stiffen, like a Guy Fawkes endowed with unreason, on the most irrelevant occasions. I would address the servants in a lucid manner, pointing out to them that I had painted Master B's room and balked the paper, and taken Master B's bell away and balked the ringing, and if they could suppose that that confounded boy had lived and died, to clothe himself with no better behaviour than would most unquestionably have brought him and the sharpest particles of a birch-broom into close acquaintance in the present imperfect state of existence, could they also suppose a mere poor human being, such as I was, capable by those contemptible means of counteracting and limiting the powers of the disembodied spirits of the dead, or of any spirits?—I say I would become emphatic and cogent, not to say rather complacent, in such an address, when it would all go for nothing by reason of the Odd Girl's suddenly stiffening from the toes upward, and glaring among us like a parochial petrifaction.

Streaker, the housemaid, too, had an attribute of a most discomfiting nature. I am unable to say whether she was of an unusually lymphatic temperament, or what else was the matter with her, but this young woman became a mere Distillery for the production of the largest and most transparent tears I ever met with. Combined with these characteristics, was a peculiar tenacity of hold in those specimens, so that they didn't fall, but hung upon her face and nose. In this condition, and mildly and deplorably shaking her head, her silence would throw me more heavily than the Admirable Crichton could have done in a verbal disputation for a purse of money. Cook, likewise, always covered me with confusion as with a garment, by neatly winding up the session with the protest that the Ouse was wearing her out, and by meekly repeating her last wishes regarding her silver watch.

As to our nightly life, the contagion of suspicion and fear was among us, and there is no such contagion under the sky.

Hooded woman? According to the accounts, we were in a perfect Convent of hooded women. Noises? With that contagion downstairs, I myself have sat in the dismal parlour, listening, until I have heard so many and such strange noises, that they would have chilled my blood if I had not warmed it by dashing out to make discoveries. Try this in bed, in the dead of the night; try this at your own comfortable fireside, in the life of the night. You can fill any house with noises, if you will, until you have a noise for every nerve in your nervous system.

I repeat; the contagion of suspicion and fear was among us, and there is no such contagion under the sky. The women (their noses in a chronic state of excoriation from smelling-salts) were always primed and loaded for a swoon, and ready to go off with hair-triggers. The two elder detached the Odd Girl on all expeditions that were considered doubly hazardous, and she always established the reputation of such adventures by coming back cataleptic. If Cook or Streaker went overhead after dark, we knew we should presently hear a bump on the ceiling; and this took place so constantly, that it was as if a fighting man were engaged to go about the house, administering a touch of his art which I believe is called The Auctioneer, to every domestic he met with.

It was in vain to do anything. It was in vain to be frightened, for the moment in one's own person, by a real owl, and then to show the owl. It was in vain to discover, by striking an accidental discord on the piano, that Turk always howled at particular notes and combinations. It was in vain to be a Rhadamanthus with the bells, and if an unfortunate bell rang without leave, to have it down inexorably and silence it. It was in vain to fire up chimneys, let torches down the well, charge furiously into suspected rooms and recesses. We changed servants, and it was no better. The new set ran away, and a third set came, and it was no better. At last, our comfortable housekeeping got to be so disorganised and wretched, that I one night dejectedly said to my sister: "Patty, I begin to despair of our getting people to go on with us here, and I think we must give this up."

My sister, who is a woman of immense spirit, replied, "No,

John, don't give it up. Don't be beaten, John. There is another way."

"And what is that?" said I.

"John," returned my sister, "if we are not to be driven out
of this house, and that for no reason whatever, that is apparent to you or me, we must help ourselves and take the house
wholly and solely into our own hands."

"But, the servants," said I.

"Have no servants," said my sister, boldly.

Like most people in my grade of life, I have never thought
of the possibility of going on without those faithful obstruc-
tions. The notion was so new to me when suggested, that I
looked very doubtful.

"We know they come here to be frightened and infect one
another, and we know they are frightened and do infect one
another," said my sister.

"With the exception of Bottles," I observed, in a meditative
tone.

(The deaf stable-man. I kept him in my service, and still
keep him, as a phenomenon of moroseness not to be matched
in England.)

"To be sure, John," assented my sister; "except Bottles.
And what does that go to prove? Bottles talks to nobody, and
hears nobody unless he is absolutely roared at, and what
alarm has Bottles ever given, or taken? None."

This was perfectly true; the individual in question having
retired, every night at ten o'clock, to his bed over the coach-
house, with no other company than a pitchfork and a pail of
water. That the pail of water would have been over me, and
the pitchfork through me, if I had put myself without announcement in Bottles's way after that minute, I had deposited in my own mind as a fact worth remembering. Neither
had Bottles ever taken the least notice of any of our many up-
roars. An imperturbable and speechless man, he had sat at his
supper, with Streaker present in a swoon, and the Odd Girl
marble, and had only put another potato in his cheek, or prof-
ited by the general misery to help himself to beefsteak pie.

"And so," continued my sister, "I exempt Bottles. And
considering, John, that the house is too large, and perhaps too

lonely, to be kept well in hand by Bottles, you, and me, I propose that we cast about among our friends for a certain selected number of the most reliable and willing—form a Society here for three months—wait upon ourselves and one another—live cheerfully and socially—and see what happens."

I was so charmed with my sister, that I embraced her on the spot, and went into her plan with the greatest ardour.

We were then in the third week of November; but, we took our measures so vigourously, and were so well seconded by the friends in whom we confided, that there was still a week of the month unexpired, when our party all came down together merrily, and mustered in the haunted house.

I will mention, in this place, two small changes that I made while my sister and I were yet alone. It occurring to me as not improbable that Turk howled in the house at night, partly because he wanted to get out of it, I stationed him in his kennel outside, but unchained; and I seriously warned the village that any man who came in his way must not expect to leave him without a rip in his own throat. I then casually asked Ikey if he were a judge of a gun? On his saying, "Yes, Sir, I knows a good gun when I sees her," I begged the favour of his stepping up to the house and looking at mine.

"*She's* a true one, Sir," said Ikey, after inspecting a double-barrelled rifle that I bought in New York a few years ago. "No mistake about *her*, Sir."

"Ikey," said I, "don't mention it; I have seen something in this house."

"No, Sir?" he whispered, greedily opening his eyes. " 'Ooded lady, Sir?"

"Don't be frightened," said I. "It was a figure rather like you."

"Lord, Sir?"

"Ikey!" said I, shaking hands with him warmly: I may say affectionately; "if there is any truth in these ghost-stories, the greatest service I can do you, is, to fire at that figure. And I promise you, by Heaven and earth, I will do it with this gun if I see it again!"

The young man thanked me, and took his leave with some

273

little precipitation, after declining a glass of liquor. I imparted my secret to him, because I had never quite forgotten his throwing his cap at the bell; because I had, on another occasion, noticed something very like a fur cap, lying not far from the bell, one night when it had burst out ringing; and because I had remarked that we were at our ghostliest whenever he came up in the evening to comfort the servants. Let me do Ikey no injustice. He was afraid of the house, and believed in its being haunted; and yet he would play false on the haunting side, so surely as he got an opportunity. The Odd Girl's case was exactly similar. She went about the house in a state of real terror, and yet lied monstrously and wilfully, and invented many of the alarms she spread, and made many of the sounds she heard. I had had my eye on the two, and I know it. It is not necessary for me, here, to account for this preposterous state of mind; I content myself with remarking that it is familiarly known to every intelligent man who has had fair medical, legal, or other watchful experience; that it is as well established and as common a state of mind as any with which observers are acquainted; and that it is one of the first elements, above all others, rationally to be suspected in, and strictly looked for, and separated from, any question of this kind.

To return to our party. The first thing we did when we were all assembled, was, to draw lots for bedrooms. That done, and every bedroom, and, indeed, the whole house, having been minutely examined by the whole body, we allotted the various household duties, as if we had been on a gipsy party, or a yachting party, or a hunting party, or were shipwrecked. I then recounted the floating rumours concerning the hooded lady, the owl, and Master B: with others, still more filmy, which had floated about during our occupation, relative to some ridiculous old ghost of the female gender who went up and down, carrying the ghost of a round table; and also to an impalpable Jackass, whom nobody was ever able to catch. Some of these ideas I really believe our people below had communicated to one another in some diseased way, without conveying them in words. We then gravely called one another to witness, that we were not there to be deceived, or to deceive—which we considered pretty much the same thing—and that, with a serious sense of responsibility, we would be strictly true to one another, and would strictly follow out the truth. The understanding was established, that any one who heard unusual noises in the night, and who wished to trace them, should knock at my door; lastly, that on Twelfth Night, the last night of holy Christmas, all our individual experiences since that then present hour of our coming together in the haunted house, should be brought to light for the good of all; and that we would hold our peace on the subject till then, unless on some remarkable provocation to break silence.

We were, in number and in character, as follows:

First—to get my sister and myself out of the way—there were we two. In the drawing of lots, my sister drew her own room, and I drew Master B's. Next, there was our first cousin John Herschel, so called after the great astronomer: than whom I suppose a better man at a telescope does not breathe. With him, was his wife: a charming creature to whom he had been married in the previous spring. I thought it (under the circumstances) rather imprudent to bring her, because there is no knowing what even a false alarm may do at such a time; but I suppose he knew his own business best, and I must say that if she had been *my* wife, I never could have left her endearing and bright face behind. They drew the Clock Room. Alfred Starling, an uncommonly agreeable young fellow of eight-and-twenty for whom I have the greatest liking, was in the Double Room; mine, usually, and designated by that name from having a dressing-room within it, with two large and cumbersome windows, which no wedges *I* was ever able to make, would keep from shaking, in any weather, wind or no wind. Alfred is a young fellow who pretends to be "fast" (another word for loose, as I understand the term), but who is much too good and sensible for that nonsense, and who would have distinguished himself before now, if his father had not unfortunately left him a small independence of two hundred a year, on the strength of which his only occupation in life has been to spend six. I am in hopes, however, that his Banker may break, or that he may enter into some speculation guaranteed to pay twenty per cent; for, I am convinced that if he could only be ruined, his fortune is made. Belinda Bates, bosom friend of my sister, and a most intellectual, amiable, and delightful girl, got the Picture Room. She has a fine genius for poetry, combined with real business earnestness, and "goes in"—to use an expression of Alfred's—for Woman's mission, Woman's rights, Woman's wrongs, and everything that is woman's with a capital W, or is not and ought to be, or is and ought not to be. "Most praiseworthy, my dear, and Heaven prosper you!" I whispered to her on the first night of my taking leave of her at the Picture Room door, "but don't overdo it. And in respect of the great necessity there is, my darling, for more employments being within the reach of Woman than our civilisation has as yet assigned to her, don't fly at the unfortunate men, even those men who are at first sight in your way, as if they were the natural oppressors of your sex; for, trust me Belinda, they do sometimes spend their wages among wives and daughters, sisters, mothers, aunts, and grandmothers; and the play is, really, not *all* Wolf and Red Riding-Hood, but has other parts in it." However, I digress.

Belinda, as I have mentioned, occupied the Picture Room. We had but three other chambers: the Corner Room, the Cupboard Room, and the Garden Room. My old friend, Jack Governor, "slung his hammock," as he called it, in the Corner Room. I have always regarded Jack as the finest-looking sailor that ever sailed. He is grey now, but as handsome as he was a quarter of a century ago—nay, handsomer. A portly, cheery, well-built figure of a broad-shouldered man, with a frank smile, a brilliant dark eye, and a rich dark eyebrow. I remember those under darker hair, and they look all the better for their silver setting. He has been wherever his Union namesake flies, has Jack, and I have met old shipmates of his, away in the Mediterranean and on the other side of the Atlantic, who have beamed and brightened at the casual mention of his name, and have cried, "You know Jack Governor? Then you know a prince of men!" That he is! And so unmistakably a naval officer, that if you were to meet him coming out of an Esquimaux snow-hut in seal's skin, you would be vaguely persuaded he was in full naval uniform.

Jack once had that bright clear eye of his on my sister; but, it fell out that he married another lady and took her to South America, where she died. This was a dozen years ago or more. He brought down with him to our haunted house a little cask of salt beef; for, he is always convinced that all salt beef not of his own pickling, is mere carrion, and invariably, when he goes to London, packs a piece in his portmanteau. He had also volunteered to bring with him one "Nat Beaver," an old comrade of his, captain of a merchantman. Mr. Beaver, with a thick-set wooden face and figure, and apparently as hard as a block all over, proved to be an intelligent man, with a world of watery experiences in him, and great practical knowledge. At times, there was a curious nervousness about him, apparently the lingering result of some old illness; but, it seldom lasted many minutes. He got the Cupboard Room, and lay there next to Mr. Undery, my friend and solicitor: who came down, in an amateur capacity, "to go through with it," as he said, and who plays whist better than the whole Law List, from the red cover at the beginning to the red cover at the end.

I never was happier in my life, and I believe it was the universal feeling among us. Jack Governor, always a man of wonderful resources, was Chief Cook, and made some of the best dishes I ever ate, including unapproachable curries. My sister was pastrycook and confectioner. Starling and I were Cook's Mate, turn and turn about, and on special occasions the chief cook "pressed" Mr. Beaver. We had a great deal of out-door sport and exercise, but nothing was neglected within, and there was no ill-humour or misunderstanding among us, and our evenings were so delightful that we had at least one good reason for being reluctant to go to bed.

We had a few night alarms in the beginning. On the first night, I was knocked up by Jack with a most wonderful ship's lantern in his hand, like the gills of some monster of the deep, who informed me that he "was going aloft to the main truck," to have the weathercock down. It was a stormy night, and I remonstrated; but Jack called my attention to its making a sound like a cry of despair, and said somebody would be "hailing a ghost" presently, if it wasn't done. So, up to the top of the house, where I could hardly stand for the wind, we went, accompanied by Mr. Beaver; and there Jack, lantern and all, with Mr. Beaver after him, swarmed up to the top of a cupola, some two dozen feet above the chimneys, and stood upon nothing particular, coolly knocking the weathercock off, until they both got into such good spirits with the wind and the height, that I thought they would never come down. Another night, they turned out again, and had a chimney-cowl off. Another night, they cut a sobbing and gulping water-pipe away. Another night, they found out something else. On several occasions, they both, in the coolest manner, simultaneously dropped out of their respective bedroom windows, hand over hand by their counterpanes, to "overhaul" something mysterious in the garden.

The engagement among us was faithfully kept, and nobody revealed anything. All we knew was, if any one's room were haunted, no one looked the worse for it.

II

THE GHOST IN MASTER B'S ROOM

When I established myself in the triangular garret which had gained so distinguished a reputation, my thoughts naturally turned to Master B. My speculations about him were uneasy and manifold. Whether his Christian name was Benjamin, Bissextile (from his having been born in Leap Year), Bartholomew, or Bill. Whether the initial belonged to his family name, and that was Baxter, Black, Brown, Barker, Buggins, Baker, or Bird. Whether he was a foundling, and had been baptized B. Whether he was a lion-hearted boy, and B was short for Briton, or for Bull. Whether he could possibly have been kith and kin to an illustrious lady who brightened my own childhood, and had come of the blood of the brilliant Mother Bunch?

With these profitless meditations I tormented myself much.

I also carried the mysterious letter into the appearance and pursuits of the deceased; wondering whether he dressed in Blue, wore Boots (he couldn't have been Bald), was a boy of Brains, liked Books, was good at Bowling, had any skill as a Boxer, even in his Buoyant Boyhood Bathed from a Bathing-machine at Bognor, Bangor, Bournemouth, Brighton, or Broadstairs, like a Bounding Billiard Ball?

So, from the first, I was haunted by the letter B.

It was not long before I remarked that I never by any hazard had a dream of Master B, or of anything belonging to him. But, the instant I awoke from sleep, at whatever hour of the night, my thoughts took him up, and roamed away, trying to attach his initial letter to something that would fit it and keep it quiet.

For six nights, I had been worried thus in Master B's room, when I began to perceive that things were going wrong.

The first appearance that presented itself was early in the morning when it was but just daylight and no more. I was standing shaving at my glass, when I suddenly discovered, to my consternation and amazement, that I was shaving—not myself—I am fifty—but a boy. Apparently Master B!

I trembled and looked over my shoulder; nothing there. I looked again in the glass, and distinctly saw the features and expression of a boy, who was shaving, not to get rid of a beard, but to get one. Extremely troubled in my mind, I took a few turns in the room, and went back to the looking-glass, resolved to steady my hand and complete the operation in which I had been disturbed. Opening my eyes, which I had shut while recovering my firmness, I now met in the glass, looking straight at me, the eyes of a young man of four or five and twenty. Terrified by this new ghost, I closed my eyes, and made a strong effort to recover myself. Opening them again, I saw, shaving his cheek in the glass, my father, who has long been dead. Nay, I even saw my grandfather too, whom I never did see in my life.

Although naturally much affected by these remarkable visitations, I determined to keep my secret, until the time agreed upon for the present general disclosure. Agitated by a multitude of curious thoughts, I retired to my room, that night, prepared to encounter some new experience of a spectral character. Nor was my preparation needless, for, waking from an uneasy sleep at exactly two o'clock in the morning, what were my feelings to find that I was sharing my bed with the skeleton of Master B!

I sprang up, and the skeleton sprang up also. I then heard a plaintive voice saying, "Where am I? What is become of me?" and, looking hard in that direction, perceived the ghost of Master B.

The young spectre was dressed in an obsolete fashion: or rather, was not so much dressed as put into a case of inferior pepper-and-salt cloth, made horrible by means of shining buttons. I observed that these buttons went, in a double row, over each shoulder of the young ghost, and appeared to descend his back. He wore a frill round his neck. His right hand (which I distinctly noticed to be inky) was laid upon his stomach; connecting this action with some feeble pimples on his countenance, and his general air of nausea, I concluded this ghost to be the ghost of a boy who had habitually taken a great deal too much medicine.

"Where am I?" said the little spectre, in a pathetic voice. "And why was I born in the Calomel days, and why did I have all that Calomel given me?"

I replied, with sincere earnestness, that upon my soul I couldn't tell him.

"Where is my little sister," said the ghost, "and where my angelic little wife, and where is the boy I went to school with?"

I entreated the phantom to be comforted, and above all things to take heart respecting the loss of the boy he went to school with. I represented to him that probably that boy never did, within human experience, come out well, when discovered, I urged that I myself had, in later life, turned up several boys whom I went to school with, and none of them had at all answered. I expressed my humble belief that that boy never did answer. I represented that he was a mythic character, a delusion, and a snare. I recounted how, the last time I found him, I found him at a dinner party behind a wall of white cravat, with an inconclusive opinion on every possible subject, and a power of silent boredom absolutely Titanic. I related how, on the strength of our having been together at "Old Doylance's," he had asked himself to breakfast with me (a social offence of the largest magnitude); how, fanning my weak embers of belief in Doylance's boys, I had let him in; and how, he had proved to be a fearful wanderer about the earth, pursuing the race of Adam with inexplicable notions concerning the currency, and with a proposition that the Bank of England should, on pain of being abolished, instantly strike off and circulate, God knows how many thousand millions of ten-and-sixpenny notes.

The ghost heard me in silence, and with a fixed stare. "Barber!" it apostrophised me when I had finished.

"Barber?" I repeated—for I am not of that profession.

"Condemned," said the ghost, "to shave a constant change of customers—now, me—now, a young man—now, thyself as thou art—now, thy father—now, thy grandfather; condemned, too, to lie down with a skeleton every night, and to rise with it every morning—"

(I shuddered on hearing this dismal announcement)..

"Barber! Pursue me!"

I had felt, even before the words were uttered, that I was under a spell to pursue the phantom. I immediately did so, and was in Master B's room no longer.

Most people know what long and fatiguing night journeys had been forced upon the witches who used to confess, and who, no doubt, told the exact truth—particularly as they were always assisted with leading questions, and the Torture was always ready. I asseverate that, during my occupation of Master B's room, I was taken by the ghost that haunted it, on expeditions fully as long and wild as any of those. Assuredly, I was presented to no shabby old man with a goat's horns and tail (something between Pan and an old clothesman), holding conventional receptions, as stupid as those of real life and less decent; but, I came upon other things which appeared to me to have more meaning.

Confident that I speak the truth and shall be believed, I declare without hesitation that I followed the ghost, in the first instance on a broom-stick, and afterwards on a rocking-horse.

The very smell of the animal's paint—especially when I brought it out, by making him warm—I am ready to swear to. I followed the ghost, afterwards, in a hackney coach; an institution with the peculiar smell of which, the present generation is unacquainted, but to which I am again ready to swear as a combination of stable, dog with the mange, and very old bellows. (In this, I appeal to previous generations to confirm or refute me.) I pursued the phantom, on a headless donkey: at least, upon a donkey who was so interested in the state of his stomach that his head was always down there, investigating it; on ponies, expressly born to kick up behind; on roundabouts and swings, from fairs; in the first cab—another forgotten institution where the fare regularly got into bed, and was tucked up with the driver.

Not to trouble you with a detailed account of all my travels in pursuit of the ghost of Master B, which were longer and more wonderful than those of Sinbad the Sailor, I will confine myself to one experience from which you may judge of many.

I was marvellously changed. I was myself, yet not myself. I was conscious of something within me, which has been the same all through my life, and which I have always recognised under all its phases and varieties as never altering, and yet I was not the I who had gone to bed in Master B's room. I had the smoothest of faces and the shortest of legs, and I had taken another creature like myself, also with the smoothest of faces and the shortest of legs, behind a door, and was confiding to him a proposition of the most astounding nature.

This proposition was, that we should have a Seraglio.

The other creature assented warmly. He had no notion of respectability, neither had I. It was the custom of the East, it was the way of the good Caliph Haroun Alraschid (let me have the corrupted name again for once, it is so scented with sweet memories!), the usage was highly laudable, and most worthy of imitation. "O, yes! Let us," said the other creature with a jump, "have a Seraglio."

It was not because we entertained the faintest doubts of the meritorious character of the Oriental establishment we proposed to import, that we perceived it must be kept a secret from Miss Griffin. It was because we knew Miss Griffin to be bereft of human sympathies, and incapable of appreciating the greatness of the great Haroun. Mystery impenetrably shrouded from Miss Griffin then, let us entrust it to Miss Bule.

We were ten in Miss Griffin's establishment by Hampstead Ponds; eight ladies and two gentlemen. Miss Bule, whom I judge to have attained the ripe age of eight or nine, took the lead in society. I opened the subject to her in the course of the day, and proposed that she should become the Favourite.

Miss Bule, after struggling with the diffidence so natural to, and charming in, her adorable sex, expressed herself as flattered by the idea, but wished to know how it was proposed to provide for Miss Pipson? Miss Bule—who was understood to have vowed towards that young lady, a friendship, halves, and no secrets, until death, on the Church Service and Lessons complete in two volumes with case and lock—Miss Bule said she could not, as the friend of Pipson, disguise from herself, or me, that Pipson was not one of the common.

Now, Miss Pipson, having curly light hair and blue eyes (which was my idea of anything mortal and feminine that was called Fair), I promptly replied that I regarded Miss Pipson in the light of a Fair Circassian.

"And what then?" Miss Bule pensively asked.

I replied that she must be inveigled by a Merchant, brought to me veiled, and purchased as a slave.

(The other creature had already fallen into the second male place in the State, and was set apart for Grand Vizier. He afterwards resisted this disposal of events, but had his hair pulled until he yielded.)

"Shall I not be jealous?" Miss Bule inquired, casting down her eyes.

"Zobeide, no," I replied; "you will ever be the favourite Sultana; the first place in my heart, and on my throne, will be ever yours."

Miss Bule, upon that assurance, consented to propound the idea to her seven beautiful companions. It occurring to me, in the course of the same day, that we knew we could trust a grinning and good-natured soul called Tabby, who was the serving drudge of the house, and had no more figure than one of the beds, and upon whose face there was always more or less black-lead, I slipped into Miss Bule's hand after supper, a little note to that effect: dwelling on the black-lead as being in a manner deposited by the finger of Providence, pointing Tabby out for Mesrour, the celebrated chief of the Blacks of the Hareem.

There were difficulties in the formation of the desired institution, as there are in all combinations. The other creature showed himself of a low character, and, when defeated in aspiring to the throne, pretended to have conscientious scruples about prostrating himself before the Caliph; wouldn't call him Commander of the Faithful; spoke of him slightingly and inconsistently as a mere "chap;" said he, the other creature, "wouldn't play"—Play!—and was otherwise coarse and offensive. This meanness of disposition was, however, put down by the general indignation of an united Seraglio, and I became blessed in the smiles of eight of the fairest of the daughters of men.

The smiles could only be bestowed when Miss Griffin was looking another way, and only then in a very wary manner, for there was a legend among the followers of the Prophet that she saw with a little round ornament in the middle of the pattern on the back of her shawl. But every day after dinner, for an hour, we were all together, and then the Favourite and the rest of the Royal Hareem competed who should most beguile the leisure of the Serene Haroun reposing from the cares of State—which were generally, as in most affairs of State, of an arithmetical character, the Commander of the Faithful being a fearful boggler at a sum.

On these occasions, the devoted Mesrour, chief of the Blacks of the Hareem, was always in attendance (Miss Griffin usually ringing for that officer, at the same time, with great vehemence), but never acquitted himself in a manner worthy of his historical reputation. In the first place, his bringing a broom into the Divan of the Caliph, even when Haroun wore on his shoulders the red robe of anger (Miss Pipson's pelisse), though it might be got over for the moment, was never to be quite satisfactorily accounted for. In the second place, his breaking out into grinning exclamations of "Lork you pretties!" was neither Eastern nor respectful. In the third place, when specially instructed to say "Bismillah!" he always said "Hallelujah!" This officer, unlike his class, was too good-humoured altogether, kept his mouth open far too wide, expressed approbation to an incongruous extent, and even once—it was on the occasion of the purchase of the Fair Circassian for five hundred thousand purses of gold, and cheap, too—embraced the Slave, the Favourite, and the Caliph, all round. (Parenthetically let me say God bless Mesrour, and may there have been sons and daughters on that tender bosom, softening many a hard day since!)

Miss Griffin was a model of propriety, and I am at a loss to imagine what the feelings of the virtuous woman would have been, if she had known, when she paraded us down the Hampstead-road two and two, that she was walking with a stately step at the head of Polygamy and Mahomedanism. I believe that a mysterious and terrible joy with which the contemplation of Miss Griffin, in this unconscious state, inspired us, and a grim sense prevalent among us that there was a dreadful power in our knowledge of what Miss Griffin (who knew all things that could be learnt out of book) didn't know, were the mainspring of the preservation of our secret. It was wonderfully kept, but was once upon the verge of self-betrayal. The danger and escape occurred upon a Sunday. We were all ten ranged in a conspicuous part of the gallery at church, with Miss Griffin at our head—as we were every Sunday—advertising the establishment in an unsecular sort of way—when the description of Solomon in his domestic glory happened to be read. The moment that monarch was thus referred to, conscience whispered me, "Thou, too, Haroun!" The officiating minister had a cast in his eye, and it assisted conscience by giving him the appearance of reading personally at me. A crimson blush, attended by a fearful perspiration, suffered my features. The Grand Vizier became more dead than alive, and the whole Seraglio reddened as if the sunset of Bagdad shone direct upon their lovely faces. At this portentous time the awful Griffin rose, and balefully surveyed the children of Islam. My own impression was, that Church and State had entered into a conspiracy with Miss Griffin to expose us, and that we should all be put into white sheets, and exhibited in the centre aisle. But, so Westerly—if I may be allowed the expression as opposite to Eastern associations—was Miss Griffin's sense of rectitude, that she merely suspected Apples, and we were saved.

I have called the Seraglio, united. Upon the question, solely, whether the Commander of the Faithful durst exercise a right of kissing in that sanctuary of the palace, were its peerless inmates divided. Zobeide asserted a counter-right in the Favourite to scratch, and the fair Circassian put her face, for refuge, into a green baize bag, originally designed for books. On the other hand, a young antelope of transcendent beauty from the fruitful plains of Camdentown (whence she had been brought, by traders, in the half-yearly caravan that crossed the intermediate desert after the holidays), held more liberal opinions, but stipulated for limiting the benefit of them to that dog, and son of a dog, the Grand Vizier—who had no rights, and was not in question. At length, the difficulty was compromised by the installation of a very youthful slave as Deputy. She, raised upon a stool, officially received upon her cheeks the salutes intended by the gracious Haroun for other Sultanas, and was privately rewarded from the coffers of the Ladies of the Hareem.

And now it was, at the full height of enjoyment of my bliss, that I became heavily troubled. I began to think of my mother, and what she would say to my taking home at Midsummer eight of the most beautiful of the daughters of men, but all unexpected. I thought of the number of beds we made up at our house, of my father's income, and of the baker, and my despondency redoubled. The Seraglio and malicious Vizier, divining the cause of their Lord's unhappiness, did their utmost to augment it. They professed unbounded fidelity, and declared that they would live and die with him. Reduced to the utmost wretchedness by these protestations of attachment, I lay awake, for hours at a time, ruminating on my frightful lot. In my despair, I think I might have taken an early opportunity of falling on my knees before Miss Griffin, avowing my resemblance to Solomon, and praying to be dealt with according to the outraged laws of my country, if an unthought-of means of escape had not opened before me.

One day, we were out walking, two and two—on which occasion the Vizier had his usual instructions to take note of the boy at the turnpike, and if he profanely gazed (which he always did) at the beauties of the Hareem, to have him bow-strung in the course of the night—and it happened that our hearts were veiled in gloom. An unaccountable action on the part of the antelope had plunged the State into disgrace. That charmer, on the representation that the previous day was her birthday, and that vast treasures had been sent in a hamper for its celebration (both baseless assertions), had secretly but most pressingly invited thirty-five neighbouring princes and princesses to a ball and supper: with a special stipulation that they were "not to be fetched till twelve." This wandering of the antelope's fancy, led to the surprising arrival at Miss Griffin's door, in divers equipages and under various escorts, of a great company in full dress, who were deposited on the top step in a flush of high expectancy, and who were dismissed in tears. At the beginning of the double knocks attendant on these ceremonies, the antelope had retired to a back attic, and bolted herself in; and at every new arrival, Miss Griffin had gone so much more and more distracted, that at last she had been seen to tear her front. Ultimate capitulation on the part of the offender, had been followed by solitude in the linen-closet, bread and water and a lecture to all, of vindictive length, in which Miss Griffin had used expressions: Firstly, "I believe you all of you knew of it;" Secondly, "Every one of you is as wicked as another;" Thirdly, "A pack of little wretches."

Under these circumstances, we were walking drearily along; and I especially, with my Moosulmaun responsibilities heavy on me, was in a very low state of mind; when a strange man accosted Miss Griffin, and, after walking on at her side for a little while and talking with her, looked at me. Supposing him to be a minion of the law, and that my hour was come, I instantly ran away, with the general purpose of making for Egypt.

The whole Seraglio cried out, when they saw me making

off as fast as my legs would carry me (I had an impression that the first turning on the left, and round by the public-house, would be the shortest way to the Pyramids), Miss Griffin screamed after me, the faithless Vizier ran after me, and the boy at the turnpike dodged me into a corner, like a sheep, and cut me off. Nobody scolded me when I was taken and brought back; Miss Griffin only said, with a stunning gentleness, This was very curious! Why had I run away when the gentleman looked at me?

If I had had any breath to answer with, I dare say I should have made no answer; having no breath, I certainly made none. Miss Griffin and the strange man took me between them, and walked me back to the palace in a sort of state; but not at all (as I couldn't help feeling, with astonishment), in culprit state.

When we got there, we went into a room by ourselves, and Miss Griffin called in to her assistant, Mesrour, chief of the dusky guards of the Hareem. Mesrour, on being whispered to, began to shed tears.

"Bless you, my precious!" said that officer, turning to me; "your pa's took bitter bad!"

I asked, with a fluttered heart, "Is he very ill?"

"Lord temper the wind to you, my lamb!" said the good Mesrour, kneeling down, that I might have a comforting shoulder for my head to rest on, "your pa's dead!"

Haroun Alraschid took to flight at the words; the Seraglio vanished; from that moment, I never again saw one of the eight of the fairest of the daughters of men.

I was taken home, and there was Debt at home as well as Death, and we had a sale there. My own little bed was so superciliously looked upon by the Power unknown to me, hazily called "The Trade," that a brass coal-scuttle, a roasting-jack and a birdcage, were obliged to be put into it to make a Lot of it, and then it went for a song. So I heard mentioned, and I wondered what song, and thought what a dismal song it must have been to sing!

Then, I was sent to a great, cold, bare, school of big boys; where everything to eat and wear was thick and clumpy, without being enough; where everybody, large and small, was cruel; where the boys knew all about the sale, before I got there, and asked me what I had fetched, and who had bought me, and hooted at me, "Going, going, gone!" I never whispered in that wretched place that I had been Haroun, or had had a Seraglio: for, I knew that if I mentioned my reverses, I should be so worried, that I should have to drown myself in the muddy pond near the playground, which looked like the beer.

Ah me, ah me! No other ghost has haunted the boy's room, my friends, since I have occupied it, than the ghost of my own childhood, the ghost of my own innocence, the ghost of my own airy belief. Many a time have I pursued the phantom: never with this man's stride of mine to come up with it, never with these man's hands of mine to touch it, never more to this man's heart of mine to hold it in its purity. And here you see me working out, as cheerfully and thankfully as I may, my doom of shaving in the glass a constant change of customers, and of lying down and rising up with the skeleton allotted to me for my mortal companion.

Secrets of Cabalism

or

Ravenstone and Alice of Huntingdon

William Child Green

(Dates unknown)

On the evening of the 29th of June, 1555, in one of the narrow streets near the Poultry Compter, in London, a dark square-built ruffian, in a thrum cap and leathern jerkin, suddenly sprung forth from his hiding-place, and struck his dagger with all his force against the breast of a man passing by. 'By my holidam,' said the man, 'that would have craved no thanks if my coat-hardy had been thinner – but thou shalt have a jape (a fool's mark) for thy leman to know thee by,' – and flourishing a short gisarme, or double-pointed weapon, in his left hand, with his right, on which he seemed to wear an iron glove, he stamped a sufficient mark on the assassin's face, and vanished in a moment.

'Why, thou Lozel!' said another ruffian, starting from beneath a penthouse, 'wast playing at barley-break with a wooden knife? Thou wilt hardly earn twenty pounds this bout.'

'A plague on his cloak, Coniers! – he must have had a gambason under it. – Thou mayest earn the coin thyself; – thou hast gotten a gold ring and twenty shillings in part payment.'

Get thee gone to thy needle and baudekin again, like a woman's tailor as thou art! Thou hast struck a wrong man, and he has taken away thy nose that he may swear to the right one. – That last quart of huff-cap made froth of thy brains.'

'My basilard is sharp enough for thee, I warrant,' muttered his disappointed companion, as he drew his tough hyke or cloak over his bruises, and slunk into a darker alley. Meanwhile, the subject of their discourse and of their villany strode with increased haste towards the Compter-prison, and inquired for the condemned prisoner, John Bradford. The keeper knew Bishop Gardiner's secretary, and admitted him without hesitation, hoping that he brought terms of grace to the pious man, whose meek demeanour in the prison had won love from all about him. The secretary found him on his knees, as his custom was, eating his square meal in that humble posture, and meditating with his hat drawn over his face. He rose to receive his visitors and his tall slender person, held gracefully erect, aided a countenance which derived from a faint bloom and a beard of rich brown, an expression of youthful beauty such as a painter would not have deemed unworthy the great giver of the creed for which he suffered. Gardiner's secretary uncovered his head, and, bending it humbly, kissed his hand with tears. 'Be of good comfort, brother,' said Bradford, — 'I have done nothing in this realm except in godly quietness, unless at Paul's Cross, where I bestirred myself to save him who is now Bishop of Bath, when his rash sermon provoked the multitude.'

'Ah, Bradford! Bradford!' replied his visitor, 'thou didst save him who will now burn thee. Had it not been for thee, I had run him through with my sword that day!' Bradford started back, and looked earnestly, — 'I know thy voice now, and I remember that voice said those same words in my ear when the turmoil was at Paul's Cross. For what comest thou now? A man of blood is no fit company for a sinner going to die.'

'Not while I live, my most dear tutor; I am Rufford of Edlesburgh.'

The old man threw his arms about his neck, and hung on it for an instant. 'It is twelve years since I saw thee, and my heart grieved when I heard a voice like thine in the fierce riot at Paul's Cross. Art thou here bodily, or, do I only dream? There is a rumour abroad, that thy old enemy, Coniers, slew thee at Huntingdon last year.'

'He meant well, John Bradford, but I had a thick hilted pourpoint and a tough leathern cap; I have met his minions more than once, and they know what print my hand leaves. Enough of this — I am not in England now as Giles Rufford; I shall do thee better service as what I seem.'

'Seeming never was good service,' said the divine: 'what hast thou to do with me, who am in God's hands?'

'He makes medicines of asps and vipers,' answered his pupil; 'I shall serve him if I save his minister, though it be by subtlety. I have crept into Gardiner's favour by my skill in strange tongues and Hebrew secrets, therefore I am now his secretary: and I have an ally in the very chamber of our queen-mistress.'

'That woman is not unwise or unmerciful,' replied Bradford, 'in things that touch not her faith; but I will be helped by no unfair practice on her. Mercy with God's mercy will be welcome, but I am readier to die than to be his forsworn servant.'

'Master, there can be no evil in gathering the fruit Providence has ripened for us. Gardiner was Wolsey's disciple once, and hath more heathen learning in him than Catholic zeal. There is a leaven left of his old studies which will work us good. He believes in the cabalism of the Jews, and reads strange books from Padua and Antwerp, which tell him of lucky and lucky days. He shall be made to think tomorrow full of evil omens, and his superstition shall shake his cruelty.'

'Thou art but a green youth still,' rejoined Bradford, 'if thou knowest not that cruelty is superstition's child. Take heed that his heathenish witchcraft doth not shake both thy wit and thy safety. For though I sleep but little, and have few dreams of earthly things, there came, as I think, a vision raised by no holy art, into my prison last night. And it had such a touch of heaven's beauty in its face, and such rare music in its voice, that it well nigh tempted me to believe its promise. But I remembered my frailty, and was safe.'

The secretary's eyes shone brightly, and half a smile opened his lips. But he lowered both his eyes and his voice as he replied, 'What did this fair vision promise?'

'Safety and release, if I would trust her, and be pledged to obey her.' — There was a long pause before the young man spoke again. — 'Do you not remember, my foster-father, the wild laurel that grew near my birthplace? An astrologer at Pisa told me it should not wither till the day of my death. And it seems to me, when I walked under its shade, that the leaves made strange music, as if a spirit had touched them. It is greener and richer than its neighbours, and the fountain that flows near its root has, as men believe, a rare power of healing —

the dreams that visit me when I sleep near it are always the visitings of a courteous and lovely spirit. What if the legends of Greece and Syria speak truth? May we not both have guardian spirits that choose earthly shapes?'

'My son,' replied Bradford, 'those thoughts are the diamond-drops that lie on the young roses of life; but the Sun of Truth and Reason should disperse them. Man has one guardian, and he needs no more unless he forgets that One. Thou wast called in thy youth the silken pleader, because thy words were like fine threads spun into a rich tissue. Be wary lest they entangle thee, and become a snare instead of a banner fit to guide Christians. I am a blighted tree marked for the fire, and thou canst not save me by searing the freshness of thy young laurel for my sake.'

'I will shame the astrologer tomorrow,' said the pupil; 'and therefore I must make this hour brief. She who rules the queen's secrets has had a bribe to make Mary merciful. There is hope of a birth at court, and death ought not to be busy. Fare-ye-well! but do not distrust that fair apparition if it should open these prison-doors tomorrow.' – So saying, the young man departed without heeding Bradford's monitory gesture.

Stephen Gardiner, Bishop of Winchester, and High Chancellor by Mary's favour, sat that night alone and thoughtful in his closet. He had been the chief commissioner appointed to preside at Bradford's trial: and though he had eagerly urged his colleagues to condemn him, he secretly abhorred the time-serving cruelty of Bishop Bonner and the cowardice of Bourne, who had not dared to save the life of the benefactor but had begged to save his own. 'You have tarried late,' said Gardiner, as his secretary entered – 'the stars are waning, and their intelligence will be imperfect.'

'I traced it before midnight,' replied the secretary, 'but I needed the help of your lordship's science.'

'It is strange,' said the patron, leaning thoughtfully on one of Roger Bacon's volumes, 'that men in every age and climate, and of every creed, have this appetite for an useless knowledge – and it would be stranger, if both profane and sacred history did not shew us that such knowledge had been sometimes granted, though in vain. – What is that paper in thy hand?'

'It is a clumsy calculation, my lord, of this night's aspect. I learned in Araby, as your lordship knows, some small guesses at Chaldean astrology; but I deem the characters and engraven signs of the Hermetic men more powerful in arresting the intelligent bodies in the heavens. They were the symbols used by Pythagoras and Zoroaster, and their great master Apollonius.'

'Ignatius Loyola and Athanasius Kircher did not disdain them,' replied the Bishop, crossing himself – 'But what was the fruit of thy calculation?'

'Nothing,' answered his secretary humbly – 'nothing at least not already known to one more able than myself. The first of July is a day of evil omen, and the last day of June has a doubtful influence. My intelligence says, if life be taken on that day, a mitre will be among ashes.'

'Ha! and the heretics will think it if Bradford dies, for they are wont to say, he is worthier of a bishopric than we of a parish priesthood. Thou hast not yet told all.'

'My lord, I see the rest dimly. – There are symbols of a falling star and a flame quenched in blood. They tell of a gorgeous funeral soon.'

Gardiner was silent several minutes before he raised his head. 'Thou knowest, Ravenstone, that I was like the Jesuit Loyola, a student of earthly things, and a servant in profane wars before I took the cross. Therefore I sinned not when I learned as he did. And thou knowest he thought much of heathen and Egyptian conjuration; but that is not my secret. Plato and Socrates had their attendant demons. I have seen, it may be, such a one in a dream last night. Methought there stood by me in an oratory a woman of queen-like beauty and strange beauty. She shewed me, as it were beyond a mist, a green tree growing near a fountain, and the star that shone on that fountain was the brightest in the sky; but presently the tree grew wide and broad, and the light of the star set behind it. Then I saw in my cathedral at Winchester my own effigies on a tomb, but all the inscription was effaced and broken except the date, and I read "the first day of July" – Is it not strange, Raven-stone, that a dream should so well tally with thy planetary reck-oning? Yet I was once told by a witch-woman, that the Bishop of Winchester should read out Queen Mary's funeral sermon.'

'So he may, my lord,' said the secretary, who called himself Ravenstone, 'but there may be a White Bishop of Winchester.'

'Ah! I trow thy meaning – White is a shrewd churchman, and looks for my place. Hearken to me, then – I have a thought that evil is gathering against me tonight; to profit by a dream, I will go privily from London within this hour, and abide in secret at Winchester till the ides of June are past. But take thou my signet-ring, and put my seal and countersign to Bradford's death-warrant when it comes from court.'

'Does my lord think it will be sent?' said the secretary calmly – 'They say the queen's bedchamber-woman has told her, she will be the mother of no living thing if she harms ought that has life.'

'Tush – that woman is a crafty giglet, but we need such helps when a queen reigns. It was well done, Ravenstone, to promise her Giles Rufford's lands. Since the man is dead, and his heir murdered him, we will make Alice of Huntingdon his heiress.'

Not a muscle in the pretended Ravenstone's face changed, and his deep black eye was steady as he replied – 'It will be well done, my lord, if she is faithful. At what hour is John Bradford to die?'

'Bid the marshal of the prison have a care of him till four o'clock tomorrow morning, for he is a gay and glorious talker; and so was his namesake, mad John of Munster, even among red hot irons. Look to the warrant, Ravenstone, and see it speedily sent to Newgate. That done – nay, come nearer – I would speak in thine ear. There is a coffer in my private cham-ber which I have left unlocked. Attach my signet-ring to the silver chain, and let me know what thou shalt hear; but let this be done in the very noon of night, when no eye nor ear but thine can reach it.'

Ravenstone promised, and his hand trembled with joy as he received the ring. It was already almost midnight, and Gardiner, as he stole out of his house, stopped to look at the moon's rainbow, then deemed a rare and awful omen. 'Alice of Huntingdon is busy,' said he, with a ghastly smile, 'but the dead man's land will be free enough for the blue-eyed witch – she cannot buy a husband without it.' – And stealing a look at Ravenstone, the Chancellor-bishop departed.

'I am a fool,' said young Ravenstone to himself, 'and worse than a fool, to heed how this wanton giglet may be made fit for a knave's bribe, – and yet that this dull bigot, this surly and selfish drone, should have such glimpses of a poet's paradise, is a wonder worth envying. I have heard and seen men in love with Platonic superstition under the hot skies of Spain, where the air seems as if it was the breathing of kind spirits and the waters are bright enough for the dwelling; but here in this foggy island – in this old man's dark head and iron heart! I will see what familiar demon stoops to hold converse with such a sorcerer.'

And young Ravenstone locked himself in his chamber, not ill-pleased that his better purpose would serve as covert and gilding for his secret passion to pry into his patron's mystery. He arrayed his person in the apparel he had provided to equip him as Gardiner's representative; and while he threw it over the close purpoint and tunic which fitted his comely figure, he smiled in scorn as he remembered the ugliness and decrepitude he meant to counterfeit. At the eleventh hour, when the darkness of the narrow streets, interrupted only by a few lanterns swinging above his head, made his passage safe, he admitted himself into the Bishop's house by a private postern, of which he kept a master-key. By the same key's help he entered the chamber, and ringing his patron's silver bell, gave notice to the page in waiting that his presence was needful. When this confidential servant entered, he was not surprised to see, as he supposed, the bishop seated behind his leathern screen muffled in his huge rochet or lawn garment, as if he had privately returned from council, according to his custom. 'Hath no messenger arrived from the court?' said the counterfeit prelate. 'None, my lord, for the queen, they say is sore sick.' – 'Tarry not an instant if one cometh, and see that the marshal of the compter be waiting here to take warrant, and execute it at his peril before daybreak.' The page retired; and Ravenstone, alone, saw the coffer standing on its solitary pedestal near him. It was unlocked, and he found within it only a deep silver bowl with a chain poised exactly in its centre. Ravenstone was no stranger to the mode of divination practised with such instruments. What could he risk by suspending the signet-ring as Gardiner had requested? His curiosity prevailed, and the ring when attached to the silver chain vibrated of itself, and struck the sides of the bowl three times distinctly. He listened eagerly to its clear and deep sound, expecting some response, and when he looked up, Alice of Huntingdon stood by his side.

This woman had a queen-like stature, to which the height of her volupure, or veil, twisted in large white folds like an Asiatic turban, gave increased majesty. Her supertunic, of a thick stuff, in those days called Stammel, hung from her shoulders with that ample flow which distinguishes the drapery of a Dian in ancient sculpture. 'You summoned me,' she said, 'and I attend you.'

Ravenstone, though he believed himself sporting with the superstition of Gardiner as with a tool, felt startled by her sudden appearance; and a thrill of the same superstitious awe he had mocked in his patron, passed through his own blood. But he recollected his purpose and his disguise; and still keeping the cowering attitude which befitted the bishop, he replied, 'Where is thy skill in divination if thou knowest not what I need?'

'I have studied thy ruling planet,' said Alice of Huntingdon, 'and as thy wishes are without number, so they are without a place in thy destiny. But I have read the signs of Mary Tudor's, and I know which of her high officers will lose his staff this night.'

'Knowest thou the marks of his visage, Alice?' asked the counterfeit bishop, bending down his head, and drawing his hood still farther over it.

'Hear them,' replied Alice: 'a swarthy colour, hanging look, frowning brows, eyes an inch within his head, hooked nose, wide nostrils, ever snuffing the wind, a sparrow-mouth, great hands, long talons rather than nails on his feet, which make him shuffle in his gait as in his actions – these are the marks of his visage and his shape; none can tell his wit, for it has all shapes. Dost thou know this portrait, my Lord of Winchester?'

'Full well, woman,' answered Ravenstone, 'and his trust is in a witch whose blue eyes shame heaven for lending its colour to hypocrisy; and her flattery has made boys think the tree she loved and the fountain she smiled on became holy. And now she serves two masters, one blinded by his folly, the other by his age.'

Ravenstone, as he spoke, dropped the rochet-hood from his shoulders, and shaking back his long jet-black hair, stood before her in the firmness and grace of his youthful figure. Alice did not shrink or recede a step. She laughed, but it was a laugh so musical, and aided by a glance of such sweet mirth, that Ravenstone relaxed the stern grasp he had laid upon her mantle. 'The warrant, Alice! It is midnight, and the marshal waits – where is the warrant for John Bradford's release?'

'It is in my hand,' she said, 'and needs only thy sign and seal; here is the handwriting of our queen.'

Ravenstone snatched the parchment, but did not rashly sign without unfolding it. 'Thou art deceived, Alice, or willing to deceive; this is a marriage contract, investing thee with the lands of Giles Rufford as thy dowry.'

'And to whom,' asked she, smiling, 'does my queen-mistress licence me to give it by her own manual sign?'

Ravenstone looked again, and saw his name entered, and himself described as the husband chosen for her maid of honour by Queen Mary. 'Has she also signed,' he said, the reprieve of John Bradford?'

'It is in my hand, and now in thy sight Henry Ravenstone; but the seal that will save thy friend may not be placed till thou hast given sign and seal to this contract. Choose! –'

The warrant for Bradford's liberation was spread before him, and her other hand held the contract of espousals. He smiled as he met the gaze of her keen blue eyes, and wrote the name of Henry Ravenstone in the blank left for it. She added her own without removing those keen eyes from his; and placing the parchment in her gipsire, suffered him to take the warrant of his friend's release. It was full and clear, but when he turned to seek the chancellor's signet-ring, the coffer had closed upon it. 'Blame thyself, Ravenstone!' said Alice of Huntingdon; 'thou hast laughed at the tales of imps and fairies, yet thou hadst woman's weakness enough to pry into that coffer and expect a miracle. As if thy master had not wit sufficient to devise a safe place for his ring, which thy curiosity placed there more than thy obedience! Didst thou think I came into this chamber like a sylph or an elfin, without hearing the stroke on the silver bowl which gave notice thou wast here? Truly, Ravenstone, man's vanity is the only witch that governs him.'

'Beautiful demon! when the crafty churchman who tutors thy cunning has no need of it, will thy master, the great Prince of Fire, save thee from the stake?'

'My trust in myself,' she answered; and throwing her cloak and wimple on the ground, she loosened her bright hair till it fell to her feet, and waving round her uncovered shoulders, and amongst the thin blue silk that clung to her shape, like wreaths of gold. Her eyes, large and brilliant as the wild leopard's, shone with such imperial beauty as almost to create the triumph they demanded. 'Be no rebel to my power, Ravenstone, for it is thy safety. Gardiner has ordered Bradford's death without appeal, and feigned his dream of danger to decoy thee here! But I have earned a fair estate by serving him, and thou mayest share it with me.' 'Thy wages are not yet paid, Alice!' he replied, grinding his teeth. 'That fair estate is mine, and that contract can avail thee nothing without my will – Henry Ravenstone is a name as false as thy promise to save Bradford.' Alice paused an instant, then laughing shrilly, clapped her hands thrice. In that instant the chamber was filled with armed men, who surrounded and struck down their victim notwithstanding his desperate defence. 'This is not the bishop!' one of the men exclaimed, 'this is not Stephen of Winchester; we shall not be paid for this.' 'He is Giles Rufford of Huntingdon,' answered his companion, the ruffian Coniers, 'and I am already paid.' Alice would have escaped had not the length of her dishevelled hair enabled her treacherous accomplices to seize it. They twined it round her throat to stifle her cries, making her boasted beauty the instrument of her destruction. She was dragged to Newgate on a charge of sorcery, and executed the next morning by John Bradford's side, in male attire, lest her rare loveliness should excite compassion. He knew her, and looking at the laurel-stems mingled with the faggots, said, as if conscious of his young friend's death – 'Alas! the green tree has perished for my sake!' – It was indeed his favourite laurel, which had been hewn down with cruel malice for this purpose. The people, just even in their superstitions to a good man's memory, still believe the earth remains parched and barren where John Bradford perished on the first of July 1555; and his heart, which escaped the flames, like his fellow martyr's, Archbishop Cranmer's, was embalmed and wrapped in laurel-leaves. His memory is sanctified by the religion honoured, while Alice of Huntingdon's sunk among dust and ashes, as a worthy emblem of the Cabalism she practised.

E. and H. Heron

THE STORY OF THE
SPANIARDS, HAMMERSMITH

Lieutenant Roderick Houston, of H.M.S. *Sphinx*, had practically nothing beyond his pay, and he was beginning to be very tired of the West African station, when he received the pleasant intelligence that a relative had left him a legacy. This consisted of a satisfactory sum in ready money and a house in Hammersmith, which was rated at over £200 a year, and was said in addition to be comfortably furnished. Houston, therefore, counted on its rental to bring his income up to a fairly desirable figure. Further information from home, however, showed him that he had been rather premature in his expectations, whereupon, being a man of action, he applied for two months' leave, and came home to look after his affairs himself.

When he had been a week in London he arrived at the conclusion that he could not possibly hope single-handed to tackle the difficulties which presented themselves. He accordingly wrote the following letter to his friend, Flaxman Low :

" The Spaniards, Hammersmith, 23-3-1892.

" DEAR LOW,—Since we parted some three years ago, I have heard very little of you. It was only yesterday that I met our mutual friend, Sammy Smith (' Silkworm ' of our schooldays) who told me that your studies have developed in a new direction, and that you are now a good deal interested in psychical subjects. If this be so, I hope to induce you to come and stay with me here for a few days by promising to introduce you to a problem in your own line. I am just now living at ' The Spaniards,' a house that has lately been left to me, and which in the first instance was built by an old fellow named Van Nuysen, who married a great-aunt of mine. It is a good house, but there is said to be ' something wrong ' with it. It lets easily, but unluckily the tenants cannot be persuaded to remain above a week or two. They complain that the place is haunted by something—presumably a ghost—because its vagaries bear just that brand of inconsequence which stamps the common run of manifestations.

" It occurs to me that you may care to investigate the matter with me. If so, send me a wire when to expect you.

" Yours ever,
" RODERICK HOUSTON."

Houston waited in some anxiety for an answer. Low was the sort of man one could rely on in almost any emergency. Sammy Smith had told him a characteristic anecdote of Low's career at Oxford, where, although his intellectual triumphs may be forgotten, he will always be remembered by the story that when Sands, of Queen's, fell ill on the day before the 'Varsity sports, a telegram was sent to Low's rooms : " Sands ill. You must do the hammer for us." Low's reply was pithy : " I'll be there." Thereupon he finished the treatise upon which he was engaged, and next day his strong, lean figure was to be seen swinging the hammer amidst vociferous cheering, for that was the occasion on which he not only won the event, but beat the record.

On the fifth day Low's answer came from Vienna. As he read it, Houston recalled the high forehead, long neck—with its accompanying low collar—and thin moustache of his scholarly, athletic friend, and smiled. There was so much more in Flaxman Low than anyone gave him credit for.

" MY DEAR HOUSTON,—Very glad to hear of you again. In response to your kind invitation, I thank you for the opportunity of meeting the ghost, and still more for the pleasure of your companionship. I came here to inquire into a somewhat similar affair. I hope, however, to be able to leave to-morrow, and will be with you some time on Friday evening.

" Very sincerely yours,
" FLAXMAN LOW."

" P.S.—By the way, will it be convenient to give your servants a holiday during the term of my visit, as, if my investigations are to be of any value, not a grain of dust must be disturbed in your house, excepting by ourselves ?—F. L."

" The Spaniards " was within some fifteen minutes' walk of Hammersmith Bridge. Set in the midst of a fairly respectable neighbourhood, it presented an odd contrast to the commonplace dullness of the narrow streets crowded about it. As Flaxman Low drove up in the evening light, he reflected that the house might have come from the back of beyond—it gave an impression of something old-world and something exotic.

It was surrounded by a ten-foot wall, above which the upper storey was visible, and Low decided that this intensely English house still gave some curious suggestion of the tropics. The interior of the house carried out the same idea, with its sense of space and air, cool tints and wide, matted passages.

" So you have seen something yourself since you came ? " Low said, as they sat at dinner, for Houston had arranged that meals should be sent in for them from an hotel.

" I've heard tapping up and down the passage upstairs. It is an uncarpeted landing which runs the whole length of the house. One night, when I was quicker than usual, I saw what looked like a bladder disappear into one of the bedrooms—your room it is to be, by the way—and the door closed behind it," replied Houston discontentedly. " The usual meaningless antics of a ghost."

" What had the tenants who lived here to say about it ? " went on Low.

" Most of the people saw and heard just what I have told you, and promptly went away. The only one who stood out for a little while was old Filderg—you know the man ? Twenty years ago he made an effort to cross the Australian deserts—he stopped for eight weeks. When he left he saw the house-agent, and said he was afraid he had done a little shooting practice in the upper passage, and he hoped it wouldn't count against him in the bill, as it was done in defence of his life. He said something had jumped on to the bed and tried to strangle him. He described it as cold and glutinous, and he pursued it down the passage, firing at it. He advised the owner to have the house pulled down ; but, of course, my cousin did nothing of the kind. It's a very good house, and he did not see the sense of spoiling his property."

" That's very true," replied Flaxman Low, looking round. " Mr. Van Nuysen had been in the West Indies, and kept his liking for spacious rooms."

" Where did you hear anything about him ? " asked Houston in surprise.

" I have heard nothing beyond what you told me in your letter ; but I see a couple of bottles of Gulf weed and a lace-plant ornament, such as people used to bring from the West Indies in former days."

" Perhaps I should tell you the history of the old man," said Houston doubtfully ; " but we aren't proud of it ! "

Flaxman Low considered a moment.

" When was the ghost seen for the first time ? "

" When the first tenant took the house. It was let after old Van Nuysen's time."

" Then it may clear the way if you will tell me something of him."

" He owned sugar plantations in Trinidad, where he passed the greater part of his life, while his wife mostly remained in England—incompatibility of temper it was said. When he came home for good and built this house they still lived apart, my aunt declaring that nothing on earth would persuade her to return to him. In course of time he became a confirmed invalid, and he then insisted on my aunt joining him. She lived here for perhaps a year, when she was found dead in bed one morning—in your room."

" What caused her death ? "

" She had been in the habit of taking narcotics, and it was supposed that she smothered herself while under their influence."

" That doesn't sound very satisfactory," remarked Flaxman Low.

" Her husband was satisfied with it anyhow, and it was no one else's business. The family were only too glad to have the affair hushed up."

" And what became of Mr. Van Nuysen ? "

" That I can't tell you. He disappeared a short time after. Search was made for him in the usual way, but nobody knows to this day what became of him."

" Ah, that was strange, as he was such an invalid," said Low, and straightway fell into a long fit of abstraction, from which he was roused by hearing Houston curse the incurable foolishness and imbecility of ghostly behaviour. Flaxman woke up at this. He broke a walnut thoughtfully and began in a gentle voice :

" My dear fellow, we are apt to be hasty in our condemnation of the general behaviour of ghosts. It may appear incalculably foolish in our eyes, and I admit there often seems to be a total absence of any apparent object or intelligent action. But remember that what appears to us to be foolishness may be wisdom in the spirit world, since our unready senses can only catch broken glimpses of what is, I have not the slightest doubt, a coherent whole, if we could trace the connection."

" There may be something in that," replied Houston indifferently. " People naturally say that this ghost is the ghost of old Van Nuysen. But what connection can possibly exist between what I have told you of him and the manifestations—a tapping up and down the passage and the drawing about of a bladder like a child at play ? It sounds idiotic ! "

" Certainly. Yet it need not necessarily be so. There are isolated facts, we must look for the links which lie between. Suppose a saddle and a horse-shoe were to be shown to a man who had never seen a horse, I doubt whether he, however intelligent, could evolve the connecting idea ! The ways of spirits are strange to us simply because we need further data to help us to interpret them."

" It's a new point of view," returned Houston, " but upon my word, you know, Low, I think you're wasting your time ! "

Flaxman Low smiled slowly ; his grave, melancholy face brightened.

" I have," said he, " gone somewhat deeply into the subject. In other sciences one reasons by analogy. Psychology is unfortunately a science with a future but without a past, or more probably it is a lost science of the ancients. However that may be, we stand to-day on the frontier of an unknown world, and progress is the result of individual effort ; each solution of difficult phenomena forms a step towards the solution of the next problem. In this case, for example, the bladder-like object may be the key to the mystery."

Houston yawned.

" It all seems pretty senseless, but perhaps you may be able to read reason into it. If it were anything tangible, anything a man could meet with his fists, it would be easier."

" I entirely agree with you. But suppose we deal with this affair as it stands, on similar lines, I mean on prosaic, rational lines, as we should deal with a purely human mystery."

" My dear fellow," returned Houston, pushing his chair back from the table wearily, " you shall do just as you like, only get rid of the ghost ! "

For some time after Low's arrival nothing very special happened. The tappings continued, and more than once Low had been in time to see the bladder disappear into the closing door of his bedroom, though, unluckily, he never chanced to be inside the room on these occasions, and however quickly he followed the bladder, he never succeeded in seeing anything further. He made a thorough examination of the house, and left no space unaccounted for in his careful measurement. There were no cellars, and the foundation of the house consisted of a thick layer of concrete.

At length, on the sixth night, an event took place, which, as Flaxman Low remarked, came very near to putting an end to the investigations as far as he was concerned. For the preceding two nights he and Houston had kept watch in the hope of getting a glimpse of the person or thing which tapped so persistently up and down the passage. But they were disappointed, for there were no manifestations. On the third evening, therefore, Low went off to his room a little earlier than usual, and fell asleep almost immediately.

He says he was awakened by feeling a heavy weight upon his feet, something that seemed inert and motionless. He recollected that he had left the gas burning, but the room was now in darkness.

Next he was aware that the thing on the bed had slowly shifted, and was gradually travelling up towards his chest. How it came on the bed he had no idea. Had it leaped or climbed ? The sensation he experienced as it moved was of some ponderous, pulpy body, not crawling or creeping, but spreading ! It was horrible ! He tried to move his lower limbs, but could not because of the deadening weight. A feeling of drowsiness began to overpower him, and a deadly cold, such as he said he had before felt at sea when in the neighbourhood of icebergs, chilled upon the air.

With a violent struggle he managed to free his arms, but the thing grew more irresistible as it spread upwards. Then he became conscious of a pair of glassy eyes, with livid, everted lids, looking into his own. Whether they were human eyes or beast eyes, he could not tell, but they were watery, like the eyes of a dead fish, and gleamed with a pale, internal lustre.

Then he owns he grew afraid. But he was still cool enough to notice one peculiarity about this ghastly visitant—although the head was within a few inches of his own, he could detect no breathing. It dawned upon him that he was about to be suffocated, for, by the same method of extension, the thing was now coming over his face ! It felt cold and clammy, like a mass of mucilage or a monstrous snail. And every instant the weight became greater.

He is a powerful man, and he struck with his fists again and again at the head. Some substance yielded under the blows with a sickening sensation of bruised flesh.

With a lucky twist he raised himself in the bed and battered away with all the force he was capable of in his cramped position. The only effect was an occasional shudder or quake that ran through the mass as his half-arm blows rained upon it. At last, by chance, his hand knocked against the candle beside him. In a moment he recollected the matches. He seized the box, and struck a light.

As he did so, the lump slid to the floor. He sprang out of bed, and lit the candle. He felt a cold touch upon his leg, but when he looked down there was nothing to be seen. The door, which he had locked overnight, was now open, and he rushed out into the passage. All was still and silent with the throbbing vacancy of night time.

After searching round, he returned to his room. The bed still gave ample proof of the struggle that had taken place, and by his watch he saw the hour to be between two and three.

As there seemed nothing more to be done, he put on his dressing-gown, lit his pipe, and sat down to write an account of the experience he had just passed through for the Psychical Research Society—from which paper the above is an abstract.

He is a man of strong nerves, but he could not disguise from himself that he had been at handgrips with some grotesque form of death. What might be the nature of his assailant he could not determine, but his experience was supported by the attack which had been made on Filderg, and also—it was impossible to avoid the conclusion—by the manner of Mrs. Van Nuysen's death.

He thought the whole situation over carefully in connection with the tapping and the disappearing bladder, but, turn these events how he would, he could make nothing of them. They were entirely incongruous. A little later he went and made a shake-down in Houston's room.

" What was the thing ? " asked Houston, when Low had ended his story of the encounter.

Low shrugged his shoulders.

" At least it proves that Filderg did not dream," he said.

" But this is monstrous ! We are more in the dark than ever. There's nothing for it but to have the house pulled down. Let us leave to-day."

"Don't be in a hurry, my dear fellow. You would rob me of a very great pleasure ; besides, we may be on the verge of some valuable discovery. This series of manifestations is even more interesting than the Vienna mystery I was telling you of."

"Discovery or not," replied the other, " I don't like it."

The first thing next morning Low went out for a quarter of an hour. Before breakfast a man with a barrowful of sand came into the garden. Low looked up from his paper, leant out of the window, and gave some order.

When Houston came down a few minutes later he saw the yellowish heap on the lawn with some surprise.

" Hullo ! What's this ? " he asked.

" I ordered it," replied Low.

" All right. What's it for ? "

" To help us in our investigations. Our visitor is capable of being felt, and he or it left a very distinct impression on the bed. Hence I gather it can also leave an impression on sand. It would be an immense advance if we could arrive at any correct notion of what sort of feet the ghost walks on. I propose to spread a layer of this sand in the upper passage, and the result should be footmarks if the tapping comes to-night."

That evening the two men made a fire in Houston's bedroom, and sat there smoking and talking, to leave the ghost " a free run for once," as Houston phrased it. The tapping was heard at the usual hour, and presently the accustomed pause at the other end of the passage and the quiet closing of the door.

Low heaved a long sigh of satisfaction as he listened.

" That's my bedroom door," he said ; " I know the sound of it perfectly. In the morning, and with the help of daylight, we shall see what we shall see."

As soon as there was light enough for the purpose of examining the footprints, Low roused Houston.

Houston was as full of excitement as a boy, but his spirits fell by the time he had passed from end to end of the passage.

" There are marks," he said, " but they are as perplexing as everything else about this haunting brute, whatever it is. I suppose you think this is the print left by the thing which attacked you the night before last ? "

" I fancy it is," said Low, who was still bending over the floor eagerly. " What do you make of it, Houston ? "

" The brute has only one leg, to start with," replied Houston,

" and that leaves the mark of a large, clawless pad ! It's some animal—some ghoulish monster ! "

" On the contrary," said Low, " I think we have now every reason to conclude that it is a man ? "

" A man ? What man ever left footmarks like these ? "

" Look at these hollows and streaks at the sides ; they are the traces of the sticks we have heard tapping."

" You don't convince me," returned Houston doggedly.

" Let us wait another twenty-four hours, and to-morrow night, if nothing further occurs, I will give you my conclusions. Think it over. The tapping, the bladder, and the fact that Mr. Van Nuysen had lived in Trinidad. Add to these things this single pad-like print. Does nothing strike you by way of a solution ? "

Houston shook his head.

" Nothing. And I fail to connect any of these things with what happened both to you and Filderg."

" Ah ! now," said Flaxman Low, his face clouding a little, " I confess you lead me into a somewhat different region, though to me the connection is perfect."

Houston raised his eyebrows and laughed.

" If you can unravel this tangle of hints and events and diagnose the ghost, I shall be extremely astonished," he said. " What can you make of the footless impression ? "

" Something, I hope. In fact, that mark may be a clue—an outrageous one, perhaps, but still a clue."

That evening the weather broke, and by night the storm had risen to a gale, accompanied by sharp bursts of rain.

" It's a noisy night," remarked Houston ; " I don't suppose we'll hear the ghost, supposing it does turn up."

This was after dinner, as they were about to go into the smoking-room. Houston, finding the gas low in the hall, stopped to turn it higher ; at the same time asking Low to see if the jet on the upper landing was also alight.

Flaxman Low glanced up and uttered a slight exclamation, which brought Houston to his side.

Looking down at them from over the banisters was a face— a blotched, yellowish face, flanked by two swollen, protruding ears, the whole aspect being strangely leonine. It was but a glimpse, a clash of meeting glances, as it were, a glare of defiance, and the face was quickly withdrawn as the two men literally leapt up the stairs.

" There's nothing here," exclaimed Houston, after a search had been carried out through every room above.

" I didn't suppose we'd find anything," returned Low.

" This fairly knots up the thread," said Houston. " You can't pretend to unravel it now."

" Come down," said Low briefly ; " I'm ready to give you my opinion, such as it is."

Once in the smoking-room, Houston busied himself in turning on all the light he could procure, then he saw to securing the windows, and piled up an immense fire, while Flaxman Low, who, as usual, had a cigarette in his mouth, sat on the edge of the table and watched him with some amusement.

" You saw that abominable face ? " cried Houston, as he threw himself into a chair. " It was as material as yours or mine. But where did he go to ? He must be somewhere about."

" We saw him clearly. That is sufficient for our purpose."

" You are very good at enumerating points, Low. Now just listen to my list. The difficulties grow with every fresh discovery. We're at a deadlock now, I take it ? The sticks and the tapping point to an old man, the playing with a bladder to a child ; the footmark might be the pad of a tiger minus claws, yet the thing that attacked you at night was cold and pulpy. And, lastly, by way of a wind-up, we see a lion-like, human face ! If you can make all these items square with each other, I'll be happy to hear what you have got to say."

" You must first allow me to ask you a question. I understood you to say that no blood relationship existed between you and old Mr. Van Nuysen ? "

" Certainly not. He was quite an outsider," answered Houston brusquely.

" In that case you are welcome to my conclusions. All the things you have mentioned point to one explanation. This house is haunted by the ghost of Mr. Van Nuysen, and he was a leper."

Houston stood up and stared at his companion.

" What a horrible notion ! I must say I fail to see how you have arrived at such a conclusion."

" Take the chain of evidence in rather different order," said Low. " Why should a man tap with a stick ? "

" Generally because he's blind."

" In cases of blindness, one stick is used for guidance. Here we have two for support."

" A man who has lost the use of his feet."

" Exactly ; a man who has from some cause partially lost the use of his feet."

" But the bladder and the lion-like face ? " went on Houston.

" The bladder, or what seemed to us to resemble a bladder, was one of his feet, contorted by the disease and probably swathed in linen, which foot he dragged rather than used ; consequently, in passing through a door, for example, he would be in the habit of drawing it in after him. Now, as regards the single footmark we saw. In one form of leprosy, the smaller bones of the extremities frequently fall away. The pad-like impression was, as I believe, the mark of the other foot—a toeless foot which he used, because in a more advanced stage of the disease the maimed hand or foot heals and becomes callous."

" Go on," said Houston ; " it sounds as if it might be true. And the lion-like face I can account for myself. I have been in China, and have seen it before in lepers."

" Mr. Van Nuysen had been in Trinidad for many years, as we know, and while there he probably contracted the disease."

" I suppose so. After his return," added Houston, " he shut himself up almost entirely, and gave out that he was a martyr to rheumatic gout, this awful thing being the true explanation."

" It also accounts for Mrs. Van Nuysen's determination not to return to her husband."

Houston appeared much disturbed.

" We can't drop it here, Low," he said, in a constrained voice. " There is a good deal more to be cleared up yet. Can you tell me more ? "

" From this point I find myself on less certain ground," replied Low unwillingly. " I merely offer a suggestion, remember—I don't ask you to accept it. I believe Mrs. Van Nuysen was murdered ! "

" What ? " exclaimed Houston. " By her husband ? "

" Indications tend that way."

" But, my good fellow——"

" He suffocated her and then made away with himself. It is a pity that his body was not recovered. The condition of the remains would be the only really satisfactory test of my theory. If the skeleton could even now be found, the fact that he was a leper would be finally settled."

There was a prolonged pause until Houston put another question.

" Wait a minute, Low," he said. " Ghosts are admittedly immaterial. In this instance our spook has an extremely palpable body. Surely this is rather unusual ? You have made everything else more or less plain. Can you tell me why this dead leper should have tried to murder you and old Filderg ? And also how he came to have the actual physical power to do so ? "

Low removed his cigarette to look thoughtfully at the end of it. " Now I lapse into the purely theoretical," he answered. " Cases have been known where the assumption of diabolical agency is apparently justifiable."

" Diabolical agency ?—I don't follow you."

" I will try to make myself clear, though the subject is still in a stage of vagueness and immaturity. Van Nuysen committed a murder of exceptional atrocity, and afterwards killed himself. Now, bodies of suicides are known to be peculiarly susceptible to spiritual influences, even to the point of arrested corruption. Add to this our knowledge that the highest aim of an evil spirit is to gain possession of a material body. If I carried out my theory to its logical conclusion, I should say that Van Nuysen's body is hidden somewhere on these premises—that this body is intermittently animated by some spirit, which at certain periods is forced to re-enact the gruesome tragedy of the Van Nuysens. Should any living person chance to occupy the position of the first victim, so much the worse for him ! "

For some minutes Houston made no remark on this singular expression of opinion.

" But have you ever met with anything of the sort before ? " he said at last.

" I can recall," replied Flaxman Low thoughtfully, " quite a number of cases which would seem to bear out this hypothesis. Among them a curious problem of haunting exhaustively examined by Busner in the early part of 1888, at which I was myself lucky enough to assist. Indeed, I may add that the affair which I have recently been engaged upon in Vienna offers some rather similar features. There, however, we had to stop short of excavation, by which alone any specific results might have been attained."

" Then you are of opinion," said Houston, " that pulling the house to pieces might cast some further light upon this affair ? "

" I cannot see any better course," said Mr. Low.

Then Houston closed the discussion by a very definite declaration.

" This house shall come down ! "

So " The Spaniards " was pulled down.

Such is the story of " The Spaniards," Hammersmith, and it has been given the first place in this series because, although it may not be of so strange a nature as some that will follow it, yet it seems to us to embody in a high degree the peculiar methods by which Mr. Flaxman Low is wont to approach these cases.

The work of demolition, begun at the earliest possible moment, did not occupy very long, and during its early stages, under the boarding at an angle of the landing was found a skeleton. Several of the phalanges were missing, and other indications also established beyond a doubt the fact that the remains were the remains of a leper.

The skeleton is now in the museum of one of our city hospitals. It bears a scientific ticket, and is the only evidence extant of the correctness of Mr. Flaxman Low's methods and the possible truth of his extraordinary theories.

THE RIVER OF DEATH

by Fred M. White

The sky was as brass, a stifling heat radiated from stone and wood and iron – a close, reeking heat that drove one back from the very mention of food. The five million-odd people that go to make up London, even in the cream of the holiday season, panted and gasped and prayed for the rain that never came. For the first three weeks in August the furnace fires of the sun poured down till every building became a vapour bath with no suspcion of a breeze to temper the fierceness of it. Even the cheap press had given up sunstroke statistics.

The drought had lasted since April. Tales came up from the provinces of stagnant rivers and quick, fell spurts of zymotic diseases. For some time the London water companies had restricted supplies, but there was no suggestion of alarm. The heat was almost unbearable but, people said, the wave must break soon and the metropolis would breathe again.

Professor Owen Darbyshire crawled homewards towards Harley Street with his hat in his hand, his grey frock coat showing a wide expanse of white shirt below. There was a buzz of electric fans in the hall, yet the atmosphere was hot and heavy. There was one solitary light in the dining-room – a room all sombre oak and dull red walls as befitted a man of science – and a visiting card glistened on the table. Darbyshire read it with annoyance: 'James P. Chase, *Morning Telephone*.'

'I'll have to see him,' he groaned, 'but is it possible these confounded pressmen have got hold of the story already?' Doubtless Chase was merely plunging around after sensations – the constant pestering of newspapermen was no new, thing to Darbyshire with his reputation for fighting disease in bulk, the one man always sent for when there was an epidemic to be grappled with. Still, the pushing little American might have stumbled on the truth. When he came back, he had better be granted an audience, however brief. Meanwhile Darbyshire took down his telephone and churned the handle.

'Are you there? Yes, give me 30795, Kensington . . . That you, Longdale? Step round here at once, will you? Yes, I know it's hot, and I wouldn't ask you to come if it wasn't a matter of the last importance.'

He hung up his receiver, lighted a cigarette, and proceeded to con over some notes. He was roused presently by the hall bell and Dr Longdale entered. 'I suppose it's come at last?' he asked.

'Of course it has,' Darbyshire replied, 'and in a worse form than you think. Just listen to this:' and he took from his pocket a newspaper clipping.

STRANGE AFFAIR AT ALDENBURGH

A day or two ago the barque *Santa Anna* came ashore at Spur, near Aldenburgh, and quickly became a total wreck. The crew of eight presumably took to their boats, for nothing has been seen of them since. How the *Santa Anna* came to be wrecked on a clear, calm night remains a mystery. From the thousands of oranges which have been picked up at Aldenburgh lately, the coastguards presume the barque to be Portuguese.

'Naturally you want to know what this has to do with us. Well, the *Santa Anna* was deliberately wrecked, and the crew for reasons of their own sank their boat. It isn't far from Aldenburgh to London: in a short time the Portuguese were in the metropolis. Some of them set off for Cardiff, to get a ship there. On the way three are taken ill, two of them die, The local practitioner sends for the medical officer of health. The latter gets frightened and sends for me. I have just got back – with *this*.'

Darbyshire produced a phial of cloudy fluid, some of which he proceeded to lay on the glass of a powerful microscope. Longdale fairly staggered back from the eyepiece. 'Bubonic! The water reeks with the bacillus! You don't mean . . .'

'I do. This sample comes from the Thames. Those seamen, who ran their ship aground and deserted her, have been suffering from bubonic fever – and by a series of circumstances they have infected the river which gives most of London its water supply. That deadly poison is hourly drawing nearer to the metropolis into which presently it will be ladled by the million gallons. People will wash in it, drink it, Mayfair along with Whitechapel!'

'The supply must be cut off!'

'And deprive four-fifths of London of water when it is grilling like a furnace? No flushing of sewers, no watering of roads, not even a drop to drink. In two days London would be a reeking, seething hell – try and picture it!'

'There's only one alternative – that process of sterilisation of yours.'

Darbyshire smiled, and moved towards his office. The notes were there, but they seemed to have been disturbed. On the floor lay a torn sheet with shorthand cypher: thereon Darbyshire flew to the bell and rang it violently.

'Verity,' he cried when the butler appeared, 'has that Mr Chase been here again?'

'Well, he have, sir, just after Mr Longdale. So I asked him to wait, which he did, then he come out again after a bit, saying he would call again, looking very excited, sir.'

'It's clear enough,' Darbyshire turned to Longdale. 'That confounded journalist has heard all we said – and tomorrow the whole thing will be blazing in the *Telephone*. Those fellows would wreck the empire for a "scoop". But we can perhaps convince the editor that that article must not appear.' He called the butler again. 'Get me a hansom, fast as you can.'

A minute later there was a rattle of wheels outside and Darbyshire plunged hatless into the night. 'Offices of the *Telephone*. A sovereign if I'm there in twenty minutes.'

The cab plunged on headlong. The driver was going to earn that sovereign or know the reason why. He drove furiously into Trafalgar Square, a motor car crossed him recklessly, and a moment later Darbyshire was shot out onto his head. He lay there with no interest in mundane things. A crowd gathered, a doctor in evening dress appeared.

'Concussion of the brain . . . By jove, it's Darbyshire!'

Here, police, hurry up with the ambulance: he must be removed to Charing Cross Hospital at once.'

The controlling genius of the *Telephone* sat limp and bereft of coat and vest. His greeting of Chase was not over-polite. But when he saw the sheet of notes that the journalist carried, the tired look faded from his eyes. Here was the tonic his soul craved for.

'It wants pluck . . . A scare like that might ruin the Empire.'

'Take it or leave it. If you haven't got the grit, Sutton of the *Flashlight* will jump at it.'

Grady made his decision. 'Sit down right away and make two columns of it. I'll get some statistics out for you.'

Cold facts made the story seem worse, rather than better. The upper waters of the Thames were poisoned – yet nearly all London derived its water supply from those waters. Only two London water companies did not derive their water from the Thames – the New River Company and the Kent Company. Only those fortunate enough to be served by these mains would be exempt from peril – and even they would soon be in danger from their neighbours.

The further Grady read, the more he felt that if he could get this dread information into the hands of the people before it was too late, he would be playing the part of a benefactor. Desperate as the situation looked, the *Telephone* might yet save it. Professor Darbyshire had no right to hold up such a secret when he should have been taking measures to avert the threatened danger.

An hour later the presses were roaring: presently huge parcels of damp sheets were vomited into the street. London awoke, and on a hundred thousand breakfast tables the eye was arrested by scare heads:

THE POISONED THAMES

Millions of plague germs flowing down into London. Bacillus of bubonic plague in the river. New River and Kent Companies alone can supply pure water. Stupendous discovery by Professor Darbyshire. Death in your breakfast cup today. Shun it as you would poison. If you are not connected with either of the above companies, or if you have no private supply – CUT OFF YOUR WATER AT THE MAIN AT ONCE!'

At eight in the morning London's pulse was calm and regular. An hour later it was writhing like some great reptile in the throes of mortal pain.

The one man who could have done most to help was lying unconscious at Charing Cross Hospital. Meanwhile Dr Longdale was the man of the hour – but he could not allay the panic that had gripped London. Under a blazing sunshine after days of heat and dust the packed East End was suddenly deprived of every drop of water. For an hour or two no great hardship was felt, but after that every moment added to the agony. Before long the railway termini were packed with people eager to be away from the metropolis.

By midday business was at a standstill. There was not a water cart to be seen from Kensington to the Mansion House. Every cart and tank had been despatched into the New River and Kent Water area to convey a supply as speedily as possible to the congested districts East and South-east of the Thames. By lunchtime the City presented a strange spectacle. Well-dressed business men could be seen proceeding in cabs with buckets and water cans with the object of taking a supply forthwith. Cabmen were commanding their own prices.

Mineral waters went up 200 per cent in price: by midday the supply had ceased – men of means with an eye to the future had bought up the whole stock. The streets were crowded with people anxiously awaiting developments. They were rewarded a little after two o'clock when a boy came yelling down the Strand with a flapping of papers on his shoulder: 'The plague broken out! Two cases of bubonic fever at Limehouse! Speshull!'

Perhaps if the readers had known these two cases were renegades from the *Santa Anna*, the panic might have been allayed. But nobody knew. Though no fever could have broken out so soon, it was assumed that the two poor fellows had drunk of the polluted flood and paid the penalty. It might be the turn of any of them next. There were those who shrugged their shoulders stolidly, others that crept into bars and restaurants and asked furtively for brandy.

By this time everything that could be done was being done. The artesian wells of East and South London were being tapped. Private houses which possessed pumps were besieged. Main line trains made way for trains of tanks bringing water to the city. But the problem of distribution remained – how could the little water available be distributed fairly among six million people over an area of some thirty square miles?

Night came, but brought no end to the stream of people coming and going between Trafalgar Square and such other open supplies as were available. Morning brought the promise of another sweltering day. Smartly dressed men were to be seen with grimy chins and features frankly dirty. The dust in the unwatered streets became intolerable. Tempers were strained. Small riots broke out here and there, some people were robbed of their precious fluid as they carried it home. Democratic agitators took advantage of the situation, a mob stormed the Houses of Parliament singing the Marseillaise in strident tones. Looters ravaged the markets, went off with baskets of apples and oranges. Mysteriously, as the sign that called up the Indian Mutiny, the signal went round to raid the public houses and hotels. Men stood in the Strand outside famous restaurants with bottles of strange liquids in their hands, the necks of which they knocked off without ceremony to reach the precious fluid within.

What might have happened when these last scant resources gave out will fortunately never be known. For suddenly, beneath the hubbub of the streets, the clamour and shrieks of the rioters, a strange unbelievable sound was heard. The shouting died away – and the people of London heard it now with no mistaking: the sound of water! The water supply had been restored!

The turncocks in the Strand were busy flushing the gutters with standpipes, a row of fire engines were proceeding to wash the streets down from the mains. The whole thing was so sudden and unexpected that it seemed like a dream.

And what was even less expected – what people only learnt when they read their papers that evening – was that the city's water supply was safe to drink all these days. For what Dr Darbyshire had no time to tell his colleague, in his hurry to get to the *Telephone* offices, was that as soon as he realised the pollution of the water at Ashchurch, he had applied his sterilising process on the spot. A few miles further down the river, the water gave the result of perfect purity.

But for the accident in Trafalgar Square, there would have been no untoward consequences: but Dr Longdale, having seen the bacillus-infested water, and not knowing of the sterilisation, had no alternative but to cut off the water supply forthwith.

London that night was in a frenzy of elation. Men shook one another by the hand, hats were cast into the air and forgotten: people stood under the beating drip of the fire-engines' sluicing until they were soaked to the skin: well-dressed men laved themselves in the clear running gutters. London was saved from disaster, and Dr Darbyshire was the hero of the hour.

'All the same, it was a near thing, Longdale. Some day perhaps this country will realise what a debt it owes to its men of science – and perhaps learn to foster them a little more. For nothing but science could, these past days, have prevented a calamity that would have multiplied ten-fold the horrors of the Great Plague, and destroyed not thousands, but tens of thousands.'

THE MAGICIAN

Lord Dunsany

*   *   *

It was underground.

In that dank cavern down below Belgrave Square the walls were dripping. But what was that to the magician? It was secrecy that he needed, not dryness. There he pondered upon the trend of events, shaped destinies and concocted magical brews.

For the last few years the serenity of his ponderings had been disturbed by the noise of the motor-bus; while to his keen ears there came the earthquake-rumble, far off, of the train in the tube, going down Sloane Street; and what he heard of the world above his head was not to its credit.

He decided one evening over his evil pipe, down there in his dank dark chamber, that London had lived long enough, had abused its opportunities, had gone too far, in fine, with its civilization. And so he decided to wreck it.

Therefore he beckoned up his acolyte from the weedy end of the cavern, and, 'Bring me,' he said, 'the heart of the toad that dwelleth in Arabia and by the mountains of Bethany.' The acolyte slipped away by the hidden door, leaving that grim old man with his frightful pipe, and whither he went who knows but the gipsy people, or by what path he returned; but within a year he stood in the cavern again, slipping secretly in by the trap while the old man smoked, and he brought with him a little fleshy thing that rotted in a casket of pure gold.

'What is it?' the old man croaked.

'It is,' said the acolyte, 'the heart of the toad that dwelt once in Arabia and by the mountains of Bethany.'

The old man's crooked fingers closed on it, and he blessed the acolyte with his rasping voice and claw-like hand uplifted; the motor-bus rumbled above on its endless journey; far off the train shook Sloane Street.

'Come,' said the old magician, 'it is time.' And there and then they left the weedy cavern, the acolyte carrying a cauldron, gold poker and all things needful, and went abroad in the light. And very wonderful the old man looked in his silks.

Their goal was the outskirts of London; the old man strode in front and the acolyte ran behind him, and there was something magical in the old man's stride alone, without his wonderful dress, the cauldron and wand, the hurrying acolyte and the small gold poker.

Little boys jeered till they caught the old man's eye. So there went on through London this strange procession of two, too swift for any to follow. Things seemed worse up there than they did in the cavern, and the further they got on their way towards London's outskirts the worse London got. 'It is time,' said the old man, 'surely.'

And so they came at last to London's edge and a small hill watching it with a mournful look. It was so mean that the acolyte longed for the cavern, dank though it was and full of terrible sayings that the old man said when he slept.

They climbed the hill and put the cauldron down, and put therein the necessary things, and lit a fire of herbs that no chemist will sell nor decent gardener grow, and stirred the cauldron with the golden poker. The magician retired a little apart and muttered, then he strode back to the cauldron and, all being ready, suddenly opened the casket and let the fleshy thing fall in to boil.

Then he made spells, *then* he flung up his arms; the fumes from the cauldron entering in at his mind he said raging things that he had not known before and runes that were dreadful (the acolyte screamed); there he cursed London from fog to loam-pit, from zenith to the abyss; motor-bus, factory, shop, parliament, people. 'Let them all perish,' he said, 'and London pass away, tram lines and bricks and pavement, the usurpers too long of the fields, let them all pass away and the wild hares come back, blackberry and briar-rose.

'Let it pass,' he said, 'pass now, pass utterly.'

In the momentary silence the old man coughed, then waited with eager eyes; and the long hum of London hummed as it always has since first the reed-huts were set up by the river, changing its note at times but always humming, louder now than it was in years gone by, but humming night and day though its voice be cracked with age; so it hummed on.

And the old man turned round to his trembling acolyte

324

and terribly said as he sank into the earth: 'YOU HAVE NOT BROUGHT ME THE HEART OF THE TOAD THAT DWELLETH IN ARABIA AND BY THE MOUNTAINS OF BETHANY!'